D1462517

Ireland Rose

Patricia Strefling

Patricia Strefling
8/27/11

WestBow
Press
A Division of Thomas Nelson

WestBow Press books may be ordered through booksellers or by contacting:

WestBow Press
A Division of Thomas Nelson
1663 Liberty Drive
Bloomington, IN 47403
www.westbowpress.com
1-(866) 928-1240

ISBN: 978-1-4497-2185-5 (sc)
ISBN: 978-1-4497-2183-1 (hc)
ISBN: 978-1-4497-2184-8 (e)

Library of Congress Control Number: 2011912011

Printed in the United States of America

WestBow Press rev. date: 7/15/2011

Charleston – April 1884

Ireland Rose Lovell stirred in her bed. Noises from belowstairs. *What could be the matter?*

Sitting up quickly, her heart beat faster. She heard the familiar creak as her door opened and Portia appeared out of the blackness at her bedside. The candle swayed near her face and Rose nearly laughed out loud at her housekeeper's comical expression.

"Lord a'mercy, Miz Rose, it's Captain Wyatt, yo husband's man, come callin' at dis hour!"

"You don't think anything's wrong with Captain Lovell?" Rose threw back the counterpane, thoughts of laughter swept away.

"Now don't you go an worry none. Ain't nothin' to do but go down and see Cap'n Wyatt." Portia declared. "Up with ya now. Ain't no time to dawdle. I'll get yo hair up and you put on this nice housecoat over your nightclothes."

Rose did as she was told, hands shaking, then sat at the vanity table and awaited her maid's ministrations. Portia wound her curly red-blond hair up and secured it enough to be presentable.

Captain Wyatt was her husband's trusted shipman. He looked after Captain Lovell's interests in London. She had never been formally introduced to him.

Why was he in Charleston? Rose tried not to worry. "Why hasn't Captain Lovell come himself?" Rose whispered aloud. "He is late..." she remembered his last letter, stating that he would be arriving in the spring. Perhaps he was here even now and had sent word for her to prepare.

Portia's words interrupted her thoughts.

"Now, my Emmanuel is down der. Jus' you mind that you don't let nothin' bother you t'all. If'n there's word 'bout the Captain..."

"Don't. Don't say anything more, Portia." Rose intertwined her fingers tightly and lay them in her lap, pulled in a deep breath willing her heart to slow it's pounding.

"All right then. You just 'member God knows all things, chile. Don't you borrow trouble. If'n it's coming it'll come all by itself."

Portia approved her appearance with a nod and handed her a clean handkerchief.

"What's this for?" Rose's fear deepened.

"Nothin' chile. Just so's you got something to hold onto. No more no less. Cain't go down there empty-handed."

Rose, glad for something to cling to, wadded the cloth up in her fist, and squared her shoulders. She may be a young wife, but she must do her duty to her husband.

"That's right. Stand up now." Portia smiled. "You's just walk in dat drawin' room and hear what the man haf to say."

Rose descended the stairs, her maid two steps behind. She hesitated as her hand let go of the newel post.

"Go on now. Me'n Emmanuel will be waitin' for ya in the back." Portia whispered and passed her the candle.

"Am I decent?" Rose worried.

"You decent." Portia wagged her finger. "Nuff that he came knockin' at 'da door at dis hour!"

Portia slid her a sideways glance and Rose saw fear in those huge brown eyes. She watched as Portia walked into the darkness.

One last look in the mirror hanging above the side table in the marble floored foyer, the candle bouncing in eerie reflection, Rose pulled in a ragged breath and walked slowly to the drawing room. She entered the doorway, but the man's back was to her. He had not heard her arrive. The light from the single candle on the fireplace danced eerily on the walls.

Captain Wyatt gazed upward at the oil painting of her likeness, his hands behind his back, so like her husband's stance when he was aboard ship. One black booted foot rested on the cinderblock hearth. Black hair hung several inches over his dark shipman's coat, a leather band holding it together.

She cleared her throat and he turned. Dark, sad eyes gazed back at her. His long stare sent quivers down her back. When he spoke, she nearly jumped out of her skin. His deep voice reverberated in the darkened room—accustomed to shouting orders at his crew, no doubt.

"Mrs. Lovell?" He bowed slightly. "Captain Wyatt here."

"Captain Wyatt." She said softly.

The man seemed to move in slow motion as he strode toward her, looking at her then looking away, and back again. He pulled papers from his coat pocket. She steeled her heart. Was she then to be a widow at twenty?

"Where is my husband?" Her voice faltered but she lifted her chin slightly.

"Your husband is ill, Mrs. Lovell, and was not able to make the trip over. I am here in his stead, as you can see."

Rose twisted the lace handkerchief in her hands, gazing over his shoulder at the black windows, the gaslights from the streets offering any comfort that might be had at this hour.

"I am here with a message from your husband. Please excuse my appearance and the late hour."

Rose waited, knowing fear showed in her eyes.

"Captain Lovell has sent me to inform you he will not be able to return until September. I myself have just brought the *Emerald Star* back to Charleston. I would not have called on you at this hour, but as it is, I am in of need your signature before we can unload the ship."

"How ill is my husband?" She stepped forward, hands twisting in front of her waist.

"He has caught Yellow Fever from the street vagabonds of London." He snapped.

"Will he recover, then?" Her voice sounded like a child's.

"Aye, he should."

"Aye." She answered quietly, her Irish heritage forthcoming in her distress. "He was no doubt caring for the poor?"

"Almost to his demise." Captain Wyatt grumped. "But if he stays abed, he should recover well enough to make the trip in September if weather permits."

Rose's hand covered her heart, glad for the news. She was alone in the world. If it had not been for Captain Lovell . . . she gazed at the fire.

"Mrs. Lovell, as I said, I am here for signatures."

Rose looked up. He seemed hurried and a bit cross.

"Of course."

Captain Wyatt moved quickly to a side table, and Rose followed a few paces behind. He spread the papers with work-worn hands, across the dark walnut surface, and stepped back.

Rose walked slowly to the table, then remembered her father's words of caution. "Sir, what am I signing?"

"You madam, are signing papers that give you full charge of your husband's assets, should there be an…an unfortunate event, such as his death."

"Such things are not done, Captain Wyatt." She turned to face him. "Females are unable to own assets as you well know."

"Aye. They are not, but it is your husband's wish and I will see to it."

Rose turned away from the weathered face. The man's black eyes seemed to read her very thoughts. A shiver passed through her body.

"But the law…"

"Aye. The Law." He spit out. "Your husband has bypassed the law and placed your name on the business he has acquired, and you are his heir. His solicitor has drawn up the papers."

"But…I…as you see…I'm only…"

"You are a child. But Captain Lovell is my employer and I will see to his duties, while he is ill." He repeated.

For a moment Rose's thoughts flew like bees buzzing around in a glass jar. What if Captain Wyatt is not telling the truth? He has a sinister look about him. Could Captain Lovell possibly be dead already, and his man is here to steal her inheritance? But hadn't he just said she was to be the heir?

"Mrs. Lovell."

Rose looked up from her seated position. *When had she sat down?*

"I assure you, I am not here to attain anything that is not my own. Fact is, your husband left me the *Emerald Star*. He has left you the *Ireland Rose*. What your husband has done is more than any man is required. He has left everything but the *Emerald Star* to you."

Rose heard the gentleness in his voice. She looked up to read his eyes. The sincerity there quieted her nerves.

"What am I to do with his shipping business, if . . .?"

"That is not for you to think about, ma'am. I will assist you should you find yourself in need. I give you my word. My men are tired from the long voyage and are now awaiting my return so they can unload the ship and go home to their families."

Rose's woman heart heard his plea. "Of course." She took a pen from the stand and dipped it into the well, her hand trembling.

"My husband trusts you. I shall do the same." She said, suddenly in charge of her emotions. "Where shall I sign?"

Captain Wyatt took two steps forward, but did not come too near. He pointed to the line and said, "Each page, if you please. I will inform you later of the details."

"As you wish." She signed at each place, put the pen in its stand and took a breath.

"Thank you Mrs. Lovell."

Before she could speak another word, Captain Wyatt, picked up the papers, folded them and put them in his coat pocket, bowed to her and was gone into the night.

Rose heard the heavy door close.

Her knees nearly failed her when she tried to stand. She had signed papers without her husband's instruction. *Lord, please forgive my lack of faith…but somewhere in my heart I felt persuaded. I pray Providence's blessing.*

"Child, is Capn' Wyatt gone then?" Portia flew to her.

"He is." Rose said quietly. "I would be in my bed, now Portia."

Portia's eyes sought hers.

"Captain Lovell is ill, but should recover and return as soon as he is well. Please forgive me, Portia…I am not myself this eve."

"Has dat man said somethin' evil to ya, child?" Portia's hands rested on her ample hips.

"Oh no. He asked me to sign papers."

Portia seemed relieved. "And the Cap'n's gonna be back den?"

"With God's help." Rose said quietly.

"Then it be up to your bed. Sees, I tole you, all's well. Cap'n Lovell would not 'low anything to happen to ya, child."

Rose smiled as they walked up together and she went back to her bed, but not to sleep. Her husband would not return for nearly four months. By the time he arrived it would be an entire year since he'd been home.

Disappointed, for he brought gifts and news from London; the summer would not be the same without him. Then thoughts began to trouble her mind about the papers she had just put her name to.

ꟹ

William "Ashton" Wyatt stepped off the wide entryway and without a look behind, stalked away. He had promised himself never to enter that house again. The blue eyes and red-blond hair…her tiny frame. It was too much. It was a drink he needed. Ashton Wyatt stepped up his pace.

Chapter 2

The servants were about their spring cleaning duties this rainy morn. Rose wandered through the house and then up to the fourth floor. The attic stairs seemed to call her upward. She needed a diversion from last evening's news.

She'd chosen a simple day dress without hoops so she could maneuver the servant's narrow stairs. There were no calling cards in the tray on the table. The ladies would not dare ruin their newest fashion with raindrops. Besides Rose admitted she wasn't really up to the silly society chatter today.

"Ireland Rose get hold of yourself." The whispered words came from her throat, but they were her mother's voice. Snatching the handkerchief from her wristband, she wiped at her cheeks. "Such nonsense." Rose gathered her skirts and hiked up to the attic.

"Ireland Rose, is dat you up 'der?" Came Portia's call from below sometime later.

"Aye, it is."

"The Irish lass up those stairs, and her lady o' the house." Portia pulled half her round body through the hole in the floor. "And here I is, all outta breath and you way up here." She fanned her face with a hankie.

Rose couldn't help but smile. "I need to keep my mind busy. You know I love old things." She murmured, kneeling and gently fishing through the contents of an old trunk.

Portia huffed and puffed her way through the square hole in the floor and joined her. "Oh, now lookee at ya, yo clothes all dusty."

Oh Portia, look, an old wedding dress." Rose lifted a sheaf of paper wrapping and sighed. "It's beautiful. I wonder who wore it?" Her heart quickened. "Help me lay it out...please."

"Like I ain't got nuthin' to do but dat." Portia chuckled and hurried over, her eyes big. "Shore 'nuff it is a mighty pretty one at that."

"It's magnificent. Look at the satin, the pearls, the lace sleeves."

"And heavy." Portia added as she rubbed her chubby hand over the thick material.

"Whose was it? Do you know?" Rose's eyes were questioning.

"Come to think on it...it may be the first Mrs. Lovell's." Portia looked away in thought. "They's a picture somewhere's about the house with her in it, I do believe."

"Oh, do you think we can find it? If we can just see the portrait, we'll know if it was hers."

"Chile why you wanna see the Cap'n's other wife on der weddin' day?" Portia puffed out. "Just don't seem right somehow..."

"Because it was the Captain's wife. And he loved her. I understand enough to know that he misses her."

"How you know dat?" Portia's eyes bore into hers.

"I see it in his eyes sometimes. When he comes in to speak with me. He starts to say something and then remembers I'm not her."

"You don't know sich a thing. You young, but you still be a woman."

Rose shrugged. "I may be small in stature and size, but I have eyes, Portia."

"Dat you do. Dat you do."

"Would you mind helping me find the portrait?"

"If you's tell me to, what else can a servant say?" She laughed, her low voice resonating through the rafters.

"Please Portia. I know you have your duties, but we *are* friends. Right?"

"O'course. You treat me right fine, Miz Lovell, better'n most. Let me think – seems to me it might be right up here in dis attic. Or at the Captain's other house."

"My husband has another house?"

Portia looked terrified. "Maybe I done spoke out when I wasn't s'posed to."

"Don't worry. I won't ask any questions."

Seeing Portia's relief, Rose suggested they look around. "Step carefully, these floorboards are really old."

"Ain't no older than I is." She laughed and moved away, watching her every step.

Several minutes passed and each delved into boxes, checked underneath mattresses and in dark corners. Rose kept getting waylaid at the least concern and found herself sitting on a crate with a book in her hand, when she heard, "Come see."

"Have you found it?" Rose stepped over the pile of books she'd discovered.

Portia stood next to the gothic arched window at the tiptop point of the house and pulled an old blanket off of a huge canvas. "There she is, big as you please." Portia whispered.

Rose caught her breath. The woman was beautiful. Handsome dark eyes gazed at her. Black hair shone in the cascading light coming through the window, the painting exquisitely done. Small hands lay across the woman's lap. And the dress. It was red-orange with gold trim and black pearl buttons, from the looks of it. Slender fine-boned shoulders were encased in a black lace, heavily fringed shawl. A tiny silver headpiece was barely visible in her hair.

"Was she someone famous?" Rose's whispered words barely found a voice.

"Seems the Cap'n did say somethin' bout dat . . ." Portia's eyes seemed unable to leave the portrait. "Her name was Lucinda."

"Lucinda. Lucinda Lovell." Rose repeated in a whisper. "He never mentioned her name or anything about her."

"Captain loved that woman, sure enough." Portia was evidently remembering the past.

"She is a real woman." Rose whispered, feeling a strange melancholy.

"You's a real woman, too. When Captain Lovell come home, you can get you some babies. Then you won't be all by yerself when he gone on them ships."

Rose knew there would be no babies.

And she would be by herself. Her husband was twenty-seven years her senior and only took her as his wife to repay an old debt to Rose's father.

Camden John Lovell had been born of strong Scot and Irish blood. Having come from London as a lad, he made his fortune in shipping. He had been a handsome man in his younger days; his portrait hung on the walls on the first floor.

The house she now lived in was among Charleston's finest. Located on the Battery and built in the English Tudor style, it resembled the fine homes of English royalty. He had lived here with Lucinda, who she knew was of Italian descent. She had died during the summer of 1875 of malaria while he was in London. There had been no children and it was said that Captain Lovell was inconsolable at his wife's passing.

Suddenly it became important to know Lucinda. "Are there other things that belong to her up here?"

"Thinkin' there is. I know someplace der's a picture with her in dat weddin' dress. I know it sure as I'm standin' here." Portia reached up and threw the blanket over the portrait.

"Do you think Captain Lovell would enjoy her portrait hanging below stairs." Rose questioned.

Portia spoke quietly. "You best leave sich ideas to the Cap'n."

"You are right. Would it be a sin if we looked through Lucinda's things?"

"Ain't no harm I can see. The woman be gone nigh unto eleven years now." Portia's deadpan voice sounded hollow in the space.

"Then we shall look about." Rose reached behind the painting for a large book and dusted the front. "It's their wedding portraits."

"Well, it be so." Portia whispered, her eyes large.

The book held in Rose's lap, revealed page after page of the young Captain Lovell and his beautiful wife. "She's very small, like me" Rose smiled.

"See, a child ain't a child 'cause of 'der shape . . . a child be a child because of they thinkin'." Portia pointed to her head.

"Portia, you make me laugh."

"Truth ain't it?"

"Hmmmm…." Rose agreed.

"Now you go on pokin' yo'self round here. I got to be gittin down to the galley and fix you some suppah."

"Step lightly." Rose warned her.

"Me, step lightly? Huh, you sees I cain't with this chunk o'body God done gave me. Chile, I be making three o'you."

"Well that wouldn't take much." Rose smiled and picked up another memento. "Mind you take care going down that ladder, Portia."

Portia slowly descended the steps while Rose, content to look around, spent the next hour searching for something to keep her mind busy and to learn more about her husband. He had signed her name to his worldly goods? Had he some place in his heart left after Lucinda? Heaven knows she was not a true wife to him and knew he would never ask her to be.

Chapter 3

Recalling the moments that led up to her marriage, Rose sighed as she put the wedding album back behind the painting away from the sun. She fingered old silver candlesticks, books, fine linens and other memorabilia, rolling them in her hands, thinking of the day when someone else used these items.

"Life is so fragile…" she whispered as memories flooded her thoughts.

She'd been fifteen when her parents called her into her father's office. That was the day she learned that he was seeking a proper alliance for his only child. He chose Captain Lovell, a widower. He was wealthy and had lived alone since his wife died several years earlier.

Until then Rose's life in Baltimore, the city of her birth, had been simple and free. Sean Michael McKensie and Branna Cathleen Malvina had married young. Too young, her mother always said. When the potato famine had ravaged Ireland in the mid 1840s, they fled the thatched-roof cottage her father built with his own hands. He farmed the rocks from the hills of Ireland on lands that belonged to his father.

Rose heard the story many times. Her parents were proud to be Irish but glad to be in America, where at least they had food and opportunities to own property. Sean McKensie founded a printing company and had done well. Once they established their business they were not free to return to Ireland.

No children had come to their home until 1864 when her mother discovered she was to have a child late in their lives. Rose knew her birth 3 May of 1865 changed their plans, for her mother was never well after she was born. They made a good life in America and planned a return to their homeland to spend their last days there when her mother became ill. She remembered the conversation well.

"Ireland Rose McKensie, you are old enough to understand that your mother and I are too old to continue the business. We have agreed to a sale with Mr. Smithers, who you know has been my able assistant. He has set by enough money to pay cash. He will assume the ownership two years hence."

When her father stopped speaking and looked to his wife, Rose's gaze slowly turned to her mother.

"Rose, your father and I will return to Ireland. We have been away too long and we wish to walk among our Irish hills afore we die." Her mother's firm look brooked no argument. "You may come along with us."

"We would have you in Ireland, too." Her father said quickly. "But you must decide."

"I? Leave you? But…"

"'Tis two years ya have to make yer choice, lass." Her father's gentle voice reached her brain, which was swirling.

Two years?

"If ye wish to stay in America, I have found a man worthy of ya. We will not leave our only lass without protection."

"Aye, as it is, we will not live long in this world and it would be a shame for you to be in Ireland without a man." Her mother said in her usual no nonsense manner. "Our families are long gone and we have lost touch with our auld friends because most of them fled along wi' us."

"We would not turn you out, lass. But as you are attaining the age of reason, we expect you to think about these things and give us an answer when you are ready." Her father's voice came from somewhere far away.

"Aye, and don't take long, lass." Her mother said sternly and quit the room.

"There now, don't look so downcast. All will turn out well. We have taught ya to believe in yerself and yer religion. Rose remembered the tears that fell on her lap. "You really did want me then, father?"

He had come and knelt next to her chair. "Lass, more than you know. Mother was nearing the age of forty years and had given up the hope she'd have children, so her heart was not as warm. And...she had to carry the child." He smiled.

"Aye." She wiped her eyes. "It cannot have been easy."

"Easy? It was not for yer muther. But from the moment you were born you were a gleeful, chubby child, with an angel face, blue eyes and that red-blond hair o'yours. Irish to be sure! I was proud of me wee lass."

Rose had jumped up from her chair and tossed herself into her father's arms, nearly toppling him to the floor.

"Father, you love me so well."

"Ah your mother does too. She shows it differently lass. She is sick at the idea of leaving you, yet we must return. She is not well...and ya know her wishes are mine as well. We are not long for this world and care nothing for it, except for you."

Rose sobbed on her father's shoulder.

"Ah, now. Your mother knew the day would come and has tried her best to teach you world-wise ways so that you will be safe, lass. It is unfortunate for you that ye arrived so late in our lives. But we are glad of it."

Sean McKensie released his daughter and from that day to the day of her wedding, Rose prepared her heart to be left behind. She wanted to see Ireland. But she would not go and watch her parents die in a land she did not know. It was better they have the time to be together alone again, as they had so many years before.

Rose had heard often enough from her mother, "Ireland Rose learn to take in all the facts, be wise in your decisions, you never know what repercussions they will make for the future."

Their friends had not understood her parents' wish to leave their young daughter to return to their bonny Ireland to be buried under the soft green hills. She knew, for she had seen the tears of deep despair when they told their stories of how they were forced to abandon their home. But hunger had declared war and there was nothing to do but make their way to England's shore and come to America.

And now there was nothing to do but return to their beloved home. Rose understood. Their gratefulness for freedom and deep affection for their homeland had soaked into her spirit and she learned to love Ireland as well. But this was her home

Chapter 4

One day two years later, her father came to her while she was in the garden, planting new seedlings. It was spring. "Rose, Captain Lovell will pay a visit as he is coming into port day after tomorrow."

The sun slid behind a cloud and so did her heart. "So soon, Father?"

"Aye, child, ye knew of it long ago. And ye are seventeen. Mother is unwell and we must go before . . ."

"I know." Rose squinted against the sun as the cloud passed over it. "Petunias are so pretty blowing in the winds. They are so delicate." She mused.

"As you are." Her father said softly and went back to his work, walking slowly away.

Knowing the Captain owned a successful shipping business and a fine home in Charleston, the elder McKensie's knew she would be cared for. Twenty-seven years her senior, he could offer their daughter protection and a good life.

Rose also knew the Captain was offering his life as a sacrifice because of a debt he owed her father. It seems the story was as a young man, rather for lack of money or position she did not know, he stowed away on a ship to America and had been caught in his deed. The serious charge could have sent him overboard easily enough. Her father learned of the lad's trouble and paid his way across. Pledging his undying devotion for saving his life, Camden John Lovell could now repay his debt and offered to take their daughter's hand in marriage.

By the time she reached the age of seventeen she knew what she had to do.

The ceremony was held in the Charleston House, away from her beloved Baltimore. Her mother had sewn her wedding clothes, even though her eyesight was bad enough that Rose had to finish the final stitches herself.

Memories of cooler evenings, and windblown leaves of every color in Baltimore left her heart broken. But there was nothing to be done. Her mother's words bore into her soul as if her body was being pulled down into quicksand. "Ireland Rose, you are a woman now. Your lot has fallen to this place and lucky ye are to have it."

Rose had listened that day, because for all the years she lived with her parents, they had prepared her for their leaving. In a few days they would be gone and she would be Captain Lovell's wife.

Fear skidded into her mind and raced around frantically trying to find a place to reside. She had stood by Captain Lovell and said the words that made her his. And, just that morning her mother had sat her down and told her, in her forward way, that she must make Captain Lovell a good wife in every way. The first three days of her marriage she had spent with her mother and father, per her new husband's instructions.

Four days after the wedding she stood at the dock and waved her lacy wedding handkerchief in the air bravely as the ship sounded it's foghorn and pulled slowly away with her mother's uncharacteristic last words, "Ireland Rose, will you not go with us?" resounding in her head.

"Mother I have married." Rose thought she sounded grown up.

But the words quickly faded into panic as it overtook her just like the time she almost drowned in the huge waves of the Atlantic. Captain Lovell had noted her distress and taken her arm in his and slowly walked home. Feet heavy upon the marble foyer floors, she found herself being handed over to Portia.

"Take her above stairs and see she has rest. I will be in my office."

Climbing the stairs had been the hardest thing Rose had ever done. Her feet felt like cinderblocks and sobs lay beneath the surface waiting to choke her very existence to death. Portia's ministrations, without a single word, had been her undoing.

The woman had taken her in hand, undressed her, pulled a soft white gown over her head, washed her face and pulled the covers up to her neck.

When their eyes had met, Rose heard herself whisper, "I thought I was grown up, but I'm not . . ." and the sobs had overtaken her. Her parents were gone. Forever. And she was alone with a man who was now her husband.

Chapter 5

Two years passed. The first year of their marriage her husband spent most of his time in his office at home and at the shipyard, overseeing the addition of a second ship. He had helped his crew build it. He introduced her into society and she learned quickly the Captain was a respected man among the Charleston aristocracy.

When the new ship, christened the *Ireland Rose*, had first gone into her waters, it was a beautiful fall day. The second year of their marriage, the Captain had been away commandeering his new ship abroad. He hired Captain Wyatt to man the *Emerald Star* a year ago and promised to be in Charleston more often. Now he was ill and would not be coming.

"Just because he's not coming home…" she tried. But her emotions were stronger than her resolve. Loneliness washed over her like a cascading waterfall. *Why did it matter that her twentieth birthday was today, May 3rd and their third wedding anniversary was May 23rd.*

Thoughts of her parents in Ireland pressed on her heart. Her mother had passed into her rest the second year of her marriage and father three weeks later. There was no one to care if she had a birthday or not.

"Let it go." She scolded herself. "There are other people who are much less fortunate." Again her mother's words. Right now she knew they were right. She would be about getting out again in society without her husband's help, even if the ladies despised the Captain's young wife not only for her beauty but for her Yankee upbringing. Charleston ladies, above all things, loved family connections and beauty -- in their societies, in their homes, and in their manner of dress. Portia told her these things…and glad she was that her maid and friend was honest and forthright.

She pulled the bell rope. "Lily, would you send for a carrier?" She handed the young servant a missive. "See that it is carried to Miss Estella Rose Perry on Tradd Street."

Estella's shared middle name had bonded them instantly, but a more sisterly bond formed the day Stella had grabbed her hand and pulled her – hard – through the doorway into the gardens, snapping her hoops nearly in half. Rose couldn't help but smile at the memory.

"Shhh… Stella had laughed. "Now straighten your dress and get those abominable hoops level."

Rose would never forget that moment. And it had all occurred during a most important engagement at one of the finest homes in Charleston. The banker's handsome son had recently declared his intentions to marry Celeste Antoinette Bertram. Her beauty alone would have turned any man's head, but with her added connections and wealth she was Charleston's reigning queen. Gold glittered from every available surface, from the crystal chandeliers to the necklace on the miniature pug-faced dog.

"Her name may mean *heavenly*, but she is anything but." Stella had nearly shouted in her ear, exposing their secrets to those standing nearby. That incident alone nearly cost Rose her position in Charleston's high society.

Later that evening Captain Lovell quietly suggested, "Rose, you must be careful to entertain dignity among the ladies, especially while I'm away, or you may find yourself ostracized and lonely."

"It is as you say." She agreed, "But how shall I keep Stella from repeating such musings in my ear. You know she doesn't care a whit about decorum."

"This is true. She does not. Still, should you find yourself in need of assistance while I am away. . ." he had kindly reminded her and smiled indulgently. His once-dark hair was now gray. But he was a very distinguished looking man and she felt proud to walk on his arm.

"I must be about my work. Do you need anything?"

Rose had answered *no* out of respect, but did indeed need something. She needed companionship.

"Sir, do you mind very much if I send an invitation to Stella for this evening? I could use

a bit of refreshment. And we are safe from society's eyes and ears…." She smiled.

He agreed and kindly acquiesced. Rose heard the office door close quietly. She wondered if Captain Lovell were happy in the least.

"Stella, you are like a naughty child. Why must you be staring out the windows? Someone will see you gawking."

"Look Rose, it's Miss Bertram. She's got her parasol stuck in the branch of the Myrtle tree. She's incensed but can't seem to pull it free. Now she's stomping her foot. Do you *know* those shoes just had to come from Paris?" Stella was bent over the plant, holding back the curtains laughing.

"Stella do you *know* what a spectacle you make?" Rose laughed. "You bend in such unladylike positions . . . to stare at people outside my window. "You'd best come back so you won't be seen, don't you think? And your dress. It's so beautiful, you mustn't muss it." Rose chuckled.

"Oh puff. If I could I'd trade these old things for my husband's shirt and trousers and walk around with my hair stuck under his hat just to see what it's like to be a man, I would. And right down this street I'd walk, too. At least we wouldn't have to wear these awful fake smiles and look away when the men speak, as though we had no mind at all."

"You'd wear your husband's trousers and hat? Rose laughed. "Such musings. And it'd be misgivings I'd suffer if you did such a thing, for we could never be seen together again."

"Well, when you put it that way." Stella reluctantly stepped away from the window. "What shall we do then?"

"Play the pianoforte for me. You are so accomplished."

"Fluff . . I'm not and you know it . . . you just say it because you know I hate to play."

"Play, please." Rose set down her needlework. "I will sit next to you on the bench."

"Okay you play high, I'll play low."

The two played together and found they could keep rhythm.

Indeed it sounded quite nice, Rose thought.

"You never told me you played," Stella smiled, her hands floating over the keys, Rose adding the melody.

"First of all, you never asked, second, we have only known each other for a month."

"Well, that explains it." Stella got up from the bench. "I really must go within the hour. My husband is tired of the evening. He has so many extra duties at the bank. Mr. Dalton doesn't deserve the president's position; he just sits in that fancy leather chair and gives orders. Foster does all the work for him and that wicked Mr. Dalton takes all the credit. By the time my dear Foster comes home, he is worn thin."

"I'm sorry." Was all Rose could think to say. "Come, I'll ring for tea."

"Excellent, I'm parched. But I warn you, Rose, don't take up with any of that banker bunch. They'll eat your kind for dinner and spit you out."

Stella set her teacup on the table. "You'd best see to your husband, too, for it has been quite a long time since he has appeared." Stella winked.

"Such things you say, Stella. But I am glad we are friends. Don't be overlong in coming again for another visit?"

Chapter 6

Rose kept her hands busy and tried not to think about her husband laying ill in London. Captain Wyatt would be reloading the Emerald Star and going back. Could she possibly go along? No, it would be childish behavior and all of Charleston would know she'd set sail to recover her very capable husband.

She set her embroidery table aside and flexed her fingers. Stella's pillow covers would have to wait. The rain sluiced over the clear glass until it seemed the people walking by under their umbrellas were just tall, dark squiggles.

Suddenly, Rose remembered her sketch pad and hurried to her husband's office. He had allotted her a special drawer and gave her leave to use his desk, should she wish to create her scenes. She could use a bit of amusement during these dark, rainy afternoons.

All but forgotten, she'd been reminded of Stella's cavalier behavior in the window that day. It had set her mind's eye flying. Within the space of two minutes Rose was sitting in her husband's chair sketching.

"Well, there you be." Portia presented herself in the doorway. "I's been lookin' high and low for ya. Made my heart skitter not to see you 'bout this big ole house. What you be doin' in here anyways?"

"Just drawing. I've just finished. Want to see?"

"If'n you want to show me, I guess I'd be wantin' to see."

Smiling, Rose lifted the board and waited.

Portia broke out into a chuckle.

"You like it then?"

"Miz Rose you's got that Lady Bertram dead to rights. She ain't a goin' nowhere with her parasol stuck up in the tree like 'at. You shore do know how to make a body shake." She laughed heartily filling the room with joy.

Rose smiled, cocked her head, and lay the picture on the desk. "It is rather funny."

"Best you don't be layin' that 'round so's nosy eyes can see sich things."

"I have another..." Rose lifted another scene with Stella gawking at the window, her skirts up to her knees and bent over the palm plant."

"Oh, that girl ain't fit to be seen in such a pose. You best put them in the drawer, chile. Ain't fit for society lady's eyes, nosiree."

"I will. It will be our secret." Rose stole a glance as Portia whose laughing dark eyes met hers for a moment.

Portia walked away still chuckling and then appeared at the doorway again. "Miz Bertram really get herself into that mess out front?"

"Stella said she did. I just sketched what she told me she saw."

"Well, now ain't that sumpin. You got a gif', that's for sure."

Rose set her pencil down and lay back in the large chair. She must have dozed, for a loud cracking sound rattled the windows, sending her nerves skittering.

The room was dark. Then it filled with blue light. Another spring storm was brewing.

Stirring from her husband's chair, she raised herself and sought the company of the servants. They were busy pulling windows and shutters closed. She hated thunder and lightning storms.

The sudden interruption of the door knocker sounded ominous. Emmanuel walked past her quickly and opened the door. Rose kept herself out of view, pressing the pins back into her hair, smoothing her skirts. She had not thought to have guests especially in the storm. It was the dinner hour in most Charleston homes.

Mr. Dalton? The banker. What was he doing here at this hour and in the midst of this storm?

Her maid appeared in the doorway announcing her guest. "Portia lay out my green day dress. I'll be up in a moment."

Portia disappeared and Rose picked up her skirts and ran up the servant's stairs. They met in her room and without a word, the two hustled her into a fresh dress and repinned her hair.

"Watch yourself chile. Dat man ain't no good. I hear'd it all 'round the town."

"Yes, I know. Stella told me. Thank you for your warning, Portia." Rose knew she needed no pinching of her cheeks. They were already warm. "Pray that I am strong."

"Yes, chile…I's goin' to be prayin' fer sure. Go on now."

Rose descended the stairs, slow and ladylike.

"Mr. Dalton."

Rose welcomed him into the parlor. "You know my name then?" he sounded proud.

He waited until she was seated and then took her husband's chair across the low table.

"Yes, I attended Miss Bertram's engagement party. It was a beautiful affair indeed."

"Shall we get down to business, Mrs. Lovell? I am here to get your signature, if you would be so kind." In one motion he made great work of pulling a set of papers and a fine gold pen from his very fashionable tweed coat pocket.

Rose suddenly felt like things were happening in slow motion. She looked at the pen, down at the papers and then back at the smiling face. It was a false smile. She sensed immediately that she must not lay her name to the papers. Stella's words whipped through her mind. *Don't trust him.* She'd said those very words. And since her friend was among the original Charleston families, she trusted her friend more than the man sitting before her.

And...hadn't she remembered something that Captain Lovell said about banker Dalton? *What was it?* She should have paid more attention.

His eyes narrowed every so slightly at her hesitation and the smile slowly disappeared as he gave her a sideglance.

"Is there a problem, Mrs. Lovell? For I assure you, these are necessary to keep your husband's loan afloat at my . . . at our bank."

Rose knew she would not sign. Her mother had taught her better. "Sir, you must allow me time to read the papers." Captain Wyatt had recently told her she was to be the heir. She would be responsible should her husband...she could not think of it.

Before she'd finished speaking, she saw him lay his pen on the table and slide it toward her. "Of course." He said patiently.

"I will wait while you read."

"Sir, I cannot read while you are present. I shall go over these papers and you may return on the morrow." Rose couldn't believe how bravely she'd spoken the words.

"Ah, so you are a wise, young wife. Very well, I shall return at nine o'clock sharp." He took up his pen and stood. "Please do not delay. These are very important. But then I'm sure your husband does not discuss such matters with . . . his young wife."

"I shall be forthright in my duties." Rose said quietly as she stood on shaky knees and followed him to the door. A sudden crack filled the sky as lightning shot through the air. She opened the door and watched him walk into the rain. She had just let a serpent out of her house.

Rose retrieved the papers and went to her husband's office. She pulled out her sketchbook and drew the word picture firmly planted in her mind's eye. Then she sat back to review the papers.

Two hours later she had read every word on the twelve pages. They seemed in order. A loan to be paid back in five years. The amount was staggering, but then she had no idea how much money her husband had. And Mr. Dalton mentioned that the loan was important. He also knew her husband lay ill in London.

Perhaps she should send for Captain Wyatt. It was late and eight o'clock in the morning was too early to rouse the Captain. Rose twisted her fingers together, "Lord what shall I do?"

Chapter 7

When the sun came up upon rain-washed Charleston, Rose was dressed and ready. She sent for Lily.

"Lily, I want you to hurry down to the dock. You will find Captain Wyatt there at the *Emerald Star.* Make sure he receives this note. It is of the utmost importance."

"I's got to git the eggs 'dis mornin' Miz Rose."

Rose smiled. Lily loved gathering eggs but was afraid of people. "Get Thomas then."

Lily ran like a child and in a minute brought back her elder brother. "Thomas would you please take this missive to Captain Wyatt. He is docked with the *Emerald Star.* You must hurry."

Thomas bowed slightly, a big smile on his face. Rose knew he loved more than anything to be on the wharf when all the activity of spring was about the town.

Thirty minutes later Thomas returned, his eyes downcast as he delivered the message.

"Ma'am, Mr. Wyatt, he drunk and cain't be found. His men say he… he at a woman's house." Thomas shrugged. "It's sorry I is to say I cain't find him."

"Don't worry Thomas. You did the best you could."

Captain Wyatt drunk. And with a woman. Heaven knew Charleston was known for the bad behavior of the shipmen when they came into port. She had hoped Captain Wyatt might be different.

Wringing her hands, Rose knew there was little time to catch hold of anyone who could help her. Stella's words came pouring back into her ears. Perhaps she could go for Captain Wyatt herself and speak to him, for there was no one else. She put that thought away. She could not allow herself to be seen knocking on the door of the captain's woman. Even if it was important. There would be talk.

Suddenly, she felt the need to pray. Gathering her skirts, she ran up the stairs, into her room and knelt on the wood slatted floor next to her bed and prayed to God who she knew would hear and answer. Rising to her feet, after several minutes, she straightened her dress, smoothed her hair and believed above all things that God had a plan and He would protect her.

Time was slipping away and Rose knew she had no other option than to sign those papers. Hadn't Mr. Dalton said the *Emerald Star* would not be allowed to leave port. And Captain Wyatt had seemed anxious to get back to London, because of the procured merchandise aboard.

It seemed Captain Wyatt was the one who was failing, not Mr. Dalton. She would send word through Thomas to the crew that the ship was to leave at first chance. The signed papers would see to that. Rose squared her shoulders, certain this was the path to take.

When the knocker sounded at the front door, she was ready. She would not knuckle under this time.

"Mrs. Lovell. Isn't it a pleasant morning indeed?" Mr. Dalton gushed.

"Aye, it is at that Mr. Dalton." She agreed.

"And have we had time to read through the labyrinth of legal terms?"

Rose sensed he was talking down to her, but he did so with a smile and a confident voice.

"I have."

"And you have found them in order I presume?"

She did not answer. Because truthfully, she knew she couldn't. Everything seemed in order. There was an additional loan amount due and by her signature alone the *Emerald Star* would leave port and deliver the goods straight to London as planned.

The man saw he had convinced his client and waited, hands tucked behind him, rolling on his feet as she signed the several pages and handed them back to him.

"Ah, an excellent business woman, I see. You are indeed a woman of means and character." He smiled.

Rose knew it was not really a compliment.

"Sir. You now have your duty to my husband and his business." She said gazing straight into his eyes.

"Indeed I do." He said almost giddily.

Rose shrunk back at the words.

"Thank you. You have been most kind, Mrs. Lovell." He bowed, took up his papers and headed for the door. Emmanuel was ready with his hat and cane and the man left her house.

The deed was done. Her heart whispered, "Lord please look out for us."

Rose went above stairs and changed into an old worn gown and slippers. She needed more than anything to be about her garden. The last two days had brought about too much uncertainty and she wished only to get her hands into the soil.

Hours passed as she worked her magic in the walled garden behind the house. Roses of every color sprung to life under her tutelage. She made certain of it. Evening Primrose, Blazing Star with its lavendar flowers, and Swamp Sunflower grew from every corner. Several shades of ivy grew strong as it climbed the walls in the warmth of the sun and the salty sea air.

Rose's thoughts wandered. Loneliness fell over her like the clouds that passed overhead. Sunlight burnt her back and sweat poured from her body. She wanted to feel it. The large straw hat with the ribbons blowing in the wind made her feel like she was a little girl back in Baltimore. But Baltimore had a winter reprieve; here the weather was unbearable during the summer months. Most of the low country planters of Charleston society went north to Newport or some city where they could get away from the heat.

Mr. Lovell wanted his wife safe in his huge home, and never mentioned taking off to the north. And many Charlestonians were still recovering after the Civil War so there was not as much money to be had these days. It was only the fortunate that survived the cannon balls when the first shot was fired at Ft. Sumter in April of 1861. Many of the southerners left for California, some to other countries, so discouraged were they after the fall of Charleston.

But people survived. And what didn't kill them only made them stronger. The orphanages around the city attested to that fact. Known for its huge shipyard and a perfect southern stage for travel along the Atlantic Coast, Charleston became home to many an unfortunate woman and her children. Ship captains alighted long enough to make their babies and off to the sea they went again leaving women and children to the care of whoever could raise the money. Rose knew that minute she would seek Stella the next day and see to getting herself involved with the city's unfortunate citizens. She was much too lonely and much too vulnerable staying in her safe place. Her husband was well known for his care of the poor, whether here in Charleston or in London.

Captain Wyatt had made comment to that in their conversations. Rose knew she had to follow in her his footsteps no matter what it cost her.

"Lord thank you for giving me a good husband. I'll try my best to make him proud, wherever I am."

As if her prayer had been answered immediately, she turned to find Portia calling to her. "Miz Rose, Miss Stella, she come for a visit."

"Stella?" Rose repeated dropping her cutting tool to the ground.

"As I live and breath." Portia said breathlessly.

"She out here Miss Stella, getting' her pretty hands dirty...and servants all 'round the place." Portia shook her head.

Rose shrugged as Stella came round the corner with a smile on her face.

"You don't know how good it is to see you..." Rose almost told her about her prayer.

"And you." Stella snapped her umbrella closed and sat on a bench under a Myrtle tree. "Come sit in the shade. How can you be out in the middle of the day in this oppressive heat?"

Rose smiled, "It is warm isn't it?"

"Warm? I declare upon all that's holy you have no sense." Stella fanned herself with a church cardboard fan on a stick.

Rose wanted more than anything to confess her deeds to her friend, but thought better of it. "How are you Stella? And Foster? Is he doing well?"

"Oh you know the same situations arise at work. That Mr. Dalton hasn't a care in the world except for himself." She gossiped. "Oh, let's speak of something else, I am sick to death of that subject." Stella sighed.

"Shall we go inside where it's cool? I'm about done here." Rose gathered her roses into a large woven grass basket made by the locals. She pulled off her old gloves and set her tools nearby. "Lemonade?"

Stella forgot her umbrella, ran back for it and hustled to follow. "Portia makes the best lemonade this side of the Ashley River." She laughed. "Oh, see it *is* cooler inside."

"I'll run up and change quickly, but I warn you I haven't bathed." Rose laughed and ran for the stairs. She felt giddy to have company about the house and didn't mind at all running when Stella was about.

"Don't worry. I am much too overcome by the heat to move." Stella called out from the drawing room in unladylike fashion.

She rinsed herself off with water Portia had left on the washstand, and turned just in time to see Portia holding out the dress she had laid across the bed. Rose changed quickly, choosing a soft green cotton day dress with pink sprigs. No need to impress anyone.

"You are a dear." Rose said excitedly. "I wouldn't have called you except these silly buttons down the back."

"I knows my duty. And I knows you ain't no trouble at'tall Miz Rose."

Portia said the words so kindly, Rose's eyes watered.

She donned the dress and was buttoned up in no time. Portia made her sit for a full three minutes, while she straightened her hair.

"Now lookee there. Ain't that a sight better, yo hair off'n your neck? I declare chile yo hair done looks like little pig's tails when it get too moist out der in that sun."

"It does have a tendency to curl in this heat."

"Go on now…if you ain't gonna sit still no longer, get on down dem stairs…." Portia shook her head, smiling.

"I have news." Stella said as soon as Rose appeared in the drawing room. "Sit down. I couldn't think straight out there in that heat. I nearly forgot the reason I came." She fanned herself.

Rose sat on the blue damask chair and put her hands in her lap. She felt flushed in the face. She must have been in the sun longer than she realized. She was famished, of a sudden.

"My husband has secured a fitting for me in Savannah. And I am here to ask you to attend with me. We can take the train."

Rose sat up straighter, her hunger forgotten. "Savannah. I've yet to visit there, but I hear it is beautiful. I haven't been on a train since I left Baltimore."

"You'll love the city. I was born there." Stella lifted her chin.

"I didn't know that!" Rose laughed. "You have a fitting you say?"

"Yes week after next. I wanted to give you plenty of time to prepare. Foster is not available to come along and will not let me go alone. So you see, you must say yes."

"I am not hindered. As you know my husband is detained with illness in London and I have been a bit lonely since I heard the news." Rose so wanted to tell Stella she thought she'd made a mistake signing Mr. Dalton's papers, but she could not bring herself to mention it.

"Excellent. I have family there I wish you to meet. You will see the house of my birth and meet my two sisters. My father is quite well known there. He is a member of the city council and oversees an orphanage and preaches at the Methodist Church when the pastor is away."

"My goodness." Was all Rose could think to say. She was very interested in meeting the parents who raised a sweet and free-spirited Southern girl like Stella.

Tea arrived and the two made plans, Stella exacting promises to stay away an entire week, if Rose could manage it. Rose downed her tea cakes and rang for more.

Stella laughed out loud at Rose's appetite. "You'll never get into your corset again if you eat like that." She whooped out.

Rose giggled with the young woman who, even though married to an upstanding Charleston banker, still held onto her own personality and exuded confidence. Indeed Rose would learn all she could and make her husband proud. She was a woman after all, young or not.

Chapter 8

Dashing to the side table, Rose grabbed the last tea cake and Stella laughed loudly as they made their way to her husband's office. Stella stared at the drawings Rose had done that rainy day.

"Oh you must never let these be found laying about." Stella was laughing uncontrollably, holding her side. "These are good. Really good, Rose. Old Dalton's tweed suit reminds me of a big Diamondback rattler's skin. And look at Miss Bertram, her parasol stuck in the tree with her Paris shoes getting all wet."

Suddenly there was noises from the foyer. Rose hadn't heard the door knocker. Before she could stop laughing, Captain Wyatt walked straight into the room. Portia right behind him her eyes dark and angry.

"May I speak with Mrs. Lovell. Alone." He stared at Stella like she was the enemy.

Stella put her hand over her mouth, and strangely, she scurried out without a word. Rose thought sure she'd tell Mr. Wyatt to wait in the library like a gentleman.

Portia stood aside as Stella walked past and then backed out shutting the double doors. The room became close and warm of a sudden. Rose still seated, stood, and found her knees knocking together.

"You signed papers with Mr. Dalton?" He questioned her, black eyes staring into hers, his hair disheveled, chin unshaven and dark.

"I thought…I tried to reach you…"

She was rudely interrupted. "Why didn't you send a currier?"

Rose hated being questioned. She needed time to think so turned her back and walked to the window.

"I sent a currier." She turned to face him.

"And what of it? I would have come had I received word from you." He stated, effectively calling her a liar.

"Thomas came back with word, only this morning with news that you were…were…"

"Speak up." He demanded.

Rose looked him in the eye. "He said you were drunk and with a woman. Your crew knew not where to look for you." There, he wanted truth, he had it.

This time, he turned his back to her seeking the other window. He stared out for so long, Rose wondered what his next move would be.

"Aye. It is true. I was drunk. And I am to blame."

Rose couldn't think of a single thing to say. He'd taken the wind out of her sails.

"Had I taken the papers to the solicitor the day you signed them, Captain Lovell would not be in this situation." He said firmly and turned to face her. "As it is, Mr. Dalton got word that your husband was ill and had made you owner of his fortune and made his way here. Had I done my duty, he would not be..."

"What?" Rose wondered.

Running his hand through his hair, mussing it even more, if that were possible, he actually looked...ashamed. "I will be in your husband's debt until the day I die. And servant to a man I despise." He said quietly.

Rose stared at him. She understood nothing.

The man looked up at her. She took a step back. His darkness, hair, eyes, even his sun- browned skin made him a sinister view. But his eyes were sad, hurt.

"You have done nothing wrong." He stated staring over her shoulder, hands stuffed in his back pockets. "It is I who am to blame."

"What blame is there?" She knew her voice cracked.

"The papers you signed give Mr. Dalton full reign over your husband's fortune should he be deceased. You signed off as owner. I have just come from his office."

"I read the papers. They didn't seem to say that." Rose caught her breath and felt her heart sink.

"The papers were all in order. But Dalton slipped in an extra sheet, effectively making himself your overseer and Captain Lovell is now fifty thousand dollars deeper in dept."

Rose wanted to sob. She put her fingertips over her lips. "What can be done?" She whispered.

"Nothing can be done. Had I filed the papers with the solicitor when I was supposed to this would not have happened. As it is, I will report to Captain Lovell my failure to do my duty."

Rose felt sorry for the man. "It's my fault, too. I had no idea..."

"You are a child. I knew better." His voice deepened. "It was not your fault."

"I am not a child." She suddenly felt the pang of regret at always being called a child.

Captain William Ashton Wyatt knew she wasn't any longer. For she had just learned her first real life lesson. Never trust a drunk. And never trust a banker.

Chapter 9

Rose listened to Captain Wyatt's apology.

"Mrs. Lovell, I have injured your husband's affairs, but I will not scurry away like a scullery rat. I will do my duty to him and to you. I am forever sorry for what I have done."

She opened her mouth but nothing came out. All she could do was try to catch his eye to let him know without words, that she didn't blame him.

Captain Wyatt bowed slightly and turned his back, his shoulders slumped and walked away.

There was nothing, absolutely nothing she could do. *God why? I thought you heard my prayer for direction.*

Rose fell into a chair, unable to think.

Stella came in and saw her distress. "Did that man hurt you?" Her fists balled at her sides.

"No." Rose said quietly. "He hurt himself."

"But it affects you. I can see it on your face."

"Oh Stella, you are going to be so ashamed of me…" She sobbed into her hands now.

Stella knelt and Rose told her the whole sordid story. Her friend had warned her against Mr. Dalton and now the whole town would know. How could she have been so naïve?

"There now. I'll speak to Foster. We'll talk it over. There's nothing to be done now. Charleston ladies have lived through a Civil War for goodness' sake. We will get through this." Stella said firmly.

Rose knew she was right. But it wouldn't change the fact that she, a mere child, just like everyone said, had made a terrible blunder concerning her husband's business and now his reputation.

"Get up, Ireland Rose Lovell." Stella ordered. "We are going straightaway to my house. You will be with me when Foster comes home and we will discuss the matter. Surely there is something to be done."

Rose stood as ordered.

"Call Portia and tell her you won't be needing supper this evening. You'll dine with us."

Rose did.

"We'll walk. How long have you been cooped up here in this house…and the gardens?"

Rose didn't answer.

"Come now, get your wrap, the evening air will be cooler."

Fifteen minutes later they were strolling down the Battery gazing out at the Ashley River, the fragrance of white gardenia and pink magnolia lifting on the air. They passed through White Point Garden park. Then walked down near the shipyard, the smell of fish wafting on the air.

Rose looked at the *Emerald Star* rocking on the water and knew the pain of loss. It was evident that the crew was getting ready to sail. She wanted to get on the vessel and run to her husband, to take care of him, to say she was sorry for all that had happened.

But Stella knew what she was thinking. "Now don't you think about it. You're safe. Here, where your husband wants you. He has Yellow Fever. You cannot go to him."

Rose looked at her friend and tears popped into her eyes and then Stella's. She looked away out to the ocean and wished she could go to Ireland where she belonged.

They walked in silence for a very long time, the evening coming upon them. "Time to go to my house. Foster will be home soon and I do not want him to find me gone."

Rose followed alongside her friend, glad for the company. She had never been to Stella's home.

When they stopped Rose looked up and saw a stately house with pink magnolia hanging over the balcony, the round colonnade pillars wrapped in yellow-green ivy. It was in a nice part of town and it looked so welcoming, Rose wanted to weep.

"Come inside dearie. We'll have tea. You ate too many tea cakes."

Rose ran her hand along the smooth wood of a rocker on the verandah and sat. She just couldn't go inside.

"That's right sit there. It's cooler in the shade. I will be around in a few minutes. You relax and take care to put your feet up on that basket there." Stella pointed.

Rose lay her head back and rocked, the white chair creaking on the white painted wooden planks beneath her. The sound was familiar and sweet. She was a little girl in Baltimore, waiting for her father to come home for the evening.

Later, Stella came with little brown-bread cucumber andwiches and they ate at the small white wicker table. Rose ate her food and swallowed several times before a sob could escape.

After some time Foster joined them. She knew Stella had already talked with him privately before bringing him out to her. And for that she was grateful.

"Foster, this is my friend Ireland Rose Lovell. My husband Foster John Perry."

Rose wondered why Stella was so formal. Perhaps it had been her proper Savannah upbringing.

"Mr. Perry." Rose stood and greeted him quietly.

"Stella has told me of your concerns." He pulled a chair out and after the ladies took their seats, joined them at the table. "It is useless to spend any time worrying. I will look into the matter and see if something can be done…" He offered.

"Thank you Mr. Perry. I know nothing can be done, but I thank you just the same. My signature, Captain Wyatt informed me, is all that was needed."

"I'm sorry to say that Mr. Dalton is of questionable character but we know that God himself sees to people like that."

Rose found a smile creep to her lips. "Thank you for reminding me." She whispered.

The topic turned to other subjects, mostly gardening, weather and upcoming events of the summer season.

Grateful, Rose's nerves settled. Soon, Foster and Stella walked her back home, offering the use of their small carriage, which Rose refused. "Thank you for your time and your concerns. I will be all right." She assured them and knew somehow she would be.

When they left, Rose took up her embroidery and disallowed any thoughts of the day's events. After some time she had a hankering for a cup of tea and walked through the back to the separate kitchen where she found sad faces everywhere.

"What is the matter?" She asked Portia.

Portia shooed Thomas and Lily to their duties and without making eye contact said, "We all doing our duty to ya, Miz Rose. Don't you worry none."

Portia paused and added. "Lily done heerd all you said. I was gonna whoop dat gal but I jus didn't have the heart. Was she tellin' the truth?"

"I'm afraid she was, if she told you Mr. Dalton has been dishonest."

Rose's heart sank. They all knew what had happened, it was clear. She had not considered that her and her husband's demise might mean theirs as well. "That's all right. I would have told you anyway."

"Now don't worry none. The Lord has ways of fixin' these things mind you…"

"Portia." Rose began, catching her brown eyes. "I will see to you all. I promise." The words meaningful and soft, gave her a sense of confidence. "We will be all right."

Portia nipped her apron to her eye and poked there. "Yes, Miz Rose."

And for the first time Rose saw her duty to her servants as they saw their duty to her.

"We are all God's children." Rose said quietly and left Portia to her work knowing Portia did not show her weaknesses often.

Rose realized for the first time how much she had to learn. Tomorrow was Sunday church at St. Michael's and Rose intended to be there.

Chapter 10

Church services at St. Michael's was the spiritual medicine she needed. Rose wore her best blue cotton cambric dress and bonnet. Emmanuel brought the carriage. Even though it was several blocks away, it was not fashionable to be seen walking about in one's Sunday best.

Foster and Stella join her in the four-person pew. She was glad they were near the front, for she would not like to see Mr. Dalton today. Christian duties required certain boundaries, she knew. One should not be staring bitterly into the face of another they disliked and well she knew it. It was better to be polite and distant.

As well as she loved St. Michael's, she missed her small church on the side streets of Baltimore. Her parents had lived well enough, grateful for every meal, for every dollar earned and for the fact that they survived and thrived in America. They knew what it was to be hungry and without warm clothing out on the windy hills of Ireland, neighbors starving for lack of food.

Because they were acquainted with these pains they possessed a watchfulness for those who needed food and clothing. Thus Ireland Rose learned many ways of sharing. St. Michael's served Charleston's elite and so there were many occasions for helping the poor. Mostly with money rather than service, Rose noted.

She had fallen into the same thinking; generous with her pocketbook but not involved. Today she resolved to draw closer to those who could teach her as well as learn from her. With that in mind, she raised her hand when the Reverend called for those who would be interested in feeding the children at Jamison's Orphanage. That particular one was underfunded because of its African population. The white orphanage was well endowed when many more raised their hand to assist there. There were two hands raised for Jamison's Rose noted, hers and one other. Stella's.

Satisfied with new purpose, she had a few words with Foster and Stella before Emmanuel carried her back home. Within the hour she and Portia sat at the table and discussed what Monday would bring. Tomorrow her new work would begin.

After breakfast Lily and Thomas joined their grandmother Portia in the attic and carried down the servant's stairs small items that might be of use to the orphanage. By noon, the pantry had been invaded and two small crates of fresh garden vegetables sat at the ready. Two side tables, a bench, and a child's desk were loaded into the old carriage and carried off.

The second trip Rose insisted on going along.

"You gonna go ain't ya? I can see it in yo eyes chile." Portia wagged her head. "Them ladies see you there at the Negra orphanage, you best be set for a bunch o'talk."

Rose hurried to get her small string handbag, stuffing some bills from her husband's cash drawer. Once she made up her mind, she went head over tails, she knew. But what did it matter? What one had could be swept away like beach sand on a windy day. And then what?

Besides she'd been taught everyone was more alike than different. Thanks to her frugal parents, she knew that hunger was hunger, no matter where you came from and clothing was needed for every body not just a few. Which reminded her. She had several dresses that might fit a young woman there.

Hurrying abovestairs, she went through her bureau and collected several items. Then rifled through her underthings and nightclothes. She had an armful and met Portia halfway down.

"I's got some things, too." She said proudly.

"Portia, how kind of you." Rose's face was flushed.

"Lily ain't got no use for these. She done growed up on them long legs." Portia belly-laughed. "Just like her Granmama."

Rose's eyes met Portia's thanking her.

"Come. Let's get these out to Emmanuel before he draws the wagon away from the curb."

"Portia you sit up front with Emmanuel." Rose ordered.

"Chile you don't mean sich a thing. I ain't havin' you ridin' in de back like 'at for all Charleston to see, mind you." She had her hands on her hips. "Even I knows that ain't right."

Rose scuttled to the rear of the wagon and drew up her dress gently, and stepped up with no assistance whatsoever. "Go on Emmanuel. Get on Portia, before folks start to staring."

Portia didn't know what else to do, so stepped up beside her husband and prayed that the good Lord shut every judging eye they passed.

The wagon lumbered along at a slow pace and Rose made certain that she hunkered down and enjoyed the ride, remembering times she rode to town with her father, sharing her memories with Lily and Thomas.

Before long they had arrived at Jamison's near the run down areas on the edge of town. The sewer smells brought her handkerchief to her nose and then she remembered her manners. This was home to some folks and well she should think of that. They all jumped down and children ran out from the facility, which was tattered and barely standing.

The building constructed of wood needed paint but was clean and tidy, if not modern. The smell of cornbread and beans wafted into their noses. Then the stink of stale fish from the wharves on this side of town soon covered the wonderful fragrances from within. Two outhouses stood at odd angles.

White-toothed smiles in dark faces were everywhere. Some stood back shyly while the elder children walked forward without a word and helped unload, eyes big with joy as each item was handed down.

"Come in. Sit down." Mrs. Jamison offered her guests. "We were about to partake. And there's plenty, right children?" She looked about.

Rose looked to Emmanuel. He nodded and she noticed immediately that several of the older children left. She wondered if they would be eating their dinner. She decided it was so and said, "I believe we will join, if you will allow us to pay for our meals."

"'Tis not necessary. You are guests and are welcome at our table." Mrs. Jamison said again.

"If you feed us as well as I think you will, we will pay our way." Rose said, her chin jutting out.

"Yes, ma'am." Mrs. Jamison said with a smile. "Come on then, we have hungry children. The others have gone for plates. You will not be eating anyone's meal."

Rose was glad Mrs. Jamison answered her question and lifted her skirts and found a bench. Emmanuel, Portia, Thomas and Lily followed. This was her first adventure outside her home. And a grand one it was, she decided.

Suddenly the room became silent. Prayers were offered up by Emmanuel, at Mrs. Jamison's request. Rose knew they were standing, well, sitting on holy ground. Why had she spent so many days wandering around that big old house?

After bowls of beans and cornbread, the children began to bring out their handmade items to show to the guests. Rugs made of rags. Baskets made of reeds and grasses from the swamps. Bowls made from branches and sea shells. Spoons carved from wood. And jewel boxes made of beads and polished wood.

Rose noticed one of the smaller children sitting at the desk they'd brought. Proud looks and thankfulness were on the faces. She sensed they had much to teach her in the days to come. This would be her work until her husband came home from London. Home to fix the trouble she and Captain Wyatt had caused.

Chapter 11

The next day, June 29th Captain Wyatt came to call.

"The *Emerald Star* is loaded with her stock and wares. We will set out tomorrow morning. Is there anything you wish to send to your husband?" He offered quietly barely looking at her.

"Yes, if you would be so kind…." She hurried to the hall desk and extracted several letters from a drawer.

With a bit of embarrassment, for they smelled of lavender, she handed them to Captain Wyatt. "I have explained what transpired between Mr. Dalton and I." She looked him in the eye.

"Aye. And I will be forthright with my part, as well." He was solemn as he placed the letters in his pocket.

His dark eyes were bloodshot. She wondered if drink would destroy him. And what of the woman he was with. It was certain, Captain Wyatt was put out at having to be in this position and she, Ireland Rose, had not helped one bit.

Rose cast her eyes away and sensed the man needed to be on his ship and away.

Just like every other time, he bowed slightly and stalked out, boots clicking loudly on the polished wood floors then she heard them tap on the marble as he exited.

She pulled in a breath and prayed for Captain Wyatt and his crew a safe journey across.

❧

Ashton Wyatt walked slowly this time. The woman was going to be his death. She had her coloring, her small stature. The haunting resemblance of a woman he loved stopped at Mrs. Lovell's voice and tender gaze, he reminded himself. It had been more than ten years, why hadn't he contained his bitterness? Why did her memory pierce his heart every time he entered that infernal house. And now he was obligated by duty to Captain Lovell. There was no way but to walk it through. He started for the tavern and hated himself.

❧

Rose swept across the floor and made her way to the servant's stairs. She meant to be busy today. Another storm was brewing outdoors. The rain had already begun to tap at the windows. The attic would be stifling, but she needed something to do before another bout of brooding overtook her. With firm steps she intended to search out more items for the orphanage now that she could see what it was about.

The entire afternoon was spent cleaning out the smaller trunks. Some had children's clothes, which was perfect. She hadn't noticed them before and set out to make piles.

Dust flying, she sneezed regularly and found that even her rolled up sleeves gave no comfort in the stifling heat.

She found items of interest and set them aside for another time. One a box of letters. Another what looked to be a handwritten journal. She wondered what family lived here before her husband purchased the house; her mind twittered away at all sorts of ideas. Her mother always said she was a dreamer. Perhaps she was.

Twice, she stopped and stepped down to the floor level to relieve her back and feel a bit of coolness. It was hard work walking, head bent, at the roof angle of the attic. Portia had scolded her, but to no avail. Now there was a large pile of laundry for Portia, so Rose found herself working alone until near dark.

Happy with the results, she asked Thomas if he might come up and carry several of the larger items down the narrow stairs. Whoever thought to carry trunks and portraits up these stairs into the attic must be quite daft, she concluded.

When Thomas was almost finished, she laughed out loud when one leg of a table broke off and bounced, stair by stair, like a pirate's wooden limb, to the bottom. She caught Thomas' eye and they nearly tripped over in laughter at the sound of it clunking each stair as it rattled down.

The day over, she patted her hands in the air, dust flying, and stepped down, Thomas behind her. "Well done." She said. "Now Thomas, if you would please set these items in the extra room, we will load up again for the orphanage.

Thomas said smiling with joy, "Yes ma'am."

Rose retired to her room. Portia had a warm bath ready and she climbed in filthy and came out half an hour later, smelling of lavender, and clean, hair to toe. Now what she wanted was a strong cup of English tea with cream and sugar and a book. An old book. She wanted to read history this afternoon.

Portia had hung the sheets for they smelled of fresh air. Sighing after a good day's work, she arranged her pillows and threw herself across the bed on her stomach. The thick and heavy book on Irish history came from her husband's library; she smelled it and cracked it open.

Not ten minutes later, she heard rumblings below stairs. Captain Wyatt was to leave on the morrow, so he would be preparing his crew. But who would call at this late hour, she wondered. Proper calling times were past.

Rose knew that she had been absent from Charleston's society meetings these last weeks and now regretted it. Her husband had been right, indeed. She had no invitations or calling cards on the silver tray below stairs.

Hurriedly, she found a dress, forgetting that she'd given many of them to the orphanage. She chose a soft pink lawn and slipped it over her head. It was not stylish in the least, but then no one had left their card this afternoon, signaling they would be callers, so it did not matter her appearance this eve.

Thankfully, the dress did not require buttoning up the back, for it was an older style. Her long hair, still wet from the bath needed Portia's nimble fingers. Rose fumbled with it and found it heavy and tangled. Shrugging, she picked up a brush and worked at the mess. She wished that her hair was not so thick at times like these.

Portia came bursting into the room. "No need to worry, Miz Rose, just a child from the orphanage bringing you a lemon cake."

"A child from the orphanage," she repeated. "Bother, I'll go down as I am." She scurried away before her maid could protest.

"Ah, a babe…" She heard Portia speak under her breath.

Happily, Rose didn't mind at all that she was almost running, so happy she was to know there was a young visitor at the door.

"Emmanuel, I'm on my way. Hold the door." Rose ordered. "Ah, I see I have made it before the young lass has gone her way." She cried out.

The dark eyes looking back at her were large.

"Please come in. What is your name?"

"Arella." Came the shy voice. But she did not move.

"Arella. What a beautiful name. So you have brought a cake for me then?" Rose coaxed her just inside the door.

The girl appeared to be twelve, maybe fourteen, Rose wasn't sure. She took the cake from Emmanuel. "Shall we have some? I am famished."

The girl's eyes nearly popped out of her head. She had never been invited to eat with a…a rich white woman. She started backing away and shaking her head.

"Do you have permission to stay for perhaps an hour? It is nearly dark. I will have Emmanuel take you back by wagon should it be required." She offered.

"I…I had better get back right away." She said nervously. "I ain't s'posed to come inside." Her eyes grew large.

"Okay. Then you must do your duty. Can we sit out on the verandah then?"

"Guessin' that'd be all right." She said.

"Emmanuel would you please ask Portia to bring us tea? And a knife so we can devour this lovely cake. I promise to share." She smiled at him as he turned.

"Arella, did you make this cake yourself?"

She nodded sitting stiffly in the white cane chair.

"Did your mother teach you how?" Rose made conversation as the early evening sound of crickets chimed in. The wind blew the willowy trees softly, the day's raindrops blowing away dry before they fell.

"Mama died when I was nine."

"I'm so sorry." Rose gazed at the girl. "And she taught you how to cook, then?"

"Yes'm."

"My mother died, too. And my father. In Ireland."

The girl's head swung toward her and Rose caught her eye. "Seems we have something in common."

Thankfully, Portia came with tea and plates. A strange smile rested on her lips. Rose guessed her maid was just as pleased to serve another as Rose was.

"Portia, would you join us, please?"

Portia's eyebrows shot upwards but she pulled off her apron, looked about, and sat. She reached for the teapot, but Rose gave her a look and lifted it herself and poured, then served their guest first and then Portia before she took her own. She saw Portia look left and then right and out front, she knew, checking to see if any of the society ladies may be walking by. For the house was on the Battery and many people took advantage of the boulevard and the river views nearby. Rose knew she'd hear about it later.

No one was about and Rose was glad, for it settled Portia down immediately. The three talked of the orphanage, St. Michael's Church, and the weather.

At the end of the evening, Portia and Emmanuel set out in the wagon and desposited Arella safely home. In Arella's arms were three lightweight blankets from the hall bureau and a small hand-stitched pillow from Portia.

Chapter 12

Weeks passed without word from Captain Lovell or Captain Wyatt. Rose began to feel the creeping of worry climb up into her mind. She prayed every day and wondered what would keep the two from writing, unless...no she would not entertain those thoughts.

Her work at the orphanage kept her busy. The entire house had been sorted and reduced to such as they needed. All extra furniture, dishes, clothes and shoes were given to the orphanage. Rose had never been happier. She must continue to spend the days fruitfully so she could tell her husband all that had passed. She knew he would be proud of her.

With not a little fear and trembling, she was to accompany Stella to a private women's meeting where funds were to be raised for the African orphanage. Someone had dared release that information and Rose doubted there would be many in attendance since the most prominent women of Charleston were the epitome of kindness to the white orphanage.

But Rose scolded herself for judging. What did it matter who was helped as long as it was the needy. She knew the other women were called in one direction, she in another, that was all. God expected no one to be someone else, only themselves. She thought about that for a few minutes. Who was she? What was she here for? She would never bear children. Rose felt a certain sadness, for she so wanted them. But if that was not meant to be, heaven knows, there were already many children who needed a mother. And her husband was known for his service to the poor here and in London. Why should she not join him? Her resolve firmed. She stepped up into Stella's carriage and her driver took them to the Episcopal Church where the meeting was to be held.

Rose had not set foot in this church. When they walked through the doors, she gasped at the beautiful stained glass windows at the front, the mahogany pews. The platform graduated level by level until one could see the simple white cross between the tall, colorful windows painted with scenes from the Lord's book.

The high ceilings were planked with cedar boards and two lecterns stood at the ready, one on the floor, the other on a tall pedestal.

Several ladies meandered toward the front of the church. When they had gathered Rose counted five in all, including Stella and herself. They waited a proper amount of time and began the meeting. Speaking quietly, they introduced themselves. Twenty minutes later, Miss Celeste Antoinette Bertram walked into the church, her blond hair swung up beautifully revealing her slender neck, blue eyes scanning the pews.

She put a white gloved hand over her brow and found the ladies. Slowly, she made her way up front. "Oh, I'm sorry to be late. Is there room for another?" She asked sweetly.

Rose could see the word "no" forming on Stella's lips and prayed she would keep quiet. Perhaps the rich and beautiful Miss Bertram was inclined to be of service. They could use all the help they could muster, Rose thought.

"Please join us." One kind lady said. And then there were introductions again.

Oddly, Miss Bertram sat next to Rose. There were other seats more convenient but she seemed to choose carefully.

Stella all but rolled her eyes. Rose gave her a look.

One fashionable hour of talk passed and the ladies dismissed. Stella stood to her feet and Rose watched as she lifted her dress and stomped toward the door.

"Mrs. Lovell...how good to see you." Miss Bertram stood in front of her, barring her leave.

"Miss Bertram. I hear congratulations are in order." She said sweetly. "Is there a date for the occasion?"

"We are discussing the matter. The heat is too severe for my dress, so we may wait until Christmas for the nuptials. St. Michael's is already attained." She said, her hands fluttering in the air. "And the dress must be shipped over from Paris, you know."

"Oh, that will be a lovely affair." Rose said kindly and stepped to the side. "It is good to see you. Perhaps you'll be at the next meeting?"

"Indeed." And Miss Bertram sashayed down the wide aisle leaving the others in her wake. All except Stella.

Rose hurried to meet up with Stella. She knew there would be plenty of talk all the way home. She only hoped her friend remembered they had arrived together.

The horses were dancing. Stella's man was impatient, or should she say Stella was impatient to leave. "Did you see her? She was there to spy. I'm telling you Rose, I can't abide that woman."

Rose remained quiet, letting her friend blow off some steam. It would help settle her nerves. Stella was no-nonsense and Rose liked her for that. She couldn't quite bring herself to judge her since Stella always told the truth the way she saw it.

The carriage jerked forward. Stella stewed most of the way. Rose knew she was holding her tongue for her sake.

"I'm excited about our plans for Jamison's." Rose tried a different tact. Their first assignment was to talk to friends who may be interested in donating quality items. Or they might hire out the older children for work in the gardens, the kitchen or child care assistance.

Stella still stewed, her jaw clamped shut.

Rose smiled and allowed her gaze to follow the cobblestone pathway. The clanking of hooves and wheels rolling over the cobblestone street made it impossible to talk anyway. She wondered how her husband was doing and hoped a letter may be waiting when she arrived home.

The strong fragrance of Gardenia lifted her spirits. The plantation families from the low country were away at their summer homes to escape the oppressive heat. Rose tapped her handkerchief across her brow wishing for a large glass of Portia's sweet tea. Even the vines and branches seemed to hang lower as the moist heat settled on the evening ground.

Stella said her goodbyes and Rose knew she would have plenty to tell Foster this evening. She wished she could tell Captain Lovell about her day. Sensing he would be proud of her, she stepped down from the carriage and hurried inside. Maybe a letter had come in the post.

Her hat was off and she tossed it willy nilly on the hat rack then made for the hall table where Portia always set her mail. No letter. Sighing, she lifted her skirts, glad that she'd gotten in the door without disturbing Emmanuel. No doubt they were tired from their daily chores and might even now be sitting in the garden sipping tea.

Up the stairs to her room for a quick toss of several underskirts, just enough to be decent. Down the stairs and through the back doors; she stepped through hoping to see them and found that no one was about. Where could they be? Hopefully, nothing bad had happened while she was away. Rose guarded her heart against borrowing trouble, just like Portia said.

When twenty minutes passed, Rose began to wonder and so took a walk out back to the servant quarters and looked about. There under the Magnolia tree sat Portia and her family.

Rose felt her heart relax. It was a terrible thing to think she could be here alone without her husband or Emmanuel and Portia to protect her or care for her. Suddenly she missed her parents.

"Miz Rose. We done wondered what took ya'll so long. I says to Emmanuel here, I was just thinking on worrying a mite."

"I'm here Portia. It's so hot tonight isn't it? Our meeting went well. I think we will be able to assist the orphanage."

"Now that's mighty good of ya, chile."

Rose smiled, thanking Portia with her eyes. Even Lily and Thomas were quiet tonight. There was nothing worth doing this eve, except waving a fan about one's face and so Rose joined the family for iced tea underneath the barely swaying leaves of the Magnolia.

Chapter 13

There was still no word from her husband or Mr. Wyatt. Rose had heard rumors from returning ship captains of rampant disease in London. Surely, there would be word soon.

The *News & Courier*, Charleston's newspaper, carried news of the same sort.

By mid-morning, she had written her husband a long letter, full of the summer activities, and her new position as a member of the newly established ladies mission group whose job it was to support Jamison's Orphanage. Placing the letter on the hall table ready for the post, Rose went about her duties.

The temperature was climbing now that July was almost upon them. The servants were busy keeping the insects from raiding the milled flour and tempers were fragile. Portia had appeared twice with a face shiny in sweat and Rose worried that the woman took on too many tasks.

"Come, Portia, sit for awhile. The winds have picked up and it is a bit cooler here in the garden. Take some tea with me?

"Chile you know I ain't got no time to be sittin' about. They's plenty to be done, pickin' the vegetables out back. Thomas and that silly grandchild Lily o'mine is trying their best, but I needs to help."

Rose knew Portia could not be persuaded today.

"I'll be about a short walk on the boulevard then." She called out and swiftly lifted her skirts and hurried away before Portia felt the need to attend her.

Rose put on a white straw hat, tied the blue ribbon underneath her chin and chose a light colored umbrella, a serviceable one, and headed out the front door and across White Point Garden toward the river walkway. She noticed several people standing at the guardrail watching the waves and found a place and gazed across the familiar expanse. Several ships bounced on the waters, their white sails whipping in the wind like so many sea birds.

Fort Sumter, she knew lay in ruins across the way, the Civil War almost twenty years past. The town of Charleston had been devastatingly destroyed by the cannons fired from the ships out in the Ashley and Cooper Rivers which encased Charleston's battery. But last year, 1883, had been a banner year for growth and rebuilding.

Employment was high. Banks were reestablished. Charleston fortunes were again blossoming. The harbor was full of stick-like ships with white flags blowing about in the winds. The wharves reeked of fish and boxes were piled high awaiting another destination or distribution to the locals. Crabs, oysters and shrimp merchants were making restauranteurs wealthy. Hotels of immense size and respectable accommodations, helped to build the export trade industry.

Rose felt her Northern birth had ceased to be a difficulty, at least for the time. The real estate opportunities of Charleston were booming and so were their inhabitants.

Rose smiled. She had reported all the news to her husband hoping that her letters would make him well and anxious to return. She prayed it might be soon. She shut her eyes and pictured the *Ireland Rose* sitting in the harbor.

Suddenly, she felt a bump at her arm.

"Excuse me." Came a sound out of somewhere nearby. Rose opened her eyes and turned toward the voice.

"I'm so clumsy." A young woman stared at her. "Why you're Mrs. Lovell, are you not?"

Rose shaded her eyes and peered into a pair of dark eyes. They reminded her of someone. "Yes, yes, I am Mrs. Lovell. And who might I have the honor of speaking to?" She said formally.

The woman's smile lit up her entire face.

My name is Mrs. Ava McGuire of Queen Street."

Rose returned the woman's infectious smile unfamiliar with the name. "Had we been acquainted Mrs. McGuire I assure you I would have remembered."

"We have not. My brother William Ashton Wyatt is your husband's employee."

"Captain Wyatt?" Rose registered surprise in her voice. No wonder those dark handsome eyes brought back her memory. She had seen them before.

"Indeed. He has worked for your husband for over a year now."

"I am happy to make your acquaintance Mrs. McGuire." Rose put out her hand, even though she knew it was not proper to do so in public. It seemed that Mrs. McGuire was without an escort as well.

The woman's smile was genuine. Rose suddenly found herself inviting the woman to tea at Clarinda's Tea Room. "It is only a short walk, if you have the time." She waited.

"I do." The young woman agreed and swirled her pink parasol. "Pray, what is your given name?"

"I am Ireland Rose."

"Ireland Rose. That is a lovely name." The woman whispered.

"Why thank you. Your parasol is beautiful. Where did you find such a confection?" Rose inquired as she admired it.

"Oh, it is a special gift from my brother. He brought it back from London."

Rose felt a kinship immediately. "How kind of him."

The two chatted over tea for more than an hour. Captain Wyatt was mentioned very little, but it seemed Mrs. McGuire enjoyed speaking of her banker husband. Rose listened intently and saw a woman in love.

Rose found herself rather pensive and quiet. She wished for a loving husband…even a husband at home…and spoke to herself sharply at her ungrateful thoughts.

"I am happy for you." Rose said with truth. "We shall have to get together again. I am most anxious to establish some new friendships. Perhaps you can assist me?"

Ava McGuire was happy at the request. Rose could see it in her face.

"Indeed. This very evening, I shall tell Mr. McGuire that I have met Captain's Lovell's wife and invite you to the next soiree."

"It will be my pleasure to meet your friends. I shall trust you implicitly." Rose said forthright, for she sensed Ava McGuire was an honest person.

"Indeed you may."

They parted ways and Rose felt herself step more lightly both in foot and in heart. She had made a new friend. Captain Wyatt's sister. *Providence no doubt.*

When they met again Rose meant to ask if she'd had a word from her brother. She'd been too reserved to turn the conversation to something so personal.

Chapter 14

Rose checked the table for any new posts. Disappointed yet again, she greeted the noise from the July Fourth parade without much enjoyment. The Citidel military corps made a handsome show in their uniforms. The crowd crowed with excitement as they passed. Charleston was well known for its well trained cadets.

The parade was over and White Point Garden was full of beautifully-dressed ladies and gentlemen away from their businesses for an afternoon of social connection. She had come without an escort knowing full well that she would be shunned by the ladies with husbands on their arm. But it didn't matter. She may well be a widow by now, the way it seemed.

Captain Wyatt had left days ago and there had not been a word from her husband in London. Certainly he would send word through a nurse who would write on his behalf. Rose was thinking about this when she was approached.

"Greetings on this fine day." Ava McGuire interrupted her negative thoughts.

"Mrs. McGuire. How nice to see you again." Rose's heart lifted.

"May I introduce my husband, Mr. Theodore Madison McGuire."

"Mr. McGuire." Rose nearly extended her hand and instead tipped her chin in greeting.

Ava chatted on about the weather and the newly built Drayton House on East Battery…in the dashing Queen Anne architectural style.

Rose knew the house. It overshadowed all the other homes along the street with its architectural design and size. Mr. McGuire was indeed a handsome man with distinct blue eyes and hair as black as coal. He was tall and finely dressed, but Rose noticed he did not listen to his lovely wife as she spoke. He seemed to be seeking someone in the crowd.

Ava, unaware, chattered on with a joy known only by a woman loved. Rose put her own musings to rest and engaged herself in Ava's excitement.

"You are a woman of great information." Rose declared. "You must tell me more about Charleston's history. I'm afraid Baltimore's is quite different." And was instantly regretful. She'd been remiss in mentioning any other roots than that of a well-established Charleston family.

Mr. McGuire looked down his nose at her, but Rose pretended not to notice.

The pain of the recent war was still fresh, and well she understood what a Southerner might feel like should they find themselves in Northern territory. It was all relative as to what city one was standing in, yet she must be a bit more careful not to draw attention to her Northern roots in such a manner.

And indeed she liked Ava McGuire very well. Mr. McGuire excused himself and went off to speak to another well-dressed gentleman. The man's tall gray hat and gray suit set him apart from the others. Rose wondered who the man could be.

Ava took her elbow and they strolled the boardwalk. "You must come to my home, Ireland Rose and see the beautiful chest my brother brought. It is exquisite."

Rose's hand went to her throat. "Then you have heard from your brother?" She said as pleasantly as possible.

"Oh no, not recently, indeed I have not heard from him since he left a few days ago. You have no word from your husband?" Ava looked at Rose, eyes wide.

"I have not." She admitted. "It has been longer than usual, I must admit." She gazed at a child and knelt to place a fallen toy back into the chubby hand, glad for the aversion.

"I shall write William this evening and send it in the next post." Ava declared. "Certainly, you must not worry yourself about Captain Lovell. He is a worthy man." She lifted her chin.

Rose knew she had a friend in Ava McGuire. "I would be most grateful. And please call me Rose."

"I shall indeed." Ava twirled her parasol, stopping several times to speak to other ladies.

"You are well established in Charleston then?" Rose said lightly.

"My husband is a third generation rice planter. But now that the rice fields have nearly been brought to ruin, he has gained an excellent position at the Bank of Charleston and does quite well."

Rose listened quietly. The conversation brought up old memories of the papers she had signed and how Mr. Wyatt had scolded her. Best to leave well enough alone, as her mother would say.

"Have you children running about your home?" Rose asked softly.

"Oh not yet. Mr. McGuire does not want a family for several years. He is just now establishing himself among the banking industry and things are going so well." She said sing-song-like.

Rose smiled. "What do you do to occupy your time? Mr. Lovell and I have no children which leaves me too much time to dawdle."

"My grandmother taught me to cook and embroider and garden." Ava gushed. "But I would rather be about the city looking after the poor families." She said in a whisper. "My husband does not approve."

Rose laughed aloud. "I should say I think we are kindred spirits."

Ava smiled wickedly. "Shall we find a cause and work together?"

"I have just recently joined several other ladies at the Episcopal Church and we have begun raising funds and donating material goods to Jamison's Orphanage."

"Nooo..." Ava stopped and looked about. "Do not let these ladies hear you say such things." She teased. "Else you should pay dearly."

"We have only just begun. Would you care to join us?" Rose said smartly.

"Most certainly. My husband is a very busy man most evenings. When is the next meeting?"

"Oh an entire month away, but do come for a visit. I will show you my herb garden and we can put our heads together."

"Shall I come by tomorrow then?" Ava giggled. "Morning or afternoon?

"Oh morning for tea before the sun wilts my plants."

"Eight then?"

"Yes, perfect. Do not dress for me, unless your husband insists upon it." Rose added. "For I am pleased to be at ease."

"I as well." But I do have to be rigid when I am in public for my husband has his reputation to think of."

"Indeed he does." Rose knew the importance of one's reputation in Charleston.

Mr. McGuire came for his wife, politely disengaging her from Rose's company and flew away with her. Ava turned her head and winked.

Mr. Wyatt's sister was a likable character. She wondered at his dark, almost sinister countenance. How could they be so opposite in personality and lifestyle? The two shared one prolific feature. Their dark eyes and lashes. Black they were and very handsome, Rose thought.

Humming, she made her way home and entered the house, cooler by several degrees. There were noises in the kitchen beside the garden. Southern homes had unattached kitchens due to the frequent occurrence of fire, since most of them started with the cook's fire. She thought it rather convenient most times, because it also meant the fires were not lit indoors during the broiling summer months.

The smell of cornbread wafted to her nose. She had not eaten any of the food from the purveyors at the park. Dashing up the stairs, she changed to a lightweight dress she could appear in and still be decent, then walked hurriedly through the garden to the kitchens.

"Miz Rose. You been out der in dat hot sun all this time? And you wit your fair skin." She clucked. "I's gettin' you some lemonade dis minute."

"That sounds wonderful."

"What you been doin' that makes ya so happy?" Portia was back with her cool drink.

"We will have a guest tomorrow. Early. Eight in the morning." Rose spoke quickly, throwing back her glass in a most unladylike fashion and swallowed.

"Dat early? That means I's got to get my chores done afore the sun comes up." She went about her business.

Rose thought her maid sounded happy. Portia was as good-hearted as any woman could come. She and Emmanuel were free to leave long ago but chose to stay.

"I done near forgot." Portia came hurrying back. "I don't know where my mind be at these days...you got word from over der in London. Cap'n Lovell done wrote."

Before Rose could turn, Portia called, "Lily, you get on up and get Miz Rose her letter. Hurry up now."

Lily flew on those long legs of hers and by the time Rose's heart stopped beating so fast, she had the letter in her hand.

It felt strange, and frightening all at once to see his familiar script. Rose settled on a settee near the roses out of the way and slowly opened the note. It was still unread when Lily came running up with another lemonade.

"Thank you Lily. Would you mind ever so much to pick a small nosegay of pink roses for dinner this evening?"

"No ma'am." Lily chimed. "I knows where the knife is." She hurried away.

Rose stared after her. Lily loved the gardens, especially her flowers.

She knew she was avoiding the inevitable. Yet didn't she now hold the letter written by her husband's own hand. Pulling in a deep breath, the gentle fragrance from the roses lifting her spirits, she ended her foolishness and unfolded the letter and read. Slowly at first and then quicker.

Her husband was weak from the illness, but well. He would leave for home in September. Both he and Mr. Wyatt were bringing the ships back across the Atlantic together. Rose wanted to dance. She thought of the conversations they would have, what trinkets he would bring from London, maybe even a beautiful trunk. She wanted to tell him about the orphanage. Perhaps by the time he returned, she would have good news. And she would know Ava McGuire better, too. Perhaps they all would dine together in the huge dining room that was hardly ever used.

Suddenly, she needed to survey the house. Look at it from a visitor's eye. What could be changed, perhaps rearranged more suitably. She had never really tried her hand at rearranging the furnishings. Lucinda had probably placed each item with perfect symmetry. Would her husband be angry if she attempted to change the decor?

Rose stood up taller. She wouldn't know if she didn't try. She would start this very day. Happy for the good news and something to occupy her time, she walked into each room, crossed her arms over her midsection and took a good, long look, her small foot tapping the elegant, but worn Aubusson carpet.

The colors were rich. Golds, greens, navy, and burgundy. They were beautiful, but made the house dark. She preferred muted tones. Soft blues and crèmes, soft greens with rose and tan. There was still time, but what funds she had left were in the drawer. And barely two months to do the work.

Excitement scurried through her bones as she made her way to her husband's office. She counted out four hundred twenty five dollars. That was a start. Suddenly, her brain began to bubble. She would begin with new draperies and consult with Ava McGuire on the morrow as soon as she could bring up the subject politely.

Sitting in her husband's chair Rose picked up a pencil and pad and began to draw. Walking room to room, she penciled in sketches and color ideas.

"Chile you be up so long. And you with company comin' in the mornin'" Portia followed her up the stairs. "We both best be gettin' some sleepin' done in dis heat or we ain't gonna be nothin' but wilted greens in da mornin'."

"You are right, as always." She sighed and pushed the pad away.

"See now, you done wore yoself out." Portia unwound her hair and brushed through it, tying in the rags so her already wavy hair would be even more so by morning.

"Thank you. You are so good to me. Captain Lovell will be home, if the winds are favorable for the journey. I shall go to sleep wondering what he might bring. Oh Portia, I know it's not the gifts that count, but it's knowing you have someone who cares for you."

"Chile, you need a good deal o' takin' care of." She laughed heartily. "Now off to sleep. You don't want that sandman throwing sand in yo eyes."

"Oh Portia, the things you say..."

"Dat girl, she half sleep already..." Portia patted the child's head. "Just like a tiny young'un o'my own." She whispered. "Dem blue eyes the purtiest I ever saw...

Chapter 15

The knocker sounded at a quarter to eight.

"Yo lady friend here, Miss Rose. And she early." Portia knocked at Rose's door then ran back downstairs and called for Lily.

"You go on and set her in the front parlor and mind you don't be starin' you hear chile?" Portia scolded her granddaughter then scurried, as fast as her legs could carry her, up the stairs.

Lily nodded and ran.

"Dat girl run everywhere. She don't know the first thing about walking like a lady." Portia was swinging her head from side to side, chuckling as she worked with Rose's hair.

"That's what a child does. They run freely -- as they should." Rose said, wishing for Portia to hurry. "Nevermind, she'll grow up and be a lady, you'll see. I was the same way. Father allowed me to be a child. Mother made sure I grew up knowing how to manage myself." She mused.

"An lookee here where you's at. Married to a fine man. Dis nice house, prettiest one as far as I can see wit these old eyes...dat's fo sure."

"Yes, I know I should be more grateful."

Portia stopped. "You's grateful child. Ain't ya? Lord knows you cain't get much finer than dis." She waved her arms. "Heaven be better, but while's you here, jus enjoy ever day, mind?"

Rose exhaled with a smile and Portia announced her finished after pinning one more curl into submission.

She hurried to the top stair then slowed, descending like the lady she was. It was time to practice since her husband would be home and they would be out in society again. Excitement jangled her nerves as she hurried to the parlor, slowed and entered.

"Ireland Rose, have you changed a thing since Captain Lovell brought you here?" Ava gushed.

Rose's eyes grew large. Could the woman read her thoughts as well? "I have not." She admitted with a gaze around the room. Why hadn't she noticed before? The furnishings were so formal as to be almost impossible to sit upon comfortably.

"Then it is time. See here, these colors were popular ten years ago. You must go lighter. Dark colors make a room appear too hot, especially at this time of year." Ava wiped her brow with her handkerchief. "All the best homes have the light colors."

"As it is, I was considering..."

Ava interrupted. "Shall we make a job for ourselves, then? We can talk while we work. And I know the best designers in town."

Rose knew Ava must have money to throw about, but she herself was more reserved, she was sure, than Mrs. McGuire. But she dare not be too reserved else it may reflect upon her husband's respectability. She would not be lukewarm, but would take a risk. She prayed that Providence would guide her.

Rose knew she had to be forthright at the outset or she would lose control. "I should like to change the living room and the drawing room. There are many months when my husband is in London and I can move through the house changing décor as he affords me the funds."

"Oh, Ireland Rose, I should think your husband has not a care for money. He is very well established from what I hear." Ava's perfectly shaped dark eyebrows lifted slightly.

She has no idea about our financials. Rose worried and quickly changed the topic.

"I have drawings in my husband's office. "

"Come, let's see what ideas you have." Ava took Rose's arm.

An hour passed without notice. There was much musing, nodding, and head leanings as the ladies decided upon the formal living room, to begin their task.

"The fireplace is key to the design in the living room. It is elegant in size… however it needs to be more stylish…" Ava's musical voice continued…"We must start with an idea and build from there. Your windows are especially narrow and long, so there will be much sewing to be accomplished." Her finger tapped at her chin.

Rose, with paper in hand made notes. Draperies, upholstery changes of chairs and settees would make the most impact, Ava informed her. With several project designs and colors decided, it was time for tea.

"Mrs. McGuire . . . may I call you Ava?" Rose asked quietly as Portia carried the tea on the tray and set it on a side table.

"If I may call you Rose…or do you prefer Ireland?"

"Oh definitely Rose."

"Rose it is."

Ava lifted her cup and sipped with ladylike precision, her back straight.

Rose noted her slow, gentle movements that were typical of Southern-bred ladies. She rather liked the laid-back atmosphere in most of the drawing rooms here in Charleston. Baltimore ladies were interested in education and bettering themselves and their children. Here in rice country, the people were more defined by the inheritance, the family name and estates. She knew she should adapt herself for the sake of her husband. They were not likely to leave Charleston.

"You are serious today, Rose." Ava's dark eyes sparkled. "Have you misgivings?" She inquired, gazing over her teacup.

"No. I do not." Rose stood. "I am glad you are here. Shall we roll up our sleeves and make our plans?"

"Indeed we shall."

Rose saw Ava's cup teeter in the saucer as she stood and did the most amazing thing.

The formal Mrs. McGuire disengaged herself from her light jacket and actually rolled up the sleeves of her elegant day dress. Sprigs of green decorated the skirt, while the bodice of spring green shone in the sunlight as Ava threw open the dark draperies.

Rose smiled.

Chapter 16

A quick rain rattled at the windows again two hours later while Rose and Ava decided on a new furniture arrangement. Emmanuel and Thomas were engaged several times to either move or carry off assorted pieces. The built-in cabinets in the living room were exquisite and Eva proclaimed they were "staying."

Rose, secretly glad, for she could not even think of what Captain Lovell would say should they begin destructing. In fact after the furniture was changed into a new pattern, both fell into the settee, now facing the windows for the view of myrtle outside, and fanned themselves, declaring the end of the day. The sun had come out again.

"I declare it's half past three." Ava jumped up and hurried for her jacket. "Theodore is due home and I haven't informed the servants what he shall have for dinner. Really I must go. It would not do for dinner to be late. My husband is severe when it comes to protocol and timeliness of daily duties." She called over her shoulder.

Rose lifted her tired body and saw her guest to the door. "Thank you for coming by today. I have had such a pleasant time, and," she turned to gaze at the living room, "it looks so much better with the new arrangement."

"Isn't it fun?" Ava declared grabbing her lacy umbrella. "It's good that the rain has stopped, else I should have to call for my carriage."

"Really?" Rose said before she put her thoughts in order. "Do you not like walking after a warm rain, especially looking for rainbows when the sun peeps through the clouds?"

Ava turned serious eyes on her. "I have no idea why one should do such a thing. I cannot. My husband, you know. It wouldn't do for me to be seen walking about in the rain in such a fashion." She declared.

"I will call for Emmanuel to drive you." Rose smiled, with a bit of sorrow for her friend's inability to enjoy the simple things of life. Rose thought of her father, who taught her to notice everything around her, be grateful for it all, and enjoy whatever moments there were to be had in this world. She missed him.

The moment the door was opened, she felt a slight breeze catch at her skirts. "It seems we have a bit of wind today. Will your parasol hold up?"

Ava stepped onto the porch and walked to the wide steps, leaned forward and looked upward, sticking her hand out. "The rain has stopped completely and the wind is quite refreshing, for I am warmed from the activity. I believe I *shall* walk home."

"Thank you Ava." Rose called out once again, sorry to see her visitor go. There would be an entire evening to while away. Slowly she turned toward the screen door and entered with a last look. Her friend had tipped her parasol and was looking upward to the clouds. Perhaps Ava was looking for rainbows. Rose smiled.

"Miz Rose, you be wantin' some lemonade? We done been to the market to get fresh lemons. Two ships came in just this last hour with 'em." Lily beamed.

"That sounds absolutely divine."

"Divine? You be thinkin' on God when I speak o'them lemons?" Lily wanted to know.

"Oh no. Divine has two meanings. One means wonderful. The other having to do with God. "I was saying that lemonade sounds wonderful."

Lily looked at her a long moment, shrugged and ran off.

Rose washed her face in the basin near the kitchen and pushed her hair, curly from the rain and sun, out of her face. She had no desire to mess with it this afternoon. No calling cards lay on the tray, and it was past calling time for the ladies, so she wandered into her husband's office.

Days seemed so long while she was waiting. It seemed she had spent two years waiting. Sighing, she checked the calendar her husband kept on his desk. While he was gone, it was hers to fill. Glad for the upcoming meeting with the ladies to make more plans for the orphanage, she decided, after lemonade of course, to head up to the attic and search for ... what? She didn't know, but a sense of melancholy settled heavy on her heart.

She mentally checked her emotions. She was married to a good man, living in a beautiful house in a grand city, and had everything she needed. Why wasn't it enough?

Remembering her mother's words, she lifted her chin, straightened her shoulders and headed for the garden where the sun would not be so hot with all the summer green branches hanging heavy above her head. She settled onto the bench and pulled in all the flowery scents that hung in the rain-washed air. Colors filled her eyes, pink and red roses, dark pink and white azalea, white daisies, their tops waving in the breeze. Myriad shades of green adorned her garden. Honeysuckle, the fragrance strong sent her mind fleeing to her childhood. She closed her eyes and drew in a long breath. Funny how a single moment can be recaptured by something so simple as a fragrance. Wisteria climbed nearby. Strong yet fragile. Just like her.

Lily appeared in an instant, interrupting her reverie.

"Miz Rose, you gonna die with the taste 'o these fresh lemons." She handed her a large glass, the soft yellow drink with a fragrance of its own.

"Thank you Lily. Will you have a glass with me?" She patted the seat beside her.

"Yes'm I shore will. I's gonna run back right now and tell Granmama you said I could."

Rose chuckled as Lily ran off, kicking up dirt behind her. What a good thing to be a young girl and feel such freedom of movement and mind. For some odd reason, thoughts of Ireland came to her. She shut her eyes, remembering her mother and father's visions of the country they were born in and how they stumbled over the rocky green wavy hills, as water came down from the rocks, causing their eyes to blink at its brightness. The water was so fresh from the run down the hills, when the sun glinted against it; mother said there was no greater sight in all of Ireland.

Lily came back with her own glass, sipping before she sat down. "You want me to pick you one o'them nosegays you like Miz Rose?" she offered.

"I would love that. Why don't we do it together?"

Lily's brown eyes got large. "You don't want me to do it fer ya? All by myself?"

"Would you mind much if I helped you today?"

"No. That ain't for me to say. I just wants to know if you don't like the way I do it, that's all."

Rose laughed lightly, caught Lily's innocent eyes. "I love the way you twist the vines around the stems like you do. I've learned to do that from you. But I think it might be fun if we make two of them. One for the house, one for your Granmama. It's her birthday today, you know."

"Tis? We never talks 'bout birthdays. Sometimes we don't know for sure what day we was borned." She paused. "How'd you know?"

"Well, I have her papers. And she knows her birthday. It's July 13th 1832. She was born in Jackson, Mississippi."

"She never done tole me any o'that." Lily sipped again, thinking. "How we get on over here in Charleston, den?"

Rose decided, she had said too much. And not knowing what Portia intended to share with her granddaughter, she changed the topic. "I'm finished. Shall we get started?"

"Yep." Lily put the glasses on a side table, making sure they sat dead center so they would not get knocked off. "Granmama tole me not to break these fine glasses. She was mad 'cause I took one o'em for my lemonade."

"They're just glasses, Lily, but thank you for being so careful."

"I knows where the knife is." She ran for the knife stuck in the ground for such purposes. "You be wantin' them scissors you like to use?"

"I'll get them." Rose hurried away. When she came back, Lily was rooted to the same spot.

"You don't haf to be gettin' yo own scissors. I'm to be doin' dat. Granmama says so."

"I'm sorry, Lily. It's okay if I do some of my own getting." She laughed. "I was just giving you a rest." She gave herself a few moments and then said, "You and your family are free. You're not slaves anymore."

"I knows that. Den you be wantin' us to go Miz Rose?"

Rose saw the fear in her eyes.

"Of course not. You're my paid staff."

"Well ain't we sposed to get what you need then?"

Rose laughed. "Yes." And left it at that.

Lily expressed her relief with a huge smile. "We best get goin'. Granmama goin' to be calling me to help with suppuh any minute now."

"Well, then let's go."

"What you want first?"

How about that vine over there." Rose pointed. "It's perfect for tying up the bouquet. What colors does Portia like?"

"She like blue. She *love* blue. Everthin' she got in the cabin out back is blue." Lily spit out.

"You don't like blue?"

"I likes yellow. Like the sun."

"Me, too. And greens and pinks...and the white..." Rose stopped when she glanced at Lily.

"You likes 'em all Miz Rose." She laughed out loud.

Rose's heart pitched in her chest. She loved Lily for her truthfulness, her ability to run about freely and enjoy everything she put her hands to. Perhaps that was why Lily wanted to be here.

"You can choose your Granmama's flowers, and make the nosegay."

"I can?"

"Yes."

Lily's smile was enough. "I's gonna make her yellow. When she take 'em home and put 'em on that old table with the blue cloth on it....they're going to shine like the sun on top o'the water."

"Very good idea! Just think how bright they will make the table look."

Lily was too busy to note her last sentence. She was scurrying around the garden, cutting every yellow flower, with a few white ones added here and there while the bouquet was forming in her smooth brown hands.

Rose watched and without Lily's notice, she went behind choosing the same arrangement. When they were ready to tie the stems with the vine, Lily's eyes nearly bugged out of her head.

"You done just like I done!"

"Yes, I did. I like what you made, so I chose the very same flowers." Rose announced.

Chapter 17

The birthday flowers delivered and Portia freed from her duties for the evening, Rose ate leftover ham with bread and cheese, much to Portia's dismay.

"Miz Rose, it ain't right you eaten them leftovers from yesterday. Birthdays don't mean much to us colored folk."

"You're free, remember?"

"Yes'm. I ain't trying to say nothin' unkind, but you's know xactly what I mean, right Miz Rose?"

Rose had told her a dozen times that she was free. Captain Lovell had seen to that right after the Proclamation, but Portia could not imagine herself anywhere but serving the Captain and his young wife.

"I do, Portia. I do. Could we count it then that you are free this evening to do anything you wish?"

"Chile you knows I ain't happy less I'm doing for ya. Fact, you and Captain Lovell been good to me and Emmanuel and taking in Lily and Thomas like you did…well, we thanks you."

Rose felt uncomfortable. "I'm so happy you are with us, Portia. I don't know what I'd do without all of you. I'd be here alone."

"Chile you know we ain't leavin' ya…you be like a newborn babe without yo parents, and the Cap'n gone all the time like he is. But you stand up straight and do your duty and you's love us like family. We ain't a'goin' nowhere. You tell me to take the evenin' off we's doing it! Me and Emmanuel'll sit on the porch out back o' the cabin and drink lemonade, if that's all right wit you."

Rose smiled and looked into Portia's dark eyes. "I'm so thankful for you. Enjoy your time with Emmanuel. Take that pitcher of lemonade with you. And don't forget your flowers."

Portia hurried off with a chuckle, the ice chips tinkling in the lemonade pitcher.

It was already half past four and the sun was burning down on the backyard. Glad for a bit of air, Rose hurried inside and up into the attic. She opened the one tiny window that let in a slight breeze from the tall willow tree outside.

She stepped over several boxes, lifted the blanket and peeked at the painting of Lucinda Lovell, the captain's former wife. She was beautiful and no doubt accomplished. Rose wished for some clue as to how she might become so herself.

Sneezing as she made her way, she spotted the notes and journal she had set aside. She noted three light blue boxes of the same design with ribboned cords tied around each one and opened the first one. Letters. Stacks of them. To Darbinger Pinckney Dalton.

"Dalton?" She whispered, the sound acid on her tongue. The mysterious and not to be trusted banker. "And Pinckney was a revered name in politics and local Charleston history.

She untied the string on a small batch....three letters. On the outside was the word *Darby* in a beautiful script. That, Rose noted, was a strong attachment from an admirer. He obviously meant these to be personal. She hesitated. Then slowly slid a folded light blue paper out, opened it gently and read the date. She promised herself if they were too recent she would not intrude.

They were dated twelve years past...1872. She began to read. One, then the second, the third. She read through the entire first box and could not go on. The male admirer loved a fourteen year old girl. Even before he finished his 6th level at school he had loved her, he said.

The letters grew more intimate as the two grew in age. Rose wiped tears from her dusty face and knew she would never experience the kind of love those letters described. She tangled her finger in her hair, the way the boy, turned man had said in his last letter. He had loved Darby's red gold hair and how she would wrap a curl around her finger. He longed to do the same himself.

A dozen references in the letters placed the visions in her mind. What would that be like? Rose kept reading. He loved Darby's hand in his own. Her profile when she gazed away from him. Her eyes, so blue and filled with love for him.

Rose found herself lost in the past and knew life would not offer her such trimmings. She sighed, reverently put the letters back, and wondered what had happened to Darbinger Pinckney Dalton and *W.*

Each letter was signed only with a beautiful scripted "W". Twelve years past and that would make Darby 26 years of age and "W" 29. Did the two marry? Was there any relationship to Mr. Dalton at the bank?

Suddenly, she noted the wind had picked up in the trees and shut the window, needing to get out of the dust. She scurried down the stairs with a last look at the boxes. She would read the last box of letters another day. She had images enough to last a lifetime. Perhaps she would never experience the love of a man the same way, she could only dream. Her husband was twenty-seven years her senior and Rose knew she would be a widow sooner than most women. But for the time being, she had a good life and must be grateful. Just like her mother said.

The house was quiet. Portia and Emmanuel and Lily and Thomas were enjoying the breezy evening. Smiling, she went to the kitchen, prepared some warm water and washed up in the bowl. She leaned her head over and poured warm water over her head and shampooed her hair, then combed through the stubborn curls and went out on the front verandah to watch the flowers sway in the wind while her hair dried. She hid well behind the creeping vines across the porch out of view and gazed at ladies out with their husbands for an evening stroll. Children played near the steps and she heard several ship horns announcing their arrival. Charleston was a busy town. She'd heard just yesterday that the town boasted that it could accommodate 200 vessels in its wharves. Cotton was still King of the South.

There were new businesses after the devastation of the Civil War…Charleston was beginning to make its fortunes once again. New sawmills, cotton presses, iron foundries and shipyards brought new wealth into the city. Her husband, gone so much would be very prosperous once he settled down in Charleston, which he promised to do in just a few years. She would wait and perhaps they could help the orphanage even more.

Running her fingers through her damp curls, Rose quit her musing and went inside. The wind, still strong, blew through the screened front door and straight out the back one. It had been a pleasant day altogether. Hungry, she found a slice of pecan cake sitting on the sideboard. Portia had put it there in case she wanted dessert. She smiled and ate alone at the huge dining table, gazing about the room, thinking what changes might need to be made. It was a beautiful room. The only thing she would like to change was the worn carpet beneath the dining table and chairs. Plantation shutters kept the sun out; lighter curtains at the window would be a nice addition.

Indeed the carpet looked to be ancient and Portia mentioned that it was threadbare and hard to clean.

A light pounding at the front door caused her to drop her fork, so lost in thought was she. Emmanuel was out back, and not wishing to disturb their evening, eyes focused, she walked slowly to the door. Perhaps it was Arella.

Her eyes lowered. There was a small child standing there. From the looks of it, there was some fear on the little face.

"May I help you?" Rose opened the screen door slowly.

"I've lost me mother." The little girl, with blond hair and the greenest eyes, looked up at her. She must have been four, perhaps five.

"You've lost your mother?" She repeated and stepped out. "She will not be far away. Shall we go back down the steps and see if we can find her?" The lass was Irish.

Rose found a chubby little hand in hers as the little mouth let out a sob.

"Don't worry. We will find her. She will be looking for you, you know."

"Aye." The little voice came back.

Rose's heart jumped.

"Where are you from?"

"Ireland, to be sure." The little voice, sounded like her own mother's.

"Aye, so am I."

"Ye are?" The voice raised a notch.

"Aye."

Within a minute a frantic woman came rushing up. "Oh Colleen, you're found. We just arrived, and I lost my wee lass."

Rose watched the moment the two bodies connected and her heart flipped. She knew her smile was sad.

"Thank you ma'am. We are just off from Ireland and..." she stopped unable to speak. "O how could I lose my lass so quickly? This town is too big and too busy. My home was quiet and not so...so industrial."

"Aye. I know it, too." Rose said quietly.

"Ye are from Ireland then, too?"

"Well, I was born in Baltimore, but from Irish parents. They returned home."
"Aye, it is I who wish to do the same." The woman declared. "And I've just arrived."

Rose understood.

"And you have married then? And live here in Charleston?"

"Aye."

"I am sorry for you then." She said quickly, then relented. "Ach, it is sorry I am to say such a thing. I'm sure I will find my way. My husband has come to work for the shipyards. He has christened his ship, "The Blarney Stone." She laughed. "Is that not the silliest name? I said he could have at least christened her the Patrice after me...or even his wee daughter, Colleen."

Ireland Rose laughed. "Leave to men such things! I guess he was hoping for the luck o'the Irish."

"Well, it is a point you have there. I am Patrice Elizabeth Riley, County Galway. May I ask your name?"

"Ireland Rose Lovell, my parents came from County Clare.

"Ah we are kindred no doubt." Patrice smiled.

"Indeed. My husband Captain John Camden Lovell has two ships. I think we and our husbands shall become friends."

"Aye."

Rose noted her new friend's relief as she spoke.

"And this...." Patrice leaned down to gaze in her daughter's eyes, is my little Colleen Elizabeth Riley.

Rose smile down at her, the child's face calm now that she had her mother in-hand.

"I live here." Rose pointed to her house. When you are settled, would you like to come for tea and scones?"

"Ah, it would be a pleasure Mrs. Lovell to eat an Irish scone. Your husband is Irish too, for he carries the name of the Irish on the west counties of Ireland."

"You would be correct. But he has a touch of Scot as well." Rose laughed. "Indeed we shall meet again. Now you must find your husband...it is almost dark."

"Indeed or you may find Colleen and I knocking at your door again." She said as she hurried away.

Rose's heart beat happy in her chest. She would have another new friend. And the angelic child with the Irish brogue reminded her of herself. *Lord you are so good to me, filling in the spaces where I am lonely...*

Chapter 18

The next morning, as scheduled, Ava came knocking, her arms full.

"Oh what have you brought?" Rose took some of her burden.

"These are straight from New York. My friend the designer has come to live here in Charleston and brought with her these swatches of fabric that we may look at."

The two spread the pieces over the huge dining table, tossing ideas this way and that.

"Now choose lighter." Ava reminded her. "Your rooms will look more airy and soft."

"Oh, but we haven't time to order from New York; besides that I have limited funds, of course." Rose mumbled as she pulled out three very agreeable materials.

"That's a good match. This for the curtains, this for the chairs and this for the pillows."

Rose felt the situation was rushing out of control. "We can begin with curtains. Put them up and then try the other fabrics..."

"Have you a seamstress?" Ava got to the point.

"No, I do not."

Both looked at each other.

"Shall we ask Mrs. Jamison at the orphanage? We could engage one of the girls."

"What a splendid idea." Ava gushed.

"I shall call upon her myself this very afternoon." Rose said.

"And I shall accompany you. I must see the orphanage so we can work together."

Rose tittered with excitement. "Your husband will not mind?"

"My husband will not know." She said firmly and handed a piece of fabric to Rose. "See do you like this one better...I do believe it has the shades you need."

"Yes, I think I do. Better than the one I chose." Rose smiled. "We have our three fabrics, shall we make our trip then after tea?"

With Ava's affirmation, Rose reached to pull the rope as Portia came with a tray. "We were just going to ring for tea." Rose laughed. "And here you are."

"Happy to oblige, Miz Rose." She set her tray on the table and served. "Will you be wantin' sandwiches?"

Ava spoke up. "I'm thinking it would be good to stop at Clarinda's Tea Room and lunch there to be seen together about town. We will need the ladies to join our adventure."

Rose smiled a bit worried that the ladies may not wish to join their adventure, but tucked away her worry for another time. Above all things she did not want Mr. McGuire to be shamed with his wife's associations. That would not do at all. She pushed her thoughts away and sipped her tea, grateful for Ava's friendship.

Yes, Portia we will lunch at Clarinda's. Thank you."

"Let us make a list." Ava suggested. She pulled a bit of paper from her elegant silk string bag and a pencil. "I must write things down or forget them altogether." She began writing. "First we must find the seamstress and then immediately go to my friend. She has bolts of fabric, brought with her from New York; a veritable storehouse in fact."

"A storehouse?" Rose set her cup in the saucer, having doused her thirst with half the cup.

"Indeed. She could not give up her design ideas and her very rich husband is so daft about his wife, he brought her entire warehouse to Charleston."

Rose, smarting from the letters above stairs, thought…*W* would have done such a thing for Darby. Then shook those thoughts from her head. She was becoming entirely romantic which was ridiculous. She must take on her mother's sensibilities and concentrate on the matters at hand. After all her own husband would be back from London in less than eight weeks if the winds were favorable.

"Well," Rose announced, shall we get on with our plans then?"

Energized, Ava finished her tea. "I say. My friend will no doubt be glad to assist us once we find a seamstress. And…it is nigh noon. We must use our time well."

Rose felt excitement at Ava's willingness to help and enjoyed her spontaneity.

"Indeed."

Within the half hour over cucumber sandwiches and teacakes and more tea the ladies decided they would stop next at Mrs. Jamisons and seek her advice. "Emmanuel, here is a sandwich for you." Rose handed her driver the food.

She noted he laid the sandwich next to him.

He did not wish for Miss Rose's fine lady guest see her do such a thing.

When the carriage pulled up to the orphanage Ava's intake of breath concerned Rose.

"If you do not wish to go inside it is quite all right."

Ava spoke from behind her handkerchief. "Is has such a stench. Have they no inside toilets?" She coughed.

"I'm afraid they do not. Even the outhouses are standing at angles as you can see." Rose said.

"I had no idea."

"Aye, 'tis the way of it."

"Well, if this squalor is where people actually live, I must be brave and brace myself." Ava McGuire stepped down and immediately lifted her skirt from the grounds. "Come. I must see for myself." She moved ahead, Rose walking beside her.

"Emmanuel would you mind asking Mrs. Jamison if we may visit." She noted no children ran out to greet them this time.

Emmanuel stepped forward and knocked at the door.

Within minutes Rose and Ava were being shown around by three of the older children. Mrs. Jamison, it seems, had gone to beg for food from several of the fish vendors down at the wharf.

"We are instructed never to open to strangers, Miz Rose, but we know you."

"Are you sure it is all right to come in, Arella?"

"Yes Miz Rose."

Arella gave them a short tour. The ladies noted the condition of the children's clothing. Rose noticed several of her own donated items were being worn by the girls and she smiled. The rooms were neat and picked up, even though the stench from the outhouses could not be ignored coming through the open windows.

"Mrs. Jamison goes to the wharf at this time every day. The fresh fish comes in about dis time and she takes away anything not sold."

"Is that healthy?" Ava asked.

"Seems so to us." Arella said seriously.

"We came to inquire if you have a seamstress among you." Rose got to the point. Do any of the older girls sew well enough to make curtains and pillow covers, perhaps?"

"Yes ma'am. Miz Nettie. She sew all kinds of things. Fact, she down at a rich lady's house right dis minute doin' just that very thing."

"Really?"

"I have paper. We'll leave a note." Ava fished in her purse, dropping her handkerchief on the floor.

Arella retrieved it and handed it back.

"Now then, what shall we say?" Ava looked to Rose.

"We'll ask Mrs. Jamison to send Miss Nettie with Arella. Tell her Emmanuel will come for them tomorrow at the same time unless we hear otherwise."

"Ava wrote the note and handed it to Arella." Please see that it is given to Mrs. Jamison."

Arella took the note and immediately ran off. "I'll be puttin' it on her desk right this very minute."

Rose smiled and Emmanuel helped the ladies up into the carriage and they drove off after deciding to make their visit for fabric tomorrow.

The usually talkative Ava was quiet for some time. Rose left her to her thoughts.

"I see why you are interested." Ava spoke quietly gazing at the landscape as they passed.

Rose was satisfied.

That afternoon after Ava left, Rose began her sketches. First of the new curtains hanging at the windows. She used colored wax to give the effect and was quite pleased. Next she set the fabric swatches in sunlight and then at dark checked them again. Indeed the house would be brighter. She only hoped that Captain Lovell would not be offended. She must tread lightly. After all Lucinda may have chosen these materials and she must not cause more trouble for her husband. Perhaps she had been too anxious. She bit her lip.

Needing something to assuage her worrisome thoughts, she headed up to the attic again. It was late but with all the ideas flashing about in her mind's eye she could not go to sleep. Portia and Emmanuel had retired early.

Very quietly, she pulled the rope to bring down the stairs and climbed up. She needn't worry about the noise too much, because Portia and her family chose to sleep out in their cottage out next to the kitchen on hot summer nights. But she must not let her housekeeper know she was up or Portia would not rest. She had already told her she would get herself undressed and off to bed tonight. Still she knew Portia had eyes and ears aplenty!

For some reason, she could not stop thinking about Darby and *W.* What had happened to them? Why were the letters up in this attic? Had they both died? She could almost picture them. Darby with her long curls and *W*...what did he look like? There were no descriptive letters from Darby to *W.*

The dark attic, lit only by one lantern, was eerie. It was early evening...just dark -- thankfully there was a touch of moonlight through the windows.

She found the last box, sat and arranged the light just right, and pulled out the letter on top. Rose already knew they were in the exact order Darby had received them. She read one after the other, tears falling from her face. What had happened to them? It was only 12 years ago...surely someone would know. Rose wiped away tears. There were only three letters left. She didn't want them to end.

One thing she knew. As soon as was proper, she was going to ask Captain Lovell about those names. He must have known them, because he had lived here for about that long.

The next one hinted of an elopement. Her eyes strained now to read every word, *W* was asking Darby to go with him. To trust him. He hinted of a position but did not say what. Would she trust him?

The next spoke of the joy and excitement they would soon enjoy, married, free of titles, ties and family expectations. *W*'s words exuded happiness that was soon to be theirs.

Hands shaking, and her heart wishing this was not the last letter, she slowly opened it and began to read:

My dear Mrs. Raleigh:

It is with deepest regret I am scripting my final correspondence to you.

I am informed that your father persuaded you to marry Mr. Norbert Raleigh these three days before our planned elopement. Should I have contrived the worst in my mind, I could not have suspected this. Except I know your heart is so easily persuaded that I know quite well how your father could turn your tenderness away from me.

Contrary to the fact that you were certain of my regard and my efforts to attain your father's blessing you chose this path. My one regret is that I did not have time to inform you of my recent appointment as Captain of a worthy ship with an annual salary that would surely have secured you a suitable position among Charleston society, as your father wished. But most importantly, with a man who so dearly loved you.

Alas, it is too late for such musings. I must inform you that I shall remove myself to London to avoid all embarrassment on your behalf for once associating with a man of lesser means. I cannot bear to look upon your happiness in your present circumstances.

As it is, I have lost you forever, and can now offer only my sincere wish for your happiness.

I leave the letter in our private post location hoping that you will find it.

W

Rose found the missive crumpled in her hands. After years of correspondence they had not married. He had loved her since she was eleven years of age and he fourteen. Tears fell onto the pages and she cried for Darby and *W*...for herself... for all who found love and could not attain it in the end. The wick fluttered reminding her the lantern was almost out of oil.

Slowly, she smoothed the letter across her knee grateful the tears had not ruined the ink and placed it back in the envelope, then back into the box just as she had found them. She rose slowly, opened the trunk and put the three boxes away. They were out of sight, but now she had been forever branded with the story.

Chapter 19

Rose slept little that night, thinking about love that is true and then lost. Portia pushed open the curtains and she hid her burning eyes with a hand. "Come on up chile. You got callers a'comin'. Been two knocks on the door already and you ain't even dressed.

"Who called?" Rose heard the scratch in her voice and saw Portia's concern in her eyes.

"Mrs. Jamison sent Arella with a note. And Mrs. McGuire done tole me to get you outta that bed. Lookee at the time. Come on, pick your dress and I'll get you into it. Breakfast is waitin'.

Rose sat while Portia fussed with her hair. "Der now don't you look nice dis mornin'. Go on down and keep those ladies busy. I got's plenty to do in the kitchen. You and your ladies'll be wanting some treats to go along with yo tea. And shore 'nuff I got some good lemons to make a lemon puddin' for dat cake."

Portia was trying to lift her spirits.

"It's that bad?" She gazed into brown eyes for the answer.

"Yep." Her maid said and smiled. "But this too shall pass chile...you been up in dat attic too much, looking at things that don't concern you none and now lookie here, you all sad and cryin' dem eyes out."

"How did you know I was up there?"

"I done checked on you to see if my baby girl was all right." She admitted with a huge smile.

"Oh Portia. I'm so glad you love me." Rose threw herself into the woman's arms.

"Now don't be going on like that." She took a corner of her apron and wiped away tears. "See now you got me a'cryin'. Get on down dem stairs and get talkin' to Miz McGuire. You ladies should get somthin' done today." She pushed Rose's back gently.

Rose smiled, wiped away tears from her face, leaned down to check her face in the mirror to make sure she didn't have tear lines down her face, straightened her shoulders and went down the stairs.

Two minutes later she was on Mrs. McGuire's arm. "Goodness, you stay abed too long. The coolest part of the day is nearly past." She exaggerated. "I've been awake half the night with ideas. And I must get done so my husband will not know what I've been up to." She winked and pulled Rose's arm.

"Where are we going?"

"We're headed for the warehouse. I've arranged for Mrs. Pinckney to see us today. She is going to show us her fabric."

"Already? My goodness." Was all Rose could think to say. Then the name slammed into her memory halting her thoughts. Pinckney was Darby's middle name. Was there perhaps a connection?

Ava took her arm and commandeered her to the waiting carriage. "My driver has orders not to speak of our destination. I must get back before my husband finds me out." She laughed.

Rose smiled but could think only of the letters. Pinckney was such a well known name in Charleston. Was Darby a member of that family? No wonder then the talk about the young boy's unworthiness. She forced herself to forget the contents of the love letters and concentrate on meeting the woman. Goodness, she was getting steeped and pulled into the city's elite. She must be careful to represent herself well for her husband's sake and silently vowed to do so. She must not fall prey to the gossip.

She looked again at Ava and saw that she had dressed quite properly today. Rose wished she would have chosen more appropriate attire. Thank goodness she had thought to bring her parasol.

Nervously she stepped down and then chided herself for wishing to impress anyone so thoroughly as to give oneself up completely. *Lord, please make your presence known in me and help me not to make another mistake in my dealings.*

Before she knew it, she was entering an oblong building on Greenhill Street. Once inside her eyes adjusted to the darkness. There were few windows. But a person could barely walk the two aisles, so narrow were they. "Oh my." Rose heard herself say.

"Did I not tell you?" Ava smiled. "Now we must make our way to the end where we will find Mrs. Pinckney in her office – which does have more windows." She added.

Rose followed and soon they were inside a most agreeable room. There were desks loaded with books. Long tables for cutting fabric and two young girls working. And a wall of windows.

"Ah, you have brought Mrs. Lovell." A voice came from behind them.

"Yes, Mrs. Lovell please be introduced to Mrs. Henry Pinckney."

Rose turned and found herself looking into the bluest eyes. The woman was much more elderly than she expected and very small of frame, her back straight as an arrow and head held regally.

"Pleased to meet you Mrs. Pinckney." She offered her hand and then realized she should have just tipped her head in a nod.

The older woman took it and Rose was grateful. "I'm afraid I am accustomed to hand shaking."

"A northerner?" The woman smiled.

"Yes." Rose answered simply.

"Well, young woman where are you from?"

"Baltimore."

"Ah, a lovely city."

"You've been there?" Rose knew she sounded surprised.

"Many times. I married a Charlestonian but I was born in New York."

"Really?" Rose couldn't help but smile.

"We met here but I made him take me back to New York when we married, promising in my old age to return to Charleston, setting New York society on it's ear at the time."

"I imagine you did just that." Rose received the woman's twinkle in her eye as a gift of acceptance to this new northerner.

"I detect a bit of the Irish brogue in your speech."

"Indeed you are right again. My parents came from Ireland."

"It is a beautiful country. Why do you not return home? Most Irish do." Mrs. Pinckney gazed at her.

"You've been to Ireland then?" Rose was astounded at their connections.

Many times. It is a beautiful country. My husband and I made several trips over to conduct business. I love the people, the countryside. It was unfortunate so many died during the hardships caused by the potato famine."

"That is particularly why my parents came here." She said quietly.

"If you ever want to go back, I'd be happy to go along." My Henry died two years after we moved back here and I had not the fortitude to move all this..." she waved her arms in the air ... back to New York City. And I wish to be buried here alongside my husband.

"I understand completely Mrs. Pinckney."

"Well now my friend Mrs. McGuire has been very patient while we have had a chat. Shall we get on to business, then?"

Ava smiled and asked if they might peruse the upholstery section, in the event Mrs. Lovell wished to recover her chairs.

Rose did not want to do that, but followed along...glad to have met so many good people. She was beginning to feel that her roots may find their place in the hot southern soil.

Chapter 20

Two days later, Miss Nettie Bloom was sitting at Rose's Singer sewing machine, her foot pedal rocking away. The twelve foot lengths of fabric had turned out to be outrageous in price by the time they covered four very tall windows. Rose had spent nearly three quarters of the budget on the curtains alone.

Once the curtains were sewn and duly hung, which took an entire day, Emmanuel going up and down the hand-hewn ladder, the house did look much brighter and welcoming. The opened windows whipped the lightweight material about, rippling and dancing, bringing life to the room.

Today, Miss Nettie was sewing pillows to toss upon the sofa. To make it look newer without too much trouble, Ava said.

Lily had taken to Miss Nettie and the two became friends. Nettie even taught the flighty Lily how to stitch the pillows closed. Portia was proud of her granddaughter saying, "Mebbe she'll make a good seamstress some day. Then she can own her a place downtown, now that she is free."

"Now wouldn't that be wonderful?" Rose smiled, the letters forgotten in her rush to finish before her husband came home....which was now just three weeks away, four or five if weather was bad on the crossing.

"Miss Nettie would you mind staying on another day. I'll send a note to Mrs. Jamison right away if you agree. I'd like to speak to you about making two new dresses. I found some beautiful linen for a day dress. Would you have time to sew it?"

"Miz Rose, I'd be happy to stay. I like it here. And any money I make we share with the others."

"That is a fine thing you are doing, Nettie. Shall we see how long they can spare you?"

"Most fine with me, Miz Rose. And I don't mind at all stayin' on. Miz Portia make the best food. She knows how to cook."

"Yes, she does. She would be happy to teach you, too Nettie."

"I's be willing to learn anything I can. Someday, I been asking the Lord, if he might help me meet a good man and I can work for myself doing for people, so's we can have a place of our own."

"That is a great dream. I hope it comes true." And Rose prayed that it would.

"Now shall we finish for today. I'm very hot and need a cool bath. If you'd like Emmanuel will set one out for you, too."

"A bath in a real washtub?" Nettie's eyes grew large.

"Yes." Rose said wondering. "Have you no bathing facilities there?"

"Well, no, ain't 'nough space. We need the extra room for beds and such. The toilets are about done for, too. Makes the smell bad to sleep at night and can't be good for us walkin' through all that mess with bare feet. But Mrs. Jamison, she make sure we wash up ever night. She don't cotton to bein' dirty; body soul or spirit." Nettie's eyes widened.

"That's good." Rose smiled.

She knew something needed to be done and would talk to her husband as soon as she could bring the subject up. But, she scolded herself, she must make sure he was nursed back to health first. It had been so long since he'd been home.

In the space of a week Portia cut out and fitted the fabric while Nettie sewed Rose two simple day dresses. Her stitches were excellent and Rose decided she could get more work for Nettie. It was time for her to go back to the orphanage.

Rose paid her handsomely and Nettie cried like a baby. "Just think all this goin' to help the other chilren, too."

Rose noted Portia had grown fond of Nettie. Surely there were more girls in the orphanage that needed training. Rose could teach embroidery, Portia cooking, and Ava could show the girls design ideas…how to make simple changes in a home setting without spending a lot of money. Rose's mind was humming with ideas.

She hadn't seen Ava since they'd finished the work and wondered if everything was all right. Hopefully Mr. McGuire had not learned of his wife's social indiscretions. Time had flown by and it was time to clean the house floor-to- attic. Portia and Emmanuel always scrubbed the house clean when Captain Lovell was expected. And Rose knew it would wear them out. Her job was to weed and cut back the gardens. Emmanuel did not like to let her work outdoors in the sun. That had been his job…and lately Rose noticed he was limping about ever so slightly.

Several days later Nettie was again loaned out for hire. She and Lily turned the contents of the attic upside down and rearranged it. Dust flew about the house until the job was done. Rose could not abide going up there again. Portia helped and Thomas did the heavy work, while Emmanuel worked outside trimming trees and repainting shutters.

As the time drew near, Rose decided they would all rest after the house was done and celebrate with a big dinner. She arranged for a hog to be put over the fire after Portia dressed it.

Stella had called off her trip to Savannah and Rose was glad. She could not have squeezed it in. Besides, when Captain Lovell left again, she would have plenty of time for visits. And it had been three weeks since she'd last seen Ava McGuire. There had not been a word from her. But there was no time to worry. Captain Lovell was coming home even if it was two months later than expected.

Chapter 21

News finally came the third week of November. Thomas ran in breathless announcing that the Emerald Star and the Ireland Rose were on the way....yet a few miles back came the report from another shipman who had just come in.

Rose's heart lifted as she gazed at the new curtains fluttering at the open window. The wind was strong, the weather slightly cooler. A relief after an unusually warm fall and two days of heavy rain. And the perfect day for her husband's homecoming. She knew it would take hours for the ships to anchor and tie up at the dock once they pulled in. The Captains would stay with their ships until the passengers disembarked and then her husband would be home.

"I's goin' to put on the Cap'n's favorite dinner. He love chicken and gravy on rice. "Lily, you get me three fine, fat chickens you hear? And pick a mess of dem snap beans, too."

Rose didn't know what to do. The house was in perfect order. She laughed as Lily flew through the house, her Granmama telling her to *slow down or she was gonna break one o'dem long legs and be no good to anyone.*

She stepped out onto the verandah and gazed out at the beautiful day. The sun appeared from behind a fast-moving cloud. Winds slung the wisteria and her loose curls in every direction. Portia always rolled her hair up tight on her head, but wisps continually fell around her face. She blew them out of her mouth with a smile. Soon her husband and from the looks of it, Captain Wyatt would be walking up these stairs in no time.

Rose forced herself to sit in the wide swing and tap her foot on the floor, setting herself in motion. She was so grateful her husband was coming after nearly a year's absence. She must prepare herself however, in the event he was still recovering from the fever. The cooler weather and the hope of the moment set the world aright again. Captain Lovell was a generous man. His letters told her he would be bringing special spices from the Orient, the finest rugs from Moracco and a writing desk of her very own made especially for her in France. He was a man of wealth, but also a man of the people. There would be gifts for Emmanuel, Portia and the grandchildren. She was proud to be his wife.

All thoughts of Darby and *W* flew out of her mind. She had been foolish even to think of such things when she had all this. She mentally issued herself a warning to be more grateful. And remembered she and her husband would need to talk about the signatures she had set her name to. That would be difficult knowing she had erred in the one decision she had been asked to make.

A good amount of time passed. Twice she had gone in for iced tea and twice she had seen groups of returning passengers carrying their carpetbags as well as others passing by the battery chatting about their recent trip. The ships must have been further out that she thought...and with two of them, there would be a great deal of work tying the ships to the dock since the winds were so strong.

Suddenly the sound of men's boots hitting the walkway hard came toward her. Rose stood to her feet, smoothed her skirts, a smile hovering on her lips as she waited at the top of the stairs on the front porch.

"Captain Wyatt." She heard the quiver in her voice. And felt faint when he took off his hat and looked her in the eye. Rose couldn't help herself...she looked over his shoulder looking for her husband.

"Mrs. Lovell, the men are coming with Captain Lovell. He is quite ill from the trip. Make a bed ready for him and we will bring him."

The man's words were still being processed in her brain when her eyes noted that he was already walking away. Instantly her mind kicked in. She straightened her back, walked through the screen door and called out, "Portia."

The woman came at her call instantly. She must have heard the fear. "Captain Wyatt has come to tell us to make a bed ready for Captain Lovell. He is ill."

"Lord have mercy." Portia breathed a prayer and called to Emmanuel. The two of them hurried up the stairs and Rose was left to stand in the huge foyer, all thoughts of celebrating gone. But, she scolded herself, *do not borrow trouble, Ireland Rose*. She turned in time to see several men coming up the stairs of the wraparound porch. Before she could move four young men carried her husband in on a stretcher, Captain Wyatt at one corner. She laid eyes on her husband and noted his color was white but he opened his eyes and winked, then held up his hand in greeting ever so slightly. They stopped for a moment and she could see that he was very ill.

"Welcome home Captain Lovell." She willed her voice to be strong.

Rose wanted to cry, but would not. She must be brave. Suddenly something inside her began organizing. "Up the stairs, third door to the right." She pointed and then picked up her skirts and followed the men. She noted how carefully they maneuvered her husband around the corner at the top of the stair.

Portia and Emmanuel had already turned down the bed linens and stood off, one on each side of the room and let the Captain be lifted and put on the bed. The men murmured their greetings to Rose and she tried not to look into their eyes. They saluted to the Captain one by one and immediately left the room, Captain Wyatt right behind them. In a moment she turned and saw Captain Wyatt out in the hall talking to two of the men. When she drew close the men left.

"Sir, what happened?" She asked quietly.

"There were high winds and strong gales nearly all the way across. Captain Lovell was not yet well enough from the fever and he fell ill again. This time from complete exhaustion. The airs were wet and many of the crew are sick from the salt in their lungs and no sleep trying to keep the ships afloat."

"I'll call for Doctor Case. How long has he been ill?"

"The day after we sailed we ran into bad weather. He has not been well since the first day. I fear he has consumption."

"I see." She said quietly, her hands tightly entwined at her waist.

"Ma'am" He lifted his hat and was gone. Rose's brain noted Captain Wyatt seemed always to be fleeing this house. She realized she had spoken aloud.

Portia flew past her and down the stairs before she could think what to do. She heard her say, "Thomas go for Dr.Case right dis very minute."

"Rose honey, now you just goes and sits in there by yo husband and talk to him. See what he says 'bout how he feelin' and all. I knows what to do..." She hurried away.

Rose picked up her skirts and walked up quickly, then entered the room, pulled a chair next to the bed and sat. Emmanuel was already gone. "You're awake." She smiled at him drawing near.

"Aye, 'tis what I longed to see. My wife and my home." He said, his eyes drooping closed.

"You are safe and glad I am of it. Close your eyes now and rest. Dr. Case will be along in a few minutes." She said in soothing tones.

Rose smoothed the covers and gazed at him. He was thinner by nearly half it seemed. Her heart sunk and she prayed, "Lord keep him safe."

What seemed like forever, Dr. Case arrived. "Several passengers just off the ship were in bad shape." He said as he hurried in.

Rose lifted herself, moved the chair away and waited in the hall so the doctor could examine her husband.

"Looks like consumption." He said quietly when he came out into the hall. "He's quite weak. Captain Wyatt said he had Yellow Fever in London."

"Yes." Rose said.

"He will need water, bed rest. And he is not to be disturbed nor is he to be out of this bed." The doctor ordered. "I have given him some laudanum so he will sleep. Shut the door and all the windows. Tell Portia to put a poultice on his chest. She will know what to do." He shut his case and shrugged into his coat.

"Yes. Thank you Dr. Case."

"Of course Mrs. Lovell. And do look for signs of breathing problems...if he rasps or coughs overmuch send for me. I'll be back tomorrow. Perhaps if he rests tonight we will be able to arrest the weakness in his lungs."

Rose nodded and smiled a little and Dr. Case was gone. Portia came rushing up the stairs with Lily in tow. "Now you just sit in dat chair over by the window and I'll nurse Captain Lovell." She pushed at Rose when she did not move.

Lily and Portia started their task and Rose got up and went downstairs. She and Captain Lovell had never slept in the same room. She felt like an intruder. Besides, she told herself they could work better if they didn't have to worry about her.

She took the long-necked water bucket and watered the flowers on the front verandah to keep busy. The noises down at the wharf carried on the brisk winds. She heard shouts of greetings and couples reuniting with the crew or perhaps with those who had crossed the Atlantic from Europe. Charleston was her home now, but suddenly she felt like a stranger.

After a time Portia found her and said, "Miz Rose, Captain is sleepin'. He won't wake for a long time. That poultice and the doctor's medicine will be the best rest. You don't need to worry none. I seen worse than that many times. Yessirree…I shorely have. I'm goin' to cook up those chickens and make some broth for the Cap'n. You just rest yoself…we's gonna be sitting next to him all night long, fer sure.

Rose thanked her with her eyes.

"I know chile you disappointed, but you got yo husband home. That's good 'nuff for now. Why don't you get some o'those pretty flowers and we'll put 'em in the window for him to look at."

Rose, glad to be doing something, went up the stairs, tiptoed past his door and put on an old workdress. Down to the garden she went, glad to be digging in the dirt. That was one thing that soothed her troubles and soon she wiped her brow with her gloved hand and realized the sun has nearly gone down behind the bright pink Azalea bushes out back.

"Come on in Miz Rose. We havin' dinner, same as always."

Rose went in, cleaned up at the wash bowl. She brushed away dust off her dress and sat down.

"Come on now. That broth be good for you, too. Throw'd in some vegetables and made soup. You'll need to be strong now."

Rose picked up her spoon and ate, for once glad to be alone.

A sudden and loud pounding at the door and Rose heard her spoon clatter to the floor.

"Who be comin' at dinnertime." Portia came flying out from the back.

"Maybe it's Dr. Case…"

"No, he be too busy tonight. And we ain't got no emergency here." She panted as she hurried to answer.

"Captain Wyatt she at dinner."

Rose stood, wiped her mouth and tossed the linen napkin on the table. "He may come in, Portia."

She was standing by her chair when Captain Wyatt entered the dining room. For a moment he gazed across the way and Rose wondered what he saw. Nothing there except several oil paintings that had been hanging since she'd arrived.

Coming to himself, he took off his hat, smoothed his hair and said, "I'm sorry to disturb you at dinner. I'm here to see after Captain Lovell. Has he improved?"

"He is sleeping very soundly, Mr. Wyatt and we have not heard any rattle in his chest."

"I'm glad for it."

Rose noted he seemed relieved and waited.

"Thank you." He bowed slightly and as was his usual custom, put on his hat and walked out the door.

Surprised when he said no more, when she could clearly see he wanted to, she wondered at the elusive Captain Wyatt. His voice was so deep that she felt as though he were her stern schoolmaster and she had just tipped her ink well.

She had also noted Captain Wyatt's discreet perusal of her untidy appearance.

The next moment, she picked up her skirts and feeling better ran up the stairs to visit her husband. He was in his nightclothes and sleeping peacefully. Rose listened for unusual breathing noises and heard none. Perhaps he would recover. She prayed it would be so. There was still the discussion she wanted to have with him about Mr. Dalton and the papers she signed.

Chapter 22

Portia and Lily arrived at dark to attend her husband, insisting she stay abed in her own room through the night.

"My mammy was de best doctoress back in the day." Portia announced. "And taught me ever thing she knew. Cap'n Lovell in good hands, Miz Rose. You go on now and I'll call ya if I needs ya."

Rose obeyed happy to say her prayers for the household and wait on the Lord to heal her husband. She felt helpless but remembered prayer was not helpless even if she may be. She turned over everything to Jesus.

Early in the morning she woke and stretched, listened for voices. Hearing nothing she grabbed a robe and tied it around her waist as she dashed down the hall and eased the door open tiptoeing into her husband's room. There Portia lay back in her chair, Lily sleeping at her feet on a pallet. No harsh sounds came from his chest. She could smell the vapors nearly causing her empty stomach to climb up into her throat. Rose hurried back to her room and dressed. She needed nourishment so she could take over her husband's care.

Grateful all was well, she went belowstairs for tea. Emmanuel was sweeping small limbs and leaves off the front walkway. "Good morning Emmanuel. It seems the house is asleep." She sipped hot tea and ate a scone with cream.

"Yes, Miz Rose. I be thinkin' thing's is good if'n we ain't heard nothin'."

Rose loved his smile. He was calm as a soft wind.

"Thomas be down at the wharf helping unload. Seems they got themselves some things to carry on up here." He shot her a quick glance. "Here dey come now. Best you go on and do somthin' else. Cap'n Lovell'll be wantin' to show you his gifts all by hisself, now."

She smiled and waved, stepped inside. It should be an exciting day. The winds were still blowing and Rose could only imagine the journey had been difficult across. It felt as though a storm may be brewing as the skies darkened. Teacup rattling in the saucer, she climbed the stairs and made her way to her husband's room. When she tiptoed in she nearly dropped her cup. Captain Lovell was sitting up in bed. Portia and Lily gone.

"I expected…" she began, noting his face was thin and colorless. "That you'd still be sleeping."

"Come sit." He motioned. "My sea legs have made me weak." He admitted. "But I have slept, I believe due to the laudanum."

Rose set her cup down on the sideboard and noted his breathless demeanor and the way he moved his arms slowly as though they were too heavy. She helped him with the rearrangement of his pillows. "Shall I send for broth and tea?"

"Miss Portia has already taken care of that. The reason I am sitting up, I believe."

Rose sensed he was putting on a brave front but was weaker than a newborn kitten. "Shall I draw the shutters back? Or will the sun hurt your eyes?"

"Draw them back." He said firmly. "And then I want to speak with you."

She did and sat down and waited for him to gather breath. He did it with great difficulty. "Shall I..."

"Stay." He said and with a hand across his chest, said, "We must speak of things now."

Rose folded her hands in her lap and waited.

"Captain Wyatt has informed me of the situation with Banker Dalton. I must write. Paper and ink please."

Rose felt her face flame as guilt crawled down her arms. Her legs felt weak. She hurried to her room and brought back simple stationary and pen and ink. She settled a pillow on her lap and the papers upon the wooden block Emmanuel had made for her. A sort of lap-desk.

"Take this down." He ordered.

She wrote not really understanding much until the very end, but when he finished, she rubbed her inked fingers. It was his last will and testament. Tears formed in her eyes when she looked at him.

"Do not concern yourself, child. I have kept my word to your father. And glad I am to have someone to leave my worldly goods to. My wife left this world too soon and there were no children."

She could hardly believe she had not seen the look of knowing in his face until just this minute. Rose was his wife now, but she knew Lucinda was his love. He had given Rose protection to pay back a debt owed to her father. And he had honored it. Tears plopped onto her fingers laced in her lap. She wiped the ink with her handkerchief before it ran onto her good dress.

They sat there, he closed his eyes and laid his head back. Rose imagined it had taken his every breath to finish. The only sound was of the birds outside the windows.

"It is a beautiful day is it not?" He changed the topic and opened his eyes.

"Beautiful." She agreed, standing to pull the drapery back a bit more and to be busy about the room so he would not see her distress. Her husband was dying. She knew it now.

"Call for Captain Wyatt." He ordered from the bed, his voice a hoarse whisper. "Send Thomas and tell him to be about it post-haste." His breath came in short gasps.

"I will." Rose hurried away then turned back. "Can I get you anything?"

"Send Portia with broth."

When he didn't say more, she bounded down the stairs and called for Portia and Thomas. Portia came hurrying around the corner. "What he need?" She asked.

"Please send Thomas for Captain Wyatt."

"Chile he ain't....ain't...."

"No....he wants to take care of some business." Rose felt her heart flutter. "But he did ask for more broth."

"Chile why'nt you say so? He be all right then, if he hungry." She dashed off to the kitchen and Rose heard the slam of the back screen as Thomas took off at a run. "I be up. You go on up and stay wif him."

Rose obeyed.

When she walked in again, he was laying back, his eyes closed, the papers laying across his chest in his hands. His breathing was so shallow, she worried biting her lip. Just then he opened his eyes and frightened a scream out of her.

Captain Lovell laughed lightly which started him coughing. Rose grabbed the pitcher and poured water into the glass and lifted it to his lips. It took several minutes for him to get control. And when he did his eyes seemed brighter.

"If I would have had a daughter, I would have wanted her to look just like you." His wispy words made her want to sob.

He smoothed her wayward curls that were always escaping from her coiffure and relaxed back against the pillows now in charge of himself.

"As you wrote, I wish to leave the Ireland Rose to you. Captain Wyatt will receive the Emerald Star. I have enough funds to correct the error made at the signing of Mr. Dalton's contract and you are not to let him extract any other monies from my accounts, is that understood?"

"Aye." She said, wishing they wouldn't be talking of such things.

"Listen now. I have a house on Tradd Street. It was the first house I bought as a young man, thanks to your father, who saved my life. This house belongs to you. The smaller one I wish to bequeath to Mrs. Jamison in however a manner she wishes to use it."

Rose nodded, having written it down.

"I am happy to hear that you have become acquainted with the orphanage. It has been underfunded."

"Yes, it has."

"Now, I will pay all debts off as soon as Captain Wyatt can do it for me. Also, I have asked him to hire a Captain for Ireland Rose. You need only to follow Captain Wyatt's orders. We have discussed this. He will be your overseer. If you choose to live here in Charleston you will be well cared for. The income from the goods being brought back from Europe should keep you until you take a husband."

"But...I..."

Captain Lovell interrupted. "I would have you see that you be careful and be certain of a man's intentions. They prey upon young wealthy women. Your father taught you well, Ireland Rose and I want to make sure you will find a man who will care for you."

"But won't you try and get well Captain Lovell?"

"Child it is not for me to say. I have lived a good life. And if not for your father, I would have been thrown overboard many years ago, a young man with no promise and no future."

Rose sniffed, missing her father, her mother and now she faced losing her husband. Even if it were not a conventional marriage she still belonged to someone. Overwhelmed she stood quickly before she could burst into tears and ran from the room, right into the path of Captain Wyatt.

"Oh…" She gasped and sidestepped him and ran to her room. Now he and her husband would know she *was* just a child.

Rose spent hours weeping. Lying across her bed, she knew the sun was near setting but she could still hear Captain Wyatt's voice. They had been conversing the entire afternoon.

She was to be a widow. Sensing that it would not be long…she'd heard that people knew when it was time. She could see it in his kind face. His blue eyes were weary. Her hands covered her face and she sobbed. He was a good man and had given her his worldly goods, been kind to her. Honored her. Protected her reputation. But she would be alone in the world.

It seemed she was living a bad dream. She had prepared for a time when she and Captain Lovell could work together at the Orphanage. He was to show her ways to assist and she wanted to learn. Now this.

Rose prayed for God to save her husband so they could work together.

Chapter 23

Hours turned into days as Rose stayed by her husband's bedside. Dr. Case made regular visits but she knew by his conduct that there was no hope. Stirred from her reverie, she lifted her eyes and watched Captain Wyatt enter the room after a slight knock at the door.

"Captain." He greeted her husband and nodded in her direction. "You're looking good today." He pulled off his hat and stood across the bed from Rose.

She stayed for a moment, then patted her husband's hand and left the two to talk. That was the pattern they had established; she felt uncomfortable around Captain Wyatt. He did not like her. She felt his distant manner each time he set eyes on her. Glad for a short reprieve, she wandered out to her garden and picked a small handful of flowers, chose a crystal bowl, filled it with water from the garden pump and gently laid the flowers on top of the water.

When that was done, she slipped a shawl over her shoulders and took a cup of hot tea to the front verandah and with a sigh sunk into the swing. She tipped her foot on the wood planks and pushed back and forth. Tears fell and plopped into her tea. She swiped them away, helpless to stop death from taking her husband. And so soon after he'd arrived.

"There you is. I been wonderin' where you tottered off to." Portia came out, hands on her hips, looking, Rose knew, for signs of fatigue. "Yep, I done see for myself...you's ready for some women-talk. Why don't you call your friend Stella and have her come and make you laugh for a bit. I got nothin' to do that cain't wait. You go on now. I'll get Thomas to run you a missive, soon as you write it down. Ain't nobody come calling for days, afeared of the fever. Captain don't have the Yellow Fever no more, his body done fought it but he's just too weak to fight the chill he done got coming across them rolling waters and crazy-like winds. 'Sides now the days are cooler Captain just might rest better."

Rose listened to Portia tell her things, but her heart wasn't in the mood for visitors. "Call for Emmanuel to bring the small wagon, please?"

"Child what you be thinkin' on doin?"

Since Portia's hands were on her hips again, Rose decided to avoid her questions and said, "Taking a nice, long ride. Would you mind so much Portia?"

"Chile, Emmanuel don't mind driving you a'tall. You knows that." She scolded. "Fact, he love running that pair o'horses onc't in awhile. Says they don't get 'nuff walking."

"That sounds good."

"Soon's Captain Wyatt be gone, I'll go on up and wrap some more o'them rags in that cream and put 'em on Captain's chest. Seems to help a mite, even if it stink like the barn out back."

Rose laughed. "I love the way you say things Portia…and without cracking a smile. You make me want to live my life right."

"Ya don't say?"

"I mean it." She smiled and lifted her tired body off the swing, nearly tipping her cup off her saucer.

"See, chile, you so tired, you cain't even stand up. You ain't 'et nothing. Go on up them stairs and walk right on past that sickroom and take yoself a nap. When you get up Emmanuel'll have them horses ready. And…just so's you know, I ain't gonna allow you to go to that Orphanage, you hear?"

Rose wondered how she could read her mind. Maybe she *was* overwrought.

"See's there I knew you was wantin' to get on over there again. You cain't be going there and getting sick and hauling it back into de house. Captain be worse off for sure." She scolded.

"You're right. I'm too tired to think…." Rose left her teacup and let herself in through the screen door, her feet dragging up each step. She wanted nothing more than to sleep off her tiredness. Body, soul, and mind. She hung onto the baluster to pull herself up the rest of the way and hearing Captain Wyatt's gruff voice, walked to her room and fell across the bed then pulled her shawl over her.

Portia came for her later in the afternoon. Rose sat up quickly when she heard her name.

"Everything all right?" She jumped up.

"All's well. Captain Lovell sleepin'. Captain Wyatt done gone and Dr. Case come and left some kinda drink that took the worry right out o'his muscles. He snoring, chile!" Portia said with a chuckle.

"Then he's resting well." Rose relaxed a bit.

"You go on and get yourself a ride. Emmanuel been waiting, glad to be doin' something. Dem horses clean and washed up like brand new babies." She chuckled again. "And it be a nice, nice day. Not so hot. Christmas be coming again. Seems like we just had it last month." She shook her head.

"Time goes so slow sometimes, and too fast others." Rose said quietly as she changed into a fresh dress and wrapped a light shawl around her shoulders. "Thank you, Portia…I don't know…what I'd do without…"

"Now don't you be lettin' dem pretty blue eyes water up none. Folks'll think you ain't strong. And I know you is." She wiped a tear of her own away. "And Captain Lovell cain't be seeing me a'bawling like a newborn calf." She stood straighter and busied herself in the wardrobe. Then popped her head out and said, "Go on now. I can hear them wagon wheels coming down the road…"

Portia heard the click of the little gal's heels as she descended the stairs and for all the world couldn't stop the tears that ran down her face. She smoothed the counterpane and straightened the pillows on Rose's bed, knowing she'd be alone without father, mother, nor husband. And Captain Lovell a good man, too.

"Lord I don't know how we gonna do without him." She said aloud then soothed herself and sang with her deep voice, "*Swing Low…Sweet Chariot…. comin' for to carry me home….*"

She heard the wagon creaking, the horses shoes clomping on the stone-studded streets as Emmanuel drove away.

Chapter 24

Rose knew there was one person she could go to for comfort.

"Emmanuel, drive me to Mrs. Perry's house on Tradd Street."

He pulled into a crossroad and slowly turned the carriage in the opposite direction.

Ten minutes later they were parked outside the Perry home.

"You ain't goin' in Miz Lovell?"

Rose twisted her lace hanky in her hands. "I never sent word." She whispered.

"Aw, you be needin' to talk, you's just go on up to that door and knock a bit. If'n she cain't have comp'ny just now come on back and we'll take the long way home."

Emmanuel's soft voice was nearly her undoing. "But my husband…."

"Capt'n Lovell be jus fine. Teeter be there. He be all right." He said looking straight ahead a slight smile on his face.

Rose smiled. He spoke with such confidence she relaxed. As long as they'd been together Emmanuel never once called his wife Teeter, at least not in her presence. She'd heard him once or twice when he hadn't known she was nearby. But the endearment only caused her eyes to water up even more. And no proper society woman could be caught dabbing her eyes in public view for all to see.

She squared her shoulders.,"Thank you. I believe I will go knock properly, Emmanuel."

He jumped down and came around and helped her down. "There you go. Me, I'll just drive on over to the haymarket, 'less you want me to wait right here."

"Thank you Emmanuel. Do as you please. Come for me in an hour please?"

"I shore will Miz Rose."

She waved him off and he drew away slowly.

Pulling in a deep breath she made her way up the steps onto the beautiful verandah gazing at the white wicker porch furniture, remembering their last visit.

She tapped the brass knocker and waited. A maid came to the door, her white apron a contrast against the dark brown dress she wore. "Is Mrs. Perry in?"

"I'm sorry ma'am she's gone down to Savannah."

"I see." Rose looked about for a moment, noting the woman's English accent.

The maid looked over her shoulder. "Your ride left ma'am?"

"Yes, I'm afraid it did....I ...I wasn't thinking properly." Her gloved hands twisted together.

"Would you like a spot of tea? Come in. You may be seated in the parlor." She opened the door wide.

"It's rather a nice day if you don't mind I'll stay on the verandah. Tea would be wonderful."

"Are you sure you'd rather sit out of doors, Miss?"

"Yes, I prefer it." Rose decided. "Two sugars, please and cream."

"Right away." The young woman shut the door softly and hurried away.

Rose seated herself on the white wicker chair after chasing several leaves off the seat. Indeed the winds were soft today and although it was getting chillier now with December upon them, she pulled her wrap around her neck and ears and sunk into the seat. She breathed in the light fragrance of the once potent white Gardenias in a hanging pot close by. The season of change settled all about her as she closed her eyes and thought about her mother and father resting so far away in Ireland. She longed to have her mother's keen words and her father's kind looks about her again.

The sense her life was about to change settled over her. She must make plans. Captain Lovell would not be long for this world and she would be alone in a city that was not her own. In a home she hardly deserved without a single person she belonged to. Perhaps she should try to correspond with family in Ireland. But all she had was the Bible her mother left her. The family tree was full; each entry made by her mother's hand.

Rose determined she would locate it one day soon. Right now she felt guilt creep up in her mind as her husband lay ill and she was sitting here. One hour, she told herself. One hour to think, to enjoy fresh air and time to decide where she would live and with whom. One purpose was planted firmly in her plans. She did not want another loveless marriage. One without children, without love.

The maid came with a tray and placed it on the glass-topped small table near her.

"How is Mrs. Perry?"

"She and Mr. Perry have gone down to Savannah to attend her father's burial services."

"Oh." Rose said sadly. "I see. Please do not mention I was here, then." She said quickly. "For indeed she has enough to think about now. I will send her a note."

"Yes, ma'am. Can I get anything else for you?"

"I will not need anything further and will be on my way as soon as my carriage arrives. You have been most kind."

"Just tap on the door Mrs. Lovell and I will come to you. Mrs. Perry thinks highly of you and your husband." She added quickly, bowed and hurried into the house.

Rose was surprised she knew her name and wondered at it. Then remembered Stella's loss and felt a certain heaviness of heart as she thought about her friend, and selfishly about herself knowing she would be grieving soon as well. She said a prayer for them both.

After the cup was empty, Rose placed it in the saucer and laid her head back, tipping the rocker back and forth with a light tap of her foot. She shut her eyes and listened to the sounds of children playing nearby their shouting and laughter suppressed by the wind. Her mind relaxed and she remembered playing as a child in Baltimore.... Green isles and sparkling water running over rocks and down hillsides danced in her mind. Her homeland. Ireland.

Suddenly a familiar sound crept into her dreams and she sat up. She forced her eyes to focus and realized Emmanuel was pulling up out front. She tried to push away the fuzziness in her brain and hands on chair arms, lifted herself. Her legs felt weak. She must have dozed for some time.

Instantly the maid was at her side. "Ma'am are ye all right?"

"Yes. Yes, I am....I'm sorry I must have ..." Rose felt her face turn a shade of pink.

"Not a worry a'tall, ma'am. I came to check on ya and ye was looking so peaceful...." She finished with a slight smile. "I'll be sending ya on yer way now so you can get home."

"Thank you for the tea."

"Pleased to be of service ma'am." She said and stood to the side, Rose knew, to wait until she left to gather the dishes.

She walked on legs that didn't seem like her own and was thankful when Emmanuel took her elbow and helped her up. When had she become so weak? Her mind worked overtime....what if she had Yellow Fever or Consumption. She knew from the Doctor's talk that weakness was a definite symptom. She pushed the foolish thoughts away and knew she was just plain tired.

"Home Emmanuel. I could use a bit of nourishment as I'm sure you could as well."

"Only been an hour, Miz Rose. I'm not tired at all."

"I shouldn't be." She declared and felt the heaviness of her eyelids as they wanted to shutter downward and stay that way. She allowed it, but for only a minute. Shutting out the world made her listen to the sounds. The clip-clop of the horses' hooves on the 6 inch square cobblestones, the light talk of gentleman and ladies as they passed by. A shout of a mother calling her children to come for suppah. She had herself taken on the southern drawl and smiled, eyes still closed. She was mixed up. Full blooded Irish heritage born in the North and now living in the South. *Who was she and where did she belong*?

Chapter 25

Emmanuel pulled the carriage up to the front and let her off. She stopped to gaze at the beautiful home that Captain Lovell had bought years ago. A young man with a beautiful woman he loved captaining the Emerald Star back and forth across the Atlantic dozens of times. Coming home with gifts for his beloved. She wondered what he was like then -- young, handsome, full of life. And now he lay above stairs in the same house alone.

Rose hurried inside and lifting her skirts ran unladylike up the stairs. She needed to see if he was all right. She feared walking in and stopped a few steps outside the door. No sounds came. He was all right, then. His coughing and sputtering were gone. Perhaps he would be better. She had prayed he would. That he could commandeer the Ireland Rose to London and back many more times. Hands at her waist, she smoothed her skirts and took off her bonnet. With it in her hand, she stood in the doorway and peered in.

He was alone, propped up and reading. Reading?

She called to him, "Sir you are well?"

"At the moment." He concurred and pulled the thin wire glasses off his nose. "Come."

She pressed herself next to the tall bed. "It is so good to see you looking so full of health."

"Portia has forced my hand with those awful mud-slathering treatments; a man couldn't lay still for the smell alone." He closed the book. "And how are ye child?"

"I am well." She paused. "I wish you wouldn't call me child." She said softly.

"Ah, forgive me Ireland Rose." He teased.

She could see he was still weak, when he reached up to tap her cheek.

"I cannot help but see your father in you. You will do well in life. He has taught you well."

"Yes." She agreed. "And you have been kind to me . . . more than I deserve."

"Ah, I'll have none of that." He said firmly. "Now tell me what you have been doing at Jamison's. I hear bits and pieces but I want to hear it from you. Take that chair and rest." He told her.

She pulled the chair closer and sat, resting her feet on the lower part of the bed frame. "I have cleared the attic of things that are in good condition. And some clothing as well. I hope you don't mind."

"This is your house." He said and gave her a look that said he didn't want to repeat that.

"Also, you have not been below stairs, but through a friend, we have taken the liberty of changing some draperies and upholstery in the large room." She started to add…*I hope you don't mind*…and pressed her fingertips over her lips.

"The rooms were dark. I'm glad you made changes. Perhaps I will yet see them."

She heard a slight chuckle and felt her heart lighten immediately. "Shall I get you something to eat? Broth perhaps."

"No. Indeed not. Portia has fed me more than I can manage for one day. A glass of water would do."

Rose jumped up and poured water from the pitcher and handed it to him. She noticed his large workworn hands were thinner and that he shook slightly when he drank.

He handed the glass back and she set it on the side table.

"Have I tired you?"

"I do believe I will lay back and shut my eyes." He said as his lids closed. He lifted a hand, adjusted the pillows behind his head and scooted down into the covers.

Rose slipped out of the room, content that her husband had finally come through the worst of it. He should be much better by tomorrow. She tiptoed out and flew down the stairs and out to the kitchens where she found Portia and reported the good news.

"Captain Lovell has come round." She said. "Your ministrations worked, Portia."

"Chile, don't you come sneaking up on a body like 'at." She turned, hand over her heaving chest. "Be given my heart a stop just like 'at."

"I'm sorry, Portia." She said tapping her arm. "Next time I'll come up quieter and address you first."

"Dat's okay honey. I done hear'd your good news. Captain looking good ain't he? I be thinkin' trouble may have passed. That stuff shore do make a body well. Thinkin' since they cain't stand the smell, they just wanna get up outta that bed to get away from it." She chuckled.

"Portia, you do make me laugh! What's for supper? I'm famished."

"Chile I knows you better now. You need to eat and keep yo'self strong. We cain't all be sick tw'once. We be havin' ham and grits and eggs all stirred up with butter and cream. Biscuits and honey and for d'sert, some apple pie."

"That sounds wonderful." It's been a long day. I feel so much better now. Can I help?"

"Go on now. Git. I just be out here in the garden to get some spice for dem eggs. 'Bout ten minutes you come on back and we's gonna eat inside tonight. Wind's startin' to pick up. I be thinkin' we gonna have some cold days. I'll be making some o'dat chicken and dumplin's Captain love when he come home. Maybe we can even bring him down those stairs and sit at that big ole dining table and eat like real families do."

"Oh that would be good. It's been almost a year since we've done that. Your family will join us too...Captain Lovell's back and he'll insist you know."

"I knows that. Don't be knowin' how dat man keep breaking them society rules like he does and folks don't give no nevermind. Course none of us done tole anybody 'bout that." She scurried away with a wave.

Rose didn't know what to do with herself, so she snuck back up the stairs and peeked in her husband's room. He was sleeping quietly. No odd noises coming from his chest. She ran to her room on light feet and remembered she wanted to look for her mother's old Bible. A quick rummage through the wardrobe and she had it in her hands. About that time, she heard Lily's quick, light steps running upward.

"Miz Rose, dinner done." She said softly and was off again dashing down the stairs with hardly a sound.

Rose set the Bible down, ran a hand over it and knew she would come back tonight and read the family tree and Psalms too. She had much to be thankful for.

"Please, let's celebrate Captain Lovell's health tonight. We'll eat in here. All of us."

"Chile you be the silliest thing I ever did see. You know we ain't tryin' to be mean, but you cain't have us in der like 'at if someone come to the door and see us. The help eatin' at the table."

Rose, hands on her hips announced, "Portia you worry too much. Bible says worry is a sin."

Portia's eyes grew large. "It do at that." She said, wagging her head from side to side as she walked away. In a minute or two, she came back with Emmanuel, Thomas and Lily, each carrying their plates. Portia had two. Rose's and her own.

"See now that's not hard is it. And I see I must remind you, you are free. Free. You are no longer slaves, haven't been since Captain Lovell hired you. Times aren't like they used to be, Portia."

"They ain't but it seem like it to us. Our folks was slaves and it ain't right somehow to eat with white folks...just don't seem right."

"Why?"

"Well, just don't 'at's all. Now you eat." Portia ordered.

Rose smiled. "See I knew you didn't have an answer."

Chapter 26

For two days Captain Lovell sat up in bed and read for a few minutes at a time. Even Doctor Case was surprised, but he warned Rose that things could take a turn. She never even considered that. Her husband was getting better. Now they could look at the desk he brought from France. And the other gifts he had carried back. They had been hidden in his office away from prying eyes until the Captain could tell her each story that came with each piece. Christmas was only three weeks away. Rose suggested they set up a tree in the foyer early and celebrate. There was so much to be thankful for.

Doctor Case said it might be a good idea and they should go along with it even though the Captain was still too weak to come down. Rose insisted they take a large branch up and hang little doo-dads from it so he would have something to look at. And that perhaps he could walk to the top of the stairs and see the huge tree Emmanuel had set up.

Today they would bedeck the tree with all those pretty doodads from the attic. She was beside herself with joy until she walked past her husband's room. She heard the rattle in his chest and hurried down and told Portia to make up some of that awful paste and plaster his chest again.

Portia's face darkened for a moment but she hurried away.

Rose felt sure things would be fine and dashed to the attic, pulled down the stairs by the rope and climbed up. She knew exactly where the Christmas boxes were stacked since they had cleaned and went straight there, diving into one box and another. She set four boxes next to the hole and scrambled down with the lightest one.

The box was placed in the marble hall. The tree smelled delicious and brought back memories of her own family Christmas celebrations. She was determined to make the most of the holiday, and earlier was better. Rose found Thomas and asked him to go up and haul the rest of the boxes down.

"Mis Rose, come and sit yoself down and eat. You gonna wear yoself out and then you be layin' up in yo bed sick. Chicken and sweet taters tonight." Portia called.

Rose laughed. "I'm coming. Let me wash up and I'll be there. "Make sure there's lots of butter."

She insisted on everyone eating at the dining room table and since they were allowed no visitors everyone had gotten used to eating together, expecting no interruptions.

"After supper, let's get that special broomstick with the nail that you made Emmanuel. This year's tree must be twelve feet tall."

"Not quite Miz Rose, but almost." Emmanuel said. "I'll go get it and we'll get those ornaments and doo-hatches up tonight. Won't take long with that stick. I'll bring the ladder, too."

"Thomas would you like to twirl the garland up and around the top. You and Lily can hang tinsel, too. We will have to string cranberries and popcorn, too... and I think it will take quite a while with such a large tree."

"Gotta check and see if them cranberries came on down from Maine. Hear'd they were coming in, but it's a mite early. We may have to do without this year."

"Portia... do you think so?" Rose worried.

"Ain't no sense in worryin' now. I's goin' down the block and chop some o'that Myrtle from Miz Burn's tree. She told me the other day I could get much as I wanted."

"We'll wrap it around the stair rail and get some Poinsettias from the garden shop for the entryway and the stairs."

Rose didn't see the look Portia gave her.

That baby girl knowin' something we don't know.... Portia felt jitters scuttle down her arms. She had to fight the old superstitions her mother believed in and remind herself the good Lord was the only way and not to get in His way o'things with such nonsense. *Lord have mercy*, she whispered.

Within the hour Emmanuel's stick had hung stringed ornaments and garland from the perfect tiptop to the wide bottom pine. Rose declared it perfect. She didn't like too many things catching the eye, leaving room so folks could admire the tree as well. She liked simplicity and to her less was better.

Thomas, Emmanuel and Lily stood back with Rose, all three with their hands on their hips and declared it finished except for the red cranberry string, provided they could get them, and the popcorn string which could be finished in two or three evenings.

Portia was out back chopping the Myrtle so they could be wound into a wreath...it would die after a couple of days, but they could make others. She helped Portia form circles from the vines and tied them together with string, while the scent of pine permeated the house.

"Good evening Captain. Hope we ain't been too noisy down below, Miz Rose all excited with that tree and all." Portia hustled over to the bed and poked her apron corners to her eyes. "Did I make that too powerful for ya, sir?" She inquired as she lifted off the cloth, heavy with the ointment.

"Well if it don't kill me . . ." he began and choked out a cough. "If I can still breath, I think I'll get some sleep now."

She chuckled, glad to see him in high spirits. "Looking as though you gonna get better." She said and helped him put on a fresh pajama top. "You rest now and don't pay no nevermind about us. I'll shut your door."

The next morning Rose awoke and dressed early. The fragrance of pine filled the hallway. She checked in and found her husband still asleep. Snoring even. She smiled and heart light, went down the stairs. She was famished. Funny, she thought how when the heart was light the body was as well. She had been so tired and fearful that she'd nearly run herself down.

Energy pumped through her veins as she gobbled down her toast and eggs and headed to the verandah out front to see if there was fog lifting off the river this morning. She loved sitting out early and watching the day begin. Blessings in her heart began to add up again. She could see more clearly the beauty that surrounded her. The hope she now had that her husband would be on his feet again and working. If they were careful, perhaps he could visit the Orphanage with her. Perhaps. She dreamed a bit and stood, ready for the day to begin.

Portia came out and swept the porch. Now that the winter season was upon them leaves dropped from all around and the winds were cooler mornings and evenings. The hot spell had been broken and it was her favorite time of the year. Mostly because her husband came home for the winter each year. This would be a good Christmas. God spared her husband. She watched her friend sweep and hum a spiritual as she worked.

"Captain done 'et his breakfast." She said as she passed. "'Et it all. Said he slept like a baby, too."

"Thank the Lord." Rose said quietly and jumped up from her chair. "I'm going up if you don't think it'll tire him."

"Chile you know he brighten up when he see you." She chuckled.

That was all Rose needed to hear. She bounded up the stairs, lifting her skirts and with hands behind her back, crept up to see if he was awake. He was reading.

"Have you made progress?" She said quietly.

He pulled glasses from his nose and laid them aside. "I have." He motioned for her to take the chair. "What news do you have from below stairs."

"The Christmas tree is up and beautiful. Perhaps you can see it…when Dr. Case says you can." She added

"I can smell it. It brings back good memories." He mused wishing he could smoke his pipe.

"Good." She smiled.

"Are you lonely with no callers." He rubbed his chin. Portia had given him a clean shave earlier.

"No. I'm just glad you're here. Even Captain Wyatt hasn't been round."

"I forbid him. He has two ships to clean up for our next voyage. Told him I'd send Thomas if he needed him. And Dr. Case runs by every now and again and gives him a report."

Rose liked the sound of that…their *next* voyage. Hope sprang up in her heart.

"Besides, he has family to visit while he's here and...."

Rose noticed the Captain stopped his sentence in mid-air. She figured the Captain's woman was also being visited as well as his sister Ava.

Chapter 27

The house was abuzz with talk of the Captain getting out of bed.

"Doctor Case, can we safely get him up?" Rose asked as they stood around the bed.

"On one condition. You must get Emmanuel or Captain Wyatt here and I'll see if he is able. A fall would . . ."

"Of course." Rose agreed quickly. "I'll go for Emmanuel."

She ran down the stairs and out to the stables where she knew Emmanuel would be shucking out the stalls.

"Can you come Emmanuel? Doctor Case said they are going to see if he can stand."

Emmanuel put his pitchfork aside and rambled slowly, dusting off his trousers and shirt. He stopped by a water bucket and washed his hands. Then followed her in and up the stairs.

Rose waited and then realized they were waiting for her to leave. In her anxiousness to see if he could stand, she forgot her manners.

"Oh my." She said and hurried out, shutting the door behind her. Instead of going down those stairs again, she wandered to the far hall and paced, then stepped inside her room. The Bible lay on her stand. She opened it and gazed at the family tree. They had been so busy decorating the house for early Christmas, she'd barely had time to read the names on her family tree. Her hands smoothed the front leaf and she began at the trunk and read upward to each branch. She had in her hands the names of her parents' ancestors. She wondered if they would be proud of her now.

Thinking herself daft, she set aside her thoughts for another day. There was so much to do.

A few minutes later she heard groaning and grunting. She opened her door but did not step out. She wanted to be there when he first saw the tree. It was a benchmark, an achievement that all of them together would share if Captain Lovell were to be well again. She shivered at the thought, thankful for all the good that surrounded her.

Suddenly his door flew back and hit the wall. She could hear the men talking, their deep voices echoing down the long hall. He was up!

"May I come out?" She asked from the doorway.

"Do." She heard her husband growl. "See a weak man up after weeks in a bed."

She peeked out and sure enough he had on trousers and a shirt. She walked slowly and joined them at the rail. "What do you think?"

The Captain stared down at the tree, the top of it at eye level and with a weak whistle told her it was grand. "Well done." He said breathlessly and asked to be taken back to bed, "weak as a new kitten."

"You did it." She encouraged him and watched as he painstakingly made the short walk to the bed, exhausted from the activity. "Rest now. Leave all of it up to us."

After a bit of scuffle, the men had him back in bed. She heard him grumble and knew he had to be better if he was angry about not being strong.

Four days later her husband was dead.

Portia stayed through the night when his cough had returned and insisted Rose sleep in her room. Doctor Case had come, even Captain Wyatt had been called to Captain Lovell's bedside. Rose had heard the rattle in his chest and the cough, but she was certain it would pass.

During the night he could fight no more and the doctor declared him free from this world to join the next. She had stood with the doctor, Captain Wyatt, Portia and Emmanuel. Feeling like she was in a dream she heard the words and did not believe them. She wanted to scream. To call him back. To tell him thank you one more time, but nothing came out of her mouth.

The next time she woke she was in her bed.

Twice she tried to get up and couldn't. Portia told her the doctor had given her something to sleep. Had she really screamed or was it a dream.

By the end of the day, she was sitting up, drowsy yet aware that her husband was no longer with them. Her mind tried to process the thought. She was a widow. At twenty. What had happened to him? He was getting better. Then suddenly he was gone. All the wind went out of her sails. God had spoken and nothing would change it.

Portia told her that Captain Wyatt had caught her as she fainted and carried her to her room. She felt her face color. He must have disliked that, since he hardly said two words to her and when he did they were usually growls. She turned her face away and slept. It was easier than thinking.

The news traveled fast in Charleston. She knew she had to get up and take her place at her husbands side. To be honorable, upstanding, and strong. On the day his body was taken away, she had watched two young men come and wrap him and carry him down the stairs for the last time. She had stood there, no tears, no emotion. She had learned that at her mother's knee. *Life brought good times as well as bad times and you must prepare yourself for both.* She'd said. Rose did her duty. She had a black dress refitted and carried herself like the lady she was. Condolences poured in from all over, including London. She hardly knew what to say. She knew very few of his acquaintances abroad, and those of Charleston's society paid their respects with long lines. He was well-liked. Rose never knew just how much. Regret wound its ugly head around her neck.

She could have been a better wife. Her husband had held positions of importance here and in London. He was known most especially for his care of the unfortunate in society. Men and women came and told her stories how he had helped them during difficult times without asking for repayment. Some had gone on and helped others, because he had helped them. Just like her father did for him when he was young, Rose remembered.

She had been so childish. Reading those letters up in the attic, wishing she had someone to love her like "W" loved Darby. For days notes came in with stories. She could only hope to walk in his footsteps.

At the reading of the will, Rose sat still, the black veil hiding her face from view as she sat with the solicitor, Captain Wyatt, and Mrs. Jamison who nervously wondered out loud why she should be called in for the reading.

Soon, to Rose's delight Mrs. Jamison learned that Captain Lovell's small house was willed to her to sell or use in any way she deemed appropriate to secure income for Jamison's Orphanage. Her church fan was doing double duty as she waved it back and forth, saying over and over, "Thank you Jesus. Thank you Jesus."

Captain Wyatt, whom Rose found difficult to make eye contact with knowing he had been forced to carry her to her bed, was glad for the black veil covering her face. She carried off her role perfectly and rose from her seat. Mrs. Jamison, tears falling from her brown eyes, told her how good Captain Lovell had been to the children all through the years and now this. "The Lord bless you Mrs. Lovell. Your husband was a kind man. God bless you child."

"God bless you Mrs. Jamison. I shall endeavor to walk in his footsteps."

After Mrs. Jamison left, Captain Wyatt caught her by the elbow. "We need to find a place to talk."

"Mr. Wyatt can it wait. I am most tired."

"Of course."

He said the words, but her eyes detected he was not happy. It was not her concern. She knew that should she have to stand much longer he would be carrying her to the solicitor's sofa. She felt the world tilt a bit and hurried away.

"Straight home quickly, Emmanuel if you please." She stepped up and nearly lost her footing.

Captain Wyatt saw it, too.

The wind in her face, she hardly noticed people as they passed them, each lifting a hand to wave kindly to the new young widow in Charleston. She felt sick to her stomach. "Hurry please, Emmanuel."

She made it to the house, walked straight through to the gardens and heaved up her stomach contents. Lily ran for her grandmother and Rose fell into the closest chair and fanned herself with her black gloved hand.

"Chile, you too hot in that get-up. Don't know why white folks got to wear all that black, hanging 'round 'em like grave clothes and they still alive. God done took yo husband out o'this world and glad I am for it." She muttered.

"Come one now. Take dat hat off and dem gloves. Lily, go get Miz Rose some water, and put a mint leaf in it."

Lily ran.

Within minutes she was up the stairs and freed from all the frippery, in a soft cotton gown and put to bed. She could have cried at Portia's ministrations. The woman sat on the bed next to her and without a word, petted and smoothed her hair, humming quietly. Rose fell into a sleep only the grieving know.

Chapter 28

For days Rose refused to see Captain Wyatt. Portia set him straight the third day, when she gave him Rose's message. She would not see him until Monday next.

She wandered the house in a soft cotton dress of pink with miniature green leaves. Portia had forbade her to wear black and no visitors were allowed.

Rose wished only to think without interruption. To go through the house and finger this and that. Memories she could have made. She would not allow herself to go into the room where the gifts he brought from London were kept. That would be for another day. She sat at his desk and felt strange. Like he was standing behind her watching. She could not bring herself to sift through his things. Instead she pulled out her drawings and laid them across the desk. Would he have laughed had he seen them?

She chuckled a bit. Then she remembered Stella was grieving her father and she, Rose, had not even remembered to send her a note. She pulled out a piece of paper and wrote a letter of condolence and told her about Captain Lovell. She knew that Stella would not be back for several weeks. She had to take care of her father's small estate and move his things out of the church parsonage. A new preacher would be needed. Rose felt her pain.

She tucked the drawings back into the drawer and said a prayer for Stella and her family. The house loomed large and lonely. She knew now that her husband's presence even when he was away, kept this house alive. It didn't really belong to her. Not really. She wondered if she could will it to Mrs. Jamison. Perhaps the children could come and live here. Nettie could sew. Perhaps teachers could be brought in. She could go back to Ireland. Back home.

Such strange thoughts entered her mind. Rose wondered if she was being childish or realistic like her mother taught her. Her father taught her to dream, her mother to survive. Each was important in it's own way. She much preferred to dream, but in order to make them come true one had to have some common sensibilities.

She could not imagine living here, under the very watchful eye of Captain Wyatt and his gruff ways. He already owned the Emerald Star. Would he buy the Ireland Rose from her? She could perhaps find family in Ireland and settle with the money she made from the sale of the ship. Certainly her family tree would show her the way. There was only one way to know and that was to try. In a couple of weeks, she may send off a few letters, see if she could go home to someone who knew who she was and where she came from.

Rose lifted herself from the desk and moseyed to the living room, fingered the new draperies and upholstery she and Ava had changed. He had not seen any of it. She cried for that. How hopeless it all looked. How silly now, when it had seemed so important then. Yet, she was among the living. Someone should have this house. It was made for a family. She picked a piece of stationery with her husband's name on top and began to make a list.

"Sell house. Sell Ireland Rose."

She set it aside and with one step, she began her new life. She would make it count. Somehow. Someway.

Three letters went out in Monday's post. And Captain Wyatt was due for his afternoon appointment. Rose knew he would be livid and with a second cup of tea to sustain her, she waited in her husband's office, sitting in his chair. Still her stomach fluttered from lack of food, but she could not eat a bite.

She didn't know what the good Captain wanted to discuss, but she was sure he would not be happy, no matter what it was about.

When the knocker reverberated through the foyer, she knew it was time to put aside her own feelings and give Captain Wyatt a chance to state his intentions. She forced herself to take several deep breaths. It couldn't be that bad. She had a job to do. And she would do it.

The minute he walked in the door she could feel his disdain for her.

"Captain Wyatt." She stood and motioned for him to take a seat. "You wished to see me?"

"Aye." He took off his hat and remained standing. He would not be seated for he wasn't staying long.

She wisely kept her tongue, even when he would not sit. He towered over her even from across the room.

"Why did you refuse to see me?"

"I, sir, needed time alone."

"Time alone? What you have done is waylaid the Ireland Rose. I had a Captain ready to go and the weather has now turned against us. Had he left a week ago, he would have been in front of the storm."

Rose looked down and then back at him. "I am sorry."

"Sorry. Sorry is it? Mrs. Lovell, there will be spoilage that we cannot atone for. Captain Quinn, Paxon Quinn has a family of eight to feed." His eyes, dark with anger speared hers.

Tears sprung to her eyes. She stood, placed her small hands on the desk and made herself look at him. "I am sorry, Sir. If there is something I can do, tell me what it is."

Ashton Wyatt looked away for a moment. He saw the tears form in her eyes but she did not let them fall. He wanted to take her in his arms, but she was only a memory of lost love. He forced himself to meet her gaze, all the while turning his hat in his hands.

"There is nothing we can do except wait and hope for better weather. As it is he has lost more than a thousand dollars in spoiled food. And his men are wont to get back to England as well."

"I will pay for the loss." She stated and not knowing what to do with her hands, intertwined them at her waist. She would not let him see she was weak.

"You will pay?"

"Yes. If I have caused the harm. I will pay. She drew her husband's book of checks from his drawer. She was now responsible for any monies he had. "If I have enough. I will pay." She amended.

"You have enough." He said gruffly and regret formed in his mind. She had no idea what Captain Lovell's worth was.

She paused and felt a pang. Did he think her uninformed? Even as she thought it, she knew she was. How was she going to work with Mr. Dalton if she didn't have Captain Wyatt on her side.

She expressed the thought, "Sir, I must have you work with me. I cannot handle Mr. Dalton. As you know I was foolish once. I will not be taken advantage of when there are so many ways Captain Lovell's monies could help others. Will you work with me?"

Ashton Wyatt could hardly stand up to those blue eyes. She had him soul and spirit, already. Didn't she know that? He wanted to kick himself for his inability to distance himself from the women he loved with this woman who looked so much like her. He could Captain a ship and a boatload of men, but couldn't commandeer his own heart.

And he wanted out from underneath her gaze.

"I will work with you."

He banished all thoughts of past hurts and meant what he said.

"Write the check. We will give anything we have that is still good to Jamison's Orphanage. Would that suit you?"

"You know about our interest in Jamison's?" She was surprised.

"Captain Lovell and I spoke about it."

"I see." She paused glad their conversation had taken a turn, because for the life of her she wanted to sit down and cry. "Then take this..." she wrote furiously and handed him a check. "And we will call it fair then. And finished?"

"Fair and finished." He said without looking at the check, pocketing it, bowing slightly and as was his usual way, clomping out the door, his boots heavy across the marble floors.

Rose fell into her husband's chair and let out a puff of air. *What in the world am I going to do Lord? This man does not like me and I'm afraid I do not like him.*

Tears popped out of her eyes like huge raindrops and she just let them fall.

Chapter 29

Rose stood on shaky knees and made her way to the living room. She fingered the new drapes and sat on the sofa as she eyed the newly upholstered chairs. The improvement was beautiful but she had no desire to rework an already suitable house. Something inside her had changed. She stood and wandered about, looking at each lamp, every piece of art on the wall. None of it was hers. Not even the items in the attic. She scolded herself for acting so childish. What did anything matter? Was it all about how one dressed? How one looked? How many manners one kept? How many rules one did *not* break?

Sighing, she looked out the window and saw the people coming by her house, the sidewalk full of new passengers alighting from someplace else and coming here to Charleston, for the holidays, for a visit, to live. She watched them go by. Husbands with adoring wives on their arm. Children following or being carried along.

She had to find a purpose for her life.

Days passed and finally the unspoken rule of visiting was upon her. Callers began to come and pay their respects. Portia had done a good job of waylaying them until Rose was ready. If ever she would be.

Mr. Dalton came and sashayed around, touching and almost taking inventory of her space. She shuttered. Foster Perry came and shared news about Stella. She was not yet home, having been gone a month. Ava came but she seemed preoccupied. She didn't even suggest ideas for another re-do. Mr. McGuire was not with her. Several ladies from the church brought dinners and notes asking her to call on them if she needed anything. But she knew she would not call. Everyone had their problems and hers were not theirs. She had to learn to face them on her own.

Besides day after tomorrow was Christmas Eve.

The day arrived rainy and cold, at least for Charlestonians. She remembered Baltimore Christmases and they were nothing like these. She did miss the soft white winter snows lit by moonlit nights. And she missed her mother and father. She wondered how Mr. Smithers was doing with the business he bought from her father. How her school friends fared. Were they married with children? Had they all forgotten her because she left? There was one boy in school she always liked. She'd never forget his name. Aaron Alexander. He threw paper snow at her one day and the teacher made her clean it up. And she at her fourth level and he his sixth. She had no older brother to protect her. When it came up at home, her father had said she could do one of two things. Ignore him. Or hit him.

She chose the first and from then on he pursued her diligently trying to get her attention. Rose smiled thinking of it now. No doubt Mr. Alexander was a businessman by now, for his father owned the Copper Penny hotel in downtown Baltimore. They were considered a very wealthy family in contrast to hers. She remembered something about his attending Yale. She had had two beaus but only in school. Her parents knew nothing about them.

As the night began to fall on Charleston's residents, Christmas candles began to appear in windows, lights from every room seemed to be shining. She cast a quick glance outside and smiled. Many folks were walking along the boardwalk in their sweaters and hats, many, she knew were anxious to see the Ashley and Cooper Rivers where they met in a V on the battery. She gazed through gauze curtains and wished for days gone by.

"Ireland Rose" she scolded herself aloud. "Pop out of it this instant." Her mother's words. "No time to dawdle, there's work to be done."

She fashioned her shawl tighter around her shoulders and went up to bed. She wanted nothing more than to forget Captain Wyatt's disappointment in her and all the faces she wore for each visitor hoping to keep her husband's memory in good standing in the Charleston community. She must do that for him.

Pulling on the railing for strength, she climbed the stairs then stopped at his room and pictured him there the last time she saw him. He was white and the life had gone out of his eyes. Slowly she shut the door, but could not shut out the memory from her mind.

The door to her room shut with a loud click in the quiet house. Rose changed into night clothes and crawled under the counterpane covering her head. Her eyes closed and she remembered nothing.

Chapter 30

Sometime during the night deep in sleep she heard Portia calling her name. "Miz Rose, Captain Wyatt down in the drawing room. He wants to see you. And he don't look too good neither."

The words were real weren't they? She didn't know for sure until she saw the candle dancing in Portia's face, her dark eyes large.

"What? Captain Wyatt?" She tried to sit up. "He's here? Whatever for?" She wondered. No fear entered her mind. Her husband was gone and he could not bring her bad news anymore. She trusted him enough to know he would never make an unnecessary visit. The coverlet was pushed away and as before Portia made her suitable enough for a mid-night visit.

She pulled her neck-to-toe woolen wrap around her nightgown and tied it closed. Portia tied up her loose hair in back. "It be good 'nuff." She said and handed her the candle just like before.

"I be waitin' up here you need anything chile."

Rose descended the stairs, her slippered feet making no noise.

She made her way to the room and stood in the doorway. Her mouth opened to speak but she stopped short of entering and clamped her lips shut. He was pacing across the width of the room in front of the fireplace, back and forth, his hand rushing through his hair twice. Slowly she placed herself in the square open space. At once he turned. Rose took a step forward.

"You're injured Captain Wyatt…" her voice hoarse from sleep.

He stopped pacing for a moment and as though thinking what to say, he took two steps forward, but as was his usual manner, did not draw closer. "Mrs. Lovell, I have an extreme favor I must ask of you."

Rose took couldn't help but draw closer to him. Once he'd stopped pacing she could see in the candle's light that his eye was nearly swelled shut. Blue wounds covered his face. A patch of his cheek was scraped. His dark eyes had blood in them.

"Shall I call for Portia to attend your….your wounds?" She kept her voice soft. Captain Wyatt, she knew, carried a strong undertow beneath the surface. Always had. Especially when it came to her.

"No." He said defining the moment with his sharp growl. "I'm not here because of myself. " He gave her his back again.

He hesitated so long, and swept his hand through his hair twice before turning back.

"Mrs. Lovell, I am sorry to say there is a young woman from the orphanage . . .

Rose interrupted.

"Jamison's?" she took several steps forward. She must know.

"No, the white orphanage."

"I see." She settled but was not calm inside.

"She is with child." He said quietly.

Rose's mind told her that Mr. Wyatt had some trouble on his hands. She had heard about his women. But a young girl from the orphanage. She was incensed but with difficulty, held her tongue.

"She needs a place to stay."

"Where is she?" Rose would not deny the woman assistance.

"She is waiting in the carriage. I did not know what to do with her at this hour. So I came here."

He had turned to face her. Rose could see the hurt and anger in his bloodshot eyes. She had never seen Captain Wyatt undone.

"Bring her in." Rose said. "She will stay here."

Captain Wyatt brought his eyes straight up to hers. "Are you certain. You have only lost your husband and…."

"Yes, I know." She stopped him with her words. "And I am only a child."

"That's not what I was going to say." He shot back.

Rose kept her lips glued together.

The man had enough trouble, it looked like and she knew in a few days, weather permitting he was following Captain Quinn across the Atlantic in an unusual mid-winter journey.

And, it looked as though someone had already given him a good talking to with those punches to his face.

"Go on. Bring her in, it's cold outside. She must be shivering. I'll attend her myself." She watched him turn without a word and walk rather gingerly it seemed. He must have suffered other injuries.

Rose stood back a few feet from the front door and heard the steps creak then as they walked across the verandah.

She schooled her face. "Lord please make me kind and loving. Show me what to do." Her quick prayer lessened the beats of her heart. She pulled in a deep breath and felt a soft smile come across her lips as the door opened.

She watched as Captain Wyatt, his arm around the girl's shoulders, drew her in. Blonde hair shone in the candlelight. She girl was young, perhaps sixteen. Her downcast eyes hurt Rose's heart. She could see the young girl was about halfway through her pregnancy.

"Come." Rose drew her in with a sweep of her hand. "Would you like some tea? I was about to make myself a good hot cup."

She looked to Captain Wyatt, and he nodded.

"Yes ma'am, if you don't mind."

"I would not mind at all. Captain Wyatt you must go and tend to your wounds, we will have tea." She said gently. "You may come tomorrow."

"Remember what I told you." He spoke to the girl.

"I will remember." She said shivering again.

Rose put her arm around her and called softly to Portia, whom she knew waited up at the top of the stairs to make sure no harm came to her.

"I am called Rose, this is Portia."

"Ma'am." The girl said to each, her eyes still looking at her feet.

Rose wanted to ask her name, but perhaps she had instructions from Captain Wyatt, so kept her silence.

"My name is Matilda Jane."

"Matilda Jane. What a handsome name." Rose took her elbow and drew her toward the house and into the dining room. Portia had gone out to the cookstove where water was always hot for tea.

The three of them sat in the large dining room. Out of the corner of her eye she saw Emmanuel laying logs into the fire for them on this rather cool evening.

Portia brought cups and saucers and even a plate of bread and butter with a side plate of ham. Rose saw Matilda Jane's eyes widen. She gently pushed the plate of food toward the girl and said, "Eat."

Portia's eyes met hers and Rose signaled that they should partake first. Rose took a small piece of bread and slathered butter on it generously. Portia did the same. Matilda waited and with jerky movements did the same and ate heartily.

Rose secretly condemned Captain Wyatt. Why hadn't he made sure she had food. Was he so low as to let her go hungry knowing she carried a child. She would speak to him about that on the morrow.

When it appeared the girl had her fill and it was apparent she was ready to retire, Rose suggested that Portia go up and turn down the bed in the Cottage Room. It was the smallest but the best lit during the day and coziest. Portia cleared the table and Emmanuel stoked the fire. Rose took Matilda Jane's hand and pressed it into her elbow and together they walked up.

"Your home is so…so large…and handsome Mrs. Lovell."

"Ah, you remember my name."

"Yes," she said softly. "Captain Wyatt told me and"…" she hesitated, "I have a good memory."

"Do you like to read then?"

"Oh yes, I do. Most sincerely."

"My husband has an extensive library." She saw the girl's eyes widen and then shutter the joy.

"I won't be here long. Captain Wyatt says I must go away."

Rose wanted to cry, which these days, with her husband recently gone, she did quite easily.

"Come." She forced the tears back. She had to be strong for Matilda Jane. "We will worry about tomorrow….tomorrow."

Rose took her past her room and showed her where she bedded down in the event she needed anything, then took her to her own room.

"Oh, it's beautiful." The girl's eyes grew large.

"It is yours." Rose said goodnight and left her to Portia who had come up the back stairs and lit the room with a candle sitting on the night table.

Rose walked slowly, yawning, thinking of herself at this age when she first received word she had a choice to make. Go to Ireland with her parents or stay in America and marry Captain Lovell. Somehow she knew she'd made the right decision at that time. Now, however, things had changed and even more so with this new development.

Captain Wyatt had a child on the way and she could help or refuse. If he would not do his duty perhaps Matilda Jane and her child could travel with her to Ireland. Thoughts flew awry at this hour and she stumbled into bed with unanswered questions and welcomed the safety of sleep.

Portia took the child in hand and helped her out of her clothes and into one of Rose's soft flannel gowns and tucked her in. Before Matilda Jane could say thank you, the girl's eyes closed. Portia chuckled as she patted her head. "Now we's have another little girl in dis house to care for. And Miz Rose done growed up just like 'at. Lord jus keep us all safe." She smiled, licked her fingers and pinched out the flame. Soon enough it would be light.

Chapter 31

Something woke Rose out of her reverie. She had been dreaming of sheep like white dots on green hills. Ireland. Her father's stories. There were so many sheep bleating that she could hardly think straight. When she woke it was Lily talking to her, repeating her name.

"Miz Rose. Miz Rose. It be past ten o'the morn. Granmama says to come and get you. Dat girl Matilda Jane, she be up and working already."

"What? She's working?" Rose raised herself on her elbows. She'd had so few hours of sleep, she could hardly manage to push the fuzz out of her brain.

"Yes'm. She be sweeping ever-thing she can. She done did the verandah, the dining room and now she sweepin' the walks out back in de garden."

"Lily, is she all right?"

"She fine, Miz Rose. Jus fine. She like to work is all I gotta say."

Rose laughed out loud. "Lily, please tell your Grandmama that I will dress myself and be down in a little while."

Lily ran out, through the hall and down those stairs jumping off the last step like she always did before Rose could haul her gown up over her head. Some activity in this house was just what she needed. Captain Lovell would be proud to see it. Her heart felt lighter than it had in days.

She chose a work-a-day dress, not wanting Matilda Jane to feel like a cast-off, wondering all the time while she worked her buttons, if the girl had any other clothes. She would speak to Captain Wyatt about that, too.

With so many things to think about it would be good to make notes. She sat for a moment at the small desk and made a list. Captain Wyatt may be captain of his own ship, but he was far from reliable when it came to relationships, she concluded. That was where she might offer him a bit of assistance. She held the end of the charcoal pencil to her lips. Satisfied, she held the note down with a small cologne bottle and dashed from the room.

Once at the head of the stairs, she lifted her dress and clambered down the stairs wondering what the ruckus below was about. Portia was armed with a broom and Lily was hiding behind her Granmama's skirts.

"Oh it's just a garter snake." Matilda Jane came around the corner with a writhing green serpent hanging off the end of a large branch. I'll just take it back outdoors and let it go."

"No you ain't, Miss Matilda Jane." Portia's eyes were large. "You go on and take that thing down to the river. I ain't havin' no snake in dis house, me walking around and stepping on it." She shivered. "Go on now. Ain't funny, you hauling that thing 'round in this house."

"Okay." The young girl said. "I'll walk it on down and be back in a couple of minutes. But really, they don't hurt you none."

"Lily, chile, let go of my skirts. Thing is gone, now. You see Miss Matilda Jane done took it off..." Portia lifted her skirts and watching the floor as she walked, made her way slowly to the outdoor kitchen, her eyes looking around every which a'way.

Rose pressed her fingers over her mouth. She didn't like those creatures either, but Portia's big eyes caused her a guffaw that she could not contain. She turned and found Mr. Wyatt staring at her. Somehow he had managed to get inside without her seeing, probably wondering what all the shouting was about.

If a man could look any worse, she couldn't think how. His bruises were blue and black and green and yellow. He'd gotten himself into some sort of fray. When he lifted his hand, she saw him quickly cover a wince, as he removed his hat.

"Mr. Wyatt....as you see we have had a rather disconcerting situation."

"A garter snake."

"Yes, but it was in the house."

"They are harmless, Mrs. Lovell."

His words sounded very much like she was a foolish child.

"Maybe to you sir. But to my household, it was a frightening occurrence." *Especially when you have a more serious situation yourself,* she wanted to say.

He had managed with one sentence to dull the laughter that still lingered in her throat. Every time she remembered Portia's face, Lily hanging onto her skirts, she felt a chuckle rumble in her throat.

"I will return in a moment. If you would like to wait in my husband's office, please do so.

Rose picked up her skirts, but not too high and walked up the stairs like the lady she was. Once in her room, she let out a little laugh and snatched the paper from beneath the bottle. At least Captain Wyatt had come on his own this morning. For that she gave him a notch of approval. But he would certainly have to earn future notches.

She straightened her back and slowly made her way down to the office. He was sitting there looking out the tall window, his right elbow on the chair, chin in hand. She must not be too judgmental...she had just read a few days ago that God and only God could judge another soul. She slipped in and took her husband's chair, scooted it closer to the fire from behind the desk...she did not want Providence to have to chastise her.

He ignored her presence for a few minutes so she waited, hands in her lap, forcing herself to let the room be quiet for as long as needed. This could not be easy for him, she reminded herself.

Suddenly he cleared his throat and stood. There was very little space to pace; she wondered what he would do. This was not a man who stood still for long.

He walked three steps, turned, walked two back, hands clasped behind him.

"Mrs. Lovell. There is a situation of which I cannot give you details. You will be forced to trust me."

Rose didn't know what to say. So this was it. He wanted her to cover for his sins? She was to trust him? Thoughts scattered. Then reason returned. Her husband was a good man and he trusted this man enough to leave him a ship and to oversee his young widow. She adjusted her thinking and concluded that this was God's job, not hers.

"Sir." she stayed seated, preferring not to stand face to face, and besides, he didn't stay still long enough … "My husband saw fit to leave you his ship and put me in your care. I will trust you."

Amazed at her own words, she felt a certain calmness come over her.

When she looked up, he had stopped and with his dark gaze looked her full in the eye.

"Thank you Mrs. Lovell. I shall do you no harm."

"Thank you Captain Wyatt. Now may I have a few words with you?" She pulled out the list from a pocket in her dress.

"You may." He sat, elbows parked on his knees, she knew to keep himself still.

"Miss Matilda Jane. What is her last name?"

"Ginter. Matilda Jane Ginter."

With a pause she wrote out the name on her paper. "And sir what provisions have you made for clothing. Has she any belongings from the orphanage?" she tried to keep the frustration out of her voice.

"I have spoken to the proprietor and will bring her belongings to you as soon as I collect them." He answered curtly.

Then, when should she expect to see you again?" Rose had not intended to ask that question.

He stared at her before answering. "I'll check in when I return from London."

"And that shall be perhaps six months from now?"

Again he stared, "Yes. As you well know."

The conversation was dead-ending, so she slipped the paper back into her pocket and stood.

With quick movements he reached into his coat pocket and pulled out an envelope. "This should take care of her needs until I return."

She took the offered envelope and laid it on the desk, folded her hands at her waist. "Is that it then?"

"That is it."

Rose found herself listening once again to the heavy booted steps as the long strides gave him his freedom. From this house. From her. From Miss Matilda Jane Ginter. Just when she thought she may abide Captain Wyatt, she found her liking of him returned to her original intuitions. He was a rogue and a rascal.

Chapter 32

Intuitions aside, Rose shook her head and went looking for lunch. She had missed breakfast. Portia having understood the nighttime interruption, let her sleep right through it. She found a plate in the warming oven and took her meal at the dining table. Not a single soul bothered her as she ate. Matilda Jane was gone to drop off the snake to the river, and Portia and Lily no doubt were in the garden looking for little green babies. Thomas and Emmanuel had gone to the stables chuckling.

Stomach full and the little episode having made her laugh out loud for the first time in months, she set her dishes aside, grabbed a shawl from the closet underneath the stairs and took a seat on the porch swing out front. Christmas passed days ago and so had the new year. It was already the fifth day of January 1886. Where had the days gone? There had been so much to do with her husband's passing and the services and the social rituals, she'd hardly had time to think.

There would be days ahead, especially when Captain Wyatt was now planning a special trip abroad that she would have to take care of business with none other than Mr. Dalton. She would need divine assistance for that. Quick, she ran inside and up to her room.

Her mother's Bible was full of underlining and also the scrupulously kept family tree of both her parents. She gazed at the writing and smiled. She had in her hand the ability to change her life. *Lord what would you have me do?*

Pulling her shawl closer she closed her eyes, and let her mind wander. Already the new year had arrived and she had hardly noticed. So much had happened after the Civil War. Slaves were freed. Some stayed behind and continued to work as domestic servant and laborers. Others had traveled to faraway places seeking new lives. The hurricane that her husband and Captain Wyatt had survived as they came across the rough waters. Her parents leaving and then both dying so quickly afterward. The passing of her husband and so soon after, the care of another young girl and a babe.

All the crutches she leaned on had been kicked from underneath her. At least in one sense. The people she loved most were gone. But she had been left with a beautiful house on the Battery, some of Charleston's most sought after real estate. And a ship with her name upon it and the income it brought in. She had no real idea of what her husband's property and possessions were worth. At the reading of the will she assumed the figure had been read aloud, but she had not heard. Her brain could not contain all that had happened in so short a time.

All in all, she surmised, things would work out. They always did. Just like her mother said.

Since it was Tuesday, still early in the week, Rose made a mental list of all that needed to be done. She was going to make certain she got in touch with Mrs. Jamison again, to see about the little house her husband willed to her. How she could help perhaps in setting it up. Maybe they would use the house as a place of business so they could support themselves while living there. She had the address written down somewhere. And she must go back to St. Michael's Church. She missed the pastor's sermons.

Then there was the idea of whether or not Miss Ginter should be seen in public. It would only cause a stir and questions would have to be answered. Perhaps that was reason enough to find out when the child was due and to make sure Matilda Jane would spend as many days out of doors before she had to settle in.

Then what would she tell her society friends? She tapped her finger on her chin in thought and soon enough it was apparently clear. She had hired the woman as a live-in companion from the orphanage. Ava and Stella would understand and she didn't much care who else did, come to think of it. Rose did not want to damage her husband's good standing within Charleston's society, she mused, serious in her quest to make her husband proud. But more so the Lord, she concluded.

Twice she thought of other jobs for Matilda Jane. She only knew she liked to work. Rose would need to find out her skills and see what she could do. And there would be a stipend for her services, making her a legitimate employee. Happy with that decision, she wondered what would become of Nettie at Jamison's. Rose had decided there would be no more fancy changes in her home. It was already beautiful and her monies could be used elsewhere.

Before she knew it, the sun had gone behind a cloud and she was shivering. Gathering her thoughts, she went inside and smelled something good. Chicken. Her brain instantly dashed to the thought Captain Lovell would enjoy....and then she remembered. He didn't need food anymore. Sadness settled into her heart. What was food and riches and sunshine when there was no body to receive it or enjoy it? She knew she'd only begun to understand the brevity of life. She made her way to the cookstove near the garden and smiled. Portia, Lily, and Matilda Jane were conversing about food and spices.

Rose heard enough to know Portia was informing Matilda Jane about lemon grass and what meats to pair it with, the lavender, how it made the best packets for sweet-smelling clothes. Lily finding it too difficult to stand still began to gather flowers for the table. Everything still bloomed, but many plants had gone to sleep during the cooler months. And so there were fewer choices.

Lily nearly ran into Rose as she dashed by the lemon bush. "Miz Rose. I nearly done lost my lunch. You scared me silly." Her hand rested on her stomach.

Rose laughed lightly. "I'm sorry Lily."

Chapter 33

An entire week passed with hardly a notice, until Rose received a missive from Captain Wyatt dated January 10, 1887.

It read:

> *Coming by to hand off Miss Ginter's personal possessions. I have only recently received permission to attain them from the orphanage. And to inform you that Captain Quinn and I are setting off tomorrow. We should arrive in London the first week of March if winds are at our back. Farmer's Almanac says we are in for a mild winter and experts say we can expect a safe crossing. Should you have any concerns with the bank they should be taken care of on the morrow. I will leave the key to the strong box.*
>
> *Captain Wyatt*

His printed message was of a good hand, except for his signature which was unreadable. She stuffed the missive in her pocket and sat down at her desk to write her own. Everyone had been busy with storing winter vegetables. Matilda Jane had already become part of the family. Her principles of hard work made Portia's work lighter and the girl was never still. Just like Captain Wyatt. Their child would be like those locomotives that ran down the track at full speed.

The next morning as they were taking breakfast in the dining room, she heard a loud knock.

"Captain Wyatt." She said immediately and stuffed the last bite in her mouth.

"Dat man knock the loudest of anyone I knows." Portia grumped as she picked up dishes. "He shore do. At least he comin' in da daylight."

"Would you answer Emmanuel?" I want to run above stairs and get my paper. Rose took the servant's stairs so she would not have to dash up with Mr. Wyatt standing below, snatched the list, smoothed her skirts and came down the front stairs into the foyer, with ladylike precision.

His hat was on the newel post, but he was not there. Thankful, she pressed her curls into place and making sure she was heard with the click of her shoes, made her way to the office.

"Sir." She greeted him. "It is a sunny day despite the cold." She said happily as she entered.

He looked up from whatever state of mind he was in and bowed slightly. She appreciated his manners, although his life choices were less desirable. She admonished herself immediately. *His life was no concern of hers.*

She scrambled to find the right words. "Shall we sit?" she offered and waited for him to speak since he was the one who had written, surely he must have an issue to discuss. After a lengthy wait, him pacing again, she stood. "Is there something you wish to speak of Mr. Wyatt?"

ꟹ

What he wanted to say he couldn't speak of. This young woman would not understand that he had privacy issues; if anyone found out, there would be trouble in Charleston society. Which he certainly despised, but it would hurt people he loved.

Instead he chose to exit the too small office. "I have Miss Ginter's things on the verandah. I'll get them."

Ramming his fingers through his hair, he felt at a loss, as always, trying to keep the balance between society's rules and plain common sense. For him the line had always been blurred. And this young woman, so much like the girl he once loved, had curtailed his ability to speak when he was around her.

He brought the small trunk indoors and placed it next to the steps. "Would you like me to carry it up for you?" he spoke from the doorway.

"Please, if you would be so kind." Rose came away from the window that she now stood staring out. "I'll show you the way." She watched him muscle the small trunk onto his shoulders and hurried to lead the way. When you get to the top go right, all the way to the end of the hall, the last door on the left." She stood aside unwilling to walk him down. She waited at the top of the stairs.

When he returned, she noted the bruises were barely visible and the scratches had healed altogether. But she wondered about his heart. He was stiff and she sensed anger lived just beneath the surface. She could feel its presence.

"Do you have any concerns while I'm gone?" He asked pointedly as he followed her down, noting her curly red-blond hair turned darker during the winter months.

"Oh I almost forgot …" he paused at the bottom of the stairs. "I have this for you. Your monthly allowance. Remember?"

Rose nodded slightly which was an absolute lie because she did not remember the reading of the will as she should have. "Thank you."

"Your key to the strong box." He fished in a side pocket and handed her the key. "It's the only one."

"I will take care of it." She said and pocketed it immediately.

"And the fees for Miss Ginter for the months I am away." He pulled yet another envelope from his pockets.

She smiled.

He frowned.

"I was just wondering if you had a rabbit hiding in your pocket."

Rose saw the slightest hint of a smile and then it was gone.

"If all is well, then I shall be about my business. We leave at first light tomorrow morning."

"You don't want to say goodbye to Miss Ginter?"

"Uh...of course." He tangled his hands in his hat that he has just snatched off the newel post.

Rose didn't say a word, but was shocked that he didn't want to tell his beloved goodbye. *What was wrong with the man*? She scurried away, sad for Matilda Jane. What kind of man would leave his woman with child and without even a proper goodbye. Mr. Wyatt came down another notch in her estimation.

She brought Matilda Jane and immediately excused herself. "I'll be out back in my garden." She said quickly.

Barely five minutes had passed. Rose just put on her garden gloves and was about to dig out a weed when she noticed shadows above her. Two of them.

"Why Mr. Wyatt." She stood embarrassed to the roots of her hair. "I thought . . ."

She clamped her lips shut when she noted his discomfort.

"Well then..." she heard her voice go out into the air and for the first time no sensible thought came into her mind.

"I'll be off. Miss Ginter here will be fine. I will see both of you when I return. Remember what I told you?" He gave Miss Ginter a nod as they exchanged private glances.

"Yes." She said quietly coloring to the tip of her nose.

His boots clomped across the square cobblestones that formed the sidewalk she had created with her own hands.

"Well, I'll be." She said, gloved hands on her hips.

Matilda Jane dashed off, asking if she might muck out the stables with Thomas and Emmanuel, explaining that she had once lived on a farm and loved the work.

Rose went back to work, too many thoughts buzzing like flies in her head.

Chapter 34

The next morning the foghorns sounded before daylight signaling the two ships were sailing out to sea. Rose prayed for each captain, that they would guide the ships over safely. It was rare to make a crossing this time of the year. She knew for a fact. Charleston weather was agreeable until one went northward and found the temperatures were extremely low and the waters much more dangerous.

Actually, she was quite excited about adding a tiny infant to the household. It wouldn't seem so lonely. It gave her something to think about and she decided today she would take up thread and needle after sketching a little hat and gowns to sew. Her knitting needles would be busy too, especially in the cooler weather.

Rose wondered if she might suggest to Matilda Jane that she be more careful, now that she was getting on. Rose had stopped the girl in the midst of her busyness a few days ago and suggested perhaps she should not work so hard, and with the girl's eyes staring at the floor and red-faced found out the child was expected sometime in late June. "Captain Wyatt told me to tell you that I was not to be seen in public. And the only person you should speak to is Mrs. Shevington. She...she knows everything."

The girl was so distraught, Rose dropped any more questions and showed her the little booties she had knitted. Matilda Jane smiled politely but dashed away as though she didn't want to think about such things. Rose felt certain there was more than the girl was telling her, but decided now was not the time.

Rose's duty to Captain Wyatt was to house her, feed her and see she was well cared for. She poked her finger and drew a drop of blood, sucked it and went back to the tiny stitches she was making in the little muslin gown.

Hadn't Captain Wyatt a brain in his head? She wondered aloud. He left a young girl in dire straights with hardly a care. But, to his one credit, he had left money for her.

Sitting allowed her too much time to think and soon she was feeling the weight of the world on her shoulders. She hoped Mr. Dalton did not come calling with any problems. That was one thing she missed now that Captain Wyatt was gone. He'd never mentioned it, but she knew the captain disliked Mr. Dalton, too. She could hear it in his voice every time he spoke the man's name. That was *one* thing they agreed on.

Nevertheless, after two hours, she set aside another pair of booties, thinking about the little feet that would wear them. And suddenly she felt old. There was yet time for her to remarry and have children, but that idea seemed far-fetched right now. What she needed was a good brisk walk. And she had the best view of the river point, *why not enjoy the sun*? she spoke outloud.

She stood, stretched and found her warmest shawl. No hat today. She wanted the sun shining directly on her head. Puff with the worrisome expectations and the absurd fear of a hatless woman seen walking about. Portia was informed that she would be about a walk and did not expect to be at lunch. The sunny day was welcome after so many dark, rainy ones. Her hand on the large clear glass doorknob, she paused, grabbed a hat and hung the tied ribbons over her wrist. In the end she was still a bit concerned to go out hatless. She sighed.

Rose let herself out and stood at the top of the wide stairs, the finest ones in the neighborhood, Portia said, and looked out over White Point Gardens noting lots of walkers today. Everyone had been inside too long; she set out to take her turn about the park. A fence lined the sidewalk on one side, keeping people safe from falling down the slight decline into the river. She walked along beside the fence and kept her eyes out on the water. The sunsparkled view was so bright it hurt her eyes. She put a gloved hand up to shade her face when she heard someone behind her.

"Ladies wear their hats in public instead of carrying them."

She knew that voice and a shiver ran down her spine. There was nothing to do but acknowledge him.

"Mr. Dalton. Good day to you." She did not offer her hand.

"See, your eyes are watering, Mrs. Lovell. You should protect them and put on your hat."

She smiled slightly, but made no move to obey him. He spoke as though she were a child and he had just chastised her for her unbecoming behavior.

"Have a good day sir."

He bowed at the neck and she clamped her lips together and forced a tight smile. She continued her walk trying not to hurry away. That man was going to be her death. On to other thoughts, she told herself.

A full half hour later she realized no one else had stopped or spoken. She loved the view and wondered if she would miss it should she choose to live in Ireland, so made a point of memorizing it. A sketch and water color frame would keep the memory alive. Suddenly a thought flew her head. When had she decided she was going back to Ireland?

Fear crept up into her throat -- a hand went to rest over her quickened heartbeat -- to slow it down. Realization that she had no friends here in Charleston hit her hard. There was no reason to stay. Her husband's life had been here, not hers. But, she knew it was yet too soon to decide. Setting her thoughts away, she stopped to put on her hat to shade her eyes from the sun. It was straight up and actually warm for this time of year.

Not ten steps later, she heard another familiar voice and turned. Ava McGuire. Rose carried herself with genteel movements. Mr. McGuire was in attendance and he had a dark look on his face. Ava's voice was strained too.

"Good day." Rose kept her voice low, her hands at her waist. "It's quite a beautiful day is it not?"

Ava smiled with her lips but Rose saw there was sadness in those handsome eyes. She noted Captain Wyatt and his sister were alike in their mannerisms. One knew their state of mind very quickly when in their presence. Both seemed to have a seriousness that constrained them.

"You are out so soon." Ava said quietly.

Rose didn't know how to answer. It had been several weeks since her husband's death. But she had been used to living alone most of the time. Her life hadn't really changed that much. Still, there were unspoken rules about how long one should be out of sight when one lost a family member.

"It's good for body, mind and soul to be out in the sunlight."

"Yes." Ava agreed weakly while Mr. McGuire stared off into the distance.

"Well, it is time to return. I will be on my way. Stop for tea Ava?" she made sure her voice was low. She had no idea if her husband knew of their visits.

Ava nodded but did not say she would come.

"Good day to you both, then." She said and quickly made herself scarce, saying a quick prayer for the two of them. Something was amiss.

With a faster pace she headed home, hoping to keep the visuals planted firmly in her head so she could sketch what she'd seen earlier. Since her husband's passing she felt more expressive in the arts of late and wondered why the two would mesh.

Before she knew it, she was walking up her own steps. It had been good to receive fresh air into her lungs and a long, slow walk along the rivers. It was almost February now so more days would be sunny.

Straightaway she went to her husband's office, tossed off her hat and shawl and began to draw. Lightly at first to give form to the view she held in her head. Then filling in heavier lines. There was nothing to do but finish it….she ran above stairs for her paint apron and tied the sash around her waist and prepared her paints and water. Brushes were refreshed with a dry cloth and she set the flat easel up near the window to get full light and finished her work.

Satisfied, she stood back, head cocked to one side and viewed it with a critical eye. It needed a bit more yellow…so she dashed a slice right through the blue clouds and tossed the brush down. Done. She must not add another thing. It looked right. She left it where it was in full sunlight so it could dry.

Happier than she'd been in days, she wandered to the back kitchen and found Portia cooking dinner. Her hands were busy stirring three pots.

"Chile it be time you got yoself home. You know them ladies gonna be thinking you out and about so soon after yo husband done passed."

"Oh, 'tis true Portia. For I heard it already…" she mused.

"You been out der all dis time?" Portia's hands rested on her hips.

"No." Rose heard a giggle escape. "I've been inside. Painting."

"You have? Now…then … you be doing your paintin' again? I ain't seen you do that since you got here, a little chile-woman."

"I know." Rose smiled and gazed at a nearby ivy climbing the red chipped brick wall "You know that is a beautiful scene right there."

"Dem old ivy leaves climbin' up on dat nasty wall?" Portia shook her head. "Girl, I think you done gone daft." She laughed heartily.

"You know, it's the views that are right in front of us that are special. Not everyone sees what we see. Up in Baltimore winters are dark and gray and brown. Everything is brown. Dirty snow lines the streets making spring such a welcome sight."

"Chile you musin' now. Ain't that what you call it?"

Portia's huge smile warmed her heart so much, she planted a kiss on her cheek.

"Well, now ain't that sumpin'?" Portia exclaimed and laughed out loud. "You be like my very own baby."

Tears popped into their eyes and Rose walked into those soft, caressing arms and rested there for a while. "What would I do without you Portia?"

"Girl-chile, you know you done just fine before...and you do just fine again. You got God and dat's all that matters."

"You are right. But it takes *you* to remind me."

"Chile you knows I ain't gonna let anything happen to ya. Go on now..." She pushed her away and swiped at tears. "I ain't gonna get nothin' done, you making me cry like a baby..." She swiped again.

Rose smiled and satisfied, moseyed back into the house and knew one thing. She was loved.

Chapter 35

Two weeks later Rose's stack of infant clothes grew taller. And several water color canvases lay across her husband's desk. She let inspiration take over. Each painting was better than the last. Portia accepted one painting of her choice but only after much fussing. And Matilda Jane was growing larger but seemed to ignore that fact.

Still Ava had not called on her, nor Stella, for that matter. How she missed those two! Had she made some faux pas? It was very unlike her friends to care one whit about such things.

Today, midweek, Rose decided to get out of the house and enjoy the day. It was not exactly the best of weather. It was overcast but she didn't care. She also knew her Bible said, if you want a friend, you have to be a friend. She'd read that just this morning. And she definitely missed her friends.

While she was at it, she decided quickly, she would stop by and see Mrs. Shevington at the Whitegate Orphanage. Determined to learn about the other orphanage, she could inquire at Ava's or Stella's, if either happened to be home. She knew very well that she should send Thomas out with her calling cards at least a day early, but threw that idea out. She was going, cards or no.

They would either accept her visit or they would know she was thinking of them. Rose ran to the office and prepared two small paper cards to leave with the servants in the event they were not at home. With a quick sketch on the front of each, she carefully folded them square and grabbed two envelopes to wrap them in. A charcoal pencil tucked in her reticule would do.

Emmanuel had already been informed of her plans earlier in the day. Glad to have any of the animals out and exercised, he pulled the one-horse buggy up out front and waited. Rose could see his smile as he pulled on the reins keeping the horse in place. She'd best hurry. And glad she was there would be a tarp apron over their heads for as soon as she walked out the door, she heard the first plip-plops of rain.

Emmanuel dare not leave the horse by itself, so she hooked her foot up on the high step and pulled herself up.

"You settled?" Emmanuel held the reins tight. "We gonna be bustin' out of here when I let loose of these reins." He laughed. "Hold on tight now."

Rose grabbed the railing with her right hand, her hat with the left and prepared herself.

Indeed Ready took off like a shot. Both her and Emmanuel let out a laugh. "You named this horse perfectly." Rose laughed.

"He'll slow once he's run a bit." Her man said quietly. "I'll let him have the lead for a few blocks and then pull 'im in onc't we get near Miss Stella's place. Wouldn't look good, us running down folks."

"Oh my no." Rose laughed again. "Not good. Why Emmanuel we'd have to stay low for a long time to stop all the talk."

He chuckled.

By the time they arrived at Stella's, Emmanuel had Ready under control.

"The door is shut tight against the rain, but I think there are lights lit inside." Rose hoped as she peered under the wide brim of her hat.

"I'll wave from the door if she's in. Then come back in an hour. Take Ready out for a run once you get out of town." She smiled. "He'll like that. Maybe it'll get some of that orneryness out of him."

"Yes ma'am." Emmanuel said with a laugh. "I be thinkin' you got a bit o'that orneryness yo'self today." He slid her a sideglance.

"I believe I do." She said and with great care, managed to get off the conveyance without falling into the street.

Because it wasn't proper, she did not look back, but heard Emmanuel trying to keep Ready calm until they could get out of town. That horse knew he was going to run free. Rose was sure of it.

Her heart beat excitedly in her chest as she lifted the knocker and hit it twice. She saw movement behind the colors of the oval cut glass as she stood on the verandah. Rose turned and waved to Emmanuel and stepped inside, glad to be out of what was now a pouring rain.

"Oh Rose, I am so glad you see you. I have meant to call on you but Foster and I have been moving furniture from Savannah. It has taken months to clear out father's house." She gushed and grabbed Rose's elbow. "Everyone is upstairs rearranging every room." "Oh I am sorry, you haven't even removed your hat… and here I am dragging you off for tea." She apologized. "It seems to me whenever you are around I end up breaking some rule of etiquette."

The two of them broke out into laughter.

"See, I knew there was a reason why I have come. To ruin you entirely." Rose laughed.

"I am so sorry about your husband and so ashamed I have not come to see *you*."

"I received your very kind note, Stella. And was thankful for it. I talked to Mr. Perry and he told me of your dilemma. And you are only just back."

"Oh, I am so glad you are not like the others. It is refreshing to . . . as they say, let your hair down. Come tell me everything." Stella pulled her arm.

For the entire hour words, expressions, emotions, and stories were swapped. Two cups of tea and two miniature oatmeal cakes later, Rose heard the sound of her buggy.

"Oh, I am so glad we had a visit Stella. Now I know so much more as do you. We will pick up our lives, even with all these changes and continue with what the Lord has for us to do, won't we?" Tears popped into her eyes. "It has been so good to visit. You've brought out in me the wisdom of talking with a good friend, what one's heart is truly feeling."

"Oh now." Stella wiped at the tears forming in her eyes. "We've both lost someone who cared for us and that it not easy."

"Indeed." Rose's voice failed her. She had been so strong for all these weeks and suddenly she wondered if she should continue her journey or head home and have a good cry.

With her next sentence Stella gave her courage. "Now you go on out of here, make your visit to Mrs. McGuire and the Whitegate Orphanage. You'll find Mrs. Shevington a fair and honest woman. At our next meeting, we shall sit down together, for I have many furniture pieces from my father's house. We will divvy up and carry to Jamison's once I sort through."

"I should like that very much." Rose said.

With that she exited the house with a smile and a wave.

"To Mrs. Shevington at Whitegate Orphanage." She announced. "It's good the rain has stopped and a bit of sun has pierced the dark clouds."

"Hmm…mmmm." Her driver nodded.

The short trip brought them to a large home, seven pillars lined up across the front verandah. The entire house was white with black shutters at each long narrow window. It boasted four white wicker rockers and matching glass-topped tables down the entire length. Ivy decorated the roof above it and hung down in lush thickness enclosing both ends of the porch.

There was a small sign in the yard. Black letters on white said simply, *Whitegate*. It hung from an arm and post and moved back and forth as the winds picked up. Rose tied the organza ribbon of her hat tighter under her chin and let herself down. "Have a good long lunch Emmanuel. I hope to be ready in a couple of hours. Mrs. Shevington has promised me a tour."

"Ma'am," He lifted his hat and held Ready still.

Heart beating fast, Rose felt a nervous excitement come upon her as she stood looking at the home for a moment and decided it was indeed very beautiful. No doubt a wealthy Charlestonian had donated it. It was no wonder the St. Michael ladies were busy trying to support it. Low hanging trees blew nearby and at least a dozen white ceramic pots of red geraniums made the entire scene look like a picture post-card. She embedded the scene firmly in her mind and decided this would be her next sketch.

After a light tap on the door, she was met by a slender maid, with a black dress, and a clean, crisp apron. "We've been expecting you this week, Mrs. Lovell." She said politely.

Rose smiled and wondered how the young woman could possibly know her name.

"Please come this way."

She followed taking in the size of the rooms. The fireplace in the parlor was gigantic. She warmed her hands at it and took the seat closest. She didn't want to catch a chill.

With hardly a chance to look around for long, Rose stood as she was greeted by a tall, slender, well-dressed woman with pure white hair and the bluest eyes she'd ever seen.

"So this is Mrs. Lovell." She actually held out her hand. Rose stood, took it, glad to know the woman was human. For by her appearance Rose would have guessed her to be at the top rung of society echelon. She was dressed perfectly in a long blue dress, with a wide band of black at her waist. The dress was simple elegance. But the woman wore it so well. And stood straight as a stick, her hair pulled back in a perfect French chignon.

Rose straightened her back immediately.

"I'm Mrs. Shevington. Come, would you like tea?"

"Yes, thank you." Rose said, not meaning a word of it. She'd just had two cups and would need to use the privy if she drank much more.

The woman pulled a beribboned bell nearby and instantly the young girl appeared again. She went to the door and spoke softly with her.

Rose liked her immediately. Even though Mrs. Shevington was elegant and formal she spoke to her servants with respect. She expected to like this woman very much. Another sword pierced her heart. And she had been ready to judge her. She kept that thought for another day.

Within minutes and after sharing her condolences for Captain Lovell's passing, the two were talking animatedly about their work. When they paused for a moment, Rose asked her how the servant knew her name.

"Well, you are certainly not a Charlestonian. I should have thought the gossip would have reached you by now." Mrs. Shevington smiled, her blue eyes crinkling at the edges. "Which is not to say much, because back in the day when Mr. Camden John Lovell was a young man, newly established here with the Emerald Rose, I, in my young days had hoped to marry him."

Rose smiled at the woman's perky look. "I fell in love the instant I met him. He, on the other hand, was a bit slower. He broke my heart and never knew it."

"I am truly sorry. Lost love is never forgotten." Rose said and wondered how in the world she could possibly know that. She had never been loved by a man.

Shaking her thoughts free, she continued, "And did you marry?"

"Yes, I did. I married society and money." My parents were very happy. For myself, I was very lonely. Until I turned our home into an orphanage after my husband passed."

"This is your home?"

"Indeed it is. And for the last twelve years I have never been happier. Mr. Shevington never wanted children. And now I have many of them. These have been the best years of my life."

Rose's teacup rattled as she took a sip ...wondering what an appropriate response would be. She felt sad for her. She would have made Captain Lovell a fine wife. She wondered what Mrs. Shevington thought of that at the time, but dare not bring it up. Felt sad, too that Captain Lovell had given his life and his worldly goods to her as an act of kindness instead of to a woman he loved.

"Come. We shall not visit old times today." She stood. "Let's take the tour I promised you, then we will talk about Matilda Jane."

The teacup was set aside and her heart thumped with joy. She would see what this lovely woman had done with her life. First stop was the kitchen. Several young girls scurried around, smiles on their face, voices low as they worked.

"Every young woman here is an orphan."

"Indeed?" Rose had thought them servants.

"Yes, each one has come and agreed to be trained in some form of service. Our girls are highly recommended when they finish their courses here."

"What other subjects do you offer, Mrs. Shevington?"

"First, since we are to be friends, Mrs. Lovell, I would like you to address me as Emmie. My Irish father named me Emerald . . . the green of Ireland you know."

"Emerald. What a beautiful name." Rose's mind went straight to her husband's ship. "Did Captain Lovell name the Emerald Star after you?" She inquired, her eyes wide.

Mrs. Shevington smiled. "You dear are a quick one. Yes, in fact he did."

Rose smiled. "It is good to know he loved you."

Emmie's eyes lit up. "And you are not offended."

"No indeed. Mr. Lovell only married me to repay an old debt to my father."

"Oh indeed. And what was that?"

"As a young lad Mr. Lovell had stowed away on a ship and when found out was in danger of being tossed overboard as a stowaway!"

"Huh..." Mrs. Shevington paused. "He never once mentioned that."

"When my father paid his way across, he vowed he would pay back the favor. And he did."

Rose felt her face color slightly. It was a bit embarrassing to tell someone that you weren't loved.

"Then you are a very blessed woman. He was a kind man, an honorable man. That is why my young heart was broken when he refused me, even though I knew he loved me."

"He refused you?" Rose could not believe it.

"Yes. I asked my father to 'attain' him for me when months had gone on without an offer. I'm sorry to say it, now. I wish I would have waited. I believe as a young man he did not feel quite up to par in Charleston society. His first house was very small and I think he felt unworthy. My father would have made it appear that way, I'm sure."

"Oh no...." Rose felt her pain. "And so your father went to him?" "Yes, he did and after that Captain Lovell started commandeering the Emerald Star to London himself. I believe he was trying to make his fortune...but alas... it was too late. My father arranged an agreement with Mr. Shevington and I was toted down the aisle."

Rose didn't know what to say. It was horrible. These arrangements...this interfering of human lives.

"Let's not think about what was, shall we? I have come to a wonderful place in my life and glad I am to have these girls in my life now."

"Indeed." Rose whispered as they made their way to another room.

"See, here the ladies are learning to sew. From the very youngest to the eldest. We have twenty four girls here now. Graduated from the low school."

"Low school?"

"Yes there is another orphanage here in town, called Newgate. They get the two of us mixed up."

"Ah, so that's the one St. Michael's ladies support?"

"Yes, and thankfully. If they support that one I can afford to maintain this one."

"Ah, I see."

"There are levels here in Charleston as you well know. Mrs. Jamison also has an orphanage and it is not as well supported."

"I am familiar with Jamisons." Rose said excitedly.

"Indeed? I am happy to hear that. Mr. Lovell chose his wife well." She spouted.

"I'm afraid he didn't choose me." Rose laughed. "But whatever comes, Providence works things out in the end."

"Indeed He does. Now shall we go on?"

"Oh yes." Rose gushed.

There were curved stairs ahead and the sound of a pianoforte filled the stairwell. "You teach music as well?"

"Yes all the fine arts. French, Italian, and German, thanks to local citizens who are willing to be paid a stipend. Music, and drawing. Do you play Mrs. Lovell?"

"No, I was not a good student, I'm afraid. My mother gave me lessons but I preferred sketching and dancing."

"Dancing. Hmmmm..." Mrs. Shevington's fingertip rested on her lips. "What steps to you know?"

"Oh not many, I was a young ballerina. Danced in school plays and such..."

"I'll keep that in mind. We are always looking for teachers. Perhaps you'd be more inclined to show us your sketching skills one day soon."

"I would be happy to help." Rose said.

After a full tour of the house, they returned to the front room with the largest fireplace Rose had ever seen. It covered a large part of the wall and boasted circular marble pillars on each side.

"Well, there you have it Mrs. Lovell. What have you to say?"

"Mrs. Shevington I am properly impressed to say the least. I didn't imagine for a moment that an orphanage, really a school, could be so productive or so well conducted."

"Then I have done my duty. I have impressed you?" She laughed heartily. "I think we shall be friends, Rose."

"Yes I do believe we will be Emmie." Rose returned the honor. "Will you write me the address of Newgate and I shall make a proper visit there, as well."

"Of course." She stood and wrote at the desk, handing her the address. "We shall visit again soon. I will be attending the meeting for Newgate next month. Perhaps you will join us?"

Rose did not want to hurt her friendship but felt she should be completely honest immediately. "My heart is involved with Jamison's Orphanage right now. I'm afraid I'll have to decline. But I would be more than happy to teach sketching and water color, if you find my work suitable for your students."

"Thank you for being so frank, Rose. Newgate is supported by the ladies of Charleston and most do not give thought to Jamison's. I'm glad you are on their board."

"Oh dear, I have given the wrong impression. I am not on their board, a friend and I have only brought items we could not use to them. And hired one of the girls as a seamstress."

"Well, then, you are doing your part. And I always say, it is better to use a person's natural skills and pay them than to do the work yourself, when so many need to feel their work is important."

Rose let her look of gratefulness and her smile convey her feelings.

"There now. You must be going or it will be dark. And visitors are not allowed after the dinner hour. The young women have much to do to prepare for the next day."

"Then I will be going. My driver has been waiting…" Rose stopped talking as the grandfather clock in the room began to chime the hour of 5 p.m. …"for a few minutes now." She finished.

Rose stepped out onto the lovely verandah and took one last look at the house and set her face toward the next stop. She could hardly contain herself. Confidence and joy burst inside the place where her heart was.

"Emmanuel, take me home. I've had enough excitement for the day."

Chapter 36

Several days later and with two framed water color paintings under her arm, Rose was on her way to Newgate. She had no idea what to expect, but she was definitely excited. Mrs. Shevington had spoken of the school and if she brought her girls from Newgate, it must be very well run.

Emmanuel pulled the buggy up and let her dismount. "An hour please, Emmanuel. It is a beautiful sunny day, enjoy yourself." She stepped down carefully while Ready neighed anxious to be about a good run.

With her gloved hand across her brow Rose took a good long look. Newgate had no sign out front and was located in a poorer side of town than Whitegate, of course, which she expected. What she didn't expect was the condition of the premises. She lifted her skirts and watched her step. No one had bothered to clean up horse droppings out front of the wooden steps, which were a bit rickety. The porch paint had peeled leaving gray worn floorboards. A good whitewash would put that in order.

The door knocker was missing and no pots of flowers adorned the place. It looked rather bleak. With a tap at the front, she waited. No one came. She could hear noises within. A piano played. She could hear it through the open window above.

Removing her glove, she knocked her knuckles against the dirty glass, louder this time. It brought a little girl who opened and looked up rather shyly.

"I'm Mrs. Lovell, may I come in?" she inquired.

The girl said nothing, but pulled the door open wider.

"Oh my, Harriet." An older girl bent to eye level and said, "You may go." Smiling as the little girl ran off.

"I'm afraid Harriet is deaf." She usually does not hear the door. She must have seen you and since no one came, she opened to you."

Rose nodded. "May I see the person in charge." She asked the girl who did not give her name.

"Yes, Mr. Doddle is available. Mrs. Doddle is sick today. I'll seat you here near the window."

Rose took the well-worn chair and gazed out the large window that went from the floor upwards at least six feet. The sun shot off any shiny surface creating arcs of light. The bird feeders were occupied; a different bird landing every few seconds, pecking and then flying off, as though there were waiting lines. It was a lovely view.

Thoughts interrupted, she stood when she heard a man address her.

"Ma'am, welcome to Newgate. I am Mr. Henry Doddle…my wife Georgianna and I are the caretakers." He said and nodded formally.

Rose noted immediately his haggard look. From appearances the children had done him in, for his dark hair stuck out in all possible directions. She watched with her fingertips at her lips to hide the smile that tried to make its way forward, as he ran his hand through his hair, which only served to muss it up more.

"I am so very sorry. I should have called before stopping in."

"No apology needed. Guests are welcome anytime. I don't believe I heard your name, ma'am."

"I'm Mrs. Camden Lovell. I should come back another time." She pulled on her gloves and prepared to leave.

"Please. If you wouldn't mind so much we have a problem with one of the girls and no one seems to know what to do. Would it be too forward of me to ask you to intervene?"

Before Rose could answer, he started down a dark hall adding over his shoulder, "My wife is ill and cannot come down…and you are a young woman, I daresay you could certainly do better than I."

"Take me to her." Rose heard the words and could not believe she had spoken them aloud. "I will do what I can."

She followed Mr. Doddle up one flight of stairs and then another. They were finally in the attic. Rose swatted at the dust that flew up her nose as they reached the top and bent their heads against the pitched roof. Rose sneezed twice.

"Cecelia, this is Mrs. Lovell. She would like to talk to you. Remember your manners." He said softly and left the two of them alone.

Since Mr. Doddle had not mentioned what Cecelia's problem was Rose decided to make herself comfortable and found a small stump of wood to sit on which brought her closer to the little, blond-haired urchin who sat upon the floor. The dark brown eyes looked at her with deep suspicion and Rose smiled slightly and looked out the window. She waited for the child to speak. She must have been in the range of 5 or 6, and her face was as dirty as her frock. Her bare feet were tucked in underneath slender legs. Worn shoes lay at odd angles nearby.

Instead of speaking, Rose decided she would sit quietly and picked up a book that lay on an ancient side table. Treasures she would have liked to investigate lay nearby. She looked at each one, studied and guessed at the year and possibly the family who put it all up here. Strangely, she thought about the love notes on blue paper that lay tied up in her own attic. She had almost forgotten them, except for the correspondence they contained. She remembered nearly every word. Were there letters like that up here?

Suddenly a little voice spoke. "I don't like you."

"That's okay. You don't have to." She kept her eyes averted studying a large 6-drawered side board with mirrors. "Would you mind if I looked in those drawers?" she pointed.

"Why?"

"Hmmm…no reason, just wondered if someone left treasures behind."

The small head swayed back and forth, wispy blonde hair feathering her face.

Rose also noted the frown and the crossed arms over the chest. This would require a bit of work.

She stood and immediately cracked her head on the low ceiling. "Oh my."

The little girl was startled but did not move.

Rose opened the drawers and found dusty photos, old towels, ancient flatware. "Wonder who these people are?" She took a picture and gazed at it. Then took up several more and sat down again.

"I know."

"You know who lived here?"

"Yes." The little face contorted for a moment. "My grandmama."

"Your grandmama?"

Rose did not believe a word of it. She herself, had made up imaginary siblings when she was young, but she played along.

"What was her name?"

"Charmaine Billingsly Thompson" from Illinois."

Rose was duly impressed. The child was highly intelligent to make up such a name and so quickly. "Whose mother was she?"

"My mothers." The voice faltered. "She used to live here with my father. And he died, then mama died and then Grandmama died."

Those brown eyes stared into hers.

"I see. And now you are here."

"Yes, but I don't like all the other kids here, too. They don't belong to me."

"They don't?"

"No." the little bare feet kicked at her shoes.

"Well, what can be done about that…" Rose wondered aloud, her finger at her chin.

"I don't know. But I won't go down there."

"You do look like your grandmama." She said for it was true. "You have her handsome eyes."

"I do?"

She seemed surprised, Rose noted. "Yes I believe you do."

"You're the only one who believes me."

"Can you tell me more?"

"Me and mama lived here, until *they* moved in." she pouted. "I was very little mama said, but she told me the story and I believe her." The arms crossed again and her lips quivered.

"Of course you do. And well you should."

The little face seemed to relax.

"Why don't we go down and see what is for lunch. I'm very hungry. Are you?

"No."

"All right then, I'll go down and if you should like to join me, put your shoes on and we'll eat together." Rose stood, put the picture in the little girls hand and started down the stairs.

Her toe touched the bottom stair and she heard clip-clop, clip-clop behind her.

"Well, then, Cecelia, let's go have a bit of milk or tea."

As she came down Mr. Doddle saw her and wisely said nothing to Cecelia.

"It is lunchtime? We are a bit hungry, sir."

"Indeed."

Rose saw him smile as led the way. As they approached she could hear the low chatter of voices. After a short walk and a couple of turns, they entered a very large, very noisy room, filled with tables and benches. It was an old warehouse. *Had Cecelia been telling the truth after all*? She wondered.

"We have assigned seats." He indicated Cecelia's.

"May I join her?"

"Here? Mrs. Lovell wouldn't you much rather . . ." he was suggesting another space with his hands.

"I would like to eat here, if you don't mind sir. Cecelia and I have things to discuss."

There must have been forty or fifty children, who were scurrying to their seats.

She looked at Mr. Doddle.

"They are waiting for everyone to be seated before prayer." A little voice at her elbow said as she took her seat.

"I see." Rose sat down quickly.

Mr. Doddle prayed and immediately older children poured out of several doors, with pots in their hands and began following each other down the line spooning soup into a bowl, followed by the bread girl, followed by the water girl. The three girls went from table to table serving.

Rose watched with wonder noting how well they worked together. Without a word dinner was served and no one ate until the last girl walked out of the room, then the chaos began. Talking, laughing, eating.

She saw Cecelia watching her and picked up her spoon and ate the soup that was more water than vegetables. The little hand picked up her spoon.

In less than ten minutes the children had finished. No wonder for the servings were small and no more were coming from the kitchen, it seemed. Each child picked up their empty bowls and deposited them in one of several large tubs of water after which the girls who served came out and began washing and drying the dishes, stacking them up on a side table as they went.

The entire lunchtime took less than twenty minutes.

"Well, then, Cecelia, I must be going." Rose said as Mr. Doddle joined them.

"Okay." She said, pouting.

"It's been very good to meet you."

"Cecelia?" Mr. Doddle prompted.

"Nice to meet you too." The child said, as Mr. Doddle apologized with his eyes to Rose.

"I shall come again to see you Cecelia."

The dark eyes brightened and Rose knew that she must keep that promise.

"Please come again when my wife is better. She will show you around, Mrs. Lovell."

"Thank you sir, I shall do that."

Rose walked out into the sun and helped herself up into the buggy. "Thanks for waiting Emmanuel…I know I was late."

"Hmmm…..mmmm." He chuckled. "I don't mind at all Miz Rose."

Chapter 37

The last few days had set Rose on a new course. She knew now why Captain Lovell had attracted Yellow Fever and ultimately paid with his life.

She wished they would have had more time together. He could have taught her so much. It had been almost three months. She had worn dark colors the first month or so, but in light of the fact she knew her husband rested with a life well lived and was safe with God, made it her goal to continue what he had started. God had been good to give her Captain Lovell. She saw that now more clearly than ever.

There were so many new friends. Mrs. Shevington. Mr. Doddle and Cecelia. And Matilda Jane, whom she and Mrs. Shevington forgot to discuss, they had been so overwhelmed with meeting each other they'd been unmindful of the reason she had come.

Matilda Jane continued to work at her usual pace. All day. Every day. She was unstoppable. Rose, Portia, even Emmanuel had encouraged her to rest, but the girl was undaunted when it came to work. She loved it. No doubt from Mrs. Shevington's good training. Which reminded her....she sat at her desk and wrote out two calling cards, sending Thomas with the missives and cash to pay the miller for their cornmeal this month.

One went out to Newgate to Mr. and Mrs. Doddle for an appointment two weeks hence. One for Mrs. Shevington. She had been better at sending cards and noted she now had two callers this week. Stella and just this moment one from Mrs. Shevington. Laughing, the two notes between herself and Mrs. Shevington had passed.

Rose stood from the desk in the library. The two new watercolor paintings of Whitegate were of no use to her, she may as well give them to Mrs. Shevington. Her head cocked to the side she lay both up against the books in the bookcase and stepped back for a look. With a critical eye, she chose one and wrapped it in tissue paper.

The thought crossed her mind about painting Newgate Orphanage and she tossed the idea aside; it would only enhance the fact the building was less than desirable. Perhaps she could find a more suitable subject....hmmmm....maybe she could sketch Cecelia in charcoal. She put that in the back of her mind...those brown eyes so like her grandmother's in the picture.

Rose set aside a small canvas for that project and heard Thomas' heavy footsteps approaching the office.

"Miz Rose. I brought the mail. Clerk stopped me and said I should carry these to you."

"Thank you Thomas, I take it that the miller is paid and you brought fish from the wharves for supper tonight."

"Yes'm. I sure did. I'll get 'em to Granmama. The fresher they is, the better she like 'em."

Rose smiled as Thomas hurried away. He would make a good business owner one day.

When she looked down at the letter in her hand, her heart skipped a beat. It was from Captain Wyatt. He never wrote unless there was a problem. Maybe he was asking after Matilda Jane. Her hands trembled a bit as she opened the missive. It seems Captain Wyatt was just sending word ahead he should arrive sometime in mid-June. No doubt to see his child born. *As it should be.*

"The idea." She whispered and opened other packet.

The doorbell sounded behind her and she jumped.

"Ava." Tossing the letters on the table she ran for the door excited to see her friend. They had much to talk about.

"Come in my friend." She said, but quickly saw there was trouble.

"What is it?" Rose took her hat and parasol, placed them on the hall rack.

"I've come to tell you, Rose, that I can no longer be associated. My husband has found out about my attendance at the meetings for Jamison's and he has forbid me to go. He is quite upset. I'm very sorry."

"That's all right, Ava. He has his reputation to think about. We can talk about it though…and no one need ever know. Sit down, I have much to tell you."

Ava's dark eyes lit up a bit. "I visited Newgate and Whitegate, both!"

"You didn't." Ava's voice was hushed, as though someone might hear her.

"Yes, and there are so many opportunities we can take advantage of."

"Oh Rose, I cannot be associated in any way."

"You won't need to. Do you pray?"

"Of course I do."

"Good. I'll call for tea." Rose pulled the rope.

"Now." She took a seat. "Newgate is in need of food and clothing. The children were not ragged, but close." Rose sat nearby.

"From the looks of it Jamison needs help more. They need a new location." Ava reported.

"You are right. I'm sure you haven't heard. My husband left his small home to Jamison's."

"What?" Ava perked up.

"Yes! But the house is not large enough for all the children so they have set up a business. The older girls that have skills work from the rooms and board there. It is good the house is situated on a corner lot. There is room to build."

"Oh Rose, the city officials would never let them build. You should know that."

"Why? It's their property."

"Because they are Negras. It will never happen."

Rose's bubble burst. "But there should be some way. They are already getting customers for Nettie's dresses. She can hardly keep up. Other girls are coming to help. They have been doing quite well."

"That is all good." Ava admitted. "But I'm afraid you will get a reputation, Rose. One you cannot withstand. Your husband's good name is honored. But he is gone. The bank, Mr. Dalton in particular, will slap away your every attempt to borrow funds. Do you not see that he could never be associated with funding a business such as that."

"That may well be, but I shall do my best." Rose had no idea she was so determined until just that minute.

"I'm sure you will but I cannot be known as a participator in any way."

"Then you shall not." Rose assured her. "Your power will be through the prayers of those who can participate, will it not?"

Ava nodded, but with trepidation Rose noted.

"Ah, tea. Portia made scones with apricots."

They ate in silence for a few moments. It was very unlike Ava to be so quiet.

"Ava…" Rose put her tea cup down. "Is there something you want to talk about?"

The woman, so elegant and beautiful, looked away then back again. "I cannot stay long. As you see I did not bring my conveyance. My husband has forbid me to have contact with you Rose."

"I see." Rose picked up her cup and sipped, giving her time to process the words. "That is quite all right. Perhaps I can send word through your brother."

"No. Do not do that." Ava said quickly, her teacup rattling in its saucer. She put it down and stood, paced, the back hem of her dress puffing out each time she turned.

"My husband and my brother have come to blows."

"The reason for Captain Wyatt's battered face?" Rose asked quietly.

"Yes." Ava whispered near tears. "They will not tell me what transpired. But it is bitter and final I'm afraid. My husband will not tolerate his presence and I am forced to follow my husband."

Rose kept her tongue.

"My husband took the worst of it. He had to feign illness for several days until the bruises went away." She whispered then caught Rose's eye. "Theodore accuses Ashton of having a temper like my father." She finished. "Our home was very strained.

"I see."

"It makes things so difficult. My husband has chances for promotion at the bank. And he must take them." Ava finished and turned, her eyes hard. "I must see to him. You do understand?"

Rose stood. "Yes, of course I do." She hugged Ava lightly. "Now be gone, before you find yourself in any harm, my friend, and know that nothing will change our friendship."

Rose had no idea how much her own life would change.

Chapter 38

The next morning Mr. Dalton was shown to the library before the house was fully in motion.

"Dat man from da bank, he sayin' he ain't leavin' till he sees you Miz Rose. I told 'im you was still abed. He wouldn't hear o'anything but to see you."

"That's all right, Portia. Just get my blue lawn from the wardrobe and we'll make Mr. Dalton wait while you plait my hair. Mind you, I want it perfect, so take your time."

"Miz Rose you done gone daft, you knows that? I gonna do just that too." She chuckled. "He want to see you. He gonna see you, all purtied up like dem little bluebirds, shore enough."

A full hour later and looking very radiant and upstanding, Rose trailed her hand along the rail, the hem in back of her dress dropping onto each step behind her as she descended. "Good morning, Mr. Dalton. I do hope we haven't taken overlong." She said sweetly, aghast that she could be so bold and with no husband to stand up for her.

"Not a worry in the world. I was just reviewing your material goods, Mrs. Lovell. You do have a lovely home."

Material goods? Was that all he thought about?

His words were overconfident. She had intended to give him a taste of his own pride and now she herself had been foiled by it.

"Is that what you came to say, sir?" She turned serious. "For if that is all you want you may leave."

Mr. Dalton turned to her and with acid on his tongue, "I shall leave. But I shall also come back. For in due time, Mrs. Lovell, this house shall be mine again."

"Yours? Again?"

"Indeed." He bowed slightly at the waist and with an evil grin, turned on his heel and exited.

The screen door slammed. Rose fell into a chair. What had just happened? His confidence and bitterness were sure. He had reason to make such a bold declaration. What should she do? She took the handkerchief out of her wrist and tapped the beads of sweat on her upper lip. And why had he come in the first place?

Immediately she went to the hall desk and snatched a paper and quill. With a quick scratch, she wrote a missive to Captain Wyatt and sent it immediately on it's way with directions to Thomas to make sure it went over on the next ship. She only hoped it would arrive before the Emerald Star left London.

The joy of the last few days flew away like a hawk with a dead creature in its mouth.

∞

Two weeks passed without a word from Captain Wyatt or Mr. Dalton. During that time she visited Newgate and met Mrs. Doddle, whom she found kind and worn out. Cecelia had been studying her subjects. Mrs. Shevington had been called away to a meeting and was unable to make the visit they had planned. Rose kept herself busy visiting Jamison's new house on Bull and Versey Streets.

Nettie was now in charge of the design, sewing and fitting of dresses for Charleston ladies. Her gift for creating stylish new dresses was exceptional. The older boys from the orphanage came and made repairs to the house. Rose noticed the well-kept lawn and an array of colorful flowers now stood sentinel in pots arranged very cleverly in front of the newly painted house. Several girls came once a week to scrub, she learned, for the house was spotless. A new counter separated the clients from entering the sewing rooms which boasted a brand new Singer sewing machine complete with gold lettering on the front.

Mrs. Jamison kept herself busy searching for food and clothing so Rose rarely saw her. Several children at the orphanage acquired new positions as the eldest with skills went to work at the new house. She also noted there was no sign out front. Clearly it was better for Charleston ladies to be seen entering a home rather than a business. For whatever reasons, it didn't matter, the fact was they were doing well.

Jamison's was making headway. Just the way her husband planned, she was sure.

Chapter 39

Weeks passed. It was May 3rd, her 21st birthday. She sat at the table in the foyer, checking mail. Still no word from Captain Wyatt. For now there had been no visits from Mr. Dalton and none from Ava either. Foster and Stella had come for dinner twice. The furniture Stella acquired from her father's home was divided and delivered according to need. Some to Jamison's and some to Newgate.

The ladies, at their monthly meetings, were finding ways and means to accomplish what they wanted. Some were willing to donate various used items from their homes when Emmanuel made his slow drive around with a small cart. A servant from the house would wave him in and deliver blankets, dishes, an old table, clothing, even boots and shoes.

Someone, no one knows who, dropped off two new doors at Jamison's. The others were so rickety varmints could easily squeeze in through the holes. Then another day two men came and tore down the old outhouses, and delivered two newly built ones. Rose suspected Stella and Foster had arranged that. Stella hated those outhouses. She giggled at the thought, a streak of joy running through her. Life meant something these days.

Bright yellow curtains hung at every window at Jamison's new location. And new-sewn aprons were dropped off one Saturday afternoon for the younger girls, which helped preserve their thin dresses. Nettie taught the girls to sew and delegated finishing jobs to the dresses she had styled. A box of fabric for projects mysteriously appeared on the front porch about once a month.

⁂

With a jolt Rose stood. There were footsteps. Lots of them. On her front porch. Who could it be? She opened the door to a passel of children, faces she knew from Jamison's -- wishing her happy birthday with a soft-sung song. Tears formed and before she could see each face, they all ran down the stairs, hopped on the cart Emmanuel was driving and quietly drove away waving furiously.

She watched and waved, knowing they had taken a chance appearing at her door and not wishing to cause trouble had done their deed and run off.

"Chile ain't that just sumpin'? I done heared all that singing…and thought Jesus had come." Portia gathered her apron corner and dabbed at her eye. "Dem kids shore do love you. See you got 'nuff love to go 'round and round. Now come on. I got lemon cake and warm lemon puddin' to put on it and cream too. Special for your birthday."

Rose followed feeling like the world was right again. Mrs. Shevington was due today. It was been weeks before they could find the time to meet. The note had seemed rather urgent so Rose enjoyed her birthday cake and hurried above stairs to get ready. She must be careful not to ruin Mrs. Shevington's stand in the community.

She put on her newest dress; perfect for a beautiful warm May day. A dove gray gown with white collar and cuffs, special flounces and a wide band of white silk at the waist. She was proud to wear Nettie's newest creation, which was fast becoming the style of Charleston.

It was said that even the former Miss Bertram had sent her maid to call Nettie for a fitting at her new home, one of the finest in Charleston.

Portia had just finished her hair when she heard the knocker. Everytime she did, it sent a shiver up her back. It was a bit early for Mrs. Shevington. Hopefully Mr. Dalton was not calling. "Emmanuel goin' to the door." Portia said quietly.

"Portia, I declare you could hear a mouse run across the floor from way up here."

"Miz Rose, I done heard that sound afore...only they was rats, right in the cabin I lived in. Sends waves up and down my spine." She shivered. "Them little feet scratchin' across the floor like 'at."

Rose forgot sometimes the life Portia must have lived as a child. Her parents were slaves in the Mississippi Delta.

"Now der you go. Lookin' pretty as ever. I hears a man's voice. Not one I knows. I'll go on down and see to it. You wait here like a lady."

"Thank you Portia." Rose's heart beat again as she paced back and forth.

"Miz Rose, come on down. Hurry on up now." She added from the bottom of the stairs.

It was too early for Captain Wyatt, he wasn't expected for another six weeks. She hurried to the top step and slowly made her way down.

"Come see here." Portia drew her to the library. "Look at that." She pointed. "Oh dear, I done forgot my manners. Mr. John Parker waitin' in the parlor. I'll go get him."

Portia bustled across the hall and retrieved Mr. Parker. "Sir, dis here Miz Ireland Rose Lovell." She introduced. "Dis be Reverend Mr. John Parker." She said and hurried off.

"It is good to make your acquaintance Mrs. Lovell. Your maid is quite unusual." He said quietly as he bowed slightly.

"She is my friend and confidant." Rose smiled.

"As I see. I am the new Reverend for the Episcopal Church. I have it from some of the ladies that there are monthly meetings at my church."

Rose's heart thumped. "Yes Reverend there are."

"And the work you are all doing is quite remarkable."

"It is." She agreed, waiting to make out what he was trying to say.

"I also understand you attend St. Michael's."

"Yes, I do." So he was here to persuade her to attend his church.

"That is quite remarkable as well." He said.

"And why is that?" Rose did not understand in the least.

"That ladies from the two churches are agreeable. I have it on good word that there has been quite a division between the two churches, so I am pleased to hear the ladies have worked together."

"I knew nothing about that." Rose answered. "I have been here three years and only recently involved."

Reverend Parker cleared his throat and came to the point. "I am here Mrs. Lovell to learn all I can about the meetings held at my church. I would like to be of service to the good people the ladies are serving."

"I see." Rose said. "May we meet another time Reverend? I am expecting a guest."

"Of course. I will be on my way. Will you call on me then?"

"Yes, of course I will." Rose agreed and handed the man his hat from the rack. "I should enjoy a visit."

He bowed and was gone. "My goodness." She whispered.

She found Portia and told her to have tea ready, that Mrs. Shevington said she could not stay long.

"It's all hot and ready. I got some o'your lemon cake, too…if she have time to eat some."

"Thank you…I'll go up and get a clean handkerchief…." Rose flew up the stairs.

"I'll go." Portia said breathlessly and ran for the door. "Everybody come at one time 'round here."

Rose heard voices and waited for Portia to come up.

"She done sittin' in the parlor and lookin' like she gonna fly out o'here soon's she can. You best go on down…I'll get the tea."

Rose carried herself slowly and walked into the library. "Mrs. Shevington, welcome."

The woman rose from her seat with a gleam in her eye.

"Please sit." Rose offered and waited for her guest to be seated.

"I've wonderful news. I have heard you are acquainted with Mrs. Ava McGuire. She and I are in the same circles of business and have made an attachment. I understand you know her husband is not appreciative of our work."

Rose nodded, noting the spark in her eye again.

"She has found a way to help us. Mrs. McGuire brought the attention of our situation to her friend Mrs. Pinckney after you and she visited her warehouse. I contacted Mrs. Pinckney and she and I have purchased a building for Jamison's Orphanage. We would have liked to combine Jamison's with Newgate but the townspeople would not be agreeable to that. We have decided to build for Jamisons, and then according to God's blessings we will improve Newgate as soon as we have funds."

"A building?" Rose made sure she understood.

"Yes, it is an old iron foundry on the edge of town near the industrial buildings. It boasts three levels and is situated on a corner lot. We bought it for a song." She declared. "And Mr. Dalton was unaware of what we intended to use the building for. I'm very certain, he was most glad for the sale and forgot to inquire. But the papers are duly signed and sealed. " She laughed.

Rose noted her deep voiced laugh and joy filled her heart until it hurt. *Thank you Lord.*

"I was unable to mention anything at our first meeting, until all the papers were signed and delivered."

"I am overwhelmed." Rose gushed.

"We are two widows with money. Now we have a purpose and we intend to make our lives count in our old age."

"Oh my." Rose pulled out the fresh handkerchief and wiped at her eyes.

"Here is the plan and then I must go. We have much to do during these summer months to reconstruct the interior space for the children. We will need beds, a kitchen, and space to play and work."

"Does Mrs. Jamison know?"

"She does indeed. I just came from there."

Rose thought of Ava. How she could not place her hand directly on the project, but with her persuasion, caused Mrs. Pinckney to come aboard.

"What can I do?"

"That is why I am here. I know Captain Lovell left his small home to Mrs. Jamison and from what I hear it is thriving. Your husband has begun the project and we want to carry it further. We want you to help us design the interior of the new orphanage. Rose -- you, me, Mrs. McGuire and Mrs. Pinckney will meet and discuss how we can best use the space. There is one catch. It must be done soon. Once the plans are drawn up our goal is to have the children moved away from the filth they are living in now as soon as possible."

"Mrs. Shevington, you have my complete cooperation."

"That is exactly what I came for, Mrs. Lovell."

"Of course Mrs. McGuire cannot come to meetings but she is going to tour the foundry and suggest design and colors. But she will be a silent participant."

"Ava has excellent taste." Rose smiled as she stood.

"Now I must be about the business immediately. We must not waste time and I have my own place to run. You will hear from me."

Before Rose could process the information, Mrs. Shevington was out the door and climbing into her carriage. To make her birthday even more memorable, she had one more visit to make before the day was over.

Chapter 40

Rose's mind began to work. Three levels. She must have a look and engaged Emmanuel to take her out for a long drive on this most beautiful day. The warm winds of late afternoon were already upon them. It was Tuesday and she had the rest of the week to sketch a plan if she could just see the building.

Thirty minutes later she was viewing it from the carriage. Indeed there were three floors, windows marched along all four walls on all three levels. Very unusual for a foundry she mused. There would be plenty of light for the children. She invited Emmanuel to walk the perimeter and he tied the horses to the post and joined her.

"What do you think? Will the windows need to be replaced?"

"Window glass can be changed for the few that are broken."

"One of the levels could be used for a sewing factory or somesuch idea." Rose's fingertip rested on her lips. "What do you think Emmanuel?"

"I be thinkin' Miz Rose that you best keep that sewing factory on the bottom level so's folks could get out if'n there's a fire."

"There are fire escapes at the ready. This must have been part of the offices."

"'Dat be true…the foundry is over there." He pointed. "Where them smoke stacks are. I be thinking dis is where they had storage or offices or somesuch thing."

"I see. Then we have the best building don't we?"

"Shore do, the way I see it. It was built newest." Emmanuel laughed. "God's doin'."

"Indeed it is." Rose looked upward. "The building does have newer brick, now that you mention it."

Without another word Rose and Emmanuel headed back home. Emmanuel put the carriage away and she went straight to her husband's office to sketch, excited to view the inside.

For the next few hours, she wrote down ideas. Beds and tables on the top floor. Kitchen on the bottom floor along with the sewing rooms. But the middle floor, she had no idea what they could use that for. A school perhaps.

Matilda Jane came walking through the house a bit slower than usual, Rose noted.

"Are you feeling well?" She stepped to the doorway and invited her to sit.

"Just a bit tired is all." She admitted.

"Do you think it wise to take a short nap perhaps?"

"Thank you, but all I do is think when I lay down. And I . . ."

Rose saw the tears form in her eyes. "Well, then, shall we go out and while away the afternoon in the gardens?"

"I should say." Matilda Jane stood up quick-like.

Rose had to turn her back to keep the smile on her face from showing. That girl had more energy.

"I shall go up and change and we will get our hands very dirty." She laughed. "You just rest for a few minutes. I warn you I'm going to work you…"

Rose stopped and gave her a look. She had thick blonde hair and beautiful green eyes, a lovely girl to look at. And she worked hard. Rose wondered what her story was, how she found herself at the orphanage. If it hadn't been for Captain Lovell, she may have found herself there, too. Or back in Ireland. While they were working, she would gently bring up a question or two.

Within minutes, Rose had tossed off her heavy dress and chose a soft cotton one. The warm sultry summer winds were upon them already. It was time to nip the buds so new blooms would be fresh and full this year.

Matilda Jane would have to endure some of the hot days of summer before her child was born. Hopefully Captain Wyatt would be here in time.

As Rose was coming down the stairs, Lily came walking around the corner. Not running. Walking. What was this?

"Lily, my but you look grown up today."

"Thank you Miz Rose. Matilda Jane been teaching me how to be a lady and I'm learnin' mathematics, too."

"She has?" Rose was pleased. "And a good job she's done of it I say. Aye, ye're a lady if I've ever seen one!" She used her Irish brogue.

Matilda Jane had joined them and they all laughed together.

"Would you like to work with us in the garden today, Lily?"

Rose knew she would.

"I shore would." Lily started to run, stopped and slowed her pace, calling over her shoulder, "I'm going to change Miz Rose and meet you out there."

"I see you and Lily have become friends, Matilda Jane. I am very pleased. You are very kind to teach Lily mathematics."

"I am?"

"Why, yes, of course you are. You are a fine young lady."

The girl's face turned three shades of red as she stared at her feet. Rose was instantly aware that the girl did not see herself that way.

"Sometimes things happen, Matilda Jane. We have to make the best of the situations we find ourselves in. Come now, I'll get you some gloves. By the time dinner is ready we will have topped off all the old buds, raked out the leaves and trash from the plants and have a much nicer garden."

Later Rose found herself up in the attic looking for furniture suitable for a tiny child. There was a cradle under an eave. She had seen it but gave no thought never intending to use it. Down it came before the days got hotter. Thomas came for it and Rose sent down a small chest and a child's trunk. Matilda Rose had her own room and there would be plenty of space for the tiny infant.

She wondered at how her life had changed, gazing out the colored glass, watching the river across the way as the sun danced along the smooth surface sending shards of light sharp as diamonds into her eyes. Truth, she was excited to have a wee babe in the house. Captain Lovell would have liked it, she mused. She found her way to the blue boxes. The letters. Somehow she could not part with them.

Darby and *W.*

Sighing, she came down the ladder, excited to set up a nursery. By the time her feet hit the floor she was gasping for breath. It was hot today, sultry in fact. Good sailing weather. The Carolina Yacht Club held their annual sailing and regatta contest this weekend. There would be many people coming down to White Point Garden to view the races. Which meant there would be lots of noise. Having a house on The Battery was highly desirable, but it also meant there were always people about, walking past, talking, shouting, and making merry.

Climbing the steps slowly, she wiped perspiration from her forehead and tucked a wayward curl behind her ear. She heard voices down the hall. Lily and Matilda Jane were talking. She didn't want to interrupt, so stepping to her room she lifted the tiny infant clothing she'd made. Whether from the heat or a sudden realization, she felt tears spring to her eyes. Life here was lonely knowing her husband would not be coming back. It felt strange. *Brace yourself and do your duty, Ireland Rose. There is always time for musing later.*

Her mother's voice.

She turned her ear. No more voices. Perhaps the girls were done talking. She made her way down the hall and entered Matilda Jane's room.

The two were sitting on the floor playing a game of tic tac toe on paper. Rose smiled.

"Shall we prepare the cradle?"

Matilda Jane looked up but didn't move. Lily didn't either. Rose realized at that moment. Matilda Jane was not ready to be a mother. Why hadn't she seen it before? The child barely out of the orphanage, who knows what brought her there and now growing large with child. Her heart skipped a beat. Captain Wyatt was a rake. Instantly she knew she was going to have a word with him. How dare he leave this young girl without marriage and a home. Well enough that he possessed the income to protect her. And why wasn't he? She intended to find out the moment he set foot in this house.

Down the stairs in a huff, she went to Portia and told her that when Captain Wyatt came to the door, she was to direct him to her office immediately.

Chapter 41

Before long it was the first week of June. The nursery had been prepared, but Matilda Jane and Lily took no notice. The two had become inseparable.

"Dat girl o'mine get her work done fast nowdays. She git done so's she and Miss Matilda Jane can go do 'dem mathematics and write 'dem words." Hands on her hips. "And what the two o'em talk about I got no idea."

"I've noticed." Do you think Lily is too young to be around an unmarried girl with child?"

"Noooo...dat be part o'life. She may as well know all the hard times now, 'stead of learnin' em later. I been trying to teach her better 'n I did her mama. I done spoiled that chile o'mine; she done had two babies and left 'em here with me. And then run off with a rich white man, all 'cause he had money." Portia's hands were flying in the air. "Now look at all she miss, and dem kids don't know a bit where their mama is. And neither do I." She swatted at the flies with that stick of hers, mashing a few of them.

Rose felt a trickle of laughter climb up into her throat.

"You laughin'?"

"Just the way you are smashing those flies."

"Just thinkin' on it gets me all up in de air again. And 'dis heat don't help none. I declare it be the hottest day yet."

"Maybe that's why we are all a bit sluggish. Maybe some lemonade with ice chips...."

"That be the thing." Portia trotted off. "Under the shade."

"I'll get the girls." Rose took her time, heading for the front verandah. June had come already; six months since her husband passed. She wiped her face and collapsed into a chair. The sun was beating off the water so brightly she had to shade her eyes.

"Girls, Portia is making lemonade. We're heading out under the shade tree out back. Come along...sun's too hot up front."

"We don't mind." Lily said quickly.

Rose looked in the direction of Lily's gaze. There was Thomas, talking to Nettie. What was Nettie doing around here? Then a smile came to her face. No doubt paying a visit to a local, because Nettie was dressed very nicely for a hot day like this. And in one of her own stylish dresses. She must be making a call. So...Thomas and Nettie knew each other.

Love was everywhere. Portia and Emmanuel. Stella and Foster. Upstairs in the attic. Someday, maybe she would be loved.

"Goodness gracious." She said aloud. "I must be overcome." She fanned herself with the church paddle fan she found laying on a chair.

"We ready." Lily said and took hold of Matilda Jane's hand and pulled her up.

The next second Matilda Jane gasped and there was a puddle at her feet.

"Oh my." Rose said. "Quick, run get your grandmother, Lily."

Lily was off like a gunshot.

"Let's get you inside." Rose put her hand at her waist and helped her in.

"I don't want to get your floor wet." Matilda Jane looked as though she was going to cry.

"Don't worry. I'll clean it up. It's only water." Rose said, not knowing a thing. She was happy to see Portia come hurrying up.

"Here now chile. First babies take a long time. We ain't takin' you up to the bed just yet. Too hot and all you be doing is rolling in dem hot covers. We'll get you cleaned up and walk this baby right on outta you. Best way."

The young girl looked like Rose felt. Scared out of her mind. Matilda Jane was just a child herself. And Captain Wyatt, the scoundrel, wasn't even here. Rose let her thoughts overtake her. And scolded herself . . . this was not the time.

Portia helped prepare the girl while Lily went to boil water. Rose didn't know what to do, had never been present at a birth, only heard talk from the ladies, which wasn't much; they didn't discuss such things. She felt useless.

Quick, she ran out to the garden, cut some colorful flowers and carried them up in a large vase to Matilda Jane's room. Perhaps the sight of them would soothe her pain. She turned the counterpane down, then snatched it off the bed. It would be too hot. She found a fresh set of sheets and smoothed the cotton material over the mattress, then tossed several pillows on the bed.

The infant bed must be made ready. She searched the wardrobe, found pillow covers and formed a soft bed for the baby. Thankful she had made gowns, at least the child would have clothing, even though it most likely wouldn't need much in this dreadful heat.

Done, she looked around. It was all she knew to do. Anxiety lit her up inside. She had to be about some business. Down the stairs she flew as Lily flew up with the same look on her face.

"Where's she at?" Rose inquired.

"She sittin' on the bench in the garden just this minute, but Granmama made her get up and walk."

Rose nodded and scurried toward the garden and peeked out. Sure enough Portia was instructing her to breathe and walk. The girl's face looked okay, and then she stopped, grabbed a nearby branch and Rose watched as her face screwed up tight.

"Oh dear." She whispered and noticed Portia left her alone until the pain passed.

"Should I go for the doctor?" She whispered.

"No. Women be having babies just the way God made it. Natural-like. We have trouble, we'll call Dr. Case right away." She assured Rose. "You go on now and I be lettin' you know if we need you." Portia shoved her off.

Rose pulled in a deep breath. She was going to take a walk. She went straight out the front door and down the verandah steps. The sun was still high, so she headed down the wooden boardwalk, turned and came back again. It was too hot, so she did not meet too many people. She walked until she couldn't breathe anymore. How awful it must be for Matilda Jane, she thought and walked faster.

Some time later she realized the top of her head was burning. She hadn't even had the sense to put on her straw hat, protect her creamy pale complexion which so many ladies were fond of. She dashed inside, listened for noises and hearing slight groans, dashed back out. This time she took the swing and swung. Hard.

In and out she went all afternoon catching Portia's eyes and then at the shake of her head, leaving again. It was nearing dusk and she heard louder noises and went in. Surely the girl had suffered enough, she prayed for the child to come quick.

"Time to take her up to the bed." Portia declared. "You come on up behind me and Lily now Miz Rose and make sure our girl doesn't fall down 'dem stairs."

Rose knew Portia. She was worried. It had been so long.

She helped get Matilda Jane into the bed and watched as Portia tied old dish towels to the black iron footboard. It was all she could do not to run, but birth was something every mother had to go through and if she wanted to be one, she'd better know how it went. So she stayed.

Matilda Jane labored and cried, called out and shouted, and still the baby did not come. Even if Portia said no, Rose was going for Dr. Case if this didn't stop.

Suddenly, Portia placed herself next to the bed and when Matilda Jane let out a scream, Portia called out, "It be a girl. A purty little girl." She lifted the tiny bundle. "Come on Rose, take 'dis child and wrap her up good now. She cain't get a chill. Go on, lay out a blanket."

Rose did and she watched Portia place the tiny thing into it and Rose folded her inside and picked her up, for she was mewling like a new baby kitten. She held it close and looked at the miniature eyes as they tried to open and when they did Rose spoke to her.

"My, my, aren't you something. So tiny and look at all that dark hair." She crooned and took a seat in the rocker.

Matilda Jane's hair was tossed all about and she was sweating. Portia had finished her up and now was sponging her face with a cool rag. "Der now, chile you done had yo baby and she be just fine. You rest and pretty soon you can nurse her. Right now Miz Rose done got her over der in the rocker and she be doin' jus fine."

"Thank you..." Rose heard the weak voice from the bed.

Chapter 42

Portia took the babe and washed it in warm water and gave instructions for Rose to dress her.

"I've never dressed an infant. Let me watch you do it." Rose looked up to see a bit of merriment in Portia's eyes.

"Then it be time you learn how, if'n you want your own babies some day." She declared as she handed the freshly bathed child to Rose.

"Oh dear." She declared and held it tightly against her, then relaxed. "I'm so afraid I will hurt her; her bones are so tiny and her fingers.

"She be fine. Now…" Portia spread a clean square of cotton out. "Just lay her head and feet cornerwise and wrap like de wrap them fish down at the market."

Rose, tired as she was fell into a fit of giggles. "You make things much more simple." Hand over her heart.

A shaky hand, Portia noted. "Ain't nothin' to it. They needs to be clean, bellys full, and loved up. That's it and all in a basket."

"That's all?" Rose questioned, serious now.

"Yep, 'at's it."

"Well then, I believe I could do that." Rose lifted the child and laid her just like Portia said and wrapped her up."

"Forgot one thing." Portia held her hand over her mouth. "She need a diaper first."

"Oh." Rose said and unwrapped. "I didn't think of that."

"She be ruinin' ever dress you got." Portia said matter-of-fact and showed Rose how to diaper an infant. "Now den you wrap her up."

Rose did and smiled. "She looks quite cozy and look, her little eyes are closing."

"Take her on up now and give her to her ma. She be needin' to feed her chile and grow close-like."

Rose gently lifted her to her chest and walked very slowly to the bed, all the while watching the little face. Once there she said over her shoulder, whispering, "Matilda Jane is asleep."

"Den come on over here and rock the babe. Maybe she be tired from all that long birthing, both of 'em. They'll sleep. And when that little one open up her mouth and start calling for her ma, we'll know she be hungry."

Rose took a seat in the rocker and found a comfortable position and just stared at the little piece of human being she held in her arms. She knew a babe was coming to Matilda Jane, but she didn't know it would be like this.

Sometime later Rose opened her eyes and realized she'd fallen asleep… with the infant in her arms. Startled, she looked down, afraid should she have dropped her. Still asleep. Two candles were lit in the room. Portia had been here and seen to them. The day had been so long and so intense all the snuff had gone out of them. She tuned her ear, noted that not a sound came from below. What time was it anyway? She heard two policemen talking through the slightly open window and a pole light went out and then was lit again by the gas lighter.

The world went on as though nothing had changed. But so much had changed in her own household. Her tiredness overcame her and she wept. She wanted a child of her own.

Swiping at the tears, she heard the familiar creek of the stairs. Lily stood in the doorway in her nightdress. "Miz Rose." She whispered, wiping the sleep from her eyes. Granmama tole me to come up and see if ya-all is all right."

"We're fine, Lily. Thank you dear, you go back to bed. If we need anything I'll come down and get you."

"Yes Miz Rose." She said and tiptoed away into the darkness.

The time went by slowly as Rose rocked, her head back, eyes closed, but careful not to fall asleep again. Then suddenly her eyes popped open. A sound was coming from that tiny baby and it wasn't just a mewl, which is all she had heard up to this time. It was a loud, needy sort of cry. Rose wandered if she had pinched her or something worse. She stood quickly and walked back and forth, ready to run for Portia.

But noises came from behind. Matilda Jane was awake. "Bring her to me." She said and Rose did. The young girl adjusted her gown and set the child at her breast, Rose watching intently as it began to suckle. Tears fell down her face and she didn't even know she was crying until they dropped off her chin and onto the babe's blanket. She swiped at them, realizing she was far past overtired. She was just plain daft.

Babies were born all the time, she said to herself. But none of it made sense. There was something inside her that had come alive since all this had happened. Something she could not take back no matter how long she lived. She thought about Ava McGuire who wanted a child but could not because her husband would not allow it. Suddenly she sensed Ava's desire. And she, Rose, with no husband.

Her mother's sense of practicality burrowed into her brain. She was a widow, for goodness' sake. And only six months. There was a decent amount a lady should wait. And here she stands longing for a child. She tut-tutted aloud and forced herself to think rationally.

"Will you be all right?" Rose whispered.

"Yes ma'am. Thank you. But afterward I would like to use the chamberpot."

Rose pulled it out from beneath the bed and left the room, sensing she was an intruder. Mother and child needed time to bond. Portia had said that somewhere along the way. She took a last look and found her way down the stairs to the ice box where she found cheese and boiled eggs and a chunk of bread. She slattered the bread with butter and ate, knowing she needed her bed and time to gather her senses.

"You'd think I had birthed the little lass myself." She muttered as she ate.

Chapter 43

The first three days the entire household was running up and down the stairs. No one could stay away from the room. Then something happened that Rose did not understand. Portia caught her at the bottom of the stairs and pulled her to the office.

'Dat girl won't feed the babe. She got what we call the 'baby blues.' Nothin' I say or do will make her feed that chile. I made up some herbal tea, like my mama made for times like these, but she would have none of it. Said she didn't want the babe."

"What?" Rose couldn't think why. She had carried the child and given birth. How could she not want to feed her? "Why?"

"Nobody knows 'bout these things. Human bein's be funny creatures sometimes. She be young. Could be she didn't want the babe…."

"Do you mean Captain Wyatt could have …. have…." She couldn't say the words.

"It be possible. Some men be like 'at. Where you think all 'dem kids come from down at the orphanage. Most of 'em be chil'ren from ship captains when they come into port and leave. Agin and agin." She said looking at Rose. "Miz Rose, I be sorry. You ain't a'quainted with such doins. I be telling things I shouldn't be speaking of to a lady."

"No." Rose said firmly. "I'm a grown woman. I should know about these things. It's….it's just that my life has been so protected from the world. My parents…well…we didn't speak on these subjects."

"It's only 'cause you never had to, chile. No harm in dat. We'll think o'somethin'. Emmanuel out right now gettin' milk from 'de neighbor's goat. I done fried a big batch o'dem donuts and traded her for milk."

"Oh Portia." Rose threw her arms around the woman and welcomed those loving arms around her. "What would I do without you?"

"Chile you need a husband to take care o'you. And some babies."

Rose did need a husband, but after seeing Matilda Jane's pain, she could wait for babies. A sound from the back brought Emmanuel into the house. "Got a clean bucket o'milk settin' on the table." He said and seeing the women talking low, went back outside.

"Thank you Emmanuel." Portia called out, then patted Rose on the shoulder and hustled out. "We gots to get milk in dat child. I be watching. That little girl done cried herself out and is weak from it all. I done brought her down here w'us. Lily been rocking and soothin' it til we could get milk."

Rose panicked and ran up the stairs. Perhaps she could talk to Matilda Jane. She had to do something. She knocked at Matilda Jane's door and crept in. "Are you awake?"

"I'm awake Mrs. Lovell."

Rose heard despondency in the voice. "Would you like tea? Are you hungry?"

"No, neither. I just want to be alone."

"I see." Rose twisted her hands at her waist. "Would you like me to bring the baby up? She's very hungry."

"NO. I've bound myself up."

Rose tried not to show her surprise.

"I don't want it." Matilda Jane whimpered. "I don't want it. I want to go back to the orphanage."

"Back to the orphanage?" Rose repeated quietly.

"Yes. I want it to be like it was before."

"I see." Rose said and her anger seethed toward Captain Wyatt.

"Captain Wyatt will be back soon."

"He can't help me." Matilda Jane turned her head into the pillow and Rose heard sobs like she'd never heard before. She couldn't fix this, no matter what she said, but she could send a letter! And she would do it right this minute.

Even though the door was shut the sounds of Matilda Jane's sobs lingered in Rose's ears. The quill and ink came out and she scratched off a scathing letter then tossed it aside. This would not do. Information of this sort must be handled very delicately. Finger at her chin, eyes closed, she prayed for calmness and wisdom. She thought through all she knew about Captain Wyatt. He liked his liquor. He had a woman…oh, there could be the problem. Perhaps he had a woman and . . . well Rose couldn't think about it. Captain Wyatt had a duty. He must see to his daughter and to the woman who bore him the child.

Noises at the front door. She did not wish to see anyone. No cards lay in the dish, so what guests could possibly be coming now? She sighed. Besides that no one knew Matilda Jane was here so it was better to keep guests to a minimum.

Her thoughts tangled, she opened the door and there stood Captain Wyatt. She stared at him. He was cleaned up and presentable, not in a hurry as usual. She guessed he was not here to gain permission to unload the ship since it was his own.

He took two steps in the door and Rose could not account for what happened next.

"Sir. You have finally arrived. Finally shown your face here. I will have you know your child has been born and Matilda Jane is not well. At this moment the child is receiving nourishment from a neighbor. I am undone Captain Wyatt, and quite disappointed in you."

When she saw the frown on his face, she became more angry. "Do not insult me by acting as though you know nothing of what I am speaking about. You have a duty sir, and I will see that you keep it."

"And what duty is that, Mrs. Lovell."

She heard his voice, saw the look in those dark eyes. He was calm but underneath....she could feel his ire.

"You have a daughter, sir. Born just two days ago. Unnamed. And you stand here her father. What have you to say for yourself?"

"Who said I was the father?"

"It was clear the moment you brought that young lass here, Mr. Wyatt."

He noted he had lost his title.

"You, sir, need to go above stairs and see your . . . your....the mother of your child." She stood aside, arms crossed over her beating chest.

"You are undone, Mrs. Lovell."

"I? I am undone? Sir you defraud yourself. I demand you make sense of this and go up this minute." She felt tears sting her eyes.

He softened his voice. It was clear she was distraught. If he spoke harshly now he could see he would be pounded severely by those little fists that formed. For he doubted she even knew herself, they were bound up one on each side holding her skirts. He had only to make the wrong move.

"You madam have allowed yourself to be misinformed."

"Aye, then you are refusing to acknowledge your own child?"

"If the child was mine I would stand up as her father. As it is, I am not the child's father."

Rose looked at him and afraid she would lose her self-respect, she gave him her back.

Captain Wyatt noted her tiny waist, her fragile frame and that red-blond curly hair popping out from every direction. Had the opportunity arisen he would take her in his arms and comfort her, but that would never be possible. She was too much like the love he lost and he was not sure he could abide that kind of loss again. He steeled himself.

"You sir, are a blackguard." She turned back and stared at him.

He almost laughed at that.

"You smirk?" She took a step closer.

She was a full head shorter, but the woman had spit and fire in those blue eyes.

"I do not. You accuse me of an untruth Mrs. Lovell. Shall I say I have fathered a child when I have not?"

Rose had had enough. Besides that she was too tired and could not think clearly. "I leave you sir to do your duty, whatever that may be."

Captain Wyatt watched her walk away, but he saw her shoulders shake just as she shot into her husband's office and shut the door. Hard. Hat in hands, he started to put it on and leave, yet figured he'd best go above stairs and see to Matilda Jane.

"Captain Wyatt." Portia greeted him quietly. "You be here to see the chile?"

"I am here to see Miss Matilda Jane. May I go up?"

"Mrs. Lovell ain't around?" She said. "How'd you come in?"

"We have spoken, Miss Portia."

"You have? Where she at?"

Captain Wyatt lifted his hat and pointed to the office with it.

"I see. Well, I gonna go up and see if Miss Matilda Jane want to receive you sir. Wait here."

"Yes ma'am."

While he waited his eyes traveled. He passed by the desk and saw his name on a paper and leaned over to read it. She was writing to him when he walked up to the door, else she would have hidden it. He had caught her in the midst of her righteous anger.

He moved away and looked out at the river across the way. She was so sure of his sin, she had written the letter hoping he would confess and do his duty. He only wished it would have been that easy.

This town was not a place where he felt free. Mr. Lovell had offered him the office of Captain to the Emerald Star and he now had ready cash. He had been pushed and shoved out of society by the very ones whom he now had to do business with. Mr. Dalton was the last man he wanted to have any dealings with but because of his promise to Captain Lovell, he was forced. Well he didn't have to live here.

As soon as he was certain Mrs. Lovell was taken care of…that there were no concerns at the bank or otherwise, he was going to load up the Emerald Star and make his home in London. There was only trouble for him here. Right now the situation with Matilda Jane must be handled.

"She ready." Portia called from the top of the stairs.

As he started up, he heard soft sobbing from the office. He wished he could go to her, but he could not. He took the stairs two at a time.

Portia led the way and he followed and found himself alone with Matilda Jane. "May I come in?"

"Yes."

He noticed she sat up in the bed. Her face was red and splotchy.

"The babe was a girl, then?"

"Yes, but I don't want her."

"You don't want her?" Captain Wyatt took a step forward. "What do you mean?"

"I want to go back to the Orphanage. I was safe there, until…"

"May I sit down?" he said gently and waited for her answer.

"Yes."

"Tell me what you are thinking Matilda Jane."

He waited patiently, looking away and back again, noting her lips were quivering and her face showing deep anguish.

"I'll do whatever you want."

"Whatever I want?" She mumbled blowing her nose into a handkerchief.

"Yes. You deserve that."

"I don't want to grow up. I want to go back. I want to finish learning to play the piano and talk like the French do. I know I can do it. But I won't be able to go back with a baby. And I don't want her to grow up there. Not like me."

"I understand. Would you like me to make arrangements for someone to keep her? Perhaps until you are above your age now?"

"No. I want her to go to Miz Rose. She loves her. I can see it. And when it was born she took it right off and wrapped it up and rocked it. I want her to have it."

Captain Wyatt noted she called the child 'it'. The girl had already decided. And he didn't blame her.

"I'll see what I can do. Shall we draw up papers?"

"Oh…oh yes…" she started sobbing. "I didn't know how to say it…I'm sorry…really sorry…but…"

"You don't have to explain. I understand. I'll take care of it. Do you trust me?"

"Yes, yes I do Captain Wyatt. If it wasn't for you . . . I don't know . . ."

He remembered stumbling upon them in an alley, his sister's husband forcing the girl to get rid of the child. He had her by the arm dragging her along, Ashton knew to someone who would do the deed and hide Theodore Madison McGuire's sin. He pushed the scene from his mind.

"What's done is done. It can't be undone. You are free to go out from here and do all those things you want to do. Will you give me your word you will keep yourself busy and make something of yourself?"

"I give you my word, sir. I do."

"Do not get your hopes high. Wait until I speak to Mrs. Lovell. If she refuses, I will find someone to take your child. If I cannot, I will take her myself."

Ashton Wyatt could have bit his tongue off. Why in the world did he utter those words. He had no wife…no one to care for the child. But they were out and he could not take them back any more than she could take back what had been done to her. He pressed his lips tight and prayed Mrs. Lovell would help.

"Make no comments to anyone. I will work this out and let you know. He stood, took the girls offered hand and left her to fulfill the promise he had just made.

He descended the stairs and knew Portia would be watching for him to come down. "Miss Portia, please tell Mrs. Lovell I shall call on her one week from today at the hour of 2:00. Please give her my regards and tell her it is of the utmost importance.

"I shall sir."

Captain Wyatt left this same house years ago making two vows to himself. The first never to enter it again, the second that he would never marry. He had lost the one true love of his life. And she had lived here while they courted. Most of his life had worked that way. Why should things be any different now?

Chapter 44

Rose had cried her eyes out. And once it started she couldn't stop. For the losses; of her young life, her parents, and her husband. She had never really grieved them. Only stood tall and strong like her mother had taught her. Now she lay across the love seat and felt like a rag doll. She had cried until she couldn't cry anymore, thinking about Matilda Jane and her baby. What would become of the little lass?

Portia had called to her from outside the door and left when Rose asked to be alone.

Now it was dusk, the house quiet. She hadn't even thought to get up to see if the tiny infant was eating and felt ashamed at her selfishness. When she was ready, she dipped her hanky in the wash bowl and freshened her face, then opened the door slowly. The gas lights were being lit; she could see the street come alive post by post.

She needed tea and walked on weak knees to get some. The cup rattled loudly in the saucer. The last few days had broken her strong will. First the hard birthing, then Matilda Jane refusing to feed her child, then worry that the child may die and Captain Wyatt would be...broken hearted. But she remembered he had told her he was not the father. Were such things done like that here? Did fathers deny their own children? Should she believe him? She knew he possessed a brusqueness about him but would he go that far? Had her husband been uninformed of his true character. Had he perhaps even now fooled everyone. But no, her husband had trusted him. Captain Lovell was not the kind of man to harbor judgment, but neither would he have put his wife, his business, nor the carrying out of his fortune in the hands of a man who was less than upstanding. That she knew.

Oh her mind was mush. She couldn't make tips nor tops of all that dashed around in her head. She gulped down her tea very unladylike, poured a second and gulped that down and went up to bed. All she wanted was to be in her soft nightclothes and cuddle deep into the goose feathered mattress and sleep. She trusted Portia and Lily were looking after the babe, for she heard no crying, and besides that her head ached. She would be useless to anyone just now.

Rose awoke late the next morning with a scratchy throat and a headache the size of the mighty Mississippi. She turned over and over, trying to find a comfortable position, threw a cover over her eyes to block out the sun and tried to sleep. It would not come. Slowly, she pulled herself to her feet and feeling faint, sat back down again.

"You up, Miz Rose?" I heard them little feet on the floorboards squeaking like always."

"I'm awake. Come in Portia."

"Heaven's above you be lookin' like you done seen a ghost. Your face all red and splotchy like you fell into the berry patch." She chuckled.

"Oh Portia, you find something funny in the simplest of things I declare. I have such a headache. I cried my eyes out last night until my head hurt."

"I done hears ya chile. You needed 'dat, dat's for shore. You been holdin' up like 'at since you was same age as Matilda Jane in there. 'Bout time you got some cryin' done. You and Matilda Jane got it all out at the same time...you did."

"Oh here I am talking about myself. How is the infant? Did she stop crying? Did she eat anything at all?"

"Chile, slow down. You ast so many questions, I don't know which one to answer first!"

Rose smiled and quieted herself, sitting up against the pillows holding her head.

"Here take some tea. I put herbs in there that should help the headache."

Rose sipped.

"Now first the child suckled that goat milk down like it was her mama's. That little tiny thing didn't wake up onct during the night. Me and Lily done slept all night long."

"I'm so happy about that."

"I sees you relieved. Now when you feelin' better you come on down, I gets you somthin' to eat and you can feed that little thing yo'self. She a mighty purty little thing."

"Yes she is." Rose agreed and drew a long sip from her cup.

"Now I's got to go see to Miz Matilda Jane. She feeling much better, too knowing the baby is fine. She done stopped crying right after Captain Wyatt left her.

"What? Captain Wyatt went up to see her?"

"Shore did and she ain't cried since."

Rose pondered the thought but it worsened her headache to think about all that had transpired between her and Captain Wyatt last night. She still didn't know whether to believe he had fathered Matilda Jane's child. Heaven knew the infant's dark hair was as black as his.

She scolded herself for thinking such things and tried to stand.

"Oh, and Miz Rose I nearly done forgot in all this mess. Captain Wyatt said he coming back in one week at 2 o' the afternoon. He want to see you then. Said it was 'mportant."

"He's coming back?" She figured in her head. She must work very hard at getting rid of her headache and bringing some sense back into her overworked brain.

She was sure she and Captain Wyatt had much to discuss. Since he went up to Matilda Jane's room he may want to confess and make things right. She forced herself to remember he had just stepped off from his long journey and may have been a bit overwrought and not in his right mind either when he denied her accusations. She would prepare herself.

"Go on down and get your b'fast." Portia called to her and then went to tend to Matilda Jane.

"I will. I'm feeling better now after the tea. My head is not quite so dizzy either."

"See to yourself first and go on and rock that baby. Lily and Thomas going to be busy today. We got to be gettin' that pig butchered and hung up in the smoke house afore summer gets any hotter."

Chapter 45

Rose tried her best to prepare herself. She ate heartily the day after Captain Wyatt's visit and learned how to feed the infant, still unnamed, with a tiny wooden spoon Emmanuel had carved out of a small branch. She dipped the tiny spoon and touched the little lips that opened for milk. It was like watching a bird feeding her young. Rose learned how to pin a snug diaper, too and to pat the baby to sleep across her knees.

The time flew, there was so much care with the new little person in the house. Thankfully, there had been no callers.

Captain Wyatt made himself scarce around Charleston. He did not go to his regular hangouts, although he could have. Most of the high-class people he avoided never went to those sorts of places. He had recently taken a room in town from an elderly widow who rented rooms in her large house to shipmen usually, was an excellent cook and kept their places while they crossed the Atlantic back and forth.

Ashton made his way upstairs to his private room, glad to be safely across once more. At the previous crossing he had wondered if the Emerald Star or the Ireland Rose would make it into port, so bad the weather had been. Hurricane-like in it's vengeance out at sea. Mr. Paxton Quinn, the new Captain of the Ireland Rose, quickly decided he was not the man for the job. Ashton convinced him to go over one more time; the weather was so mild during the second crossing, thankfully the man decided to keep his position. Since he was the father of six children he needed the income and on the other hand, he had said, his wife and six children without a husband or father was worse.

Tossing his coat off and crashing onto the single bedstead on his back, he considered his options. He had only three days before he was going back across, with a small crew, carrying a special shipment of cotton. His men were almost finished hefting the cargo on board. The light load would make easy sailing and if the cotton was delivered to the London mills on time, he stood to make a bundle of cash. Perhaps then he could rent a large flat and spend the hot months in England instead of the States. He had come back to Charleston because of his sister. And that was the only reason.

Hands beneath his head, he kicked off his shoes and shut his eyes. It seemed he could not get away from the past and the demons that haunted him. And it had been years. Why had he let himself drink to oblivion. It nearly cost him his job with Captain Lovell. But the good man told him someone had given him a chance and he would do the same. That, if he controlled his drinking, he would appoint him Captain of the Emerald Star. Ashton knew, that Captain Lovell had gone one step further offering to pay him well if he would help build the Ireland Rose which would provide partial compensation to buy the Emerald Star outright.

He had done it and succeeded. The first time in his life he had put down the bottle. That and the fact that Captain Lovell knew he and Ava had come from the Newgate Orphanage and still he believed in him.

Even with this new life, every now and again, he did have a drink or two more than he should have, he had managed to stay clear of the taverns where his old friends would buy him drink after drink just to have the companionship.

Now he had choices. And he was up against a big one this time. He had to find a place for this child now that Miranda Jane had refused to raise it. He didn't blame her at all. But Mrs. Lovell could not take an infant without a husband. She would be shunned by society especially now that she had no husband to protect her interests.

The townswomen would be asking where the child came from. Did Mrs. Lovell have a lover and so soon after her good husband's death. There would be questions about the father. He knew they would be tut-tutting in their little gossip circles, ruining people's lives because they had nothing else to do.

If he were to ask Mrs. Lovell if she might keep it while he secretly supported the child, how would that look? Even worse. He'd ruin her. What could he do? A thought flashed through his mind. He could marry her and stop all the talk, saying the child came from the orphanage, which it did. He could see she loved the child else she would not have cried in his presence. Who would know it was a marriage of convenience. He had created the problem by taking Matilda Jane to her home in the first place. And she had done her duty and taken care of both mother and child in his absence.

He tossed that thought out with a groan. First of all Ireland Rose reminded him of his lost love, had since the day he laid eyes on her. Second, how would she fare with him staying in London and her and the child in Charleston. People would talk.

He sat up, threw his legs over the side of the bed and ran both hands through his hair. Then thought that if he was in London, she would be free to live her own life, under his protection in name only. And the child would have a home. Would she agree to that?

It seemed to make sense until he remembered the vow he made to himself never to marry. If he did marry it would be to keep that innocent child from going to Newgate.

All the problems would be solved, all the secrets exposed. Except one. Which would never pass his lips as long as he drew breath.

Tossing himself on his back again, he ditched the idea. No way could he be married to someone. He was too free and did not want to answer to a woman, least of all one as young, kind and sensitive as Mrs. Lovell. No. He would only hurt her.

Which brought him back to the original problem. What would he do with the child? He was a man and could not – would not toss his problem in Mrs. Lovell's lap. That was not the man he had become. And he had given Captain Lovell his word he would watch out for her.

He heard the dinner bell. Struggling, he sat up, put his shoes on and went down to the dining room that was abuzz with deep voices. Several shipmen must have just come in. He caught up on the news from all along the coast. Talk of pirates and troubled crossings and prices of goods took him away from his present difficulties.

Chapter 46

Ireland Rose leapt from her bed and dashed to the cradle in her room. She had slept all night, the babe had not woke once. She touched her to be sure she was breathing and sighed with relief.

Quick, she fit herself into an old dress. She'd learned that babies spit up their milk and stained her good gowns until Portia had to scrub them clean. In a moment she had changed a very wet diaper and tossed it in the water bucket, then put a fresh gown on the squirming body.

"What a lass you are. Look. Wide awake and not a tear in your eye. My but you are a happy little one. We must find a name for you." She cuddled the babe as she spoke. "Now down for breakfast. Surely you must be hungry as an ox."

With her burden in her arms, Rose stepped carefully and made her way down to the kitchen where Portia and Lily both had a turn at holding her while Rose dipped a bowl of milk and retrieved the miniature spoon. She dipped then filled the little hungry mouth.

"That be good, Miz Rose. Her stomach is no bigger than this..." she made a circle with her fingers hardly the size of a walnut.

"Really, it's that small. Do you think I've overfed her?" Rose looked to Portia.

"No. You's did it just right. We gonna get that pig cut up and hung in the smoke house today. Emmanuel got the butcherin' done already and we cain't waste 'dat good meat. Lily and Thomas be helpin' too. You think you can take care o'that little thing until we get done? Might take all day, chile."

"I can. We'll sit on the porch between her naps. The winds are favorable today. She'll enjoy rocking in the swing."

Portia paused and with a look...

"Do you think it unwise to take her outdoors? Is it too soon?" Rose worried.

"No...no...nothin' like dat. I just be thinking what'll people say if you got yoself a little baby out there like dat for all o'Charleston to see. That's what I be thinkin'."

"Oh." Rose said

"Aw, now don't let your heart sink down. I's don't mean no harm. Just thinkin', that's all."

"You're right, Portia. I didn't think of it. Rose carried the infant to the back gardens. "We'll sit out here in the shade, where no one can see us. At least for a time until the sun comes up over the house."

"Dat's a good idee." Portia said. "Mind we gonna be gone the whole day down at the butcherin' shop. What're you gonna do if you need us?"

"I have Matilda Jane here and she's getting around well now. If there is a difficulty I'll leave the baby with her and come for you. We'll be all right, though I'm sure of it."

"All right den."

Rose saw worry in the brown eyes. "Don't think a thing. You'll be back before we know it."

"You 'member Captain Wyatt comin' at 2:00 dis afternoon doncha?"

"Oh my, I had forgotten." Rose exclaimed and after a moment, "I'll just make sure she's ready for a nap and she'll sleep right through our visit. I'm sure Captain Wyatt means only to discuss business."

Portia gazed at Ireland Rose and knew that girl's heart had already become attached, *just like she her mama*. She whispered to her husband.

"Hmmm...mmmmm." Emmanuel agreed.

"Ain't nothin' can be done about it neither." She wagged her head. "Matilda Jane wants to be free and Miss Ireland Rose, she want 'dat baby. Lord have mercy."

Rose pulled out a small tub and gave the baby a bath. She watched Portia give her the first one...she was already a week old...and dressed her. While she was humming to her, she made it a point to think about asking the girls at Newgate to stitch some little bonnets and dresses to match, for when she grew a bit older. Light weight gowns made of Charleston-grown cotton were perfect. Rose dabbed the fresh lavender scented water over her after she was clean, wrapped her in a cloth and carried her upstairs to be dressed. She hadn't thought to bring down extra clothes.

"Would you like to see her Matilda Jane?" Rose called as she came down the hall.

"No, Miss Rose. I'm busy writing out my French lessons. Lily is going to take them to my teacher when she comes back this afternoon."

"All right then." Rose answered quickly and laid her bundle on the bed and changed her clothes. She couldn't fathom a mother not wanting to see her child. But it just gave her more time with the little lass. Humming as she worked, she watched the baby's eyelids become heavy. Perhaps a bath had done the same as it did for her -- made her sleepy. She laid her down and covered her lightly, turning the cradle away from the sunny windows.

Downstairs she flew like a flash and made sure there was enough milk for the day. Lily had left the little bowl in the ice box. Satisfied, she busied herself washing out the diapers and hanging them across a short line draped between two trees. They would need more square cotton cloths for diapers too. When she was finished, she ran to the desk and started a list of clothing and incidentals they would need. She saw the letter, half written to Captain Wyatt and groaned. It was in full sight. But she had no notion if he had seen it or not. She had rushed off to the office for a good cry. She wadded the paper up and tossed it aside.

First of all they needed a name. Rose began to make a list. Jane after her mother. Beatrice. Josephina. She must go up and ask Matilda Jane. She stood, lifted her skirts and dashed up, first stopping to see the babe still asleep.

"May I come in?" Rose asked at the door, seeing the young girl was busy at her desk writing her papers.

"Yes. My hand is quite tired, but I am learning so much."

"I see. French then?"

"Yes, I love the language." She spoke a sentence in French.

"How lovely it sounds coming off your tongue, Matilda Jane.

"Thank you Miss Rose. I can't wait to go back. My teacher promised I could take German if I learned French well enough. She said I was gifted."

"You are indeed." Rose agreed.

Matilda Jane stared at her for a few seconds and waited.

"I have come up to ask what you would like to name the lass. She must have a name."

"I don't care. She's not mine. You name her, Miss Rose. I don't mind at all."

And Matilda Jane went back to her writing with a smile.

"Are you sure? You are her mother."

"You are her mother. I will sign papers saying so." The girl spoke like an adult.

"It has only been seven days, we will wait until you are sure. Meantime I will choose a name if you give me leave."

"I give you leave. Now I really must finish. Lily will be taking my work to the teacher, if I am finished…" she hinted.

Rose stood and left the girl to her work.

Chapter 47

Rose processed Matilda Jane's decision to let her name the child and went back downstairs to her desk. She must choose a name. The perfect name. She scribbled several more ideas. Amanda, Hannah, perhaps Natasha...but nothing seemed right. The pen at her cheek, she mused.

"Carolina Jane." Rose burst out. Her place of birth and her mother's name. She would always know where she came from and who her mother was. That was it.

Carolina Jane she repeated.

The door knocker sounded. "Captain Wyatt." she whispered. "Oh dear."

There was nothing to do but answer, she smoothed her skirts and groaned as she quickly tucked loose strands of hair away from her face.

"Captain Wyatt. I am afraid I have not noticed the time. Please come in. I will go above stairs and make myself presentable."

She felt her already hot face warm even more when she noticed he was dressed, not in his normal attire, but a pair of tan breeches and a navy blazer. She also noted, his hair was shorter. Still tied in back but not as long. She backed away knowing her skirt must look awful, wrinkled and feared she may not have put on enough underskirts so that he may be able to, in the sunlight, see right through.

Captain Wyatt smiled as she backed away and dashed up the stairs without ever once looking back. He hung his new hat on the peg and wandered about. She had been writing again. Hands behind his back, he leaned over the desk. This time there were scribbled names. Female names and one circled. *Carolina Jane.* He said it out loud and liked the sound of it. So the lass was named, he guessed.

He took the bench seat there in the foyer and bowed his head, closed his eyes to think. After a minute he leaned forward elbows on his knees, eyes staring at the marbled tiles. Then stood and paced. The space seemed too small and there was little air circulation. He pulled at his collar, wishing he'd be through with it. He had papers to prepare. The ship was loaded and now needed only a small crew. He was anxious to get out on the waters.

Rose quickly changed as she peeked at the sleeping baby. "*Pray you stay asleep a little longer. We know when you are hungry you make very much noise.*" She whispered, smoothed her skirts and hoped her wayward curls did not look too mussed. Portia was not here to manage her unruly hair.

"Mrs. Lovell," he met her at the bottom of the stairs. "Shall we go into your husband's office?"

"If you wish..." *perhaps there were papers to sign.*

She walked in and her stomach did a flipflop. Her drawings and paint supplies lay about just where she'd left them.

"Oh dear, I'm afraid...."

"What are these?" He picked one up and held at arm's length, then turned so the light would show it better. "You use water colors?"

"Yes. But I'm afraid they are just juvenile works..." she tried to snatch the painting but he moved it out of reach.

"No, these are good. This is Mrs. Shevington's place, if I am not mistaken is it not?"

"It is." She tried to whisk them out of his hands but he held them away. "Come Captain Wyatt, I'm sure we have other business. We will use the living room. The sun is not on that side of the house." She hurried out and led him away to the front room.

He followed, but slowly she noted. "Here take this seat." She offered.

"Ladies first." He gestured with his hand and waited until she was seated and then sat.

"You have papers you wish signed?"

"Are you in a hurry today Mrs. Lovell. You seem a bit overwhelmed."

Sure he was remembering her behavior of last time when she ran to the office and shut him out, she lifted her chin and kept her shaky hands in her lap. "I am quite at ease sir. Please state your business."

The next instant he was on his feet. He could not think sitting down. "Mrs. Lovell, I have already informed you I am not the child's father."

"Her name is Carolina Jane. I have just gotten permission from Matilda Jane."

"I like it." He shoved his hands through his hair. "Now that is taken care of, we must decide what we will do with her. I have spoken to Matilda Jane and she wants to return to the orphanage. She has a teacher she admires. And if she learns French she may be able to travel to France a year hence."

"But how could she ever afford such a venture?" Rose stood. The man did not stay in one place and she could not abide carrying on a conversation without being able to read his eyes.

"I have seen to it." He said quickly and spoke again before she could interrupt him. "Mrs. Lovell, as I said we need to rectify this very unfortunate situation and I am at the present suggesting we marry and give the child a home so that she does not have to be returned to the orphanage."

Rose stared at his back, for again he had moved to the window. Did he say marry?

"Whatever made you think . . ."

"What?" He turned.

Dark eyes bore into hers as he said, "I am well aware I am not of equal caliber as your former husband, Mrs. Lovell. I, too, admired him. And I do not wish to compare myself to him. All I am saying is I would take the position of the child's father and your husband only to look out after the two of you. You cannot stay in Charleston and raise a child alone without being eaten alive by the locals."

"You are angry without cause, sir." She said quietly. "I did not mean to compare you to my husband. It would be unkind. "I only meant to say you do not have to sacrifice your life to save mine. Or Carolina Jane's."

"You misunderstand me Mrs. Lovell. It would not be a sacrifice..."

"Captain Wyatt I remember you expressed to me once you would never marry. And since the first time I met you, I sensed you do not like me."

"That is not true...you have no idea why I...I have not been kind." He rammed his hands through his hair dislocating the band until his dark hair fell loose around his collar. He stuffed the band in a pocket to give himself a moment. The woman deserved the truth. There had been enough falseness. He was tired to death of it.

He took the chair opposite her so he could face her. Elbows on his knees, he leaned forward, his hands intertwined. "Mrs. Lovell, I am afraid you resemble the woman I wanted to marry when a young boy. She lived here in this house. Every time I walk through the door I see her here. And..." he paused, then pushed out the words, "she resembles you in coloring, height, and slender stature."

He hung his head, his hair forming walls on each side, and waited for her response. At least it was out.

"So that was why you stared at me that first night. I thought you despised me and yet we had never met."

He shook his head and sat up straight so she could see his face. "I did not despise you. Your presence, your looks brought back memories I had thought I forgot."

"I see. That makes a great deal of sense. Should I have been in your circumstances, I would have felt the same." Rose said quietly, knowing she had never been in that position. How would she have known what it felt like. She had yet to love anyone. Or be loved by anyone. Rose saw him release his breath, a sense of relief coming from his dark eyes.

"Thank you. I was not in a position to discuss such personal matters." He stated.

"Of course, nor would I have wanted you to."

"But now you . . . I . . . and Carolina Jane are in dire circumstances. The child needs a father, you need the child..."

"And you Captain Wyatt, what do you need?"

Up he went.

Rose felt his pain.

He was unused to expressing himself so frankly...and in the tight space. Once a man loved the sea, he could hardly be expected to reside in a small room with no air or wind at his back.

He didn't answer for a very long time. Rose kept her seat and watched him pace in front of the two windows.

"I don't know what I want. All I know is that this problem must be resolved and soon. I have gotten you into this position. And I will do my duty."

"Your duty being?" She stood now and waited.

"I am offering to take you as my wife and Carolina Jane as my own daughter."

Ireland Rose waited a decent amount of time before she answered.

"Sir, your offer is noble. I am humbled by it. But it would not solve any problems, it would only create more. You have stated that I remind you of your first love. And I have determined I will not marry in name only again. I will marry for love."

Captain Wyatt turned and stared. "You mean you and Captain Lovell, were, were not …" he cleared his throat.

"We were not sir. Captain Lovell paid a debt and I gained protection."

Ashton Wyatt had hardly been a man without an answer, so used to ordering his shipmen around and handling problems, but in this moment, he could not think of a proper response.

The air hung thick around them.

"There you have it. And now you understand sir, that I cannot accept your offer."

What in the world was he supposed to say to that?

"I see." Was all he could think to say. His mind was reeling. He had thought it all out and it had landed right back in his lap. She had refused him. He should run out the door and be glad. Instead he walked to the peg in the foyer, took down his hat, turned it round and round and said, "Then I will be on my way. I will continue to look out for your affairs, Mrs. Lovell as I promised your husband. If you will allow me to see the child, I would appreciate that very much."

"Of course." She barely kept up with his long strides.

"You brought Matilda Jane to me and if you are the not the child's father, then you know best. I will take the child and raise her as my own. And you, sir, will be free to go on as you were."

He stood straighter, feeling dismissed.

"But I do request that papers be written so Carolina Jane will know who she is and where she comes from. But not yet. I must make sure Matilda Jane does not want to change her mind."

"I will see to it." He backed away, turned, donned his hat and let himself out.

He had just been refused after a proposal of marriage.

Rose heard the slam of the lightweight screen door and knew things between her and Captain Wyatt would never be the same again. They had stated their truths and set boundaries that could not be moved.

The sound of whimpering reached her ears and she lifted her dress and ran up to see to her little charge. Ireland Rose's heart leapt as she looked into the cradle at her *daughter*.

Chapter 48

Stunned, Captain Wyatt left the house and automatically headed down to the tavern. Without a thought, he walked in took a seat on the stool at the bar and ordered a whiskey. He threw back his head and slugged it down. As it burned its way down his throat he realized what he had done.

Before he could get to the door, two of his old drinking buddies stopped him with crude comments, about his "coming up" in the world and looking very much like *one o'the proper gentleman* they laughed at every evening.

Their words hung in his head as he took firm steps to retrace his way back to the ship. It was too early to go up to bed, the sun still high in the west. He would work off his frustrations on the Emerald Star.

Once aboard, the familiar sway and dip of the ship in the water slowed his body and mind. He went down to his bunk, changed into work clothes and joined the crew who was still moving crates to make room for more. The sale of the cotton would bring him a sizeable sum. The higher they stacked the crates the more money he'd make. Tonight he needed to work.

Thoughts went to Captain Lovell. How he'd promised the man he'd curb his drinking and he had done it, after so many years of throwing back the glass hoping it would soothe his wounds. But no matter how hard his arms and hands and legs worked, his mind would not shut off. Somehow he'd managed to spend the years sloshing the memories away with drink. But now he was too busy with his own ship and Captain Lovell's belief that he could manage his young wife's affairs as well.

Ashton wondered now if Captain Lovell had been daft. He had just failed himself. First for sending a young pregnant female to her then for proposing to the young woman so soon after her husband was gone. What had he been thinking? His mind whirled. But how could he assign the child to the orphanage. Newgate was run by decent people now. Back when he and Ava were there the man and woman had been harsh and no-nonsense.

His own family failed. First his father left the family and his mother left Scotland hoping to give her two children a chance to make it in the world. His father, he learned later, left his wife and children, for the love of a young girl.

His mother was a saint in his eyes. She had brought them across to Ameriva and begun her own milliner shop she ran out of their small house which was on the poorer side of town. And then tragedy. She had contracted some sickness, no one ever told them what, and died, leaving them with no place to go except Newgate. Ava had been twelve, he fifteen, nearly grown. They had made it through their grades, their mother had seen to that. But no further schooling came after she died. They were made to work. He learned he had a way with numbers and was trained and given a chance to make something of himself thanks to a kind older man at the bank. He had done well after the man spent an entire year tutoring him. By the time he was twenty he was a bank employee.

That was how he met Captain Lovell. They had taken up a conversation at the bank window. When the Captain found out his dream of becoming a shipmate and traveling the world, he offered him a job. How well he remembered the first time Captain Lovell had said the words, "Good job son."

"No one had ever called him son, least of all his father. From that day to this he never quit thanking God, the God his mother served, whom he believed in but didn't know very well. He had called out to God when he was in that orphanage after both his parents were gone and asked Him to keep him and his sister safe. But with every hardship that came along, he lost a bit of trust as time went by. Even now, with all the good that had happened, he still had trouble believing God to be anything more than a harsh taskmaster, pleased only with perfection.

He slammed down the box he was bearing and berated himself for his weakness. Why had he thought himself worthy to ask Mrs. Lovell to marry him was beyond him. What had he been thinking? How would he ever be good enough for a woman like that. A woman that reminded him of Darby.

Another box slammed to the floor, and another.

He worked off the steam and the liquor he promised himself he would never touch again and realized the sun had just disappeared behind the water's edge. Tired, he made his way over to his room and after a hearty meal at his own small table, fell into bed bone- and brain-tired. In two days' time he would be on the water and free from the demons that chased him like barking bloodhounds.

Chapter 49

It was time to go. He forced himself to visit Mrs. Lovell before he left. It was the right way to separate. Keep the foolishness he had created yesterday to a minimum if that were possible.

His hard knock brought Emmanuel to the door.

At the man's nod, Ashton walked in and waited. He kept his eyes away from that desk. He need not engage himself her personal affairs from now on. His job was to make certain the Ireland Rose made a profit, that all the finances were in order at the bank and that Mrs. Lovell's well-being was protected.

"Sir, it is a beautiful day to set out isn't it?" Ireland Rose greeted him as she came from her office, wanting him to feel assured of her friendship. "I daresay, you should have an excellent crossing."

"Indeed." His heart was not racing. The comfortableness between them was welcome on both sides, he figured.

"Shall I bring Carolina Jane down so you can see her?"

Ashton loved her happy voice and the serene smile that rested on her lips. He stared at them for a moment and turned away and then back again. "If you don't mind."

"Not at all, she has been freshly bathed and fed and is quite enjoyable this morning."

He watched her lively step as she climbed the stairs and came back down with the baby in her arms, looking like she herself was the child's mother.

"Ah," he took the child's hand and the tiny fingers tightened around his finger. He could feel Ireland Rose's breath on his cheek. She hardly noticed he was there, fully amused with the baby in her arms.

"Here hold her. She's become quite chubby now that she's learned to eat."

Before he could object the woman had gently handed the child over. He had never held one this little before and wondered at his foolish offer to raise it himself.

The little lass wiggled and her open eyes seemed to seek him as he spoke. She must have heard his deep voice, for her head turned slightly and her eyes crossed.

"Isn't she funny?" She drew close to wipe a dribble of milk that ran down the miniature chin and then put the handkerchief back in the sleeve of her wrist like she had done this her entire life. And the child not two weeks old.

When the baby fussed he quickly turned it back over to Mrs. Lovell. He must remember to keep everything between them on a business level. "If you need anything send a wire. If you wouldn't mind dropping a note every now and again to let me know all is well, I will not be concerned. Matilda Jane will return to the orphanage as soon as she is able."

"I will see that Matilda Jane has whatever she needs." She said gazing at the babe.

"If there is nothing else you wish to discuss, I will be on my way." He took his hat off the peg, anxious to be gone.

"I believe we will be fine, sir. I wish you an excellent crossing. As the Irish say, *may the wind be always at your back."*

"And yours." He made eye contact, kept his back straight, put on his hat, and exited.

He hoped all would be well because he did not intend to come back until September. Distance was what he needed and it would give him time to engage a flat in London so he could…escape the sultry Charleston summers. At least that's what he told himself.

Chapter 50

Rose returned to the work at hand. First a feeding, then a nap. The office had already been straightened and her paintings put away. She doubted she'd have much time to paint these days. And there would be meetings of the ladies regarding the design and furnishing of the new property. She wiped the moisture from her upper lip and wondered when she had ever been so happy. After all the loss and sadness, she found joy.

Baby was fed and put down for a nap and Rose flew below stairs to make a list and plan dinner with Portia when they heard the stairs creak. The both looked at each other and got up.

"Matilda Jane, you are looking well. And quite rested." Rose kept her voice low and her smile genuine. "It is good to see you up and about."

"Thank you. I'm sorry I've been so laxadaisical but I had no strength in my mind nor my body."

"Chile you done borne a chile out o' dat body. That was sumpthin. You tired, that's all. Doin' that schooling was good for ya, kept you in dat bed 'til yo body and your mind got better."

"Thank you Miss Portia And Miss Rose. You have been so kind to me. I will remember it forever."

Rose saw the quivering lips and wet eyes and went to her, arms enclosing the young girl, a woman now. "It's all right. You have grown up. And God has got work for you to do. Just you wait and see."

"God? Do you think He can do something with me . . . after . . . everything." She pulled back to see Rose's eyes.

"Of course He can. First of all you did not do anything wrong. Even if you did, people may not forgive. But God does, if you just ask Him."

"I already did." She said through tears.

"Then jus' believe Him chile." Portia's apron was serving double duty. "You ask and believe, it be so. And dat's dat."

Matilda Jane swiped her cheeks dry and nodded.

"Come on now you twos, time to eat and be strong." Portia turned and hustled to the kitchen.

~

July flew by and it was mid August. Rose checked her calendar...where had the time gone. Matilda Jane returned to the orphanage and working under the tutelage of her teacher, was already teaching basic French to children under her age. All the while learning it better herself.

There had been two meetings of the women's group and much progress had been made at the new location. Mrs. Pinckney had donated all the materials for curtains, and there were a lot of windows, as well as bedding for light coverings for each bed. Rose had written a bank check for her part, because she had little time to associate outside her home. No one asked her questions and she felt quite safe. She had told no one about the child.

She had seen little of Ava, her husband quite happy with his new promotion, had taken up most of her time making calls and singing his wife's praises. When Rose did see her walking at the park or passed her in a shop, Ava looked extremely satisfied. They exchanged secret smiles. Because she was always on her husband's arm, they had not spoken privately. It was even more important to Mr. McGuire to be seen publicly now that he had posted his name as a candidate for Mayor of Charleston.

Stella and Foster had announced they were expecting a child. Ireland Rose wanted so much to tell her about her own baby. But dare not. At least not now. More and more her thoughts were to leave Charleston, take Carolina Jane and go to Ireland where no one knew her or the circumstances of how she became a mother.

The baby, chubby and looking sweet in her new cotton dresses designed by Nettie and sewn by Nettie's girl students, Rose felt she had the life she always wanted. One thing she wanted for her daughter was a father. Her own father had been so important in her life. She wondered if going back to her home country would produce a worthy husband and father for her child.

Matilda Jane would be free to continue her education without worry. And Captain Wyatt would be free from the unwarranted desire to marry her for protection. Rose began to earnestly think about leaving Charleston, South Carolina.

Chapter 51

When the grandfather clock struck the sixth hour, Rose got up from her bed and peeked into the cradle. The little lass, dark head thrown back, was sleeping on her side, her face a perfect profile. The heart in her chest did a little dance. She was a mother. The one who was responsible for this life that lay there so peacefully. She reached out and touched the pink cheek, full and plump now. She closed her eyes said a prayer of thanksgiving and hope that she would be a good mother.

When she opened her eyes, she was being watched. The little fist came flying through the air and the tiny lips started to form a smile.

"Oh you're awake lassie. The angels must have fluttered by carrying my prayers, for here you are. Wide awake and a smile too." She cooed at her.

"Come on up, now." She lifted her into her arms. "We will be about our business. It is such a hot day and I have much to do." Rose blew strands of hair out of her face. She had learned quickly that holding and feeding an infant required two hands and other things had to be managed without the use of one or both hands. She also learned her spoon feeding was not fast enough and sped up the process.

Carolina and Lily had taken to each other. Lily, having grown up right before her eyes, was careful and took the child and played on a pallet with her in the cooler parts of the house. Kept her entertained while Rose washed out diapers, Portia grumping that washing the family clothes was her job.

"I want to do my part." Rose shooed Portia away. Go on and do another task, *two together will make light our work*." A quote from her mother.

"Miz Rose, I declare you been raised in a fine Baltimore home and marry a fine man and got yerself all 'cepted by Charleston ladies and here you is washing out 'dem baby's diapers. Ain't right. Just ain't right."

"Portia every mother cleans up and cares for her babies."

Rose saw the faraway look in Portia's eyes. And knew she had struck some sad chord. "Have I hurt you?" she stopped scrubbing on the wash board.

"No, honey, you didn't hurt me none. I was just thinkin' on how I used to wash Thomas' and Lily's mama's clothes out. And now she gone out in dis world and me not knowin' where."

Rose continued working, then when Portia shook the thoughts away and began to work, said, "I'm sorry Portia."

"You's ain't got nothin' to be sorry for. Just now the Lord done let me know my girl, she okay. I cain't be sittin' round worrying. That's sin. It is. Just plain sin. God cain't take care o'you then ain't no use in livin."

Rose smiled and hung her diapers on the line and hoped they would dry in time. She was out of them again. "What is the date today? I declare days fly by. Know I'm supposed to meet with the ladies the last Friday of the month."

"It be the 26h and a hot month for August. Soon enough we'll be feeling the breezes and leaves fallen off dem trees over yonder. And all the folks be coming back from Newport, too. Streets'll be busy and school kids be runnin' up and down the alleys, playing. Too hot now." She wiped her brow.

"Oh the meeting is tomorrow at noon. I must get my thoughts ready."

Lily came carrying the baby on her arm.

"Go on, Lily watch the baby. You best get your thinkin' done afore that sun come beatin' down on dis house." Portia shooed her.

"Thank you. Please make a pallet in the dining room, Lily. She loves it in there."

"Yes Miz rose." Lily beamed.

Pushing aside the drawings she had recently done of Carolina, she pulled out a folder and began reading. She was to contact the police and fire department officers and ask for donations. They had seen a lot of the troubles the citizens living in the poor districts and knew first-hand the issues they faced. Charleston had one of the largest police and fire forces along the Eastern coastal cities. And the Citidel.

She had only to come by, for the men had taken up a collection. They had received her note of request and glad to know the old Jamison Orphanage would be torn down because it had been a fire hazard and they had already lost too many buildings to fire. They had happily offered to assist them to move out into the new facility.

Tomorrow was the meeting.

The next day Rose hurried above stairs taking Portia with her. "What shall I wear? I won't be long, but I want to represent the ladies guild well." She mused looking at dresses in her closet.

"Here Miz Rose, wear 'dis one. It be soft yellow and happy looking. 'Sides all those men down there gonna be looking at you in this pretty dress and maybe empty out them pockets a bit more." She chuckled.

Rose laughed.

It took a full twenty minutes for Portia to do her hair. Those red-blond ringlets were stubborn in the heat today. "That look nice now." Portia picked and patted, her head bent at an angle. "Get that little yellow parasol and you be the sunshine in dat office down der."

Rose didn't want any more fuss and made her way out of the house, down her wide stairs, and holding the parasol against the sun took the walkway to the station four blocks away and made her entrance.

Immediately she noted the men's eyes light up. *Was it the yellow dress*? That was strange. They tipped their hats each one and invited her to sit, even offering her a glass of lemonade to refresh herself.

Each one was so accommodating that by the time she was ready to leave she found herself surrounded and could barely make her way to the door. Finally, she was out, on her way home, with a very generous check.

When she arrived home she went inside, bent her ear. No baby sounds, and went upstairs to redress in her lightest cotton dress. "It was the strangest thing, Portia. The men were . . . so accommodating. It seemed they had nothing to do but stand around and talk." She mused. "What do you think that was about? I've been in there before, but never noticed such behavior."

"You's don't know?" Portia was belly-laughing.

"No" Rose straightened her back. "What is so funny?"

"Chile you be a widow. A young, perty one. Dem young men be looking at you for to see if you'd be ready to take callers now that your husband be gone. And you know de know you a rich woman."

"Oh for goodness' sake. It never occurred to me."

"You not like 'at."

"Well, just think what they would all say if they knew I had a baby!"

Portia finished buttoning the back of her dress and went off laughing.

Rose found herself laughing, too, as she put the check in the desk drawer for safe-carrying to the meeting tomorrow.

The rest of the day passed so quickly, Rose could barely believe she'd slept all night and was getting dressed to go to the Ladies Meeting. Was that normal? Time flying by just because a tiny lass came to live in the house?

How did mothers do this with 4 and 5 children?

Chapter 52

The Ladies Meeting went exactly as planned yesterday. Rose came home with a long list of ideas and began to paint again. Stella had told them about her sketches and water colors before she could quiet her.

Mrs. Shevington suggested she bring several to the next meeting so they might, if she agreed of course, auction them off at their first public auction. They would need every hand-designed item to sell.

Rose agreed, but only if the ladies thought they were worth selling. Today she sketched Lily holding Carolina Jane. And one of Emmanuel and Ready with the buggy. Once those were finished she put away her pencils and finished hemming two new little dresses. She had missed several church services, unwilling to leave little Carolina Jane at home. But she had promised to read an announcement at church about the upcoming auction so was arranging for a cool bath and the laying out of her clothing.

Once finished Portia had come up and was combing the tangles from her hair when they heard someone at the door. Carolina Jane was already asleep. Lily came bouncing up the stairs. Papa Emmanuel said 'dis come for you." She handed Rose a telegram.

Rose eyed it, then quickly tore it open. Who could it be? Her eyes fell on the first line.

"It's from Captain Wyatt." She said. "He's never sent a telegram before. He's always written. What could be the matter?" She wondered aloud, then read.

"It ain't bad news is it?" Portia's eyes grew large.

"No." Rose stopped and read again. "It seems Captain Wyatt has informed me that he will be spending the winter months in London, and should I need any assistance I am to send a telegram."

"He ain't coming back 'til next year?"

"That's what he is saying. Says further that he has attained a flat."

"Well, I'll be. Captain Wyatt done got hisself a place in London. Don't dat beat all."

Rose set the paper aside and thought about his last visit, how nicely he dressed and his new hat. Perhaps that load of cotton he took over did bring him enough funding to make himself comfortable. Well, she decided that was good, then. Her one dread was that she did not want to deal with Mr. Dalton. She still remembered that strange comment he made about getting *his* house back again. This house.

He was an odd man, but she had other things to worry about and set the telegram aside.

Sunday Church was the best thing that she'd done all week. Emmanuel had driven her alone just like he always did and she was glad to see two new ladies raise their hand to consider helping Jamison Orphanage make their new move.

The ride home was hot and dreadful. She came in and up the stairs in a flash to find her daughter awake and in her cradle. She bent over and before she could get her Sunday bonnet off, the child had tangled her hands in the ribbons. Rose laughed out loud.

By Tuesday morning it was so hot, Rose told Portia to shut both doors against the heat. She had absolutely no motivation. Thank goodness tomorrow was the first day of September. At least in a month or so the air would begin to lose the sultry wetness that now lay upon them like a rain-soaked blanket. Tonight she was thankful her bedroom was at the back of the house overlooking the gardens. The front of the house was too bright from the sun reflecting on the water in the morning hours.

Rose slipped into a cotton gown and tied her hair up so it didn't hang on her neck and climbed into bed early.

Suddenly Rose found herself not in a dream but falling from her bed. The floor was shaking beneath her. And the noise! Was it a hurricane or were they cannonballs? Her mind would not work. Were they at war again?

She heard screams that were not her own. The baby! She crawled on hands and knees her stomach roiling and saw the cradle pitching back and forth violently. There were explosions of light outside her windows. She could see in the dark. When the cradle swung her way she held on and turned it on it's side and felt ceiling plaster raining down on her as she grabbed the child with both hands and covered her with her own body. The fearsome screams were muffled beneath her breast. She held herself away slightly to keep from smothering her.

There were bricks falling outside, she could hear the clicking together over and over again as they slammed against each other. What evil was upon her and why didn't the noise stop?

Rose wondered if the house were going to topple down on top of them. Dust and plaster kept falling across her back. She grabbed the counterpane and threw it over her head. As suddenly as it began the infernal shaking stopped. Afraid to move, lest the roof caved in, she waited. They were tented in the blanket, so she lifted herself away and heard only whimpering.

"There there..it's over now." She heard her own voice, then others calling from below. There were screams outside. Fire exploded again and again outside her windows. It was the dead of night. Had the world ended? What could be the matter. People were yelling. It wasn't just her own house…something dreadful had happened to the entire city.

"Miz Rose. Miz Rose." She heard someone calling her name. So this was not a dream, then?

It was Thomas. "I'm here. I'm here." She yelled back.

"Are you safe?"

"Yes I am safe."

"And the child?"

"Yes, we are both safe."

"Don't move. Stay there. They's cracks in the walls. I be coming up the steps slow-like, Miz Rose. You stay right there you hear?"

"I hear Thomas."

Now that the shaking had stopped she lifted the blanket off and dust flew and clumps of ceiling lay all over the floor. The noise outside increased as people came out of their homes yelling for family members, crying, some screaming for help.

Rose rolled away from the baby careful to protect her eyes from the dust. And what she saw nearly ripped her heart out. She was smiling!

Suddenly, her heart gave way. She began to sob. The little thing was safe and looking at her as though she were a hero. Rose gathered her to her breast and cried all the harder.

"Miz Rose, you hurt?" Thomas yelled up.

"No Thomas, just happy." She yelled quickly. "We're fine. We're fine."

"Thanks be to God." Rose heard him say.

"Indeed." She agreed and took another look at her child to be sure she wasn't dreaming again. The noises outside increased. It sounded like the whole town was gathering in White Point Gardens. What disaster had befell them?

"Almost there Miz Rose."

"Don't hurry Thomas."

Each time another explosion occurred outside it lit the inside of the dark house. The gas lights along the street were dark. There must have been a hurricane. It was the season for it. She spit white dust out of her mouth and took in a short, shaky breath.

She heard Thomas making his way down the hall. And then heard Portia's voice below.

"You be up der yet Thomas?"

"I'm up Granmama. She safe. Dey both safe."

"Thank you Jesus." Rose thought she heard Portia say.

"Thank you Jesus." Thomas repeated.

Rose agreed.

"What happened?" She asked Thomas, never so glad to see someone.

"Earthquake. Bad one. Done shook the bricks right off'n the house. We nearly got caught, too." He said quickly assessing the situation as best he could in the dark.

"Come on now, we gonna get you down before dis house cracks down on us all. Best we get outside and over to the park. Dat's where everybody's goin'. I hear them out there. And if it is a quake we gonna get some more shakin'. Here, give me the baby, whilst you stand up."

She tried to stand, but her legs were so weak from fear, she had to grab the foot of the bed and pull herself up.

"You take the baby and hold onto my shoulder. I'll go ahead and take each step. Feel along the wall and don't let go the wall. Another quake starts, get away from de walls okay?"

"Yes." Rose said. "Hurry, Thomas..."

"Yep, we going down now...mind you watch the steps and put one foot down first before you trust the step...each one now."

Rose followed his every instruction and when her toes touched the marble floor, she gave a sigh. About that time the earth began to shake beneath their feet. "Here get in the doorway." He shoved her from behind and stood next to her. Carolina Jane began to whimper again. Rose murmured comfort to the baby and prayed.

"Der dat one not last as long as the other. But it was bad."

Another explosion from down the street lit up the scene. Bricks from the house were strewn across the porch which listed to the right, it having come off it's foundation like a ship sinking in the water. Telegraph poles lay tangled among the still sparking wires and shouts of fear and anguish filled the darkness.

"Oh Thomas." Rose closed her eyes tight and wished when she opened them the scene would be gone. "We are undone."

"Bricks fall Miz Rose, but we can put 'em back up again. I feared that people done died in their beds." He said quietly.

Rose couldn't speak a word.

When the shaking stopped and the dust settled again, she heard Portia and Emmanuel as they made their way through the dining room. Glass was crushed everywhere. Rose hadn't even noticed. She was barefoot.

"You okay?" Portia's voice was nearby.

Rose reached out with one hand. "Yes. Are you and Emmanuel and Lily all right?"

"We fine. Our little carriage house in the back be fine. Thinking the big house done got the worse of it."

"Thank God we'll all accounted for."

"Amen. Amen. Thank you Jesus." Portia said over and over. "I done heared dat baby cry and cried myself."

Rose's knees began to shake when she realized how they could have all been dead right this minute and tossed the thought out of her head. They were still here, talking, breathing, alive. That was enough for now.

"We all headin' for the park." Emmanuel said. "Grab anything you can for the baby there and I'll bring some blankets and pillows and something to make a tent. We can't go back in the house till morning. We gonna get more shakin' afore the night's done."

Portia called over her shoulder she was going to get the diapers off the line and the milk for the child. "You go on over." She called.

Rose needed shoes and gave the baby to Lily and went to the closet beneath the stairs and tried to open the small door.

Thomas came and jerked the door open and stood back, letting the dust settle. "Best we wait, make sure dem steps don't come down."

He leaned in and felt around until he found two shoes to match and took her elbow and hustled her out to the porch. There was a small space where they could stand. She got her shoes on and took the baby, afraid to let her out of her arms.

Thomas cleared a path for them throwing bricks as he went. The sound of the clicking bricks reminded her of the noise that woke her up. She flinched each time one hit another.

The Oleander bushes out front were crushed and the beautiful white flowers, poisonous as they were beautiful, lay beneath tree branches from the live Oak nearby. She didn't want to see the damage to the beautiful tree. And she did not turn around to look at the house.

Portia soon joined them with a tablecloth filled with items they might need. "We get some wood and build a fire over yonder and make do."

Thomas led the way. People were tripping over large and small debris that had been shaken loose. Lily had not uttered a single word. Rose could see she was in shock. They walked together and found neighbors with the same looks on their faces. Some folks were coming down the brick-laden streets stepping over poles, holding bedding. Some were sobbing, others were yelling instructions to family members, hoping to keep the living alive.

Then there were other sounds. There were fathers holding onto grief-stricken mothers who'd lost their children and would *not* leave them in the houses alone in the dark. Rose cringed. Darkness and death and dread filled the air.

Some already had gas lamps lit and were helping others. Portia laid out a huge blanket on the ground, then Emmanuel came with sticks and poles cut off the trees with his knife to make tent-posts.

"Come on inside here, Portia ordered Lily. Rose followed. Pillows were tossed around and they all found a place to lay their heads. Portia insisted on holding the baby and feeding her. "You go lay down now. You take care of her tomorrow. I'll hold onto her tonight so's you can rest."

Rose watched her wrap up the little girl, just three months old and hold her to her large breast. She was within arm's reach and Rose shut her eyes, which were dry from the dust, but soon were watered by thankful tears. She turned her face away and hoped she could sleep.

Chapter 53

Rose hardly slept, but kept her eyes closed and her lips praying. Voices of death were all around. Some crying out for lost children, others having recently received news their loved one had died in their bed. She never slept and before dawn most were up and moving about the makeshift campsite. Portia was already at the fire with the baby in her arms, Lily gathering sticks that were plentiful. Thomas was off helping other families and Emmanuel fed and watered the horses and went inside the house to assess the damages.

"The front of the house was hardest hit. The winds off the water and the earth shaken below made big cracks in the roadways. Watch yer step. Stay 'way from the house, too. Days and days they'll be aftershocks. We done been in one before."

Rose, wide-eyed, listened to each comment.

"You's need anythin' you let me go back into dat house." Emmanuel warned.

Portia came with a cup of tea. It was sweet and Rose gulped it down. Then toast appeared and she chewed and swallowed, knowing she would need the sustenance for the long day ahead after a near sleepless night.

Rose fed the infant with her little spoon and handed her to Lily who seemed to need something to hold onto, while she tidied up. Soon everyone was wandering about wondering what to do. The looks on their faces mirrored what she herself felt. Shock. Unbelief. And fear.

She soon learned, through talk of the ladies, that Patrice and her daughter Colleen had perished in their beds. The husband and father was found wandering the streets. The Irish captain was without his wife and daughter so soon after they had come to this new land. Tears boiled over as Rose thought of the little blue-eyed lass and her mother's worry she had lost her child. Now the two of them were together. In another place. She couldn't stop crying so went to the tent and let the tears flow, her face buried in a pillow.

News kept coming in and each time Rose wanted to put her hands over her ears and stop the world from spinning. No word yet about her friends, Ava and Stella. They lived on the other side of town, but couriers coming back said hardly a building stood without some sort of damage. Bricks lay cast down in piles, porches and verandahs were most badly damaged. It was reported that hardly a chimney was still standing in the whole of Charleston.

Two days passed, the wagons with wooden boxes rattled by. Rose was glad she didn't have to watch the parade of death march by her house. But the park became eerily silent everytime a wagon passed two streets over, the metal wheels clunking over each cobblestone. God seemed so far away she wondered if the inhabitants of their beloved city would recover. It would take months maybe years.

Their family group was getting into a routine. Water was easily had from the Cooper and Ashley Rivers. Lily spent a great deal of time, her eyes lifeless as she made trip after trip to the river, looking at her feet most of the time. Thomas had found himself digging holes in the ground wary of sinkholes to bury the dead. He came back each evening for three solid days, ate and slept. Finally the fourth day they were finished. There were 60 people dead and many more laying in Roper Hospital. That building had been shored up first to care of the injured.

Between meals Portia took Lily and they went to help others any way they could. Rose stayed with Carolina Jane, feeling each time she held her and fed her, that she was one of the blessed ones who still had her child. On the seventh day after the earthquake Rose looked up and saw Stella and Foster coming her way. She was so full of joy she ran to them and threw her arms around both at the same time. The funniest thought shot through her head.

Charleston ladies did not allow themselves such silliness, shaking of hands, hugging or showing any sort of affection in public. Now it didn't matter a bit. Everyone was on the same level, living in tents and makeshift houses. News came from Foster that the bank's vault was safe and people were beginning to draw out monies to buy or trade for food at the markets that were still cleaning up debris, actually using the debris to built lean-to's against the weather.

People, if nothing else, were clever. They used whatever they had to find a way to keep themselves together and help those who had needs.

Rose laughed as Stella and Foster looked around their new living quarters. "Smart tent you have there." Foster smiled.

"Yes, Emmanuel was very creative. It seems he lived though an earthquake before. We have our own closet that doubles as our clothesline." Rose pointed. He wrapped a good long line of rope around two trees and brought hangers so it looked like someone's closet.

"Very inventive." Foster agreed.

Rose noted Stella was not saying too much. She was halfway through her pregnancy and looked tired. "Sit down, Stella. Tell me. How did your house fare?"

She noted her friend was unusually quiet until they got off together. Rose spread a quilt and while Foster went for a bucket of water for them, the ladies talked. Rose didn't know how to ask, but decided with all that had happened, it was best to come right out.

"Is the babe all right?" She leaned close and caught Stella's eyes.

"I don't know."

"Can you find Doctor Case?" Rose was afraid to ask if he were still alive.

"No, there are too many other people he needs to take care of. But I have been so tired and I can't think straight. Our house is one of the least injured in the quake, but I am afraid to go back inside."

"As you see, we haven't gone back in either. Any day now, but I'm in no hurry." Rose admitted. "We've done just fine and thank the Lord it hasn't stormed or rained once. But Emmanuel and Portia said it's almost time for a good rain. There will be little shocks, but hopefully none as large as the first few days."

Stella actually looked relieved.

"Tea?" Rose stood and motioned for Stella to remain seated. "I'll be back in a moment." She hurried to the fire and poured two teas and put two strainers in the cup and two blocks of sugar, thankful for the sweetness and energy it would give them.

Stella wrapped her hands around the cup and sipped, a look of hope in her eyes. "Drink up now. Tell me is your chimney gone?"

"Yes, in a pile outside the house. We have broken windows and a bit of damage on the second floor verandah, it will have to be removed, and much loss of trees, but we have been blessed. Other houses on the block suffered much more damage than ours."

"You are blessed." Rose agreed, finding a smile on Stella's face when she looked up.

"What?"

Rose noticed her hand covered her belly. "I felt movement. The child is all right." She laughed then tears came right behind.

"Ah, Stella," Rose set her cup down and scooted close so she could embrace her friend.

"I thought…I thought that because we were so blessed with our house and so many…so many…"

"So many died that you didn't deserve to have your house and your baby?" Rose finished.

Stella sobbed into her hands. "Yes."

"God is God Stella. There is nothing else we need to know." She soothed her friend, tears falling off her chin because she, too, had her little baby.

Chapter 54

Ten days after the quake the people were slowly moving back into their homes. The men had traveled in groups, going to the houses that had young children or the elderly and cobbling up windows and doors so people could move in and begin their inside work. There were meetings in St. Michaels. That church had lost its beautiful spire. It lay crashed on the ground nearby. There were several cracks visible on the outside walls in Charleston's oldest church.

The glassmakers and bricklayers were so busy they could hardly keep up. No ships had left the harbor, most having been tossed about like paper cut-outs with mere sheets for sails. Food supplies were low. Fishermen rowed boats out to fish.

Crews went about the streets clearing debris so wagons could be loaded and brought down the street. Another crew worked day and night to set up telegraph poles so the townspeople could be in touch with the outside world. Word was that the quake was felt as far north as New York. But no city was damaged more than Charleston and nearby Summerville which had the worst of it including open ground craters and sinkholes. Few houses were sitting square on their foundations in that small town.

Slowly families removed their tents from in front of their houses and the bravest moved inside without trepidation. Others worked inside and slept outside.

Rose's family was back in their house. Thomas was quiet and somber, Rose knew from all he'd seen when he helped pick up and bury those who had died. Lily was quiet and reserved as well.

"It shore be good to be back in 'dis house. Thank you Lord." Portia declared one late September afternoon.

"It is." Rose declared, picking up Carolina Jane and rocking her. And look how much she's grown even since then."

Suddenly a hush fell over the house. The chandelier in the foyer began swaying, slightly at first then the glass crystals started clinking. Portia knocked them all from their reverie when she shouted for everyone to get out of the house. Rose picked up the baby and flew out the front door and down the makeshift stairs Emmanuel had rebuilt.

Once all six of them were accounted for, Rose relaxed and stood out near the roadway. Then when she thought it had passed she heard a deafening crash. Glass shattering on marble…the chandelier.

Then the oddest thing. Bricks began falling from above. The parapet began a slow tumble. Everyone rushed further away just before it crashed as the noise split the air like a bolt of lightning. They just stared at it.

"Wait." Emmanuel held his arm out, keeping anyone from going closer. "It ain't done. Look up there." He pointed.

Shingles from another part of the house began raining down and Rose saw a horrific hole in the roof on one side of the house as it collapsed inward where the parapet had been.

Once the noise stopped, no one spoke. Rose knew it was bad. Thankfully none of them had been inside. Others had suffered the same malady. Anytime there was another shake, someone's already weak structure was weakened further.

Her heart stilled and in a single moment, she knew she could not stay. It would not be safe for any of them. Several people rushed over after they heard the noise, each one warning them not to go back in tonight. There might be more shocks.

Several men gathered to look over the new damage, among them Mr. Riley, the Captain from Ireland. He stood at the back alone and watched, hands in his pockets, a look of grief on his sunburnt face, his dark beard heavy on his face. Rose hurt for him.

With the baby still in her arms, she made her way over to him as he stood alone under the live Oak, what was left of it and stayed nearby. When he seemed to notice her, she spoke to him in a bit of Gaelic and when he turned his eyes toward her, she thought he was going to cry.

"I'm very sorry. Have I pained you?" she inquired, wishing she could pull the words back into her mouth. "I only meant…" What did she mean? She had no idea…and snapped her lips together.

"A lass from Ireland then?"

His voice possessed a tender timbre.

"Born to parents from Ireland. County Clare. I was born in Baltimore."

"Ah. I see. County Galway here."

Rose moved a bit closer and didn't know what to say. She had planned to tell him that she met Patrice and little Colleen. But how could she now?

"Sweet little lass ya have there." He gazed at the child.

Oh no, the infant reminded him of his daughter.

"I had a lass."

His voice was so sad. She saw his Adam's apple climb up and back down again.

"Yes, I know."

"You know?"

"Yes, I met your wife and little Colleen."

She saw him suppress tears and then smile. "Bonny lasses."

"Indeed." Rose agreed.

"Then ya met my girls? I'm glad to know it. My wife told me she met a young Irish woman straight off the ship. Seems my little….little one…scooted away from her muther and found you."

"Yes, she found me." Rose's voice quavered.

"Then it be glad I am that it was so. That very first day."

"I am glad, too." She wiped away tears and felt her child wiggle.

"Well, then."

Rose watched him straighten up and with a quick move, he removed an old hat, smoothed his hair back and said, "What needs to be done?"

"We have a hole in the roof, it seems."

"Tis hours until dark. We can get a cover over it, if it isn't too large."

He joined the other men and Rose saw he was back with the living. She shook her head wondering at the power of men to suffer great pain and yet stay on their feet and fight for those who are left. She admired Captain Riley and reminded herself, she must do the same.

"Come on little lass. Time for your dinner."

Chapter 55

Within a week's time Rose had tickets to Ireland. The men she trusted in the community said it would take weeks if not months to repair the damage at the top of the house. Captain Riley had hired a crew to repair his ship and was headed back with a load of specialty hand-crafted furniture that the owner had in a storage building. The man had already lost some of his best pieces and since it would take weeks to repair the structure, he decided to send his most expensive pieces to England on the first ship out of the harbor. He was a well-known furniture maker and the sales would help raise money to rebuild.

Captain Riley made the offer to carry it over and was set to sail as soon as his ship was seaworthy. Rain threatened and his crewmen loaded the last piece before the first drop touched a single one. Plus he had an immense order for special furniture coming out of London's best shops to carry back for Charleston's wealthy citizens who had lost everything.

Rose headed to the bank to visit Mr. Dalton. They had set up the tent again but rain was coming their way and Stella insisted she bring the baby and stay at her home. She didn't want to leave Portia and Emmanuel but they had sent Lily along to help and insisted they would do much better knowing she and the child were in a safe house.

As it turned out, Rose, Lily and Carolina Jane got the last room in the Perry's home. Foster and Stella had taken in children whose parents had died or were in the hospital. It was a lively house and Rose was glad to be with her friend, who now had a purpose to fulfill.

When Captain Riley had found out she had moved from her house, he came knocking at the Perry's and offered to take her to Ireland when he heard she may be wishing to go back to her family. Rose accepted immediately.

Today she was going to put Emmanuel and Portia and Thomas' name on a portion of her bank monies so Emmanuel could hire help to repair the house. He learned bricklaying as a young man and planned to teach the trade to Thomas. This would be the opportunity. The four of them rode in a buggy together, leaving the baby with Stella.

She never felt more sure of anything in her life. Captain Wyatt was not here and she knew he would not hear of their circumstances for weeks. She would face the banker herself and hopefully never set eyes on him again.

"Sir, Emmanuel wishes to open an account with you."

"Mrs. Lovell, as you know you must have a considerable sum before you can open an account."

"I don't wish to open an account. Mr. Smith does." She turned to Emmanuel.

"As I said…"

"How much is required, Mr. Dalton?" Rose interrupted.

"Five thousand dollars."

Rose's eyes narrowed, but she kept her peace.

"Then I wish to withdraw ten thousand dollars in cash."

"Why of course." He bowed slightly and made his way to the vault and came back with a large envelope.

She turned, dug into the envelope and handed Emmanuel five thousand dollars. She heard Portia gasp behind her. Thomas' eyes were large.

"Now sir, Mr. Smith has five thousand dollars."

"Mrs. Lovell, I'm afraid you'll have to come back tomorrow. I must make sure who I am signing on as a patron of this bank. You understand I'm sure. It seems I remember you had to read the entire content of the last contract before *you* signed."

He was reminding her of the time she asked him to come back for her signature. Again she schooled her features.

"Of course, Mr. Dalton. But I assure you, if that account is not open tomorrow, I shall withdraw all – all of my money from your bank, sir."

Rose turned her back and the four of them walked out.

When they were safe in the buggy, Portia started whispering. "Miz Rose, you shouldn't of done that. Dat man evil. He repay evil for evil."

"Portia, Mr. Dalton will have it ready."

"How you know that chile?"

"Captain Lovell's entire fortune is in that bank. Mr. Dalton cannot afford to lose money. Especially in light of the fact he will make much more when people come to borrow for their homes. Believe me, he will open that account."

Portia shook her head and chuckled. "You may be a slight little thing, but onct you set yo Irish mind on somethin' you ain't gonna change yer mind, dat's for shore."

"My father taught me the basics of fairness and to know there is a time for kindness and there is a time for firmness; it is time for the latter."

They stopped in front of the Perry house. Emmanuel got down to help her and said, "Thank ya, Miz Rose."

"Emmanuel, you are going to have that bank account and any money you need for the house repairs because it is going to belong to you and your family. I intend to make my way in Ireland."

He stared, she knew, believing she had lost her mind like some of the people had done during their recent hardships.

"Miz Rose, we cain't…you cain't…."

"I'll not hear another word. And…tomorrow, we'll have money for repairs. You may want to make a list of supplies and men you wish to hire, Emmanuel. I hear bricklayers and builders are coming in from all parts of the country to work."

"Yes ma'am."

She heard the joy in his voice and saw the tear in his eye. "Go on now." She said. "Tomorrow is going to be a busy day. Oh…and mind you and Portia can make whatever revisions to the house that you see fit. I do know Portia loves blue…." She waved and they were off.

Running up the stairs, her steps light as air, her heart singing, she burst into the house and called for Stella.

Her friend came running. "What is it. Another quake?"

"Oh dear no. Nothing like that. I've made a decision Stella. I'm going back to Ireland on Captain Riley's ship. He leaves in exactly sixteen days!"

Stella embraced her, happy at first, then in tears. "Oh my, I've never cried so much in my entire life." She wiped tears off her cheek as they stood arm in arm. "You are going back home to your beloved Ireland."

"I never thought Ireland my home, but it is what I'm made of. Irish to be sure." She said as she realized for the first time, she truly was going home to family. "Let's eat before my daughter wakes up. I'm famished." She announced.

Stella followed, her hand across her growing belly. Rose hoped one day she would be as big as Stella was right now, with her second child.

She never felt more sure of anything in her life.

Chapter 56

The next morning Rose chose her finest dress. A rose colored satin with crème lace, matching bonnet and parasol. Today was going to be special. Emmanuel, Portia, Thomas and Lily would have their bank accounts.

When they entered the bank, through a side door, since the front entrance was still unsafe, she saw Mr. Dalton in his office. His secretary announced their visit and they were shown to a large room with a long table. Each took their seats.

"We look all right, Miz Rose?" Portia pulled at her sleeves nervously, stuffing her handkerchief in and out of her sleeve at her wrist.

"Very fine." She said and set her parasol aside. "It's an incredibly sultry day." She fanned herself with a cardboard fan left on the table for such times.

Mr. Dalton walked in, looking like, Rose thought, that he'd not had a wink of sleep. She doubted he did. For he was in a quandary. Either he opened an account or she would ask for her husband's entire fortune to be withdrawn via a bank check. She had only learned the true amount when she asked for it yesterday and could easily have fainted dead away. She had somehow managed to hide the surprise on her face. The first time she was ever strong enough to act unconcerned as though she knew the figure all along.

"Mrs. Lovell." He grumped ignoring her friends.

"Sir." She held her head high, her shoulders back, as her mother always said to do. "Have we papers to sign?"

He shoved papers her way with a false smile. The same one he used on her as a young woman months ago when he came for the signatures.

Rose studied them an overlong time. She could see he was pulling at his sleeves and nervous as a cat. The figures were correct right down to the penny. She passed the papers concerning the new account to Emmanuel.

"Mr. Smith, I believe your signature is required here."

She gave Mr. Dalton the envelope with the other five thousand dollars in it and said, "I wish to invest in Mr. Smith immediately."

"All of this is to go in *his* account?"

She heard the ugliness in his voice and gave him a look. "It is."

"Is ten thousand enough to repair the house Emmanuel?" she asked politely. For if you need more . . ."

"I believe it is, Miz Rose."

"Then once you have agreed and affixed your signature, I believe we are through here."

"Yes ma'am. Emmanuel signed his name in perfect penmanship."

Rose felt proud to know him.

"Oh Mr. Dalton, since I have invested the full amount of my withdrawl, I shall be needing a bank check for an additional thirty thousand immediately."

"What? Thirty thousand more?"

"Yes, sir. Thirty thousand."

He got up and huffed out. Rose expected him to tarry long, but he was back in five minutes with a check. He wanted them out of there.

When all papers were duly signed, Rose stood.

"Mr. Dalton, thank you." She turned to leave and remembered something.

"Oh by the way are you still interested in buying my house back? I believe you mentioned something about owning it again."

He gave her a good, long stare.

"Because if you are, Mr. Emmanuel Smith owns it now. You may make him an offer if, of course, he wishes to sell."

Rose felt a bit of shame creep up into her face.

"I never wish to own *that* house." He spit out and left them standing there.

Chapter 57

"Miz Rose you done growed up into a woman." Portia said when they were out of earshot."Got yourself a little baby and going to Ireland . . ."

Rose heard Portia's voice give way.

"Oh Portia don't talk like that. I need to go home and you need this house."

"Chile I don't need no house. I's got everthing I want. My Emmanuel, my grandchildren. Jesus done said 'dis ain't our home anyways."

"Yes he did." Rose agreed. "But blessings come to the faithful. When you sow you reap. And you have been faithful to us. Long before I arrived you took care of Captain Lovell and his wife and then me. You can do with the house what you wish. Perhaps the Lord has something for you to do."

Portia stopped in her tracks. "You think dat be why He done give it to us?"

Rose could see Portia's mind working.

Sixteen days was not enough to time prepare. Rose's trunks were packed with clothes and a few special items. But their hearts were not so easy to pack away. Goodbyes had already been said with the Perrys and Rose knew she could not leave until she spoke with Ava. The ladies at the church meeting were truly sorry to see her go. She left them a donation in Captain Lovell's name for the orphanage, which suffered very little damage, except a few more broken windows. The building was newer and it would be a safe place for the children.

Then she had gone over to Newgate to leave a check. One for Cecelia and one for the building fund. She visited with Cecelia and told her she was leaving. The child had had enough people leaving in her life and Rose wanted to make sure they would correspond and left enough money for a ticket so Cecelia to come over when she was old enough.

Today she decided to take the long walk to Ava's home and found her there alone. Their house had suffered the most damage of any on the entire street. But her husband's family money had taken care of that. Rose looked at Ava's dark beautiful eyes and saw profound sadness. This friend had the house, the successful man, the best position in society and was the most unhappy. Ava was distant and on the verge of tears, so she made the visit short.

"Rose take care. I wish you the best. Little Carolina Jane is beautiful."

Rose could hear the hurt in her voice. Ava wanted a child more than anything but her husband would not permit it. He didn't want her to lose her beauty or be busy with other affairs.

"Thank you Ava. I will and please keep in touch. I'll send my address." Rose gave her a hug. "Captain Wyatt will come soon. Please give him my best. I will send him a note informing him of everything. I'm sure once he hears about the quake he will come to you." She reassured her friend.

Ava nodded and turned away, shoulders shaking. Rose let herself out and walked slowly tucking every scene away in her mind to remember Charleston. It still lay in ruins, but there was busy activity day and night. She made a detour to have a look at St. Michael's. Men were still working on it…the spire had been taken away for repair and the cracks were being plastered over this evening, she noted.

She missed her daughter and picked up her pace. The sun was going down and the soft warm winds made her melancholy. Ireland was so far away, yet seemed to be calling her. Rose could only hope her heart was right. She would have to leave Portia, Emmanuel and Thomas and Lily. She had asked them to come with her but they could not. Their daughter was in America and might need them one day.

Rose stood outside for a long time and then ran inside to the office. The child still slept. She pulled off her gloves ran outside and began sketching. One canvass, then another and another.

That's how Captain Riley found her. Drawing madly with her charcoal pencil.

She was so busy, having found a thick fallen branch to sit upon, she jumped when he spoke not three feet away.

"Mrs. Lovell." He greeted removing his hat.

"Mr. Riley, I did not see you approach." She quickly turned the canvass over and laid it aside, pencils falling from her lap as she stood.

"You were drawing."

He smiled but his eyes were sad.

"Yes, I'm afraid it occurred to me that I should render Charleston to memory while I can still see it."

"Very good." He said and gazed away for a moment and then back. Rose could see something made him remember his grief. The pain was apparent, for he uttered just a few words about coming to get her things on Thursday and walked away.

Rose felt his pain. She gathered up the supplies and took them inside. She had three completed and a fourth she would finish tomorrow. The minute she walked in the door she was greeted by Lily coming down the stairs.

She tossed her items on the foyer table and eyes on the outstretched arms of the babe, she ran for her and took her into her arms. Already she knew her mother on sight.

In three days they would board the ship to Ireland.

Chapter 58

Judging from the weather they should have an easy journey. The trunks had been safely set by the door. A carpetbag lay beside them with the clothes they would travel in. But for now, Rose was using every spare minute to sketch. Some odd desire took over her. She wanted to remember Charleston. Her first marriage. Her first home. The birth of her daughter in this home. She must create a legacy for Carolina Jane's sake.

"Oh." She set aside her work. "I must go see your mother." She said to the child who lay on a palate on the office floor her fists swinging in the air. The winds blew the curtains at the open windows and Rose suddenly felt the urge to unpack and stay. *What was that about?*

Shaking her head against the thoughts, she hurriedly found Lily to watch the baby; then to Emmanuel to get the small carriage ready.

Within the hour she was standing inside the orphanage waiting for Matilda Jane to come down the stairs. She appeared at the top and Rose could see the change in her. They hadn't visited since the day she left. The girl was slender again and her hair was swept up in a stylish coif.

"Matilda Jane." Rose put out her hand.

"Yes." She lowered her eyes.

"I have come with news. I am leaving for Ireland in a couple of days. Would....would you like to see your daughter before I go?"

Matilda Jane looked up and away and then back at Rose. "No. Thank you Mrs. Lovell. I cannot. I have a new life now."

Rose nodded and understood. "May I wish you the best Matilda Jane. I....I...I thank you for your gift." Her voice waivered. "You have my word I will raise her as my very own daughter."

"That's why I gave her to *you* Mrs. Lovell."

"Yes. Well, then." Rose smoothed her hair. It seemed Matilda Jane had made up her mind a long time ago. "Shall I send you my address?"

The young woman hesitated for a long minute. "No. Thank you." She said and with a slight hug, turned and straight-backed, went up the stairs. Rose heard the piano playing softly as she stepped out the door.

~

When Captain Riley sent his men with a carriage for her trunks, Rose's heart jumped about like a wild bullet in a fire. Her eyes shot here, then there, then finally at Portia who stood off under the Willow tree, what was left of it, and lifted the corner of her apron time and again.

"I believe all our papers are signed and delivered Emmanuel. She kept her voice smooth. Should you need assistance I will inform Captain Wyatt of our changed circumstances and will ask him to stop by. If that is suitable." She added quickly. This was Emmanuel's house now.

"Miz Rose…uh…ain't no one gave me a chance all my life to be a man. To own a fine house like this. Folks' gonna talk, that's for sure. But I'll stand up and be a man. Take care of this place and if you and Miss Carolina Jane come back, you be owner of this house again."

"Thank you Emmanuel. You've earned this house for all those years you served. It is your turn to receive. And I am so glad it is you who will occupy it. I have enjoyed it for a season, but I feel the Lord is sending us elsewhere. May God rest his hand upon this home and your family." She gave him her blessing and shook his hand.

Lily ran off in tears, after running up and hugging Rose and the baby. Thomas nodded and stood next to his grandmother.

Finally Portia came out from under the tree and had herself a good cry in Rose's arms. "Chile you be like my very own. Now here you goin' off so far and that little baby goin' too." She swiped at the tears with both hands.

"Now, then. You have a life here Portia. And God has something for you to do. Find out what it is and I shall do the same. Do we agree?"

"Yes'm we agree all right." She cried out and enclosed Rose in her soft embrace for a long time.

"Now den, you been loved up. Don't you forget Miz Portia now you hear? And when you write dem long letters, I be gettin' Lily to read 'em. Already Lily know her letters thanks to Matilda Jane. And she learnin' to read better ever day. She read that Bible to me ever night."

Rose smiled and felt tears sting her eyes. "If you need anything, have Lily write. Anything at all Portia."

"Yes ma'am."

The goodbyes had taken so long Rose wondered that Captain Riley's men hadn't driven off without her.

She turned and was helped up while one of the young men held the baby and then handed her up. Rose turned to look over her shoulder engraving in stone the vision of her home, partly tumbled and crushed but she remembered every window. And had the sketches to help her never forget.

Chapter 59

Captain Riley was commandeering his ship. New men had been hired to handle the heavy load. There were only a dozen or so passengers that decided they would travel over rather than wait for the repair of the passenger ships. There was so much activity with construction supplies coming in now that people were aware the City of Charleston had been devastated by the earthquake.

She was given a large private berth. With so few passengers they would have the run of the main deck. The sun was just going down when they set off. Good weather was a godsend and Captain Riley knew to take advantage of it. Rose prayed God would carry them over safely.

The first day waters were calm but the second day had Rose in her bed with a bucket next to her. One of the mothers saw her dilemma and sent her twelve year old daughter to care for Carolina Jane. Every time the young girl lifted the little spoon to her daughter's mouth, Rose wanted to heave. She turned her back and tried to close her eyes which made her feel worse. The entire trip was miserable. Green in the face from the smells of others who had the same malady just made it worse.

When the waters calmed Rose ventured up on deck and gulped in fresh air. Her knees were weak from lack of nourishment and the constant swaying finally sent her below deck again. Too many days later, someone shouted "land ahoy" and Rose felt tears spring to her eyes as she held ~~Matilda~~ Jane close and looked out over the waters.

"Ireland." She whispered as on the horizon she could spot a church spire. A sign she was home at last. "Thanks be to God we are safely over."

By the time the ship docked and all papers were duly recorded the passengers were released. Carolina Jane lay heavy in her arms as Rose made her way down the gangplank, concentrating on each step. She was still weak-kneed and dizzy. She had meant to use the time aboard to study the family names in her mother's Bible. She had not been able to focus her eyes.

"Mrs. Lovell." Captain Riley slipped by passengers to catch up. "I understand you did not fare well."

"No. I'm afraid I'm not made for swaying ships on roiling waters." She admitted, glad to be breathing in fresh air.

"Have you established connections with your family?"

"I'm afraid I have not. There was not enough time to send a letter of enquiry."

"Then you must stay with my family."

Rose stopped to catch her breath and the child began to whimper. "Sir doesn't your ship need to be unloaded?"

"The crew is handling it. I am headed home to my family."

She nodded noting the sadness in his eyes. *How thoughtless of her. Of course he must be beyond grief knowing he'd left with his wife and daughter and come home alone. And now he must go tell his family.*

"Here let me take your bag."

He took it from her hands without waiting for an answer.

"Thank you."

Rose walked on, stomach sore from heaving and legs weak from the long trip.

"Me sister owns a B&B nearby in Dublin."

The man sounded so tired and here she was thinking only of herself. The babe was asleep on her shoulder now, but so very heavy.

It must be difficult to return without his wife and sweet little daughter. Suddenly tears popped into her eyes before she could process the thought that he must feel so lost and alone. His family had come to the States on their maiden voyage to find a new life. But to come back alone. She could only imagine.

She was so deep in thought that she didn't notice he had stopped until she heard someone call her name and turned.

"Our carriage."

He stood holding the door open. His and her carpetbags had already been tossed in the back rack.

"I'll take the child." He said and gently pulled the sleeping babe from her arms.

She managed to get herself up into the carriage and with relief found a seat. He hopped up easily and seated himself then handed her the infant.

Soon, the carriage was rocking and rolling. Rose tucked the baby in her elbow and pulled her close then her eyes slowly closed. At least they were on the ground and not rolling east and then west and then east again on rushing waves. Her last thoughts were of the earthquake rearranging the earth beneath her.

Something didn't seem right. She tried to open her eyes and found they did not want to cooperate. Where was she? Last she remembered rocks were falling about her. The nerves in her body jerked all at once waking her. They were stopped. She heard voices. Soft voices. And Carolina Jane was not in her arms.

She slid across the seat and nearly fell getting out.

"Take care Mrs. Lovell. Your child is right here." Captain Riley said from a few feet away.

Swiping her hand across her eyes to remove the dust she turned and at the sight of the little one chortling aloud, her heart began to pace itself again. She wanted to shout at him never to take her child without waking her first. But the joy and fear at once had mingled together.

"Mrs. Lovell, my sister, Ryanne."

Rose nodded and wondered what she must have looked like. An orphaned waif off the boat, no doubt.

"And where is me wee Colleen?"

Rose froze.

She hugged her child close and backed away and turned her back to gaze out over the green hills rolling up and down, dotted with white rock. She lifted her hand against the sun and walked slowly, past the house and away.

In a moment she heard soft crying. Tears filled her eyes and ran over. And once they started they didn't stop. They rolled down like two raging rivers. For her parents who were here somewhere, for her husband, for Matilda Jane, for Ava, for....for herself. She was even now looking on the land from which she came. What she had only heard about now lay before her. Something in her heart calmed. She was home.

Chapter 60

Before she knew it, she was further away than she'd thought. The thick grass beneath her feet and the freedom she felt looking at the glorious green hills filled her soul. Tired, she stopped beneath a small tree and let her child play. Somehow, someway she was going to make it. She thought about Captain Lovell and his gift to her. She only now realized how ungrateful and assuming she had been. If it were not for him she would not have the money to settle herself...and Carolina Jane here. She wished the little girl would have come along while her husband was alive.

"He would have loved the wee little lass wouldn't he?" She said to the miniature smiling face that was looking up at her.

The wind blew her unwashed hair. Turning her ear, she heard voices carrying on the wind and turned.

"Mrs. Lovell. I must be about my business. Come. Ryanne needs a woman. Would you mind. She'll help you with the lass and . . ."

Captain Riley walked away. His voice had caught...Rose knew why.

"We have work to do...baths and food. In that order." She popped the tiny nose with her finger. "Women need their friends. And we shall become a friend to Miss Ryanne...or perhaps it is Mrs. Ryanne."

Rose pulled fresh air into her lungs and found new strength.

"Come in Mrs. Lovell." Ryanne straightened her back. Me brother tells me you have left Charleston for good."

"Yes, we have." She said firmly. "This is our home. I have family here." Rose noted the woman's eyes puffy from crying.

"And your folks come from County Claire?" She took the baby from her arms. "Now 'tis a bath you'll both be needin'. Hearings from travelers say those ships are dirty places indeed. Shall we?"

Rose sensed she was talking about anything and everything but what her brother had just told her.

She followed Ryanne into a small room and saw a tin hip tub sitting in the corner. "Water's boiling in the pot....you get ready and I'll bring hot water....cool water's already in there. You plan on a good soaking and I'll wash the babe."

"Thank you." Rose felt her throat tighten. "I'm so grateful."

"Ah now there ye go...we Irish take care o'our own and . . ."

Ryanne stopped speaking and Rose watched her turn, pull the child closer to her breast and walk away. Patrice and Colleen were missing from this house. And she and Carolina Jane were not the two souls Ryanne wished to see.

Rose undressed and all her dusty clothing went into a pile. She missed Portia instantly. She wondered if she had made the worst mistake of her life. How would she live without Portia and Emmanuel? And she only just arrived. Knowing her mind was too tired to process her thoughts, she slipped down into the water, recently warmed, and washed her hair then laid her head back on a folded cloth. Nothing was more wonderful than being clean. Which had been a luxury in Charleston these last several weeks.

When she heard the sounds of a fussy babe, she stood and dryed, then fished in her carpetbag for the one change of clothing she and Carolina Jane possessed. They would have to wait for their trunks.

The instant her daughter saw her, she began to cry. "Oh now…oh now…" Rose soothed. "We are overly tired. I have your spoon."

She fed her freshly washed baby, still wrapped in a drying towel. "Now we shall get your clothes and you will sleep like the baby you are." She teased. "See Irish milk is the same as ours."

Rose made a pallet in the small room on the floor near the window and before she laid her down, Carolina Jane was already asleep.

"She is a beautiful lass."

Rose smiled at Ryanne.

"Go on now and take a nap. I'll fix potatoes and carrots and leeks for dinner while you rest."

Rose could not think of more beautiful words…and said so.

Chapter 61

There were noises about. Rose turned on her side and opened her eyes. It was nearly dark. She sat up and scanned the room. The baby was still asleep. Captain Riley was in the house. She could hear his deep voice. Stomach growling, she raised up quietly and gathered their dirty clothes.

Soon Carolina Jane must have sensed her movement for she stirred. Rose picked her up and let her stretch her chubby arms and legs. "Oh dear, time for a diaper change."

In minutes both were freshened and combed. A knock sounded on her door.

"Come dinner is ready." Ryanne announced from the other side.

Rose opened the door slowly and entered the largest room with the fireplace. It was so homey she wanted to cry. The smell of food wafted toward them and instantly Carolina Jane began to wiggle. Rose hustled to feed her. When that was done and a pallett arranged just the right distance from the fireplace, Rose sat down with Captain Riley and his sister and ate. He lifted his spoon but she noticed he didn't eat much. Grief settled down on one like a blanket soaked with rainwater. She knew it well.

The meal was eaten mostly in silence, no one looking up. Ryanne picked up empty plates and about that time the baby squealed, causing them all to jump. It broke the silence and all eyes were on the little rascal who kept trying to watch her own fists waving in the air.

Before long Captain Riley retired to a room on the other side of the house. Ryanne cleaned up quietly and whispered,"The little one is asleep again. Perhaps you two should bed down. There'll be plenty to do tomorrow. Guests are coming from Edinburgh."

Instantly Rose looked up as she gathered the sleeping baby in her arms. "We must be on our way as soon as our trunks arrive. We can travel by carriage from Dublin tomorrow if we have our belongings."

"Na, we have two cottages. One in the back for guests who wish to be alone or those with larger families. This one is for overnight travelers who wish to get up and be on their way." She explained. "You and the babe may stay as long as ye like."

"Thank you. If I might wash some of our clothes, I would be glad to do any washing you have."

"Ye are a guest and a guest does na wash their own clothes nor do they wash mine." Ryanne said firmly. "Besides there's a special man coming to help repair the roof on the morrow. And I have na seen him in a month." She winked at Rose.

That's when Rose noticed how beautiful Ryanne was. When they'd arrived she had been dressed in a gardening frock…a long gray dress with a black apron on top. Today she had piled her thick dark red hair atop her head. It was shiny clean. And she had put on a soft brown dress with a wide colorful print band around her small waist. She resembled Captain Riley only in hair color. He was taller. She was slender and light of foot.

Rose thanked her and excused herself, leaving Ryanne to her preparations for tomorrow. She couldn't imagine why she should eat and go back to sleep again.

Morning came so soon, she thought perhaps she had not slept an hour. Washing sleep from their eyes, Rose noticed first that their trunks had arrived. Instantly she began digging inside to find clean clothes. She must make her way back to Dublin to find a conveyance that would take them to County Claire. But to what city she had no idea. She unpacked the Bible and sat down at the table. There she found several names with cities, thankful for her mother's detailed accounts.

The next moment Captain Riley came in wiping sweat from his forehead. "Ah, ye're up and about." He spoke quietly. "Sorry for the noise. Rethatching is hard work and it takes daylight to finish."

"Thank you for bringing the trunks." She watched him take a good long slug of water. He nodded.

"May I find a ride to Dublin? I'll stay there, until I find enough information to locate my family."

"I'll take ye myself. In about four hours we'll have more help so I can get back to the ship. There's still furniture to be taken off and delivered.

"Then it won't be a bother?"

"Twill not." He said and was out the door.

Rose knew he needed to work. Hard work cured what ailed a man…so her father said.

Ryanne was scarce this morning, but there was a fine smelling stew bubbling in the black kettle hanging on the arm over the fire. She straightened their things and stuffed the dirty clothes in a flour bag. They would be in Dublin tonight.

Just as Captain Riley said, he came for her and the baby, lifting her up to Rose. "There are good records, the best in Ireland, there in Dublin's courthouse. It is wise to make use of them before you go looking. And mind, it would be better if ye let me drive ya over. It'll be no charge. Straight line over to from Galway, half a day's ride."

"I would thank you sir for your kindness, but I will pay you same as anyone else."

"Ye'll not do that." He said firmly. "We Irish take care o'our own."

Rose knew there was no sense arguing with an Irishman.

Two days later Rose and Carolina Jane were settled into a small house near downtown. They could walk and hustle about getting everything they needed, just as Ryanne said.

Her trunks were even now in the small receiving room waiting to be unpacked. She had paid two month's rent in advance to be sure there was enough time for research. The hustle and bustle of Dublin was different than Charleston's. More pubs and fisticuffs were common. It was true the Irish had a penchant for beer and a good shout-down.

Twice she had had to avoid a tussle in front of a pub while she was pushing the baby in her new carriage. Already the little one was too heavy to carry about. But her research work was paying off. She had found the line of the McKensie family and also learned that her father was more Scot than Irish.

The days flew by. Captain Riley stopped whenever he was in town to make sure she was all right. The ship was reloaded with some new furnishings. Next stop was London to fill it up completely. "The shipping business is booming." He said quietly. Rose noted he still did not have light in his eyes and his voice was always low and quiet. He said very little.

At the end of the second month in Dublin, Rose asked Captain Riley to take them to the place of her parents' birth. He had just returned from Charleston and brought news that the town was in a building frenzy. Rose knew once he had her settled, he was set to go back. New furniture was in great demand and he was doing quite well for himself.

He found a young man on the street and asked him to heft the heavy trunks into the wagon and paid him. Rose hated to leave the city that she was only beginning to love. Baltimore, Charleston and now Dublin. She only hoped living out in the country would not be displeasing. Once she'd located her father's family she had sent letters enquiring if there may be land to purchase nearby. It looked as though there were family members who needed to sell several parcels and she may have her choice.

The wagon creaked as they pulled away from the city and ventured out into the softly rolling hills. The sun glinting off the waters made her eyes water.

"Ye'll need a hat. The sun on the water and the hills reflecting will burn ye're eyes."

Rose noticed he'd fallen back into the brogue of the Irish as soon as he returned. It brought back memories of her father and mother when they spoke. She had learned a bit of Gaelic but little enough to get around. The road signs were in English and Gaelic. She tried to memorize the names as they passed. This would be her country now and she must acquaint herself with their language and customs...many of them she already knew. Her parents loved America and the freedom to pursue their dreams. But their sad stories of hardship during the potato famime seemed to be most remembered in her mind.

Indeed the people had been driven apart like a huge axe thrust in a tree until it had come crashing down, splitting entire families into pieces. Rose felt sorry and began to understand the reason they wanted to come back home.

She twisted around to make sure the baby was still asleep. Satisfied, Rose settled in and made good use of her eyes. Captain Riley spoke very little. Most likely planning his next trip.

Hours later they stopped to use the woods and feed Carolina Jane who was now awake and fussy.

"Won't be long now." He said when they climbed back up to continue. "Good land around here. You won't have trouble making a garden and flowers if you are wont to do that."

"Oh yes. I love gardening." Rose began to titter at the idea of lush green, rolling hills. What wonderful walks she and her babe would have.

She was dreaming away when the Captain's deep voice broke the reverie in her left ear. "Mrs. Lovell." He stopped to clear his throat. "It may be too soon, both for you and for me..." Pause. "But if you'd give some thought to us joining up in wedlock...."

Rose gasped but corrected herself by placing her fingers across her mouth to keep any foolishness from spilling out. "I've lost a wife and a lass...and you've lost your man."

Afraid to move, she waited for him to finish, but the only sound she heard was wheels grinding across the stony roadway and the child gurgling playfully behind her.

Her mind worked. So that means we should replace them with each other? She wanted to say. Indeed her mother's practicality was at work in her own mind. What foolishness that would be. She was free and did not intend to marry any man for convenience. Captain Wyatt had offered the same. What was it about her that men seemed to want to fix. Was she lacking? Did no man want to be with her because he *wanted* to, not because he *had* to? She felt tears come and looked away glad the wind was blowing, because they dried up quicker than they could fall.

When it was apparent he did not intend to speak further, she put him at ease.

"Captain Riley, it is good of you to ask, but I'm afraid Carolina Jane nor I could replace what you have lost. We would no doubt let you down. It is too soon for either of us. And it would be a mistake." She kept her voice low, soft.

Silence again. Rose didn't mind it so much when they were on good terms. But now the question hung between them like bad blood.

Then after they had passed a couple miles, he let her off the hook. "Mrs. Lovell, you are most wise. It was from grief I spoke. And too soon at that."

Rose took a deep breath, and felt the wind washing away all the hurt. "Sir, you are a worthy man. I have benefited from your assistance in many ways. I am honored that you consider me and my child worthy of such an offer." She gave him a soft smile as they glanced at each other.

"Well, then. I'm thinking about five more miles and you will be home Mrs. Lovell."

Rose noted the lift in his voice, no doubt because he himself was glad she had declined. She felt joy and sadness all wrapped up in one emotion. Maybe some day she would be loved.

Chapter 62

Captain Riley helped her down and Rose could not take her eyes off the scene that lay before her. White rocks dotted the gently rolling hillsides. Bright blue skies met emerald green and silver streams ran behind the houses. A more beautiful place she had not seen. Cities were alive with people and conveniences, and public places. Here she sensed, a person could be alone and still not be lonely.

Captain Riley was muscling the smaller trunks off the wagon.

"Look CJ, your new home." She lifted the child and kissed her cheek realizing she'd just given her a nickname like her father had given her at birth. Rosalette.

"Mother disapproved. But when we were alone together he called me *Little Rosalette*." She whispered to her daughter. "And I shall call you CJ."

Rose sighed, overwhelmed with the beauty and a sense of belonging.

"Your mother has brought you to the place where your grandmother and grandfather…." Rose stopped just realizing they would never know they had a grandchild. Tears popped out. Again. She was tired of crying. She swiped at them and made herself a promise.

"We will learn all we can and be satisfied with what we have now. And you, lass, will grow up to be grateful and thankful for what you have…as simple as it may be." This day she realized the blessings her parents had given her. And she would make the effort to give to CJ what she herself had been given.

Rose smoothed her hair and the wrinkles out of her dress with one hand and whispered a quick prayer, "Lord I pray from this day forward we find a good life."

She realized she had been musing and turned. Captain Riley's back was to her. He was looking out at the view himself. Rose felt sad for him and shook the thoughts from her head. One day he would find someone, but she was not the one.

Before she could think another thought an older gentleman, a full head of white hair came out of the cottage; his jaunty walk and smile drew her.

"And ye would be our niece." He held out his hand in greeting then walked over and introduced himself to Captain Riley. And this be your husband?" He turned to Rose.

"No sir. Captain Riley has been kind enough to bring us from Dublin."

Rose could not take her eyes off of him. He was so much like her father. She watched him talk, the way he motioned with his hands, his gentle voice. Hawthorn McKensie, her father's brother.

"I'm Hawthorn, Haw for short. Ye're father's eldest brother. Come in for tea. The wee babe will be a welcome sight for me wife. She misses the grandchildren.

Come Captain Riley, we shall talk of ships while me good woman serves up the best food in the whole of County Galway."

Rose walked into a small thatched cottage and blinked. The inside was lit with candles and looked every bit like her mother's description of their first home when they were newly married. Her eyes took in every nuance. The smell of food reminded her they had not eaten since breakfast many hours ago.

"Come sit down. I'm Elsa McKensie. The men are already busy talking ships and weather." She smiled.

Rose was completely surprised by his wife. She had beautiful white hair and blue eyes the color of a summer sky. The Scandanavian accent still had a hold of her tongue.

"Ah, a wee babe. My arms are needin' a little one to hold." She turned quickly.

Rose heard the waver in her voice. "Would you like to hold the lass? I think she is tired of sitting on my lap. I could use a bit of moving about as well. I'll set your table if you tell me where to look."

"Ah, my dishes and cups are in that cupboard." She pointed and took the baby from her mother's arms talking and soothing her.

"She is used to people. She will not cry." Rose smiled and washed her hands at the basin and set the table.

"Wait until she has one year behind her, she'll cry." Mrs. McKensie said firmly. "But now she is little and doesn't mind who holds her. Oh such a pretty little thing. Blue eyes and the blackest hair."

Rose felt a pain stab her in the stomach. The next question she expected to hear was. "And where is the wee lass' father."

"There. Table set for four. Carolina Jane is her name, ma'am."

"Carolina Jane." The woman repeated and stood.

"Here she will eat better with her mother." She handed CJ to her mother. "I'll call the men."

Mrs. McKensie called and they appeared instantly. Everyone was hungry, including CJ who was now beginning to fuss. Rose found the spoon in her bag and began to feed her milk.

"What a strange way to feed the lass." Mrs. McKensie stood nearby and watched.

"This is the way she learned and it has worked quite well." Rose smiled and commented how good dinner smelled.

"Oh dear, and everyone hungry. Come now let's say our prayers and have our fill."

They gathered around the table standing behind their chairs.

Mr. McKensie prayed a blessing upon the food and the guests then everyone sat and filled their plates. Rose loved the lively conversation and the food.

Twice Captain Riley looked at her and then away. Rose felt there needed to be words of gratefulness said to him before he left. Before her thoughts were completed she heard his chair as it scooted back on the wood floor. "Tis enough time for me to make my way back yet this eve."

"Are you in such a hurry then?" Mrs. McKensie inquired.

"Aye. The wagon will be lighter and if I get far enough before the sun sets, my horse will know the way back. I have a ship ready to leave the harbor and must return. Thank ye for your good meal Mrs. McKensie." He took his hat off a knob and started for the door.

"Sir, may I speak with you?" Rose handed the baby to Mrs. McKensie and followed him out.

He watered his horse and straightened his back. Rose watched him for a few moments.

"Thank you for taking time to bring us to my family Captain Riley. And I thank you for your offer. It is because of your kindness we are here." She held her hand up to her eyes. The sun was still bright in the sky, but she knew it was well past noon and he must be going.

"Aye."

Rose saw a slight smile on his face as he tipped his hat and drove slowly away.

Now her life would begin here in Ireland. With family.

Chapter 63

The weeks flew by. Rose met her father's younger brother Donal and his family. She listened to their stories at the table. The same ones her parents told, except she knew now what happened after they left. While they were starting out in America, Hawthorne, the eldest had already left home and established a life with Elsa. They survived by moving to Denmark with her parents for several years and then coming back to Ireland.

The youngest brother had a much sadder story. He had been lent out to a family in Dublin. They had mistreated him which set him to drinking. He had not fared as well and there was trouble between the brothers. Although Donal and his wife had joined them for dinner one evening, Elsa had said they would probably not come often. Their lives were very different. The reason they did come, was they were the party that had the land for sale.

It seems Haw had come back with savings earned from working at a shipping business in Denmark and bought back the land his father and mother lost during the famine. And, in fairness he had given half to his brother Donal with the expectation of his paying for it over time. From that day to this Donal had not paid a single penny. Yet he built a small cottage on the farthest lot away without asking Haw if he could. There had been bad blood ever since.

Now Rose was sitting in the middle of the pond without a paddle for her boat. She wanted to buy land that belonged to Haw, but was occupied by Donal. She sought counsel from Haw once the first dinner meeting was over.

Haw suggested she take an opposite corner from Donal's home and build there on his section. That way each would have their own land and perhaps Donal, with the money Rose paid him, would pay Haw.

While Elsa and Rose worked in the kitchen, Elsa confided that Haw didn't really expect the money, but all the same, he felt Donal should pay his part so that he would be free of the guilt.

Rose agreed. "Ownership requires money. But for those without it, the strain causes hardship."

Within weeks a deal had been struck. Donal was so anxious to receive the cash from Rose he sold her off a good portion, saying his children were gone anyway and didn't need so much. Rose now owned 42.6 acres of Irish soil.

Now to build a dwelling.

Haw and Elsa had the gift of design. And Rose was so grateful for the time she spent with Ava who showed her ideas to improve the Charleston house. Plans were drawn up at their kitchen table.

"Donal," Haw said, "has the gift of working with his hands. He will build your house. I can only assist." Haw went down to see Donal and settled on a price.

The building began the last week of October. Haw and Donal worked side by side many an evening, along with other young men hired from around the area. They had to get the shell up before winter. There would be time to work inside during the colder months.

Life was simple and it was good. While the men worked, Rose helped Elsa cook for the workers. Many an afternoon was spent writing letters to Portia and Matilda Jane and Stella and Ava. She learned a bit more Gaelic from Haw and several words of Dutch from Elsa. Already CJ was bonding with Elsa and Rose felt like she had found the life she was made for.

Good weather and enough money brought her house up in six months. While the men worked Elsa showed her how to prepare a small garden spot in the rocky soil. They dug up and carried small rocks and formed an edging along the front of the house for the flower bed. Rose couldn't have been happier.

The day she moved in, everyone had come and Haw stood at the front door and prayed a prayer for the house, the lands, the occupants and any visitor who might pass by.

Dinner was made over the fire with her new kettle. When the younger men left, she, Elsa Haw and Donal sat at the table and admired their work.

"Donal, you have the gift of building. I never knew how much until now." Haw said. He tapped the table with his fingertips and tipped his cup to his lips.

Rose felt the tension in the room. As long as the brothers had been working together everything was fine. She noted that Haw never made a decision on how the building was constructed, only worked at jobs he could handle.

Donal sat quiet for a long time . . . and when Rose looked up, she saw him struggling.

Then when Elsa's eyes filled, suddenly hers did too.

"No one has ever told me that." Donal's low voice filled the room.

"Well, now they have." Haw stood and lifted his cup. The four stood and clinked cups over the table.

Rose could have died with joy on the spot. If this were any indication of how God was going to use this house, she was going to love being a part of it.

Chapter 64

It was mid-April 1887 and Rose had just planted her first seeds. The bed had been prepared while the house was going up and it was finally time to start the garden. Carolina Jane was ten months old. Each morning she took the little one for a stroll over the new pathway created by walkers coming from the main road.

The fireside at night was her favorite time. Even though the winds blew warmer, still the nights could be chilly. The winds whistled around her house creating a soothing sort of sleep.

Elsa and Haw came to visit her often, Donal less often as days progressed. Donal McKensie had taken the money from the sale of the land, bought new tools and started finishing off newly built homes. His work with wood was becoming known throughout the parts. And he started making payments to Haw for the land. Haw and Elsa were so proud they helped spread the word about Donal's fine workmanship. Soon wealthy people from Dublin paid his travel fees and provided room and board to come and build for them.

So much was so good, Rose could hardly believe she had been reluctant to return with her parents. Her one regret. Yet some things in life had to happen in an order of which one cannot understand -- she mused one day as word came via mail from Portia. Charleston was still rebuilding. Rose loved the news from Portia...dictated to Lily. Lily's handwriting was so much improved, Rose commented on it to her. Jamison's Orphanage was nearly finished. Workers from parts all around the country had come to help Charlestonians rebuild and the timing was perfect. Jamison's had the help they needed. There was room for double the children with the new accommodations. The good ladies from St. Michael's church, after suffering their own maladies, realized the importance of helping others in less fortunate situations.

Mrs. Pinckney donated yards and yards of material for curtains to cover the entire top level set of windows. Thirty-two in all. Nettie knew because her girls had sewn every single pair with the addition of two more Singer sewing machines, also donated by Mrs. Pinckney. Lily learned how to sew. And Emmanuel was respected in the streets. He had put up every last brick and repaired every last window. He and Thomas rebuilt the chimney.

Stella's baby boy had been born with much difficulty but both were doing well, she wrote. They were planning a move to Savannah to take over her father's house. It seemed much safer, away from the quake area and Foster had finally found another position as a bank officiant. They were bursting with joy...she could feel it in Stella's letters.

Ava had written only once and the letter had been about the weather, the rebuilding, her husband's position at the bank. Nothing about herself.

Rose set aside Ava's letter and gazed at the writing on the envelope of the last post. It was familiar. She sliced the envelope and opened a one page note.

> *Mrs. Lovell, it is imperative that I speak with you. I am bound for London at the first thaw of the Atlantic. You may expect me sometime in late April, early May.*
>
> *Sincerely, Captain Ashton Wyatt*

Her heart did a triple beat. What was imperative? Trouble at the bank. Had Mr. Dalton given Emmanuel difficulty. Even though Rose had left everything in his name Mr. Dalton had refused to speak to Emmanuel. Her mind worried. She set the letter aside and forced herself to be patient. Whatever it was, there was nothing she could do about it now.

What day was it? The time flew by so quickly and she rarely checked the calendar except when writing a letter. She dashed to her art room. It was April 16th. Her hand flew to her mouth. Less than two weeks away? CJ fussed and she went for her.

"Soon missy, we're going to take your socks off and set you on the grass so you can learn to walk." She laughed when CJ laughed. "We will be having a visitor. Thanks to Captain Wyatt I have a daughter. We shall show you off and see what he thinks of you now."

Rose felt like creating today. She set up her easel out of doors first, then put a finely stitched light yellow dress on CJ and set her on her best quilt. One her mother made. She set her just right so the hills and trees would form a good background. The sun shone on her dark curls perfectly. Rose's heart fluttered inside.

She was hard at work turning her head this way and that for the best view because the pencil in her hand was magic today. When she was finished, she had a beautiful rendition of her daughter. Memorizing the colors of the grass, the sky, and the soft yellow of her dress, she would set to work tonight and color in the details with her paints.

The day flew by once again. Twice she gazed at Captain Wyatt's note and twice she forced her thoughts elsewhere. Portia said trouble will come all by itself, we must not go looking for it, she reminded herself.

Late into the evening the colors were added to CJ's portrait, Rose careful not to move the paper so the colors would not run together. She dabbed carefully then set the heavy paper flat on a towel in the middle of her hand-made table. She ran her hand over the smooth wood table thinking of Donal McKensie and felt proud to have his work in her home.

ᘛ

The weeks went by and still no word from Captain Wyatt. Perhaps he had not known where to find her. Lily had said in a letter he had come calling and needed her location; he had urgent news for her. Rose shrugged and finished yet another painting. Perhaps it was good news.

The hand-drawn coal pencil sketches from Charleston were hung as a series, another design by Donal, in a square. Nine frames perfectly the same and perfectly symmetrical had taken up one wall. She loved gazing at them. Remembering her people. Her husband. One was of a trunk with blue envelopes laying across the top, a lacy handkerchief and a ladies watch alongside. She still remembered the love that flowed from those letters.

Someday, perhaps someone would love her that way. Right now she was so satisfied with her life, she didn't need more.

Chapter 65

May arrived with sunshine and promise. New buds had opened in her garden, an array of wildflowers across the front of the house enclosed by the low rock wall she and Elsa had built.

Pansys and Primrose, Daisy and Cowslip, even some beautiful purple Violets were just beginning to show their colors. The long leaves and white puffs of Cottongrass flowed in the winds.

Elsa brought starts from her own garden every time she visited. So the beautiful colors would soon be full and vivid. A view that would call for another sketch and color, Rose mused.

In a month CJ would reach her first birthday. Rose wanted it to be special and planned for a picnic out of doors -- a simple dinner on the grounds with her two uncles and aunts, time for her daughter to play. On a recent trip to Dublin with Elsa, Rose and bought a large roll of canvas for her paintings. Haw was building her a frame; one a little larger than her usual twelve inch square ones. This would be a special sketch. Rose couldn't wait to celebrate. The color portrait would hang in her daughter's room. One for every birthday would follow.

Excitement reached her ears when she heard CJ calling her. "Mama."

Rose's heart never failed to lurch when she heard the little voice trying out her first word. She tiptoed to the door and peeked her head around and saw the chubby arms go out straight in front of her. No mother could resist that. Rose hurried to her and pulled her out of bed and into her arms.

"Oh we must change you." She said sweetly and kissed her neck, making her giggle; a sound Rose could hardly abide without a tear coming to her eye. What a treasure God had given her.

When that was done and she was freshly washed and dressed, Rose knew she would have to be quick about breakfast, so set her down. CJ crawled off her pallet and came straight for her skirts. She liked to hide herself in them. She did not try to walk and Rose was in no hurry to rush her. A babe needed time to be a child. She reveled in the noises she made as she pulled herself up by her skirts and teetered, landing on her bottom again and again.

"One of these days....one of these days...little Carolina Jane....you will be at your first year. And here we are in Ireland. Did you ever think of such a thing?" She talked aloud.

"I think that even though you were born in Charleston you are an Irish lass to be sure."

Four days later, Rose saw a horseman heading across the hills. Since there was not another cottage nearby, she knew someone was coming to her. She was not afraid, because the rider would have been directed to her place, most likely by Haw or Elsa. They made a point to know who was traveling past their place.

She shielded her eyes against the noon sun. CJ had just gone down for her nap and Rose was taking a walk looking for the perfect picnic sight.

The man and his horse rode directly for her house. She started back, knowing she was probably not in his sight. At one point she was afraid he would reach the house and knock on the door and her child was in there alone. She started to run and by the time she walked through the back door of her cottage she could hear the loud banging on her front door. She stopped a moment, listened for CJ and hearing nothing rushed through the house to stop the noise. Jerking the door open without looking through the window first was not wise.

Hand over her heart she caught her breath and standing large in her doorway was Captain Wyatt. She couldn't actually see the top of his head. He was tall enough that he had to bend his knees to show his face. She gasped when his deep voice reverberated, "There was no time to write another letter."

For a moment she stood stuck in her thoughts. It was so strange to see him in Ireland at her door, she forgot her manners, then recovered.

"Captain Wyatt, please come in." She stood aside and watched as he ducked and entered her house. He looked huge in there. She put her hand over her mouth to hide a smile.

"What is it? " He grumped.

"It's just that…that you're so tall, the house seems smaller." She told him truth. "Are you famished after the long ride, sir?"

"Yes."

"Well, then hang your hat on the peg there." She pointed. "And come have soup. It's been cooking since early this morning." Rose went to get bowls, knowing the best thing to do was feed a man after a long journey.

"Wash up there at the bowl." She pointed again.

He took off his coat and hung it on the peg next to his hat. Rose's nerves tittered. A man in her house. A child asleep in the other room and food cooking over the fire in her kettle.

Suddenly she felt fear shiver down her back. He had said he had urgent news. By the time those thoughts formed, she found him standing aside watching her, waiting to be invited to sit down.

"Please sit." She motioned to a chair and realized she forgot the bread. She brought it wrapped in a towel and placed it in the middle of the table then spooned up a full bowl of soup for him and a half bowl for her. She doubted she could eat until she knew why he had come all the way from London.

He settled his tall lanky frame on the chair and gave her a quick look when she didn't proceed.

"Do you mind. We pray at mealtime."

"No." he said and lowered his head.

Rose's heart skipped a beat and she said a quick prayer, hoping the Lord understood she didn't remember a word she said.

"Now, sir, enjoy. Have you been to Ireland before?" Rose took a knife and sliced off big chunks of bread.

"No. It is my first time." He picked up his spoon and ate.

She ate, actually enjoying the taste of the food. She could see by the look on his face that he, too, was eating heartily and she liked that.

He enjoyed the food, but she could see he was not himself. He did not smile. He did not make conversation only answered her questions politely. She sensed that he was filling his stomach and then he would be decent to hold his temper and tell her what he had come for.

When he had finished a second helping, Rose laid her spoon down.

"Captain Wyatt, why have you come?"

His dark eyes found hers for a second and then he stood pushing his chair back noisily as he got to his feet.

He was going to pace.

And indeed he did. Back and forth he went thinking. Hands behind his back.

"Please be out with it." She stood and cleared the dishes from the table and set them aside. "It cannot be that bad."

"It can and it is." He stopped and stared at her as though she were the problem.

She laid the last bowl on the sideboard and turned to him.

"Has someone died?"

He stopped and stared again. "Then you know?"

"Know what?" Now her heart began to prepare for bad news

"Ava's husband has been killed. Gunshot to the back. Unknown person."

Captain Wyatt had said the words so coldly, she wondered that he could say them without flinching. For she was looking straight at him when he said it.

"Mr. McGuire?" She knew why Ava had not written.

"But..."

"There is more." He said and gave her his back, ducking down to look through her windows.

"Is the child asleep?" He turned to face her.

"Yes."

"Then would you mind if we stepped outside. I can't abide . . ."

She knew his trouble. He could not stand small spaces. Seamen couldn't. She understood.

"Of course." She snatched a shawl from the back of the rocker, stepped into the room to check on CJ and went out with him, her thoughts of Ava and she in her grief alone.

"He was killed by someone. They don't know who yet."

"Killed? Why?" Rose whispered.

"You don't need to know the circumstances. Take it from me that he probably deserved what he got."

Rose wanted to turn and shout at him. *No one deserves to die at the hand of another.* But she kept her peace until she could learn more. Captain Wyatt was a hard man. But she knew he and Ava had come from the orphanage and there was usually a hardship story to go along with each one who found themselves there.

"But Ava…did she deserve that?" She asked quietly.

"No, she did not. She was only hoping to make a good life for herself. Her beauty drew Theodore Madison McGuire. He wanted her for his trophy. And he knew she would be grateful to be married into one of Charleston's wealthiest families."

Rose didn't understand.

"He married her for his gain." That was it. "He was a coddled and corrupt man born of riches, noble blood and cold hearts."

Rose heard those words from behind him. He had given her his back again, talking over his shoulder. She couldn't disagree with the statement. She sensed something was not right when she first met Mr. McGuire. But murder? She watched him run his hands through his black hair and turned to face her. She felt frightened for the first time. Something in her heart rushed to fear.

"Mrs. Lovell. There is a secret that I have kept until now. And it concerns you."

Rose felt a tightening in her throat. In an instant she knew it was about Carolina Jane. The only thing she and Captain Wyatt had in common between them. She glanced out at the hills and back at him.

"What I didn't tell you that night. What I couldn't tell you that night…was that Theodore McGuire fathered Matilda Jane's child."

Rose's heart sunk to the ground and she couldn't speak. Her mind raced. Of course he couldn't tell that. It was his sister's husband.

"Did Ava know?"

"Of course not. Why do you think I came to you? McGuire and I fought it out once I found out. But I couldn't tell my sister."

She felt his pain even in his harsh words.

"I came upon McGuire mishandling Matilda Jane in a back alley. He wanted her to get rid of the child. We fought. Matilda Jane wanted to give the child to Ava but McGuire said he'd deny it all and he threatened her. Matilda Jane knew Ava and I had been at the orphanage, so she trusted me."

"I'm so sorry." Rose said.

"Sorry isn't going to help now." He spit out the words.

Rose gave him her back. She knew more was coming and wondered if she could hear it and not die.

"You want my daughter back?"

The deep voice behind her confirmed what she already knew.

"Yes."

"Ava knows now?"

"Yes of course she knows. She's my sister. How could I keep it from her that her lying, cheating husband has a child. It's all she has left, Mrs. Lovell. And I intend to do what I can to help her get the child back."

Rose understood. It was Ava's husband's child.

Even though papers had been signed, Rose knew she had no right to Carolina Jane. Just like the two women in the Bible. When two women claimed a child was theirs, the judge said we will cut the baby in half and give each of you a half. The real mother shouted she would give the child up to the other woman. The judge gave the child to the women who did not want her child dead, even if it had to go to someone else.

Why Rose thought of that right now was beyond her, but the story was there in her mind.

"Why didn't you tell me that night?" she could not face him.

He came around and stood in front of her. Rose looked away.

"I don't know. I couldn't hurt my sister. She'd been hurt enough already."

His voice wavered and Rose wanted to…she wanted to bang her fist on his chest and next minute to hug him like a child and tell him it was okay.

Instead she walked away from him because she could no longer hold in her grief. She knew what she had to do. But how in the world was she going to do it? She needed time alone and hurried away, stopping under a tree and gazing out not seeing a single thing. Grief had darkened her sight on a bright sunny day.

Captain Wyatt stayed where he was, pacing and jamming his hands through his hair enough times to keep himself from going over there and picking her up and carrying her to the house. He had broken her heart. The same way his was broken so long ago. And the sight of her shoulders shaking was his undoing.

Several long strides later, he did exactly that. Without a word he came up behind her, swooped her up and carried her sobbing to the house. She shouted in his ear to be put down, but he ignored that.

Ducking the doorway, he didn't know what to do now. Where was her room. His boots clicked heavy over the wooden floors and he checked each doorway until he found a bed and gently laid her there.

"I'll be back tomorrow." He said, stalked out the door, jerked the reins off the rail and galloped away. She hated him and he didn't blame her.

Chapter 66

The way the horseman flew by their house, Elsa knew something was wrong. She called Haw in from the fields and said. "We have to go to Rose."

Haw didn't question his wife, just pulled up the cart, drove over and knocked on the door.

Rose didn't answer. The house was too quiet. Elsa stepped in calling her name, and then hearing the sobs went straight to her.

"There, there. What is it. Did that man hurt you?"

Rose tried to control herself. "Yes, but not in the way you may hink." She blubbered.

"He…he came for Carolina Jane." She sobbed again. "The child is not mine and I cannot keep her, but oh Elsa how am I going to give her up. She's all I have in the world."

"There, there. Haw and I will pray for you lass."

Rose let herself be held and put her arms around Elsa. "I wish my father were here." She cried. "He would know what to do."

"Your Father is here and He does know what to do." Elsa whispered.

Rose could feel her tears plopping on top of her head and cried all the more.

~

After a time Rose heard the soft soothing sounds from the other room of Haw and Elsa as they talked to her child. She must have fallen asleep.

She forced herself from the bed and pushed tear-soaked strands of hair away from her face. There was nothing to do but face what came. Hadn't she learned that from her mother enough times?

The minute she walked into the room her little one threw her arms out and said, "Mama."

Rose couldn't get to her quick enough and pulled her into her arms crushing her against her chest. "Mama's here. Mama's here." She plopped down in the rocker and noticed that Elsa and Haw shot out the door saying they were going for a walk.

"Oh aren't you pretty after your long, long sleep. I bet you want to go outside don't you?" Rose smoothed the dark hair away, the blue eyes gazing into hers.

If her heart had not been broken before, it was now.

Before she could think another thought a slice of courage cut through. She had to be strong. Had to be firm or else the child would suffer. And that was one thing she would not do. Cause her child to suffer.

She stood and firmly made her way out the door and walked, talking to her child, explaining things. The older couple were far away, still in sight but leaving her alone. If Captain Wyatt meant to come back tomorrow for her, what could she possibly say or do to change his mind? Maybe Ava could come here to live, she reasoned, or I could go back to Charleston.

Two mothers? She whispered. *How foolish.* She scolded herself. She would have to give the child up to save her from knowing two women each wanting her affection. Rose would not do that. She firmed her mind and her heart. She would be ready when Captain Wyatt came tomorrow. And she would do it with honor, knowing the sacrifice would be worth it in the end. What she would rather do is state her case, throw a fit, saying she had been promised the child and Matilda Jane had signed papers saying she was hers.

Rose wondered if she could sign papers saying she wasn't hers and tears came rolling down again. When CJ looked at her Rose saw the blue eyes noticed she was sad. "I'm just crying because I'm happy, she lied to the little one. So happy because your father and your mother had you. You are here because of them. And I'm just so…so happy God let me have you for a time."

Rose couldn't believe she was actually saying those words. It had not sunk in yet that she would not be a mother anymore. How could she not be a mother? She was already one. That love would never leave her. Ever. She would always know she was Carolina Jane's mother no matter what happened. She hugged her closer and swirled around, so she would laugh. It was amazing to realize that a child this young could see a mother's sorrow.

In time, her heart strangely became calm. She knew it was not from her own will but from God's somehow. Knowing what she must do, she walked out to the McKensie's and told them she was going in the house to pack CJs things. Elsa insisted on coming and sent Haw home to his work. He could come for her later.

The evening was spent sitting on the floor, Elsa, Rose and Carolina Jane. Playing. Rose wanted to rush to her art room and sketch CJ playing with her little toys, sitting on the brightly colored rag run and smiling. But she didn't want to lose a minute with her. The child was innocent of what was about to happen to her. Rose couldn't think of her being in Captain Wyatt's care alone. She must go with him, and stated that to Elsa.

"Of course you must. The little lass would sob her way across the Atlantic without her mother near. You must go. I will insist upon it." Elsa knew the whole story now.

Rose's felt fear crawl up into her mind again. Would Captain Wyatt allow her to accompany him back to Ava? Would Rose come back to Ireland or want to stay in Charleston. How would CJ fare with her new mother? Would she need to stay a week, a month or longer to be sure CJ would be all right with Ava? Could she leave her behind and come back to Ireland?

Too many questions. Finally CJ was put to bed late. Rose lay her down and patted her back until she slept. She did not want to leave her alone in the room, until Elsa came for her and gently reminded her, they needed to get the child's things together.

Rose reluctantly left her sleeping daughter and began gathering up her toys, reminding herself if she really loved CJ she would do whatever it takes to make her happy.

Then a thought occurred to her. She could refuse to let the child go. Could say that Matilda Jane had signed papers and that she was her mother. And let Ava figure things out for herself. After all Mr. McGuire was not a nice man. Why would she want his child?

Rose brought her thoughts back into line. Yes, she could do that. God would let her, but did she want to? Would being selfish help CJ. She knew it would not.

Elsa saw her dilemma. Second thoughts?

Rose nodded.

"That's all right. You need to consider all sides." Elsa assured her.

But both kept packing. The house silent and the windows dark. Rose pulled the curtains closed.

A knock at the door, frightened both women at once.

"Haw has come. He stayed away as long as he could." She said and took Rose by the shoulders. "I'll be back tomorrow, if you want me. But I won't come unless you send word. I'll have Haw come down in the morning."

"Thank you Elsa." Rose hugged her for a long minute. "I'll be all right. I'm going to ask Captain Wyatt if I can come with her."

"Don't ask…insist on going Rose." Elsa patted her arm and walked out the door with Haw.

Rose listened to the wagon wheels roll over the rocky soil.

It was time to sleep. She'd had enough for today. Her eyes were swollen and burning. Once in her gown and in her bed, she picked up her mother's Bible and let it open, praying for a word from the Lord. It fell open to the middle. Psalm 46: 10. *Be still and know that I am God.* Rose shut the book and laid it back on the table. That was all she needed tonight. To know that God was God and somewhere in all this there was a plan. And Rose had no idea where she fit into it.

Chapter 67

At first sign of light, Rose was up. She could not waste a single hour of the time they would have alone. Carolina Jane was woken early and bathed, Rose talking to her the entire time, telling her of her love for her, how one day maybe she would know the mother of her first year.

At least she knew Ava would be a good mother, had so wanted a child. Rose tried to think of herself as a cog in the wheel, because if Captain Wyatt had not brought her to Rose, the child could have been adopted out and sent away. At least Ava would have her husband's child. There was good in this. But it was going to cost her everything.

When the sounds of wagon wheels approaching caught her ear, she went to the door. It was not Haw, it was Captain Wyatt.

He had brought a small wagon to take Carolina Jane's things. Her heart melted like snow on a hot day. He had come too early. She resented his presence. Even though it was noon, it was still too early.

Nevertheless, she opened the door at his loud rapping.

"I know it's early. I have to catch my ship. I'm sorry..."

"We prepared last night." She said. "Have you eaten breakfast?"

"Yes, I have. At the McKensie's down the way, he tipped his head in their direction.

"What?"

"They stopped me this morning and would not let me pass until I came in and ate."

"And heard their counsel?" A small smile came to her lips.

He nodded and twisted his hat in his hands. Round and round it went.

"Here let me take that for you." She reached out and he gave it into her hands. "I have packed a trunk for her."

"And for you as well, I hope."

"Then you want me to come." She felt the constrictions in her throat release with a puff of air.

"Mrs. Lovell, I know I have wronged you, by keeping the secret. I don't know what else to say to you."

"It's enough that I can go and see to her . . . her transition from one mother to another." Rose couldn't help herself. Did he see the harm he had done to the child as well as to her. Then reminded herself, didn't he just say he had wronged her. She struggled with her emotions and forced herself to get back on task.

"Here is her trunk." She led him to the child's room.

He hefted it and carried it to the wagon. And came back in. "And where is yours?"

"There, but I wasn't sure I was going, so I have a few more things to put in it."

Did he have to rush so?

Within the hour the cottage was shut up tight and locked. She wondered when she would see it again. She had planned never to leave this place. And always had thought Carolina Jane would grow up running these hills.

She carried her child close, memorizing every nuance. The way her blue eyes turned ever lighter in the sunlight. The darkness of her hair, the softness of her skin. The sweet fingers wrapped in her skirt as she tried to stand and declare her first independence.

Captain Wyatt chucked the horses and they began the long trip back to Charleston. He was so quiet, Rose snuck a look or two, but he never glanced her way. CJ was asleep in her arms and she could not put her down, even though her arms ached. They would ache even more in the days ahead, she knew and cuddled her closer.

Looking down at pure innocence and worrying what would happen, and the fact that Captain Wyatt did not speak, she felt hot tears scald her face. There was nothing she could do, but let them fall. Any notion of holding back her emotions was gone.

A good hour passed in silence. Then he glanced at her. She could see from the corner of her eye. She'd been careful to avert her face.

He pulled back on the reins and stopped. She feared to look at him, so she kept her face to the hills and waited for him to get down. She needed to go to the woods herself and assumed the same of him. He tucked the reins on a post and got down, and walked into the woods. He came back and to her side of the wagon.

"Take your walk. Hand her down. I'll keep her."

She nodded and ducked her head, knowing every emotion she was feeling was plastered on her face. She handed CJ down. He helped her down with his other hand. Not a word was spoken between them. Rose wondered if he had any feelings at all.

She hurried to the woods, glad to be relieved. It seemed water was flowing from every place in her body. When she returned his back was to her and she saw him shoulder the child and pat her back. Carolina Jane was not happy. Rose hurried to her.

"Mama's here." She soothed and took her back.

"Look, Mrs. Lovell, I'm not happy to do this." He looked down at her, his hat shading his eyes.

"I know." Her voice low.

"If there were any other way. I've thought about it." He turned adjusted his hat, then headed for the wagon. "We have to make good time. My men sailed around to Dublin to save time as it is."

"I know. The perishables will spoil."

She followed and handed CJ to him and she began howling. CJ never howled. Rose felt his hand at her waist as he pushed her upward. The baby, heavy now, was handed up once again and the little head laid on her shoulder and whimpered. How under God's heaven was she going to hand her over to a stranger. That last sentence a prayer from a heart heavy with wondering if God even heard her.

The last part of the trip was the hardest. Rose knew now she was not going to fare well on the ship and dreaded the voyage. And spring storms were the most violent.

As they got closer to Dublin, Rose began to recognize the city, it's streets familiar to her.

"Captain Wyatt you will want to avoid that road. It is muddy and a wagon is easily rutted."

"Which way then?" He spoke looking straight ahead.

"There." She pointed. Then heard her name being shouted.

"Stop, please." Her head twisted around. It was Captain Riley. He came running up, sidestepping people.

"Mrs. Lovell. You are in Dublin again."

"Yes. Captain Riley, Captain Wyatt, my husband's friend." She made introductions over the noise in the streets.

They tipped their hats at each other. "I'm afraid we are in a bit of a hurry." She apologized.

Captain Riley nodded and waved them on their way.

"Who was he? He looked familiar."

"He captains the *Blarney Stone*. I met his wife and daughter the day they landed on their maiden voyage to Charleston." She said quietly.

"From Ireland, then?"

"Yes. But his wife and daughter were lost in the earthquake. He brought Carolina Jane and I over."

"And no doubt proposed marriage?"

Rose could not have been more surprised. She gave no answer.

"And you refused him."

She was burning mad now. "Captain Wyatt, that is none of your affair."

"Ah, so he did ask." He pulled up on the reins as they neared the livery stable. "I'll turn in the horses and the wagon and we'll walk down to the dock."

He jumped down and took care of business and then helped her down, baby first. Thankfully CJ did not awaken.

"My crew will come back for the trunks. You'll be needing the small bag for the child?"

"Her name is Carolina Jane." She said stiffly. All of a sudden she did not feel she could tolerate his attitude.

He tipped his hat without a smile and grabbed her bag from the back. "This the one?"

She nodded and waited for him to show her the way.

"They should be down at dock bay number seventeen."

Rose noted they were at dock three.

"I'll take the lass while she is asleep." He offered and without waiting lifted her from Rose's shoulder.

Thankful, for she was tired, and the child was heavy now, she walked alongside him but said nothing.

"There will be time to eat on the ship, unless you are unable to wait."

Obviously he was in a better mood now that they'd reached their destination… and she was in a worse mood.

"I can wait."

"Suits me." He kept walking.

And she burned. That was a lie she just told him. They'd traveled half the day and she knew she would be sick the entire journey. This was her only chance to eat anything that would stay down.

"Sir, would you mind if we stopped and picked up a meal. I'm afraid I'm not the seaworthy sort."

Without a word he led them to a restaurant and ordered what she wanted. "We'll take it along and you can eat before you board. I'd like to get out yet tonight."

Rose nodded, too tired to care. She smelled the food in the box she carried and was grateful to have it. Once the ship was in sight, Captain Wyatt went into his duties. His men were ordered to go get the trunks, she was ordered to sit on a bench and eat. He engaged a lady he must have known well, for he ordered her to sit and hold the child while she ate.

His voice was strong and loud as he went about his work. If he had anything to say about it they would be off before the sun went down behind the water. She could only eat, savoring each bite hoping she would have help with CJ, for she would be useless.

Chapter 68

The trip back was worse than the one coming over, Rose decided once she'd heard "land ahoy". She actually cried. Carolina Jane had been older and much more difficult to keep happy, not to mention that she hurled up once or twice and Rose could do nothing but watch miserably from her bunk. She made a new friend, however, in a young mother with a tiny infant. Her little one slept and this woman was not averse to the pitching of the ship.

Rose could not wait for Captain Wyatt, whom she'd not seen once, to come for her so they could be on land again. The passengers above board were talking and laughing glad to be going ashore. The young girl had left with her baby son. Rose sat on the bunk, her hand holding up her head while CJ played near her feet. The rocking had slowed so much since the ship was moored to the dock.

When she felt like she could stand, she picked up her child. She felt much heavier then remembered that she was weak. Even now she felt green around the gills, enough she thought she might hurl again. That's when she heard his voice. He was coming below. She grabbed a wall nearby and forced her eyes to focus.

His hair windblown and loose made him seem like a madman. She realized her mind was working overtime.

"Where have you been? Thought you would have been off by now." He said as he walked up, his boots clicking on the wood floor, echoing in her ears. Then his walk slowed and he caught sight of her.

"Whoa there." He steadied her. "You weren't joking when you said you aren't seaworthy. Without asking, he took CJ off her hip and she felt instantly able to stand again. He grabbed her tight around her waist to steady her and brought her alongside his hip. "Hold on we'll be on land soon enough."

Soon enough wasn't soon enough. Rose had to cover her eyes in the daylight. She'd been down below the entire time not even attempting to walk up and look at the sky and ocean twirling together.

She noted CJ wasn't crying either. They were both past their limits.

"Where are we going?" She managed to say after a few breaths of fresh air.

"Straight to my place."

"Wait..." she tried to talk but had to run behind a barrel. All she could manage was the dry heaves. She didn't care a whit what he thought. She only wanted a bath and a bed.

"Take me to my house."

"You don't have a house. I heard you sold it."

"I can stay there. Portia will take care of me." She swallowed hard.

"Not this time. There's an empty room where I stay. Mrs. McClure will see to you and the lass both."

Rose didn't have the heart to disagree.

Before she could think straight they were inside a large house. Rose took the first chair offered her and the woman lifted CJ away from Captain Wyatt. They had a few words Rose couldn't hear.

"We've got a seasick gal here and this little lass needs a diaper change and a bath." He told the woman who was already heading for a little tub to fill.

Rose held her head.

"I'll take you up. There's a room you and CJ can have. I'll arrange a bath if you can manage it."

"I can manage it." Rose said and pushed on the chair arms. Once up, she felt herself being hauled up. She almost hurled at the quick movement.

She heard the clunk of his boots on each step and couldn't wait to be put down and left alone. Rose also felt the beating of his strong heart against her ear and relaxed.

By the time they reached the room she was almost asleep. Rose remembered him laying her on something soft and she groaned and turned on her side, promising herself she would get up in a few minutes and look after CJ.

The next thing she knew it was morning. She woke, still in her awful smelling clothes and sat up, instantly causing her head to hammer. There were voices. The light from the window hurt her eyes and she turned on her side. Five more minutes and she would get up. The world was still tilting left and then right in her brain.

Miserable, she pulled herself upright and hung her legs over the side and sat for a few more minutes until she could get her bearing.

Then up on her feet, she shuffled and opened the door. The smell of meat frying sent her into a frenzy. She clapped her hand over her mouth and nose and shut the door. Mrs. McClure must have heard it for the next thing she knew someone was standing over her bed.

"Ah, Mrs. Lovell, you are still unwell. Are you carrying again?" The woman looked concerned.

"Carrying?" Rose couldn't understand her meaning.

"Are you with child again?"

"Oh no." she felt her face flush.

"Then you are not seaworthy?"

"I am not." Rose agreed and groaned.

"Stay where you are. Little Carolina Jane is doing well. The men are taking turns feeding her off their plates while I attend to you. I'll bring the tub in and fill it for you."

"Oh that does sound good." Rose tried to smile.

"Do not move. It will take a few minutes but from the looks of you, you won't mind waiting."

An hour later she woke again to a flurry of activity. Mrs. McClure was running up and down the stairs with large tin pots of hot water. Finally she leaned over and told her there was soap and a drying towel and she should lock the door. This was a house full of shipmen.

Rose was about to get up and go down and get her daughter, but sensed Captain Wyatt would not bring them to a bad place. Instead she trusted him and peeled off her clothes and slid into the water, dunking completely under the clean water and washing her hair first and then the rest of her. The water had cooled by the time she lifted herself out, refreshed and clean.

That's when she realized she didn't have a change of clothes. She wrapped herself in the towel and for good measure one of the sheets from the bed and called down to Mrs. McClure.

"Captain Wyatt has not returned with your trunk. I will bring you a dress. We'll have to sew it around you." She laughed, for Mrs. McClure was a large woman.

Rose wondered what in the world they were doing for diapers and clothes for CJ, but she could hardly step outside her door, although there were no more voices of men. They must have all gone.

She waited sitting on the bed and jumped when the woman came bustling in. "Here ya go. Needle and thread will help you a bit. If you double up and just quick-stitch you'll be decent. The men are gone down to the last one and I've locked the front door against visitors. That little lass of yours is asleep on a pallet in the library. It's darkest in there."

"Thank you so much Mrs. McClure. I am grateful for your hospitality."

"Bother. " She laughed. "I'm used to it. Been running this house since me husband died. And we Irish take care o'our own." She winked. "Captain Wyatt told me you come from here and I knew it by the little bit o' brogue you still have on your tongue. He mentioned, too, that I was to take special care of you." She winked again.

Rose looked away. What must the woman think? Her a widow with a small child traveling with an unmarried man. Rose could only shake her head. She had other things to worry about this morning. One of them getting decent so she could be with her daughter. Time seemed to be working against her.

She sewed herself into the dress and looked like one of the ragamuffins running the streets but was decent. She descended the stairs very slowly, keeping her eye out for anyone who might be about. She heard CJ and found her rocking on her hands and knees on the pallet whimpering.

"Oh little one." She ran and dropped to her knees. "Mama's here. Mama's here." Rose cried and held her close. "Oh how are we going to do this Carolina Jane? How are we going to do this?"

Mrs. McClure came in through the back door with clothes hanging over her arm. "I do the washing for the men, too." She explained and tossed the pile onto the dining table and began to fold.

"I've got food left from breakfast in the warmer oven. Help yourself. The men won't be home until lunchtime."

"They come for lunch?" Rose's eyes grew large. She would have to hide upstairs.

"Oh never you mind, Captain Wyatt said he would leave your trunks on the front verandah and you'll be dressed proper by then no doubt. That man always keeps his word." She added.

Rose found her way to the kitchen carrying her child. She fed both of them at the dining table while the older woman finished folding and stacking.

Rose just stood to carry her dishes to the kitchen when she heard that familiar knock. "Oh dear it's him." She said. "Don't let him in. I'm not decent for company." She ran to hide.

"I'll answer." The woman hustled away.

Rose could hear their conversation. He insisted on seeing her. He had news he wanted to deliver.

"She's in the kitchen."

Rose's hopes fell. She was sewed into a dress twice her size. At least she was clean. She stayed in the shadows away from the windows and appeared.

He took his hat off. "You look better today."

Rose saw him look at her dress then bring his eyes back up to hers. "We're both fine." She said. "What is your news?"

"Ava is ill. The doctor is worried it could be something the child should not be around. So you may want to stay at your house on the Battery for a few days."

"Really? Rose couldn't help but smile and stepped out. "That means I'll have a few days with my daughter before . . . ?"

"Yes, it seems that is the case."

Rose thought she saw a glint in those dark eyes.

"Are you sewed into that dress?" He leaned closer to look.

"What does it matter to you, sir. Did you bring our trunks?"

"I did."

She gave him a look when it seem he was amused.

He plopped his hat on and turned on his heel. Rose heard the door slam hard.

She handed CJ to the older woman and looking both ways, she stepped out and fished through the trunks and found clean underthings and all she needed, ran upstairs and dressed her daughter and herself in their own clothes.

She made herself useful about the house while CJ played nearby. That evening, while the fire was crackling and she was helping with Mrs. McClure's mending, she heard the men in the other room talking, laughing and eating. Among them Captain Wyatt. She shut herself and her daughter in the parlor after they'd eaten their fill before the men came.

Chapter 69

The next morning Rose and CJ came down after the men left. Mrs. McClure had word from Captain Wyatt that he would send a couple of his crewmen to carry her and the trunks to her home. She took a deep breath, thankful that she could visit Portia and her family. It would be a complete surprise because she had not had time to write.

She thanked Mrs. McClure for her kindnesses, especially that first night. Two young men had come to convey her and her things across town.

Rose's heart beat faster as they neared the Battery. She remembered the city she left. This was a brand new one. None of the bricks lay in piles. There was hardly a trace of the devastated city she left behind. Her eyes fell on her house. The chimney was new brick. The porch had been painted a soft cream color and new spindles had been added. Emmanuel's work. She didn't have money to pay the young boys and apologized.

"Captain Wyatt said we're not to take money." One said on his way down the stairs after they had transferred her trunks to the front verandah.

Rose knocked at the front door and waited. While she did she looked about. New flowers were growing up a trellis, the old swing had survived. She would rock CJ soon. Lily came and opened the door wide and Rose could not believe her eyes. There stood a young woman, not a gangly shy child.

"Miz Rose, that you?" Lily invited her in. "That be little Carolina Jane." Lily took the child in her arms.

"Lily it is so good to see you." She hugged the two together. "You've grown into a young lady." Rose smiled.

Lily headed for the kitchen calling out, "Granmama come out. See who's here. It be Miz Rose and Carolina Jane."

Rose heard Portia's outcry and saw her coming from the kitchen, pulling off her apron. "As I live and breathe, it's my babies."

She pulled them into her embrace and cried which set Rose to crying which set Carolina Jane to crying.

"Oh dear, look what I've done. Jus look at dat pretty baby. She done growed up."

Rose couldn't stop the tears.

"Aw, you done come home to us." Portia said. "Come on I'll get some lemonade. You hungry?" She looked at Rose and stopped.

"What's de matter chile?"

"Oh Portia...I've come..."

"Come on now. Dis house is yours. You sit right down and tell me about it. I'll get tea and some orange cake. Lily take that chile up and rock her."

Lily smiled and carried the little one up the stairs humming a spiritual to her.

At tea Rose told her all that happened. "Chile we knows that Mr. McGuire wasn't no nice man. But we was sad to hear he was kilt like that."

"Like what?" Rose asked.

"Shot in the back he was. Everbody know that ain't fair, but somebody done hated him 'dat much. Mighta been one o'those girls he kept."

Rose nodded, having no idea how Portia would know these things. And Ava was her friend. She felt sad for her.

"You just stay here and be safe until Miz McGuire get well again. You don't want dat baby sick. And we had some fever here, all them folks coming from all over the world here to Charleston." Portia shook her head.

For the next two weeks Rose had her family again. Just the way it was before she left. She saw all the repairs that Emmanuel and Thomas had finished. The debris was gone from the front and the new gable replaced at the top of the house. She was so proud. Seems banker Dalton had tipped his hat once or twice to Emmanuel when no one was looking.

Rose's favorite addition to the house was two new girls from the orphanage. Girls who would use their time to study and learn music. A brand new piano sat in her husband's old office. Rose smiled and ran her hand over the piano keys. Mrs. Shevington's gift.

Rose was so proud.

Then Captain Wyatt showed up with that loud knock of his, breaking into her reverie.

Portia answered and came for her, brown eyes sad. "He here."

"Thank you Portia."

Rose went. It was nearly dark. Just like the first time she met him. He joined her in the front parlor and she invited him to sit. "Ava is released from the doctor. She did not have the fever. Doctor Case says she is well.

"I'm glad to hear she is better."

"Look, Mrs. Lovell, she would have come with me, but she understands what you have done for her. I'm here to tell you she would like to meet Carolina Jane."

She nodded and stood. "I'm ready."

"Not today. Keep her tonight and then we'll come two days hence, if that is all right with you. I'll bring my sister then."

Captain Wyatt was standing now.

"Thank you…" she started for the door.

"Are you well?" He looked into her eyes."

"Yes, I am well. Thank you for bringing me safely over."

"You're welcome. You look much better than when you first came off." His slight smile made her heart feel lighter. Life was so hard at times, that any little flutter of light lifted one's soul.

"I was a sight wasn't I?"

"I'd have to agree. And you didn't smell as good as you do today."

Rose laughed lightly. "I don't imagine I was very happy either."

"You could say that." He agreed. "Well, I won't take up your time."

Rose saw him to the door. He took his hat off the knob and hesitated then she heard his heavy bootsteps going down only this time the new steps made the sounds different.

Chapter 70

The next two days passed so quickly Rose could not believe it when she heard the sound of Ava's carriage. CJ was napping. Captain Wyatt came to the door with Ava on his arm. This was the first time she had seen them together. They looked so much alike.

"Ava." Rose invited her in and saw instantly the pain in her handsome dark eyes. "I'm so sorry for everything."

Ava nodded, but did not speak.

Captain Wyatt took her shawl and put it and his hat on the peg. "Would you ladies prefer to meet alone?"

Both said, "No."

He hoped to be excluded from this difficult scene…but he had helped create it and Rose felt he needed to be nearby. She had chosen a new dress to wear; a beautiful emerald green reminding her of Ireland, but now that Carolina Jane was here she wondered if it was wise to go back. Especially now that her daughter would not be there…there would be so many memories.

"Mrs. Lovell?" Captain Wyatt's voice caught her attention.

"I'm sorry…I must have…"

Ava interrupted. "Rose I'm so sorry for everything."

Rose nodded and invited them to sit in the large formal front room. She couldn't abide a small intimate meeting.

"I like the changes you made."

Ava spoke so softly Rose could hardly hear. "Yes, I am so glad you helped me. It looks so much lighter and brighter in here."

"But you don't own the home anymore Rose."

"No, I don't. I've made my home in Ireland now."

"I see."

She saw Ava fold and refold her hands. "Carolina Jane is upstairs for her nap. When she wakes, we'll go up and get her."

Ava's smile of relief set Rose's heart on the right track. She found courage building up in her. Portia came with tea and set the silver tray on the sideboard and made a quick exit. "Thank you Portia." She called after her.

Captain Wyatt stood at the window gazing out, one palm on the wall.

The room grew silent. Rose stood and excused herself and brought back some items that were CJ's favorite toys. She handed them to Ava, who began to weep. Rose couldn't stand it any longer. "Captain Wyatt, would you excuse us ladies, please?"

Glad for the exit, he bowed his head, snatched his hat and before Rose could have counted to three, she heard the carriage wheels rolling down the street.

"There, now we won't have to watch our words." Rose said and took a seat closer to Ava. "Tell me all you wish to share."

Ava sat for a long moment reining in her emotions. Rose waited.

Then she started talking. "Oh Rose, I knew before I married him he had a roving eye for women. How could he not. He is . . . was so handsome and talented. He came from one of Charleston's finest families. He had everything to live for, everything he could want, except for one thing. Women. He couldn't stay away from them. His mother died when he was young and I think he missed the companionship of a woman. The only thing is he couldn't stop with me, his wife. He had to conquer. And when we were alone he was so kind, so loving, I would not allow myself to believe the things I'd heard. I forced myself to make excuses even when I saw clues."

Rose sat silent as Ava looked away, she knew, gathering strength.

"Then he came home one night and told me he and Ashton had fought. I questioned him but he only got angrier. I think he was embarrassed to admit they had come to fisticuffs. He was a gentleman. He told me Ashton started it and I believed him. Then when he was . . . was killed Ashton came several weeks later and told me about the child. I was so distraught all I could think of was getting her back. Ashton told me that you didn't know my husband fathered the child."

"I did not."

"I know my brother was trying to protect me, but now that I know...well, she's all I have left of him. And I did love him, Rose. I truly did."

Rose's eyes filled with tears. Again. She was sick to death of crying.

"I didn't know about Matilda Jane at first. When I did learn of her, I went to the orphanage, but she wouldn't see me. And now she's left to go to France. I wanted to apologize to her."

"Matilda Jane is all right, Ava. She straightened things up by giving her baby to someone who would care for her. When you see how happy CJ is you'll understand what a gift Matilda Jane gave her daughter."

"CJ?"

"Yes, my endearment for her. Father gave me one when I was little and I always loved it."

"Would you mind sharing yours?" Ava asked quietly.

"Rosalette. He always called me his Little Rosalette."

Ava struggled then spoke. "I remember my father and mother in the good days. They loved us so much but my father's temper ruined our happy times. When Ashton and I lost them we were assigned to Newgate. The people there at that time made us work too hard. Ashton especially was picked on for he was sensitive and kind. And when he lost her. . ."

The air was thick. Rose went and opened a window.

"Father called mother his little woman. I do remember that." Ava stared, remembering.

Suddenly a voice was heard. Both women looked at each other. Rose knew it was time. "She's awake. Shall we go up and greet her?"

Ava stood, her hanky twisted tight around her fingers. Rose hooked her arm and they went up the stairs together. Slowly they walked toward the child who was calling, *Mama, Mama*. Ava halted, "I don't know if I can do this." She started to weep. If she looks like Theodore I...don't know if I can stand it."

"Now that I now he's her father, she does look like him, Ava. But you should be glad. No matter what troubles your husband had you loved him and this is his daughter."

Rose walked slowly and entered the doorway. Ava waited.

"Mama." Rose walked to her and picked her up, closing her mother's heart as best she could. Her voice quivered as she soothed her and hugged her. "Someone is here to visit you." She smiled as water filled her eyes. "Someone who wants to know you." She motioned for Ava to come in.

Ava stepped just inside the door and stared. Tears popped into her eyes, too. They exchanged glances. "She is beautiful. So like her father." Ava whispered. "Oh Rose...."

Rose leaned close to Ava and waited to see if CJ would warm to her. She did not. She put her face in Rose's neck shyly. "Aw, you are not quite awake are ye lass?"

Ava took a step back and waited for a moment, then walked out of the room. Rose thought she was upset until she realized she left her alone to say her goodbyes. How could she say goodbye. Now or ever? It wouldn't happen. This was her daughter. But it was not, she told her heart, but it did not listen. Rose knew she could not just hand the child over to a stranger.

"Ava. I cannot...I cannot just hand her over. Would you consider letting me come for a few days, just until she gets used to you. I can't abandon her. She doesn't know anyone else except me."

"Would you please?"

Ava looked relieved. "Everyone will know she is my husband's child." She whispered and with everything that's happened, how can I go out in public and take her along. It's too difficult here." She told Rose.

"I see your point. Perhaps we can talk for a few days and introduce her to the people that mean the most to you. The rest don't really matter do they Ava?"

"You are right, Rose. We can take her to Mrs. Shevington. She'll understand."

"Indeed she will." Rose agreed, happy that Ava did not see her as a threat.

"Shall we go to CJ's new home then?" She carried the child on her hip as they made their way down the steps. "I have her things packed. There in that small trunk by the door. If I come I can show you what she likes to eat and what we have done. The way we play. The things she likes to do."

Ava nodded, unable to take her eyes off the child's face. She took her fingers and held them for a moment, but the little lass was wiggling to get down.

"Oh, she likes to stand and hide in my skirts. And lately she has been pulling herself up. Soon she'll be walking, I'm sure of it…"

Ava looked at Rose, who had lost her ability to finish her sentence. "Come let's go to my house together. Ashton will bring your trunk. He'll be back in a few minutes."

"Yes." Rose rallied. "I'll feed her and you can help. I'll warn you, though, she makes quite a mess even with a towel wrapped around her neck."

"I imagine she does."

"Do you live in the same house?"

"Yes. Although I'm afraid my husband did not leave much. It seems he gambled. I have a little money set by but I think I will have to sell and purchase a much smaller home."

"That's all right. CJ won't mind, will you?" She chucked her under the chin.

"She is fed and changed. Now for some floor time. She loves it best when I spread a quilt and give her toys. She'd much rather, now that she's older, be on her own instead of on my lap."

The two watched her play. Then the carriage was back. Rose looked at Ava. "It's time to go. I'm sure Captain Wyatt has work he must be doing."

"I'll let him in." Ava offered.

Soon, the three of them stood together, Captain Wyatt gazing at the two women.

"Ashton, Rose has agreed to come stay with me a week or two, so Carolina Jane can become accustomed to me."

Rose had only mentioned a few days.

"Yes, we feel it is best."

He nodded and went out to load both trunks.

Rose called for Thomas to help with her large one.

Once they were settled, CJ on Rose's lap, he pulled slowly away from the curb.

"I've told Portia and Emmanuel not to expect me for a couple of weeks."

No one said anything.

Once they were at Ava's the air seemed to clear. They had a plan. Even CJ wriggled to get down. She set her eyes on something and wanted to go. Rose found a quilt and spread it on the floor and gave her toys.

Chapter 71

Two weeks passed too quickly, but Rose was satisfied that Carolina Jane would go to Ava. For the last two days she had stayed completely out of sight, taking long walks, working in Ava's garden.

They visited Captain Lovell's solicitor on Carolina Jane's first birthday to give her the McGuire name, then celebrated with a tiny cake. Rose burnt the images in her mind so she could set them to paper when she got home.

It was time to go back. Rose couldn't abide being near her daughter without seeing her, holding her, bathing her. Jealousy was going to set in if she didn't get away. Determined, she packed her trunk and couldn't imagine what in the world she would do from here on out. The cottage would be full of sketchings of Carolina Jane. She would have to hide them beneath her bedstead for the time being.

"Ava, I'm going to walk down to the dock and find Captain Wyatt and see when the next passage will be ready."

Rose went out the door. Ava was busy with the child's bath. She heard the joy in her friend's voice. A heavy rock settled where her heart was supposed to be. But wasn't this what they had been working for? To clear the way for Ava to parent her husband's child. And it was Ava who had lost a husband in the cruelest of manners. Whereas Rose reminded herself she was well taken care of. At least that's what she told herself as she walked, her arms aching to hold CJ one more time.

She passed people she'd come to know while they lived in the park after the earthquake, and had polite conversation but barely remembered. Or when she finally arrived at the dock. The Emerald Star sat rocking on the water. The winds were high today. The sun strong. The skies blue. Blue like Carolina Jane's eyes.

Wandering around she found Captain Wyatt engaged by two women. They were talking animatedly and swirling their parasols. He looked bored. Rose smiled. The man was hard to talk to. Even though the ladies were lovely he kept looking out over the water, every now and again looking at them long enough to be polite.

Rose thought to save him and walked up and stood away where he could see her.

"Excuse me ladies. I have business to attend to." He tipped his hat and hurried over.

He took her elbow firmly, turned her in the opposite direction and escorted her to White Point Gardens where he found an empty bench.

"You were quite engaged." Rose smoothed her skirts and gazed at the sparkling water.

"Engaged is not the word for it. Trapped would be more like it. They were gaggling like school girls."

Rose smiled at his deep-voiced disapproval.

"You smile. Mrs. Lovell have you ever been trapped like that?"

"I believe I have. A time or two." She admitted.

He came straight to the point. "Are you ready to go back to Ireland?" He turned to look into her eyes.

She avoided him by looking out over the water. "I believe I am."

"Ava says you have done a fine job of it." He said gently.

Rose nodded, not wishing to talk about it and said so.

"Would you like to join me for dinner?"

Rose checked his eyes to see if he meant what he'd just said.

"I'd count it a favor of immense proportions, Mrs. Lovell. I have declined dinner with the two of them saying I had other plans. Would you consider being my *other plans*?"

That was the first time Rose found him funny.

"Well, if you put it that way..."

"Are you engaged right now?"

She could see an idea just popped into his head.

"As a matter of fact, I am not."

"Would you like to go for a carriage ride? It is a beautiful day and Ava's horses have not been run often now that her husband is gone."

Rose looked away and back again. "I would consider it a favor of immense proportions if *you* could keep *me* busy for the next few hours. I have kept myself away from CJ for the last two days hoping the two of them would bond. It seems they have. For me to appear now would ruin all we have worked for."

"Done, then." He stood and took her hand to lift her up.

They walked along the boardwalk. I must tell you however, that I will need to say my goodbyes to Portia and her family."

"That can be arranged."

"When do you plan on sailing?"

"Day after tomorrow. There is a storm blowing in tonight and it should pass and then we can be off."

"I will stay with Emmanuel and Portia tonight and tomorrow evening."

He nodded and increased their pace. "We want to get in before the skies start pouring."

They walked to Ava's. He went inside and told his sister of their plans and pulled the carriage around. For an hour he drove slowly. The spring flowers were in full bloom and the weather was perfect. Rose wondered if the good Captain had made a mistake about the weather. Twenty minutes after that thought the skies began to darken. Soon raindrops were plopping on the warm streets, dust turning to mud.

He dashed to put the horses in the stable and park the carriage while she waited inside. It was pouring now. Then all of a sudden it stopped.

"Let's make a dash to the restaurant. It's not far from here but we'd better go now."

He took her elbow and they made quick work of getting there, and just in time for it poured again. "Such fickle weather." She shook her parasol.

"Just like a woman." He grumped.

Well he was back to his old self, Rose noticed. He didn't like women much.

But always the gentleman, he pulled out her chair. They were seated in a corner with tall glass windows and candles lit the space. It was quiet and rather dark since the clouds had rolled in. Rain sluiced down the windows next to their table. Rose found it comforting.

"Why is this your favorite place?" she felt a bit uncomfortable since this was the first time they had ever sat down together.

"It's quiet. A person can think in here."

The menu offered a large assortment of dinners. They made their choices and sat back. Because of his latest comment, she did not wish to interrupt his thoughts, so she studied the design in the restaurant and the flowers outside the window, now listing to their sides under the weight of the fast falling rain.

The food came and she watched him eat. He had the manners of a gentleman and the personality of a shipman, she noted. And he was most certainly accustomed to giving orders.

In the middle of their meal, a woman walked up to the table. He was looking down and at the sound of her voice calling his name, he put his knife and fork across his plate very slowly and stood, his chair nearly falling backward at the quick movement.

Rose could see his dark eyes shutter anger or hurt. She couldn't tell which. But his jaw was working and his stance was hard.

"Captain Wyatt." How good to see you again. "Will you not introduce me to your guest."

He stared at her then seemed to remember he did have a guest. Rose thought he was going to refuse for a moment, but he chose manners instead of temper. She could see his mind working.

"Mrs. Lovell." He indicated her. And said nothing else.

Rose waited for him to introduce this woman to her.

"Darby Raleigh – Mrs. Norbert Raleigh." She stated staring at him. "Pleased to meet you Mrs. Lovell." She nodded like the perfect lady Rose was sure she was. The woman was dressed in one of the most exquisite gowns she had ever seen.

But tension was like a tightly pulled rope between them. The name Darby shot through her memory like an arrow. The same name as on the blue envelopes in her attic…speaking of undying love and then rejection by the suitor at the last. Darby was such an unusual name she would never forget it.

"Well, it is nice to see you. I hear you've done quite well for yourself." Mrs. Raleigh gazed at him through hooded eyes.

Now he was being rude. He never answered her and sat down, saying, "If you don't mind, we were in the middle of a conversation." And picked up his fork summarily dismissing her.

She huffed and just to taunt him Rose noticed she stayed an extra minute and then slowly walked away, her beautiful parasol acting as a cane. She watched her pop it up and wave for a footman to bring her carriage.

Rose picked up her fork and began to eat. He on the other hand, was so angry, she was waiting for him to slide an arm across the table and send the dishes crashing to the floor. His jaw muscles worked and his eyes were black. Very slowly he laid down his fork, flexed his fingers and then picked it up again and started eating as though nothing had happened.

Indeed Captain Ashton Wyatt did not like women. She wondered that he had invited her to eat with him. But then realized she was just a friend. A very safe woman. A man didn't worry about a woman he wasn't in love with. And she believed he had been in love with this woman.

"I'll explain later." He said and finished eating, stabbing his food like it was alive.

Rose nodded and enjoyed her meal, for there was no conversation after that. She had learned that when a man didn't want to talk, nothing short of a disaster was going to change his mind. At least in Captain Wyatt's case.

It was completely dark outdoors. He wiped the carriage seats dry with a towel and helped her up, then drove the horses slowly. The night police were walking along lighting the gas lanterns. When they pulled up in front of her house on the Battery, he parked, brushed the horses and asked her to wait until he was finished. He walked her to the front door and just as she was going in he touched her arm.

"If you have time, I would like to explain what happened tonight."

Rose turned back and knew he was uncomfortable asking her to stay. She hesitated and then decided. "I wouldn't mind at all. It will keep my mind busy, so I won't be thinking about leaving."

"Well, then." He indicated the swing and followed joining her on the seat. She was careful to sit as far away as possible.

He leaned forward elbows on his knees and hands folded under his chin.

She lifted her feet as the swing moved. The night noises were loud. Pesky insects were buzzing around their heads. She stood, untied the mosquito netting and let it fall around them and nearly laughed out loud when it caught on his boot. He tried to move but it clung, until he reached down with his big brown hands and released it.

The netting pooled around them keeping the worst of the bugs away. Otherwise they would have to go inside and he would pace again.

"I'm sorry about tonight."

Rose nodded in understanding.

"I loved that woman one time." Pause. "She and I were youngsters when I fell in love with her. And we secretly became betrothed. We were going to run away one night and get married, but her father interfered and she chose another man."

Rose knew the story. The blue envelopes. Darby and W. But his name was Ashton..."

"I never forgave her. And to make it worse, her father is Mr. Dalton."

"The one at the bank?" Rose's voice rang out. He turned his face and his eyes met hers.

"Yes."

"You mean you had to deal with him for me all this while?"

"One of the reasons I was not happy to be left with that duty. It had nothing to do with Captain Lovell or you..."

She felt her face warm knowing she had read those personal letters and looked away.

"Am I making you uncomfortable?"

"Oh no...it's just...just that I am sorry, that's all."

"Sorry for me? Sorry?" He repeated. "It should be *her* you are sorry for. She had the chance for love. What she has now is money and no love."

Rose knew that pain. Money, no love.

"She married a man that is under her father's thumb. He can't make a move without permission. That was why I moved to London. I had to stay and do my duty for Captain Lovell, and I would do it again. Fortunately I had not seen her since that day twelve years ago...until today. I'll have no reason to be here once you are settled in Ireland, except of course for my sister and now for CJ."

Rose loved hearing him call her CJ, but it brought back all the hurt of knowing she had to leave.

When she thought back to Captain Wyatt's proposal she had to ask. "So your proposal to me citing convenience was not for love then?" she teased him.

He turned his head and she saw the slightest smile come across his face. She was so accustomed to his snarl she smiled back.

"I didn't want you to be a widow with a child. And I had caused you the trouble in the first place by bringing Matilda Jane to you."

"I'm glad you did. It gave me something to do, someone to love. My life took a turn for the better that day."

"But now look what my foolishness has caused."

"Well you could have hardly avoided telling Ava. She would have broken hearted." She said softly.

"I owe you an apology Mrs. Lovell. I am sorry for the way everything has turned out."

"And I for you, Captain Wyatt that you lost the woman you loved."

"Well, there it is said. And done as far as I am concerned. Shall we speak of other matters? There isn't anything either of us can do to change the circumstances." He concluded.

"Indeed." She agreed and tipped her foot to the floor setting them swinging gently.

After about two minutes, he untangled the netting and released himself. It is late Mrs. Lovell and you need to be abed."

He lifted the netting so she could get out and helped roll it back up and tie it in place. "Thank you sir for the carriage ride, for dinner, and for your honesty. All were refreshing. I was kept busy as were you."

He tipped his hat and Rose heard his footsteps as she let herself in the door. She had seen another side of Captain Wyatt this evening.

Chapter 72

Rose spent the next day with her family in her former residence. She never thought to be back in Charleston and wandered around the house memorizing every room. Yet she longed for the smaller, cozy rooms of her cottage; for the views from her window of the bright green carpet as it rolled away, lifting then dipping with each hill. She missed the quietness, the slow, easy pace of the people there.

Crashing noises from the kitchen pulled her back to the present.

Portia and Lily were cooking her favorite meal. Rose felt like she was taking the last meal before her beheading as Queen of England. Then laughed at herself…such musings. Maybe she should take up the pen and write a story for every sketch she made. God knew she was going to need something she could throw her life into, now that she would no longer have CJ.

The smells coming from the kitchen and her sincere desire to *not* grow morose, sent her flying toward the fragrances. She was hungry and told Portia so.

"Chile it almost ready. We done made you yo favorite. Chicken with some o' that good low country rice and string beans and the best lemon cake."

Rose smiled. That was Captain Lovell's favorite dish, but it didn't matter. It all smelled so good, especially since she dreaded the awful knowledge she would once again be starved and miserable all the way back. Most likely even more since her grief would be added to the seasickness.

Emmanuel came and helped her and Portia into their chairs while Thomas held Lily's for her. Rose's eyes lit up.

Rose did not sit at the head. She chose a chair at the side. Emmanuel gave her a look and she fussed with the napkin in her lap. All of a sudden, each chair scooted back and they all stood. She looked around wondering…then did the same.

"We pray standing and holdin' hands ever meal, Miz Rose." He said with a smile. "Grateful for everthing we got."

Rose nodded and took Emmanuel's hand on her left, Lily's on her right and then Lily took Thomas' long arm that stretched across the table and Portia took Emmanuel's.

"God we thank you for this home, we thank you for this food. Bless Miz Rose in her troubles, Lord, and in her good times. Thank you Lord for your blessin's. Amen."

Rose felt tears prick her eyes. It seemed she had spent a lot of time this last year crying and hoped those troubles Emmanuel talked about were over. She was only 21 yet had been a wife, widow, and mother. Now she was just a widow. Alone again. It was good her father and mother were not here to see it. She hoped, there was still time to make a good life.

She knew one thing, as she set the napkin across her lap. Her life just had to count for something.

Portia's smile stretched from ear to ear. Rose gave her a glance. "What are you up to?" She set her fork down and gave her the eye.

"Nothin' you just eat chile."

A giggle escaped from Lily's mouth. And from Thomas, a shy smile.

Rose looked at Emmanuel who was also in on whatever was going on. She ate but wondered what in the world had them all atwitter.

After dessert, Thomas asked to be excused. Rose had almost forgot the earlier silliness when suddenly she saw a little puff of brown fur waddling into the dining room. Portia had excused herself and Rose was picking up dishes as usual.

Then they erupted, Portia standing in the kitchen doorway, her hand over her mouth in laughter, Emmanuel chuckling and Lily beside herself. Thomas stood to the side watching, a quiet smile on his face.

"What is this?" Rose exclaimed and bent down for the little puppy who was coming straight for her. "And who are you?" She picked it up and nuzzled it.

"Captain Wyatt done brought you a puppy. Said to tell you it cain't make up for Carolina Jane but it was the best he could do." Portia smiled, her hands on her hips, proud she had kept the secret. "We been a'feedin it all day. Captain Wyatt done tole us to wait until after dinner."

Rose's face felt warm.She buried her face in the soft fur and missed her beautiful little daughter even more. Still she had something soft and wriggling in her arms and that had to do for now.

"Oh dear." Rose said aloud.

"What, somthin' wrong?" Portia eyes grew large.

"I get seasick. Who's going to take care of him?"

"Oh don't you worry none. Captain done told us about 'dat and he said he'd keep the pup with him until you made it over."

"Oh." Rose sighed. "I guess he's thought of everything."

"He shore did. Acted like a little boy hisself bringing that pup over here dis mornin'."

Rose smiled. The man had a tender spot after all.

Chapter 73

Rose spent the last night with Portia and her family sitting by a small fire out back in the gardens. The puppy was flopping around playfully.

"Chile you know Jesus see all 'dis happening to ya."

"I know."

"We all got troubles."

Rose looked up. "You're right. I know there is a reason. But I'm afraid after having CJ for so long and thinking she was mine forever, I ... well, I don't know how to go on from here."

"We aint' got nuthin' to do but go on til Jesus comes." She said staring at the fire.

Emmanuel put another small log on and the flames jumped higher and sparks flew. Rose stared at the flames wondering how in the world she was going to find purpose and motivation to move forward.

"Dat little puppy over der'll keep you company for a bit. And me and Emmanuel, we been a'prayin' for you a man."

Rose thanked them with her eyes.

"You could stay here and work in 'dem orphanages like you did."

"Oh Portia, I don't think I could stay. Every time CJ saw me she'd want to come to me. And Ava would be hurt...it would be like tearing the child in two."

"Yep, just like in the Bible." Portia agreed. "It be gettin' late Miz Rose, you better climb up dem stairs and get yoself in dat bed. He be coming at dawn."

"Dawn?" She stood and shook the dust out of her skirts. "You're right."

"I be up early. Get you some breakfast. Captain Wyatt says he eat over at his place and for you to be ready. Lily'll keep the puppy tonight so's you can sleep and then he be all yours tomorrow. You best think of a name..." She stood

Rose gave Portia a hug and forced herself to climb the stairs. Tomorrow she would be gone and her little Carolina Jane would stay.

❧

The next morning when all the goodbyes, handshakes and hugs had been delivered, Rose went out to the front swing, while Portia went flying out the back door with her apron covering her face. Lily followed in the same fashion. Thomas bid her goodbye and Emmanuel said, "Ain't nowheres you can go Miz Rose and Him not see ya." He pointed upward.

Rose nodded and tipped her foot, setting the swing going. Her heart was breaking but there was no place to put the broken pieces. So she rocked back and forth her eyes closed to the world.

A few minutes later she heard the wheels cranking their way closer and closer and then silence. Portia had a fear of watching someone off, she had said her goodbyes and gone to work. She wasn't indifferent Rose knew, just couldn't see someone she loved leave.

She heard the front door slam. "Here he be, Miz Rose." Lily handed her the puppy.

She looked into the brown eyes and saw a great deal of sadness. "Have you named him Lily?"

When she nodded Rose asked the name.

"Nibbles." She said.

"Nibbles?" Rose smiled.

"Yes, all he does is nibbles on my toes everwhere I am."

"Well, then Nibbles it is." She said forcing a smile, seeing clearly Lily didn't want to part with him. She had a notion to leave the little puppy behind, but it was a gift from Captain Wyatt.

"I knows you need him, Miz Rose. More'n me. I know that."

Rose stood still and caught Lily's eyes. "Lily, you are a kind girl. I've watched you grow into a young lady. The first thing a person can tell about another is in their unselfish ways. I see that you."

Lily smiled.

Rose could see her spirits had lifted. Which in turn lifted hers.

"I shall make it a point to come back sometime when you are grown and see how you and Thomas have done. Remember, too…if you and your family need anything, please write me won't you?"

"Yea ma'am I will."

The dog squiggling in her arms, Rose hugged Lily and then watched her walk into the house. She held herself erect and plunged into her duty.

Rose watched Captain Wyatt, in his shipmen's clothes, come walking up with one of his crew.

"Good morning Mrs. Lovell." He greeted and walked right past to her trunk. "We'll load this up. That's all you've got?"

"Yes." *Of course it was all she had. CJ's trunk was staying and she'd had so little time to prepare for the trip over, she wondered at the man.*

She had been careful to eat only toast and one cup of tea, dreading the awful journey to come. Rose knew what she had to do. After all she was a grown woman, a widow for goodness' sake and weren't there so many others out there worse off than she was?

At least that's what she told herself when the crewman helped her up to her seat, handed the little dog up to her and then climbed in back. Captain Wyatt had already taken himself up to control the horses.

The clipclop of the hooves on the cobblestones reminded her of the carriages carrying the dead to the cemetery after the earthquake. Mrs. Riley and little

Colleen among them. Wild thoughts flew through her head. Why had she, Ireland Rose Lovell not been one of them? Why was she here and they were not. She was a widow at the time. Mrs. Riley and Colleen had a husband and father. And now he was alone. Where was the justice in the world? Their family had been broken apart. So had hers.

Maybe God had turned his back for a minute.

Rose felt a fear climb over her body. She was leaving Charleston forever. Without her daughter. What good could God possibly make out of that? She swallowed hard, angry at herself for not trusting. For not being more faithful to what she knew was true. She was having trouble grasping truth right this minute.

Captain Wyatt sat stiff, looking straight ahead. The dog wriggled in her lap.

When they reached the wharf she was helped down again. Two men came running down the gangplank and snatched her trunk and hustled it up. She felt the anxiety. Something was amiss.

"Is there something wrong?" She turned to the Captain.

"Winds are averse this morning. We are late getting away." He grumped.

Rose knew it was because of her. He didn't have to say it. She left him to his work, grabbed her skirt and ran up the gangplank. Her resolve was gone. She clapped her hand over her mouth and ran below stairs. Now familiar with her quarters, she passed several people and flew into her room and slammed the door shut.

Chapter 74

Captain Wyatt watched her run. She had clapped her hand over her mouth and with the little dog in her arms looked like a child running to her mother. And he died a little bit inside.

He'd spent a sleepless night. Weather reports had changed. One crewman had been caught stealing and had to be let go and one decided to join another ship.

But he knew the real cause for his misery.

Seeing Darby, hearing her voice, setting eyes on her after all these years had been his undoing. He had built a wall so strong against the hurt, he hardly knew how to knock it down now.

He'd run from the pain most of his life. And wondered why he spent so much time hating her and hating her father. In the few times he conducted business with Mr. Dalton there had been tension so strong in the room, he had had to keep his fists from punching the man in the face.

Mr. Dalton found out about their plans to marry and sent one of his spies to locate their secret hiding place. They were found out. All was lost.

As a young man he had waited out by the gate all night pacing up and down, careful to keep hidden behind the bushes. She had not come.

"Ready to sail Captain?" He heard his name being bellowed out.

"Aye, set her off." He ordered the ship to her waters.

Once they were off and he was at the helm he could rest. At least his body could. He had to focus out ahead, watch for danger zones and try to forget that she was downstairs crying her eyes out. And he had been the one to hurt her. All because he had kept Theodore McGuire's sins secret. And now regretted it.

Once they were on the way he began to perform mental list of checkpoints. The young boy assigned to the crow's nest was new. He looked up and saw he was doing his job. Checked the compass. Checked the sails. Checked the skies. Everything was in order.

The next few hours were relatively calm sailing even though the crew was two men short.

His skin crawled as his thoughts returned to Darby…Darbinger Dalton, the girl he had loved, married to that twit of a man, Norbert Raleigh. Everyone knew he was one of the richest men in the Carolina's thanks to his father's tobacco business. But everyone also knew he was a mama's boy straight from the bluebloods in England and could not make a decision if his life depended upon it. Raleigh's father was rough, gruff and fearless. The Father's only son, who was supposed to be groomed to run the business was nothing but a laughingstock to the bank employees where he worked. Somebody had embezzled his manhood. He actually felt sorry for the man.

Once when he'd had to go into his office, the squirrel of a man refused to give him a loan, stating that his ship did not have enough income to allow the loan. Ashton knew it was a lie but her husband also knew he was Darby's first love. He was sure her father had told him to refuse the loan. Nobert Raleigh had a high position at that bank because his father had knuckled somebody. That he knew.

And Darby in her outlandish outfit. Feathers flying off her hat, jewels jangling at her wrists, makeup too thick stealing all the beauty she once possessed. Her voice grated on his nerves when he first heard it. She sounded like her husband . . . false-voiced. One look at her at the restaurant and he wanted to leave her standing there, but he could not. Mrs. Lovell would have been publicly embarrassed.

The cologne she wore. Ashton thought he would never forget the overly pungent scent. He shook the memory of it as he watched the sea birds flying and dipping in the air. He pulled fresh air deep into his lungs and settled himself to his work. He wondered how Rose was doing below. They were in calm waters, at least for now. He checked his navigation numbers on the map and satisfied, walked the deck. Passengers were standing at the rails enjoying the winds. The sun was just up and soft white clouds floated on air. They were still in warm waters. As they made their way North, things would get a bit pitchy. He hoped Mrs. Lovell was getting her rest now.

Below Ireland Rose kept to her bed, her face to the wall. She had pulled a light blanket over her head so she could sob into a pillow. The puppy whined and cried while she let all the hurt and pain flow. Then when she stopped hiccoughing and crying, the puppy slept in the crook near her belly. She had cried until there were no more tears. It couldn't be helped. She had come this far in life and had never sobbed until it hurt the muscles in her stomach.

Much later, she turned, her eyes burning, her nose stuffed, her head beating like a drum. She opened an eye and saw through the porthole that it was dark. She felt her stomach roiling inside but as yet it was mild. Then a blue light lit the cabin. Lightning. A storm. She quickly disentangled the puppy and used the chamberpot, then spread an old paper and hoped the puppy knew what to do. She couldn't imagine cleaning up after him and hurling at the same time. Her head swirled.

Dreading the next few days, she laid back down on her side, covering her eyes with her hand and tried to rest.

Not two hours later she woke to violent rolling. She grabbed the bucket and began heaving dry air. The puppy whined. He needed food. Somehow she would have to get off the bed, up those stairs and walk out there where the water was at eye level one second and then the sky at eye level the next. She didn't know if she could make it. But she had to. The dog would be tossed around and there was no little box to keep him in. Captain Wyatt had forgotten to take him.

For more time than she meant to, she lay in the bunk, the storm continuing outside on the water. Finally, there was nothing to do but grab anything nearby and hang on for dear life. She first held on eyes wide open. If she closed them the room would be upside down. She waited until her eyes and stomach settled and picked up the pup and tied it into her apron.

She needed both hands to maneuver those stairs. Twice she fumbled and passed two other passengers that looked as sick as she did. Twice she gagged and finally when she was at the top of the stairs, she could smell fresh air. Rain hit her in the face the moment she was on deck and it actually felt good.

For a bit she would walk, then stop, get her bearings. One of the crewmen asked if she needed help. She nodded one hand over her mouth. He pulled her arm and led her to the sideboard where she had dry heaving again.

That's how Captain Wyatt found her. His crewman holding her shoulders while she hung over. His steps quickened. "What seems to be the matter?" He grumped. The man had his hands on her.

"She needed help, sir."

The crewman walked away, but not before Captain Wyatt barked an order at him.

When she finished, Captain Wyatt took her arm, pulled her next to him with a hand around her small waist and walked from post to post so she could hang on. The storm had almost passed but the waters were still agitating.

"Sit here." He took her elbows and lowered her to the seat. "Stay there."

"Wait." She garbled as thunder rolled across the waters. She unwrapped the puppy from her apron. "He needs food and he's so … so small he'll get hurt."

He took the furry little body and went below to his cabin. Found some food from the cook and set water and paper on the floor, then shut his door.

As he cleared the stairwell, he saw her zigzagging. She was going to smash her head or worse. He caught up with her and offered his arm. "You can stay in my cabin with the dog. I'll find another place to sleep."

Rose shook her head, but it made things worse. "I'd rather stay in my own place."

"You've hardly got a voice. Do you want me to get the doctor?"

"No….no…I just want to…" She stopped wide-eyed.

"Hold on. Swallow. Look at me not at the water.

She did. He held her gaze.

He noted both her hands were holding tightly to objects nearby and her stance was wide, trying to keep her balance.

"I'm taking you below."

His voice was loud in her ear because he had leaned down to speak close to her head.

Before she could form a word he had lifted her slowly and she heard the clunk of each step as he carried her below. He let go of her legs and she slid to the floor, one arm stil around her waist, and opened the door.

He walked her to his bunk and helped her in. She still had a tight hold on his sleeve. "You're safe. Storm's slowing. We should be in calm waters soon."

She turned on her side and he lay a blanket across her and made his way back up. Something in him nearly snapped when he'd seen his crewman taking advantage of the situation back there.

Chapter 75

Morning light was burning Rose's eyes. She moaned and groaned trying to sit up. The puppy was asleep in a little box. She forced her eyes to focus and got down on hands and knees and crawled the short space, put the puppy in her lap and sat on the floor.

"Oh Nibbles I never want to cross the Atlantic again. I doubt I'd survive it. Her throat was dry and sore from too much activity. She hadn't needed to use the bucket he'd placed by the bed. She actually felt her stomach had settled down. Glad for even a small reprieve there was time to peruse the cabin. A rain slicker hung on the wall, next to a pair of boots. There were no personal items about. Just a simple room.

Then she saw something shiny. She got up carefully and made her way. It was a necklace pinned to the wood walls. A beautiful one. It was hardly noticeable because it was behind his pillow which she had knocked aside as she tumbled out of his bunk.

The sun was shining at just the right angle making it sparkle. She fingered it and admired the beautiful work.

The door flew open and he found her looking at it. His dark eyes, sleepless from the looks of it, found hers.

"I happened to . . ."

"It doesn't matter. Are you feeling better?"

"Yes, I am."

"Can you make it to your room or do you need assistance?"

His straightforward questions made her wonder what he was getting at.

"Yes, I believe I can." She tried unsuccessfully to push her hair out of her face. She must look like a waif . . . and her clothes were wrinkled beyond smoothing.

"I need my bunk. Take the box for the dog and try to rest yourself. You look white and should probably get some sun and air up on deck."

He began to remove his jacket. She scuttled to pick up the box, got to her feet with fair success and grabbed the door handle. "Thank you for…last night. Oh I almost forgot…" she laid the necklace over his palm.

Rose slipped through the door, box, puppy and herself and closed it, leaning against it for a moment. The quick movements reminded her brain it was still not working correctly.

In a moment she grabbed the railing and made her way to the top. She took his advice and pulled fresh air into weak lungs. Thankfully the sun was behind clouds today, because the water was smooth as an ice skate pond and the day fair. She hung on, slowly closed her eyes and filled her lungs again.

Most of the people at the rails looked as mussed as she was. And sleepless eyes were beginning to look normal. Then there were others strolling arm in arm as though they were walking on the boardwalk near her house in Charleston.

It was time to wash up. She found water, cleaned out her bucket and refilled it with fresh water and sponged herself off. Her trunk was in her room. Someone must have brought it last night. Grateful, she fished through her things and found a cooler lightweight dress in brown. It would have to do. She didn't much care. Pulling her hair down from its tangled mess, she brushed through it and rewound it enough to get by. Curly tendrils fell around her face.

There. So much better.

"Nibbles, we can only hope the rest of the voyage will be like this. I think I could make it if it were." She smiled watching him eat. Once finished, she lifted him out of the box and let him waddle and play. An old handerchief tied to a long string made a toy. "You…" she picked up the puppy and hugged it…."are my new friend. When you grow we're going to take long walks on the Irish hills, just the two of us."

Her eyes filled. CJ would not be walking the hills with her as she had planned.

With most of her senses back, she thought about CJ, wondering how she was doing. Did she call Ava *mama* from her bed in the morning. Rose's eyes spilled over. Then about Mr. Riley. Wondering how he was doing. If he was faring well at all. She chose to think about something else and thought about putting words to her water color sketches. Perhaps she could find a paper source and make a book. Send it to CJ telling her a little story. But then decided against it. That would cause division when Ava would have to explain who Rose was. She put that idea to rest. Perhaps she could work in Dublin with an orphanage there. She could teach drawing, water color painting.

Musing, she missed the call for dinner. The same crewman who helped her last night knocked on her door even as it stood open. "Sir."

She saw him look her up and down and shivers ran up and down her arms, alerting her senses.

"Ma'am the dinner bell rung. Will you need assistance?"

"No sir, I will not." Rose said firmly. "Thank you."

She gave him her back, but instead of leaving, he stood watching her for a long minute and finally left. Rose thought it best to shut her door and mingle with others.

Chapter 76

Two days later strong winds whipped the sails and the ladies' dresses. Rose made herself stay on deck, with quick trips below to check on Nibbles. The storm passed so quickly Rose gave a sigh of relief. She was actually doing better.

Twilight began to fall. The sails had done their duties well and now the winds were low. The ship rocked and glided along slower than usual. She was gazing at the stars and wondering how many people had crossed this vast body of water and how amazing it was that one could visit countries back and forth. She was anxious to see Haw and Elsa.

Something told her she was not alone and she glanced at several people next to her at the railing. And beyond them stood the crewman she did not like. He was looking her way. Rose made her way toward the front of the ship hoping to find Captain Wyatt. She felt safer near him and dared not go below.

When the Captain was in sight, she felt a tug on her arm. It was him. She pulled away. "Sir you are behaving in an ungentlemanly way. Please remove your hand from my arm."

Rose was careful to speak in a low, firm manner. No one had ever made her feel this way before. Her heart raced a bit, but she could see Captain Wyatt and knew she could scream.

The man did and stepped back, putting both hands behind his back. "I meant only to steady you." He said, his eyes never leaving her face. "You have beautiful hair."

Rose put more distance between them, turned and walked away. By the time she got to her safe place, she was unnerved.

"What's wrong?" Captain Wyatt asked her as soon as he turned. "Has he bothered you again?"

Rose's eyes told him without saying a word.

"I'll break…."

"Sir, he is pushy, but harmless, I believe."

"Harmless? No man is harmless when there is a woman around. Let alone a beautiful woman." He growled, his eyes concentrating ahead.

"Stay here." He ordered and went below for a moment and returned. "Take this." He handed her a small pistol.

"Whatever for?" Rose could not make herself touch the thing.

"In the event you need it. Use it." He pushed it into her hand. "It's already loaded. You have one shot."

She wanted to throw it down, but worried it may go off.

"I cannot protect you everywhere on this ship, Mrs. Lovell. Do as I say."

Rose pressed it into a hidden pocket of her dress and moved slightly closer to him.

"I'll escort you to your room when you are ready. And I suggest it be soon."

Now she was worried. If Captain Wyatt thought so, she must not be foolish.

"Then take me when you are ready. I'll go in and put a stick of wood under the door handle."

"Start on, I'll join you in just a moment. The deck is beginning to clear of passengers. Ladies should not be above board at this hour."

She looked around, and began walking slowly, her eyes scanning. About the time she was out of his sight she felt a hand grab her elbow. She started to scream and heard him say close to her ear. "Just walk with me. That's all I ask."

The next moment she felt the hand in the crook of her arm jerk her back. All of a sudden two men were fighting. She saw several men run and the young boy at the top of the crow's nest shimmied down and landed on the deck with a thud. They were surrounded. Captain Wyatt picked the guy up by the scruff of his neck and jerked the man's face to his.

"I should throw you overboard. Feed you to the sharks." He said through gritted teeth. "You touch another woman on this ship and I'll see that you are tossed over. You understand that?"

The man nodded and started to say something and snapped his mouth closed. The crewmen stood ready, fists at their side to assist.

"Jacob lock him in the brig."

Captain Wyatt tossed the man hard enough to cause him to stumble.

Rose watched thinking this was all a dream. She felt the gun in her pocket, pulled it out and handed it back to him. "I'm sorry for the trouble."

"Keep it." He ordered as long strides took him away. He shoved his hands through his hair, straightening his clothes as he went. "Take her down to her bunk, Will." He ordered.

One of his crewmen stepped forward and indicated she should go ahead. He followed and made sure she was safely in her cabin.

Rose shut the door and wondered where the brig was located on the ship.

Chapter 77

Finally after nearly three weeks at sea…the winds had slowed enough to hinder their trip, Ireland Rose set foot on dry ground.

She never saw the crewman again.

The puppy had grown larger and she became accustomed to having him at her feet at night. She was thankful to be on home soil. This voyage had been so eventful she'd had little time to think about anything but getting home.

Captain Wyatt was busy and stayed to himself, assigning Will to watch out for her and the other ladies. It hadn't just been her. Other ladies had reported the young man was equally brazen with several of them.

Captain Wyatt made the regular stop in London and then with a skeleton crew, sailed to Dublin. He had insisted. She had insisted otherwise, saying she could hire a driver to take her overland to County Clare.

So they sailed to Dublin and docked the ship. His men, all of them unmarried, a requirement for the job, she learned, went their way with instructions to meet back in a week's time. She and Captain Wyatt set out with a small horse and carriage he rented from the livery stable.

He was distant and Rose wondered what she could have done. It seemed she was trouble for him at every turn. First assigned by her husband to handle her business affairs, having to deal with Mr. Dalton on her behalf, and now this. She needed to find a way to let him go.

Perhaps she could see how Captain Riley was doing these days. Relieve Captain Wyatt from his duty to her.

And…she mused, it seemed every man she came in contact with was a ship's Captain. And she a fiercely unseaworthy woman.

Wondering as they drove along, the puppy asleep in the wagon, she realized they were getting closer to home. This had been a hard trip in many ways. Her heart hurt for the loss of CJ. Her stomach hurt from all the heaving. Her bottom hurt from bouncing on the hard wagon seat and on top of that she managed to ruin the hem of her dress from the muddy rain. She glanced at him, his long legs stretched out, elbows resting on his knees.

He caught her looking and she turned away, embarrassed to the roots of her hair.

"Are you all right, Mrs. Lovell." He asked, face forward.

"I'm fine Captain Wyatt. Although it has been quite an adventure."

"I want to apologize." He started.

"For what?"

"Woman, don't interrupt me." He ordered.

She put her hands in her lap, but knew her chin lifted a level. He was forever bossing people around.

"I made a grave error and I'm sorry for the trouble I caused you."

She watched as he ran his palm over his darkened chin, looking pretty ragged himself. "You already apologized." She said quietly."It's somehow for the best."

"Why would you say that?" He demanded.

"Because, sir, I sincerely believe that God does not do anything without purpose. Whether we see it or not, is immaterial. I have begun to look for it now. After having much and having little, I prefer to have little and joy, rather than much and menace.

"Menace?"

"Banker Dalton." She informed.

He readjusted his hat and tapped the reins.

She smiled. The man was in a hurry to get back to his home in London. She was sure, handsome as he was, he had a woman waiting in every port.

"Anxious to get home?" She made light talk.

"Why?"

"Oh, no reason. Just wondered." She shrugged. He sure was touchy.

Soon she saw her place from far off, gasped and lifted her bottom off the seat half standing.

"Sit down. You want to fall out and break every bone in your body." He stuck out his arm like a fence in front of her.

She sat but could not contain the smile that came across her face. She was home and she was not…not going back across the Atlantic and said so.

He gave her a sideglance. "I don't blame you. You are one of the most sickly women I've met."

She saw his cheeks working. Did he have a bit of fun in him, then?

"You, are right." But I'll bet you can't run like the wind."

"Run?"

"Yes, run. I imagine that if I challenged you to a run across the hills you'd decline."

"I would not. Since when could a woman, especially one as small as you, beat a man running?"

"Well, why don't we just see? My legs are so anxious to be running, I can hardly contain myself another minute." She said knowingly.

"As soon as we unload your things, I will accept your challenge."

Rose just smiled. Little did he know she was the best runner of all the children on the playground, boys or girls. First level or eighth level. Not one boy could beat her.

"You never said anything about running before." He pulled the wagon to a stop.

"Why ever would I have needed to?" She did not wait for him, but lifted her skirts and let herself down, picked up her puppy, box and all, and started for the door.

"I'll get your trunk."

Rose ran ahead and opened the door and took a good look. She put the puppy down and set his box nearby. "Welcome home Nibbles." Her eyes roamed the room, happy to be home to her own cottage.

Then she saw it on her bed. Carolina Jane's little doll Elsa had made.

She couldn't look at that doll right this minute and shut the door. "Are you ready?" she challenged him without a smile. What she needed was a good run. One that would pound out all the pain she would have without Carolina Jane in that house.

"I'm ready. Say the word." He lined up with her.

Rose took a deep breath said a private prayer, *Lord help me to run like the wind and with it carry away the pain that I feel.*

"Keep your eyes straight ahead." She watched him hawk-eyed as she tucked her skirts up. "See that lone tree over there?" She pointed.

He followed her finger and nodded.

"First one there is the winner." She pulled in a breath.

"Go!"

She started running purposefully holding herself back. Let him think he was going to beat her hands-down. Then when he began looking over his shoulder with a smirk, she picked up her pace caught up with him, stayed just behind him so he would think she was never going to pass, and then at the perfect time she let loose and sailed past him and to the tree.

"How did you do that?" He came sputtering.

"I may be the worst seaworthy passenger you've ever had, but I can beat you running." She said barely breathless.

"Indeed you can." He laughed.

Rose looked up at his face. "You're laughing."

He looked away and back again. She saw his eyes darken and something in his look changed. Before she could read it, he closed off and started back, walking big strides again. Would the man ever stand still? She caught up with him but wisely said nothing.

"Are you hungry? I am starved." She said as he followed her in, ducking under the doorway.

"Yes." He said evenly and put his hat on the nail by the door. "I am. Have you got anything to eat around here?"

"I'll look. Not likely too much. We could go down to Haw and Elsa's and ask for some bread and cheese."

He grabbed his hat and went for the wagon. "I'll brush the horses. You have any feed?"

"Just on the side in the small shed."

He fed his horses and she saw him carrying a bucket with rainwater from her barrel. She watched his movement as his big hands brushed then smoothed the horseflesh and saw a gentle man.

She pulled her shawl over her shoulders and got up on the wagon without assistance.

"Why are you always doing that?"

"What?"

"Getting up yourself."

She shrugged. "No one is around. I just thought it might save time. I'm hungry."

"Well just so you know. I don't feel like a gentleman when a lady doesn't act like a lady."

Instantly she looked away. He thought her unladylike? Well if he could give it, he could take it. "Sir I hardly feel like a lady when a gentleman walks around barking out orders and tossing dark, menacing looks at her."

He snapped the reins and they rode in silence.

Rose wondered what happened.

Chapter 78

Haw and Elsa shared their dinner with them insisting they stay and eat. But it was awful quiet at the table.

Elsa sent several slices of buttered bread, some cheese and enough meat for the next day. Haw pointedly told Captain Wyatt he could sleep at their cottage that night. They pulled out.

Rose felt like crying. The stars were out. She was happy to be home and now they were angry at each other and she didn't know why.

"I'll get your trunk situated where you want it. Unless you think you can move it all by yourself."

That statement wounded. Was he mad because she beat him at running?

"Of course I can't lift it by myself. Just because I can run doesn't mean I can lift something three times my weight."

She got down herself and with firm steps let herself in and lit the gas lanterns.

"I'll get wood." He said from outside.

He came in and put a few small logs in the fireplace and lit it with the candle she handed him. Then he muscled the trunk to a low side table. She lifted the lid and began unpacking things, wondering when he was going to shoot out the door without another word, stay at Haw's and Elsa's and go back to London.

She worked carrying things and dropped something to the floor. He reached down to pick up . . . oh no . . . the blue envelopes.

Rose tried to scoop them up, but he had already seen them.

"Where did you get these?"

His voice was low. She knew enough to recognize when he was forcing himself to be reasonable. And this was one of those moments.

"Up in the attic. At *my* house." She held her hand out but could not look him in the eye.

"These are not yours. You had no right to read them."

"They were dated so long ago…I thought…I…" she couldn't finish.

He looked down at them and picked up a stray one and stacked them together and put them in his coat pocket.

"Did you enjoy reading about my private affairs."

He spoke too calmly and Rose knew to step lightly.

"I … I did read them. And I found them to be…" she hesitated "very lovely."

"Lovely?" He looked at her hard.

"I read them and I . . ." she started to tear up. "But I had no idea it was you. They were all signed by *W.* I didn't know it was you until Darby, came by the table that afternoon." She gave him her back.

He grabbed her elbow and swung her back to face him. His dark eyes were accusing.

"All right, if you must know, I fell in love with the man who wrote these." She cried, jerked her elbow free, put her hands over her face. "I couldn't help it." She blubbered backing away.

"Don't go."

She felt strong hands at the tops of her arms pulling her back. Rose could not look at him. Whatever possessed her to say those words, she had no idea. No idea that she had fallen in love with the man who wrote those notes. But these two men were not the same. How would she explain that?

A finger lifted her chin. She dropped her hands clumsily and their hands entangled. He took hers firmly into his and pulled her closer. "Look at me, Rose."

Her heart went banging again. Her name on his lips did something to her. She forced herself to look at him. His eyes were soft, hurt.

"I fell in love with this woman." He pulled the letters from his pocket and waved them in the air, but it wasn't her I was in love with it was you."

Rose thought he had lost his mind. But the look in his eye told her differently. When had he loved her? She'd never seen it. He'd protected her. Done his duty to Captain Lovell…when had he loved her?

"But I thought…your duty to my husband…when did you love me?" she looked him in the eye and waited. She would see the truth.

"The moment I walked in the first time and saw you standing there in the night, waiting for news of your husband…you were so young, so beautiful in the candlelight. But your features were so much like hers…that I couldn't separate the two of you. Not at first. And my anger was so deep for so long. When I saw her at the restaurant I knew it was over. My hatred for what she'd done melted away. Not at first but later that night." He stopped. Then continued.

"I was glad that she had not come out that night--that we hadn't run away. Glad that I wasn't the son-in-law of Mr. Dalton. I could see clearly for the first time you were nothing like her."

Ireland Rose stood still for fear the spell would break. Had her ears heard right? He had loved her from the first day. She must be too tired, for she couldn't seem to put all of that altogether.

"Why didn't I see it?"

"Because I shut you out. I closed the door so fast that night. I went to the bar after I had promised your husband I would stay away from liquor. And I hated myself for it."

She processed his words. "I see."

"You are not convinced are you?"

"Not totally." She said honestly.

"Well then I'll show you Ireland Rose..." she watched as his dark bearded face came toward hers and felt her eyes close slowly. He kissed her tenderly at first and then his arms tightened around her and he kissed her breathless.

She pushed with both hands on his chest. "I can't breathe." She heard herself say.

"Rose, I've waited so long. Promised myself I would not push you so soon after your husband's death."

His soft gaze made her realize he was telling the truth. Not to mention that kiss. Her first kiss.

"Is that why you were so grumpy?"

He laughed aloud. "Yes."

"Hmmm....." Rose didn't know what to do. Should she stand back. It wasn't decent, the two of them alone in her cottage. And heaven knows she wanted him to kiss her again. Was that proper? She decided it was not.

"I think you'd better go to Haw's place."

She saw he hesitated, but stood back and without his gaze leaving her eyes, he picked her up and carried her out through the door. "Not yet."

"What are you doing?" She felt fear at first and then laid her head on his shoulder instead of squirming. She trusted this man.

"I want you to remember this night. He dropped her down and pulled her tight to him, his hand at her waist. Look up."

She did. "See those stars and the moon."

"Hmmmm...." She mused feeling safe in his embrace.

"Ireland Rose Lovell, I want you to be my wife. Will you?"

She pulled away slightly and in the moonlight made sure he meant what he said...that she wasn't dreaming.

"I believe I will." She said.

"So serious." He laughed and threw his arms around her middle and swung her until her skirts billowed out like the sails on his ship.

Rose laughed. Exquisite joy like she'd never known filled her. When he stopped swinging she pulled his head down to her lips and kissed him lightly and said, "And that's the last time I kiss a Captain."

"I thought you said this was your first kiss."

"It was."

"Captain Lovell loved you didn't he?"

Rose knew what he was asking. "He married me out of duty. But we never ... I've never...been kissed or made love to..."

William Ashton Wyatt was now the one who was shocked. She could see it.

"You've never been loved have you Rose?"

"No. I just told you Captain Wyatt."

"Call me Ashton...I'm William Ashton Wyatt." He said without taking his eyes from hers.

Rose knew he was going to kiss her again. And she didn't mind one bit.

After a long, sweet kiss in his arms, she murmured, "No wonder God made me wait. It was worth it." She lay her head on the tall man's shoulder wondering why it could have possibly taken so long for her to see what was right there all the time. His chin rested on top of her head.

Chapter 79

Captain William Ashton Wyatt went reluctantly down to Hawthorn McKensie's house and spent the night. But early the next morning he was banging on Rose's door. He had to be sure that last evening had really happened.

When she opened the door, dressed, hair up, and smelling like lavendar, he couldn't take his eyes off her.

"Breakfast?" She asked and turned. Rose heard him growl and grab her again, swinging her round and round. "I've been dizzy enough lately." She laughed.

"Not near enough." His deep voice at her ear.

Rose pulled away, wondering how long they had to wait for a marriage certificate.

He, on the other hand, was wondering where they would live. Did she want to move to London -- to be in the city. Did she want to stay here? He voiced his questions.

Rose tipped her head and thought about it. She saw Carolina Jane's little doll. "I want to stay here. I want my children to grow up here. In Ireland. In this cottage."

His dark eyes roved over her face. "How many?"

"How many what?" she felt him close in on her.

"Children."

"Oh dear." She whispered.

Rose forced herself to get away from him. Her mind could barely process the fact that he had kissed her. Twice. Something inside her wanted to run into his arms and never look back, but her practical nature needed to make sure this was real and true. He had a past she knew nothing about. She needed to hear his story.

"Come. I have breakfast." She couldn't help the smile that lingered on her lips. "We can talk."

She saw immediately Captain Wyatt, William Ashton Wyatt, she remembered him giving her his full name, was going to be a handful. Slipping away, she placed herself on the other side of the table and waited for him to sit, meanwhile she noted he hadn't taken his eyes off her. She must be wise.

"Sir, you sit there." She pointed and made her way past him and set the food out. This was not going to be easy.

"You address me so formally. Call me Will."

Rose nodded, "All right. Will."

"You will be the only one who calls me Will." He said firmly and sat down.

She looked up and caught those dark eyes looking at her, his mouth lifted at the corners. "You mock me?"

Instead of answering he just gazed at her, making her nerves titter all up and down her arms. She picked up a spoon and stirred sugar in her tea, the noise loud in the silent room.

"Say the prayer." He said his eyes never leaving hers.

She did, hardly remembering a word, and prayed a silent one that God would help her keep her senses. The goal this morning was to make sure this man was the right one. She could ill afford to make an error.

When he picked up his fork to eat, she looked down at her food and wondered how she would swallow, him sitting so close. And the kisses he gave her were downright unexpected last evening. She had never thought Captain Wyatt had a romantic bone in his body.

This man, whom she'd thought of as a grump, was sitting there eating, knowing she was at all odds. Confused, she picked up her teacup and sipped, but could not bring herself to eat a bite.

"You're not hungry?" He said, that beguiling smile resting on his lips.

She shrugged.

He put his fork down and gave her a look. "Go ahead, ask the questions you need answers to."

How did he know?

"I'll answer anything you want to know. Nothing will come between us Ireland Rose. Nothing. I won't live like that. There's been enough secrets and we will be honest and forthright in this marriage."

Her shoulders straightened. "I have not said yes to your proposal, sir."

Actually she had said yes. Last evening. He remembered the words. *Yes I believe I will*, making him the happiest of men. But he knew she was leery of his past. And she was weary of proposals that were made out of convenience. In total, she was unaware of her ability to make a man crazy in love with her.

"You need time don't you?" He saw her need.

"How is it you know that Captain Wyatt?" She felt her chin lift.

"Because you wear your feelings on your face."

Rose looked away and grabbed her cup again. She knew she was unable to hide her feelings, but did he have to announce it. Especially not now when their relationship had turned so quickly. Perhaps a bit too quickly. She stood and brought the teapot to the table.

"Perhaps you should make your trip over and we should talk about this when you come back." She suggested.

"You are refusing me, then?"

He still wore the smirk.

"I did not say that."

He could play along.

"Then I shall be on my way." He put his fork down. "Thank you for breakfast Mrs. Lovell. I will call on you for your answer when I return."

Rose watched as he scooted his chair back, picked up his hat on the way and walked out the door. The same way he always did. Without another word.

When she heard the horse's hooves, she couldn't believe her ears. He was gone. Just like that. Burning tears popped into her eyes. She was alone. Again. CJ was gone and now she'd let this man, the man with whom she shared her first kiss, walk out the door. He had kissed her hadn't he? And proposed marriage for love, not convenience hadn't he? Why had she been so proud? She wanted to run after him, but it was too late. Captain Wyatt was not a patient man.

She processed all these things and realized it was more fear than pride. She had to be sure. And how could she be certain? They'd only known each other a year's time. And none of that time had been fruitful until he'd seen his first love. Did he actually care for her or was he infatuated with her because she looked like Darby?

Likely he had stopped at Haw and Elsa's place, maybe even told them of their first disagreement. And only a few hours after his declaration of love.

Rose was sick at heart.

Chapter 80

William Ashton Wyatt did stop at Haw and Elsa's to ask them to watch out for Ireland Rose. She had only recently lost Carolina Jane and he worried that his proposal had been made at an inoportune time. He was headed back to the America's and could not put off the voyage. But he would be back.

"Send word if she needs me." He left his address. "I will be back as soon as I can."

Haw and Elsa watched him walk out their door.

"He loves her." Elsa said quietly. "But I don't think Rose knows that for certain. She's had too much to think about in such a short time. Her husband passes, she loses a child she loves. And a man she knows only as an acquaintance proposes marriage. She doesn't believe him."

Haw smiled. "In time, she'll see."

"You're right. Providence works in ways we don't understand." Elsa reluctantly turned to finish clearing the breakfast dishes off the table. "I'm going over there."

Haw smiled. He knew she would.

Rose heard someone coming. She ran to the door, ready to throw herself in his arms and tell him she would be his wife. When she saw Elsa, she sobbed. First because it wasn't Captain Wyatt, second, because she needed a woman to sort out all her misgivings.

"I came as soon as I heard." Elsa said and Rose threw herself into her arms.

"He told you? Is he coming back? I'm so foolish…" she blubbered.

"There now." Elsa soothed. "Let's go for a walk. We can talk much better that way. And besides you need to decide what you want in your life. A body can do that well enough out of doors walking these hills. Get your shawl. The morning mist is cool."

Rose cast her eyes about and obeyed, covering her shoulders.

Wisely Elsa did not say anything. They followed the footpath upward into the hills.

"I don't know why I acted like I did." Rose said quietly.

Elsa nodded.

"I believe Captain Wyatt was sincere, but I cannot be sure, Elsa. I found recently that he could not abide me because I looked so much like the woman he lost. Can he separate me from her? I don't know. Does he want me because I look like her? And I'm so…so distraught…am I acting foolish because I lost Carolina Jane? I just don't know…."

"Lass, you've lost a husband, lost your home, lost your good friends, Portia and Emmanuel, and now your child. It is no wonder you are questioning. It is not bad to question. God knows all these things about you. He knows you need time to be sure. Making a marriage is not a small affair."

Rose nodded, but her heart felt broken and unsure.

"Captain Wyatt said he would return as soon as he could and asked us to watch out for you."

"He did?" Rose felt awful. "And he has so many troubles of his own and I'm just adding to them."

"Loving someone is not trouble, Rose."

"I found he was forced into dealing Darby's dreadful father, because he had to take care of my affairs. And all this time I never knew."

"That tells me the man honored your husband's wishes, even when it cost him personally to do so."

Rose snatched her handerchief from her wrist sleeve and wiped her eyes.

"And that he never mentioned it, tells me he didn't want you to know." Else finished.

"Ummmmm…..hmmmm." Rose started to cry again. "And look how I acted this morning. Do you think he will come back?"

Elsa looked at her friend. She had just told her Captain Wyatt would be back. She didn't think herself worthy.

"Rose, you must measure yourself, not the losses you have experienced, but the real reason you are here. When you worked at the orphanages during the time your husband was gone, did you find fulfillment?"

"Oh yes, I did. I loved the work."

"Then you must be about finding yourself work like that again. You are not here to just survive you are here to help others. I see that in you."

Rose sniffled. "You are right. I need to find something to do that will matter, Elsa."

"Indeed you do. There is a family of six. Four children under the age of ten. The mother is very ill. She is an hour's ride from here. Would you like to go visit her?"

"Yes. Yes. Could we go tomorrow? I'm in no condition to visit today."

Elsa took her arm. "Let's head back. I've work to do at home too. We'll take some vittles over to the family. But I warn you, they are a lively bunch. The father is a fun sort of man and will play tricks on you, so you must watch your back. But he keeps his wife and children smiling."

"Good. I'll make a pot of soup." Rose sniffed and swiped her nose again.

"I'll make a cake and bake some bread."

Rose waved as Elsa trotted down the worn path. She entered the house and knew she could now grieve losing Carolina Jane. She was alone with God. Prayers began and didn't stop. She peeled vegetables, cried when she saw CJ's doll, and prayed for her beloved Captain Wyatt. That he would not give up on her and that she could find a place in her heart for him that would be true and faithful. They had been at odds for so long, Rose knew now, she had not truly believed he cared for her. Until those kisses. How could she not know after that?

Back and forth, her heart swung. This way, then that way. She had to be sure, above all things, that she would make a good wife for him. He had lost his parents and she sensed that he wanted to settle down. She wanted the same thing. Could he live in that small cottage? Would he be happy with an unseaworthy wife? Would she be able to withstand all the weeks he would be gone captaining his ship?

Chapter 81

The weeks passed. No word came from Captain Wyatt. Some days she wondered if he would come back. Perhaps he would go for comfort to the other women she was sure waited for him. There was no lonelier feeling than regret.

She vowed that when he walked through the door, if he ever did again, and if he still wanted her, she would throw herself into his arms and declare her undying love. Smiling at her romantic foolishness, she kept busy. The new family was a godsend. Twice she and Elsa visited and twice Rose had come back more fulfilled than ever. The woman lost a three year old son and recently her newborn daughter. Rose saw the suffering of others and counted herself blessed to have had Carolina Jane for the time she did. At least her child was still alive.

Rose wondered if Will, she tried his name on her tongue, would bring a report from Ava and let her know how CJ was doing.

One rainy day about a month later, she heard someone coming. Probably Elsa or Haw. She set aside the bread she was kneading and waited for the knock. When she heard it, her heart jumped out of her chest. She knew that knock. And here she was bedraggled, working over a hot fire making stew for the large family.

She smoothed her skirts, wishing she had time to put on a pretty dress. Pressed her wayward curls behind her ears and heart beating, opened the door.

There he was standing in the pouring rain, water sluicing off his hat and wide shoulders.

"Come." She took his hand and pulled him in.

Before she could say a word, he tossed off his hat and pulled her tight into his arms. Rose began to sob. He still loved her. His arms around her broke all her resolve. She needed this man.

After a moment, he pulled back, his beautiful dark eyes gazing into hers with love. She could see it. "I'm so sorry…Will…I didn't…."

She couldn't finish, because he was kissing her. Hard. She could feel the water soaking into her dress as he held her and branded her forever with that kiss. He knees began to buckle and he held her up, else she would have melted to the floor.

"Ireland Rose Lovell, will you be my wife?" He growled into her ear.

"I will. I will." She sobbed again. "I'm so sorry for ever doubting you, Will." She gushed.

"I'll make sure you'll never doubt me again, Rose." He whispered back.

She laughed. Laughed with joy.

He swirled her around and set her on her feet.

"Sorry about your dress. You're soaked."

"It'll dry. Hungry?"

"Famished."

"Have you dry clothes."

He laughed heartily. "No, I came straight from the ship as soon as I docked in Dublin. It rained all the way here."

Rose loved the look on his face. He was happy. She had made him happy. And, she resolved that minute, on doing that every day of her life.

"Did Haw stop you?"

"Nobody was going to stop me." He pulled her into his arms again. "Feed me woman."

Rose disentangled herself from the big hunk of man and set the table for two. She watched from the corner of her eye as he grabbed the towel near the wash bowl and dried his hair and patted the water off his clothes. Her heart did pitter-patters.

"Elsa will be by this afternoon. We intended to take food to a family."

"I'll go with you." He stated and pulled out a chair, putting the towel on the seat.

"But it's an hour's ride and you've just gotten off the ship . . . don't you want to . . ."

He interrupted. "I'm going along."

She smiled and served up a portion of that pot of stew she was making and cut two large slices from the first loaf.

Rose watched as he ate heartily, his black hair wet. "Did your trip go well?"

"What do you think?" He looked grumpy.

Her eyes widened.

"I was miserable. I should never have left like that. I knew you needed to know about my past. And that you had just lost CJ."

"I was miserable, too."

He looked up and locked eyes with her, she knew reading them to see if she meant what she said.

"I know I didn't give you much reason to even like me. I was hung up with the past, Rose. I'm sorry for that. It wasn't your fault that ..."

"That I reminded you of Darby?" She finished with a shy smile.

He stopped and put his spoon down. She thought for sure he was going to get up and pace. Instead he looked her in the eye.

"You are not Darby. You're nothing like her. I was a fool. I'll make it up to you, Rose."

"You don't need to." She smiled. "It was because of her that I got to know the real you."

He laughed out loud. Rose loved it.

Chapter 82

"William Ashton Wyatt do you take this woman Ireland Rose Lovell, to be your wedded wife?"

"I do."

Rose heard the conviction in his deep voice. The pastor of the small kirk, Captain Wyatt wanted to be married in a church, smiled and asked Rose the same question. She heard her voice waver with emotion as she said "I do."

She found the love she was waiting for. True and honest. Strong and faithful. God had been good to her.

The pronouncement that they were husband and wife felt surreal. Her new husband gave her a look and her heart thrilled. He was going to be a handful. Haw and Elsa and the good parishioners of the little kirk planned a small dinner. And they didn't even know the bride and groom. Rose knew that in time her husband would understand that God was not cruel, like some fathers were, but loving to His children.

Their wedding day in the tiny church in County Clare, Ireland became the starting point for their marriage from that day forward.

Epilogue

Not a year later Rose knew what poor Matilda Jane knew. She was ready to scream and wondered how in the world she was going to survive childbirth. Her husband was ordered away from the house while she and Elsa did this thing only women know how to do. More than two hours later, hair tangled and finally relieved, she held a son. Black hair and dark eyes, he came quietly into the world. He lay now on his mother's arm, eyes wide open.

Captain Wyatt said it would be a boy. But he wouldn't know for a little while. Haw had hauled him down the road to keep the peace. The man had made both women crazy after pacing back and forth outside the door for hours. They had finally ordered him out of the house. And certainly out of hearing distance, because Rose, no matter how hard she tried could not keep the noises she made quiet. It was too hard.

And the child, Elsa said, was large for her. "No wonder ye had a hard time, lass. But the others that come will be easier after this lad."

"Others?" Rose wanted to cry. "I don't think I can do this again."

"Lass, look what ye did. Brought a fine strapping man into the world. In a home where God is. Now tell me that isn't a blessing."

Rose knew the love of a man. One who wanted her, loved her, and would die for her. All the times she doubted whether God loved her slipped away. Little William Henry Wyatt was proof of that! This time no one would come and take her child away.

She heard her husband bellowing at the door and invited him in. The look on his face was enough for Rose.

"It be a big strapping lad." Elsa said, smiling and joined her husband outside.

Ashton's eyes met his wife's with the question all men ask on this occasion. "Are you all right?"

"Yes. Look." She pulled back the blanket.

The tall dark-haired man at her side gazed down at the babe and then back at her.

"You're sure you're all right?"

"Now I am." And lifted her son to her husband's arms. Immediately a loud bellow came out of that tiny mouth.

"Oh my, just like his father." Rose sighed.

Two more sons and finally a lass joined the Wyatt family. Rose was forever grateful for every single loss she suffered, for it brought her to this place.

CPSIA information can be obtained at www.ICGtesting.com
Printed in the USA
267605BV00001B/5/P